AUTOBIOGRAPHY

OF A

FEMALE SLAVE

WORKS BY MATTIE GRIFFITH

Poems... Now First Collected
Autobiography of a Female Slave
"Madge Vertner" (serialized novel)

AUTOBIOGRAPHY

OF A

FEMALE SLAVE

By *Mattie Griffith*

With an afterword by *Joe Lockard*

Banner Books
University Press of Mississippi/*Jackson*

TO ALL PERSONS

INTERESTED IN THE CAUSE OF FREEDOM,

This little Book

IS

RESPECTFULLY AND AFFECTIONATELY DEDICATED,

BY

THE AUTHOR.

First published in 1856 by
J. S. REDFIELD

Afterword copyright © 1998 by
University Press of Mississippi
All rights reserved
Manufactured in the United States of America
01 00 99 98   4 3 2 1
The paper in this book meets the guidelines for permanence and
durability of the Committee on Production Guidelines for
Book Longevity of the Council on Library Resources.

Browne, Martha Griffith, d. 1906
Autobiography of a female slave / by Mattie Griffith; with an afterword by Joe Lockard.
p. cm.
Originally published: New York: J. S. Redfield, 1857.
ISBN 1-57806-046-X (cloth). —ISBN 1-57806-047-8 (pbk.)
1. Afro-American women—Kentucky—Fiction. 2. Women slaves—Kentucky—Fiction.
3. Slavery—Kentucky—Fiction. I. Title.
PS1145.B35A95   1998
813'.3—dc21   97-42192
                                                                        CIP

British Library Cataloging-in-Publication data available

CONTENTS.

CHAPTER X.

CHAPTER XI.

CHAPTER XII.

CHAPTER XIII.

CHAPTER XIV.

CHAPTER XV.

CHAPTER XVI.

CHAPTER XVII.

CHAPTER XVIII.

CHAPTER XIX.

CHAPTER XX.

CHAPTER XXXIV.

CHAPTER XXXV.

CHAPTER XXXVI.

CHAPTER XXXVII.

CHAPTER XXXVIII.

CHAPTER XXXIX.

CHAPTER XL.

CHAPTER XLI.

CHAPTER XLII.

AUTOBIOGRAPHY

OF A

FEMALE SLAVE.

───────•───────

CHAPTER I.

THE OLD KENTUCKY FARM——MY PARENTAGE AND EARLY TRAIN-
ING——DEATH OF THE MASTER——THE SALE-DAY——NEW MASTER
AND NEW HOME.

I WAS born in one of the southern counties of Kentucky.
My earliest recollections are of a large, old-fashioned farm-house,
built of hewn rock, in which my old master, Mr. Nelson, and
his family, consisting of a widowed sister, two daughters and
two sons, resided. I have but an indistinct remembrance of
my old master. At times, a shadow of an idea, like the reflection of a kind dream, comes over my mind, and, then, I conjure
him up as a large, venerable-looking man, with scanty, gray locks
floating carelessly over an amplitude of forehead; a wide, hard-
featured face, with yet a kindly glow of honest sentiment;
broad, strong teeth, much discolored by the continued use of
tobacco.

I well remember that, as a token of his good-will, he always
presented us (the slave-children) with a slice of buttered bread,
when we had finished our daily task. I have also a faint
reminiscence of his old hickory cane being shaken over my head
two or three times, and the promise (which remained, until his
death, unfulfilled) of a good "*thrashing*" at some future period.

My mother was a very bright mulatto woman, and my father,

I suppose, was a white man, though I know nothing of him; for, with the most unpaternal feeling, he deserted me. A consequence of this amalgamation was my very fair and beautiful complexion. My skin was no perceptible shade darker than that of my young mistresses. My eyes were large and dark, while a profusion of nut-brown hair, straight and soft as the whitest lady's in the land, fell in showery redundance over my neck and shoulders. I was often mistaken for a white child; and in my rambles through the woods, many caresses have I received from wayside travellers; and the exclamation, "What a beautiful child!" was quite common. Owing to this personal beauty I was a great pet with my master's sister, Mrs. Woodbridge, who, I believe I have stated, was a widow, and childless; so upon me she lavished all the fondness of a warm and loving heart.

My mother, Keziah the cook, commonly called Aunt Kaisy, was possessed of an indomitable ambition, and had, by the hardest means, endeavored to acquire the rudiments of an education; but all that she had succeeded in obtaining was a knowledge of the alphabet, and orthography in two syllables. Being very imitative, she eschewed the ordinary negroes' pronunciation, and adopted the mode of speech used by the higher classes of whites. She was very much delighted when Mrs. Woodbridge or Miss Betsy (as we called her) began to instruct me in the elements of the English language. I inherited my mother's thirst for knowledge; and, by intense study, did all I could to spare Miss Betsy the usual drudgery of a teacher. The aptitude that I displayed, may be inferred from the fact that, in three months from the day she began teaching me the alphabet, I was reading, with some degree of fluency, in the "First Reader." I have often heard her relate this as quite a literary and educational marvel.

There were so many slaves upon the farm, particularly young ones, that I was regarded as a supernumerary; consequently, spared from nearly all the work. I sat in Miss Betsy's room, with book in hand, little heeding anything else; and, if ever I manifested the least indolence, my mother, with her wild ambition, was sure to rally me, and even offer the tempting bribe of cakes and apples.

I have frequently heard my old master say, "Betsy, you will spoil that girl, teaching her so much." "She is too pretty for a slave," was her invariable reply.

Thus smoothly passed the early part of my life, until an event occurred which was the cause of a change in my whole fate. My old master became suddenly and dangerously ill. My lessons were suspended, for Miss Betsy's services were required in the sick chamber. I used to slyly steal to the open door of his room, and peep in, with wonder, at the sombre group collected there. I recollect seeing my young masters and mistresses weeping round a curtained bed. Then there came a time when loud screams and frightful lamentations issued thence. There were shrieks that struck upon my ear with a strange thrill; shrieks that seemed to rend souls and break heart-strings. My young mistresses, fair, slender girls, fell prostrate upon the floor; and my masters, noble, manly men, bent over the bowed forms of their sisters, whispering words which I did not hear, but which, my mature experience tells me, must have been of love and comfort.

There came, then, a long, narrow, black box, thickly embossed with shining brass tacks, in which my old master was carefully laid, with his pale, brawny hands crossed upon his wide chest. I remember that, one by one, the slaves were called in to take a last look of him who had been, to them, a kind master. They all came out with their cotton handkerchiefs pressed to their eyes. I went in, with five other colored children, to take my look. That wan, ghastly face, those sunken eyes and pinched features, with the white winding sheet, and the dismal coffin, impressed me with a new and wild terror; and, for weeks after, this "vision of death" haunted my mind fearfully.

But I soon after resumed my studies under Miss Betsy's tuition. . Having little work to do, and seldom seeing my young mistresses, I grew up in the same house, scarcely knowing them. I was technically termed in the family, "the child," as I was not black; and, being a slave, my masters and mistresses would not admit that I was white. So I reached the age of ten, still called "a child," and actually one in all life's experiences, though pretty well advanced in education. I had a very good knowledge of the rudiments, had bestowed some attention upon Grammar, and eagerly read every book that fell in my way. Love of study taught me seclusive habits; I read long and late: and the desire of a finished education became the passion of my life. Alas! these days were but a poor preparation for the life that was to come after!

Miss Betsy, though a warm-hearted woman, was a violent advocate of slavery. I have since been puzzled how to reconcile this with her otherwise Christian character; and, though she professed to love me dearly, and had bestowed so much attention upon the cultivation of my mind, and expressed it as her opinion that I was too pretty and white to be a slave, yet, if any one had spoken of giving me freedom, she would have condemned it as domestic heresy. If I had belonged to her, I doubt not but my life would have been a happy one. But, alas! a different lot was assigned me!

About two years and six months after my old master's death, a division was made of the property. This involved a sale of everything, even the household furniture. There were, I believe, heavy debts hanging over the estate. These must be met, and the residue divided among the heirs.

When it was made known in the kitchen that a sale was to be made, the slaves were panic-stricken. Loud cries and lamentations arose, and my young mistresses came often to the kitchen to comfort us.

One of these young ladies, Miss Margaret, a tall, nobly-formed girl, with big blue eyes and brown hair, frequently came and sat with us, trying, in the most persuasive tones, to reconcile the old ones to their destiny. Often did I see the large tears roll down her fair cheeks, and her red lip quiver. These indications of sympathy, coming from such a lovely being, cheered many an hour of after-captivity.

But the "sale-day" came at last; I have a confused idea of it. The ladies left the day before. Miss Betsy took an affectionate leave of me; ah, I did not then know that it was a final one.

The servants were all sold, as I heard one man say, at very high rates, though not under the auctioneer's hammer. To that. my young masters were opposed.

A tall, hard-looking man came up to me, very roughly seized my arm, bade me open my mouth; examined my teeth; felt of my limbs; made me run a few yards; ordered me to jump; and, being well satisfied with my activity, said to Master Edward, "I will take her." Little comprehending the full meaning of that brief sentence, I rejoined the group of children from which I had been summoned. After awhile, my mother came up to me, holding a wallet in her hand. The tear-drops stood on her cheeks, and her whole frame was distorted with pain. She walked toward me a few steps, then stopped, and suddenly shaking her head, exclaimed, "No, no, I can't do it, I can't do it." I was amazed at her grief, but an indefinable fear kept me from rushing to her.

"Here, Kitty," she said to an old negro woman, who stood near, "you break it to her. I can't do it. No, it will drive me mad. Oh, heaven! that I was ever born to see this day." Then rocking her body back and forward in a transport of agony, she gave full vent to her feelings in a long, loud, piteous wail. Oh, God! that cry of grief, that knell of a breaking heart, rang in my ears for many long and painful days. At length Aunt Kitty approached me, and, laying her hand on my shoulder, kindly said:

"Alas, poor chile, you mus' place your trus' in the good God above, you mus' look to Him for help; you are gwine to leave your mother now. You are to have a new home, a new master, and I hope new friends. May the Lord be with you." So saying, she broke suddenly away from me; but I saw that her wrinkled face was wet with tears.

With perhaps an idle, listless air, I received this astounding news; but a whirlwind was gathering in my breast. What could she mean by new friends and a new home? Surely I was to take my mother with me! No mortal power would dare to sever *us*. Why, I remember that when master sold the gray mare, the colt went also. Who could, who would, who dared, separate the parent from her offspring? Alas! I had yet to learn that the white man dared do all that his avarice might suggest; and there was no human tribunal where the outcast African could pray for "right!" Ah, when I now think of my poor mother's form, as it swayed like a willow in the tempest of grief; when I remember her bitter cries, and see her arms thrown franticly toward me, and hear her earnest—oh, how earnest—prayer for death or madness, then I wonder where were Heaven's thunderbolts; but retributive Justice *will* come sooner or later, and He who remembers mercy *now* will not forget justice *then*.

"Come along, gal, come along, gather up your duds, and come with me," said a harsh voice; and, looking up from my bewildered reverie, I beheld the man who had so carefully examined me. I was too much startled to fully understand the words, and stood vacantly gazing at him. This strange manner he construed into disrespect; and, raising his riding-whip, he brought it down with considerable force upon my back. It was the first lash I had ever given to me in anger. I smarted beneath the stripe, and a cry of pain broke from my lips. Mother sprang to me, and clasping my quivering form in her arms, cried out to my young master, "Oh, Master Eddy, have mercy on me, on my child. I have served you faithfully, I nursed you, I grew up with your poor mother, who now sleeps in the cold ground. I beg you now to save *my child*," and she sank down at his feet, whilst her tears fell fast.

Then my poor old grandfather, who was called the patriarch slave, being the eldest one of the race in the whole neighborhood, joined us. His gray head, wrinkled face, and bent form, told of many a year of hard servitude.

"What is it, Massa Ed, what is it Kaisy be takin' on so

'bout ? you haint driv the *chile* off ? No—no ! young massa only playin' trick now ; come Kais' don't be makin' fool of yoursef, young massa not gwine to separate you and the chile."

These words seemed to reanimate my mother, and she looked up at Master Edward with a grateful expression of face, whilst she clasped her arms tightly around his knees, exclaiming, "Oh, bless you, young master, bless you forever, and forgive poor Kaisy for distrusting you, but Pompey told me the child was sold away from me, and that gemman struck her ;" and here again she sobbed, and caught hold of me convulsively, as if she feared I might be taken.

I looked at my young master's face, and the ghastly whiteness which overspread it, the tearful glister of his eye, and the strange tremor of his figure, struck me with fright. *I knew my doom.* Young as I was, my first dread was for my mother ;. I forgot my own perilous situation, and mourned alone for her. I would have given worlds could insensibility have been granted her.

"I've got no time to be foolin' longer with these niggers, come 'long, gal. Ann, I believe, you tole me was her name," he said, as he turned to Master Edward. Another wild shriek from my mother, a deep sigh from grandpap, and I looked at master Ed, who was striking his forehead vehemently, and the tears were trickling down his cheeks.

" Here, Mr. Peterkin, here !" exclaimed Master Edward, " here is your bill of sale ; I will refund your money ; release me from my contract."

Peterkin cast on him one contemptuous look, and with a low, chuckling laugh, replied, " No ; you must stand to your bargain. I want that gal ; she is likely, and it will do me good to thrash the devil out of her ;" turning to me he added, " quit your snuffling and snubbing, or I'll give you something to cry 'bout ;" and, roughly catching me by the arm, he hurried me off, despite the entreaty of Master Ed, the cries of mother, and the feeble supplication of my grandfather. I dared to cast one look behind, and beheld my mother wallowing in the dust, whilst her frantic cries of " save my child, save my child !" rang with fearful agony in my ears. Master Ed covered his face with his hands, and old grandfather reverently raised his to Heaven, as if beseeching mercy. The sight of this anguish-stricken group filled me with a new sense of horror, and forgetful of the presence of Peterkin, I burst into tears: but I was quickly recalled by a fierce and stinging blow from his stout riding-whip.

" See here, nigger (this man, raised among negroes, used their dialect), if you dar' to give another whimper, I'll beat the very life out 'en yer." This terrific threat seemed to scare away every thought of precaution ; and, by a sudden and agile bound, I broke loose from him and darted off to the sad group, from which I had been so ruthlessly torn, and, sinking down before Master Ed, I cried out in a wild, despairing tone, " Save me, good master, save me—kill me, or hide me from that awful man, he'll kill me ;" and, seizing hold of the skirt of his coat, I covered my face with it to shut out the sight of Peterkin, whose red eye-balls were glaring with fury upon me.   Oath after oath escaped his lips.   Mother saw him rapidly approaching to recapture me, and, with the noble, maternal instinct of self-sacrifice, sprang forward only to receive the heavy blow of his uplifted whip.   She reeled, tottered and sank stunned upon the ground.

" Thar, take that, you yaller hussy, and cuss yer nigger hide for daring to raise this rumpus here," he said, as he rapidly strode past her.

" Gently, Mr. Peterkin," exclaimed Master Edward, " let me speak to her ; a little encouragement is better than force."

" This is my encouragement for them," and he shook his whip.

Unheeding him, Master Edward turned to me, saying, " Ann, come now, be a good girl, go with this gentleman, and be an obedient girl; he will give you a kind, nice home ; sometimes he will let you come to see your mother.   Here is some money for you to buy a pretty head-handkerchief; now go with him."

These kind words and encouraging tones, brought a fresh gush of tears to my eyes. Taking the half-dollar which he offered me, and reverently kissing the skirt of his coat, I rejoined Peterkin; one look at his cold, harsh face, chilled my resolution; yet I had resolved to go without another word of complaint. I could not suppress a groan when I passed the spot where my mother lay still insensible from the effects of the blow

One by one the servants, old and young, gave me a hearty shake of the hand as I passed the place where they were standing in a row for the inspection of buyers.

I had nerved myself, and now that the parting from mother was over, I felt that the bitterness of death was past, and I could meet anything. Nothing now could be a trial, yet I was touched when the servants offered me little mementoes and keepsakes. One gave a yard of ribbon, another a half-paper of pins, a third presented a painted cotton head-tie; others gave me ginger-cakes, candies, or small coins. Out of their little they gave abundantly, and, small as were the bestowments, I well knew that they had made sacrifices to give even so much. I was too deeply affected to make any other acknowledgment than a nod of the head; for a choking thickness was gathering in my throat, and a blinding mist obscured my sight. I did not see my young mistresses, for they had left the house, declaring they could not bear to witness a spectacle so revolting to their feelings.

Upon reaching the gate I observed a red-painted wagon, with an awning of domestic cotton. Standing near it, and holding the horses, was an old, worn, scarred, weather-beaten negro man, who instantly took off his hat as Mr. Peterkin approached.

"Well, Nace, you see I've bought this wench to-day," and he shook his whip over my head.

"Ya! ya! Massa, but she ha' got one goot home wid yer."

"Yes, has she, Nace; but don't yer think the slut has been cryin' 'bout it!"

"Lor' bless us, Massa, but a little of the beech-tree will fetch that sort of truck out of her," and old Nace showed his broken teeth, as he gave a forced laugh.

"I guess I can take the fool out en her, by the time I gives her two or three swings at the whippin'-post."

Nace shook his head knowingly, and gave a low guttural laugh, by way of approval of his master's capabilities.

"Jump in the wagon, gal," said my new master, "jump in quick ; I likes to see niggers active, none of your pokes 'bout me ; but this will put sperit in 'em," and there was another defiant flourish of the whip.

I got in with as much haste and activity as I could possibly command. This appeared to please Mr. Peterkin, and he gave evidence of it by saying,—

"Well, that does pretty well; a few stripes a day, and you'll be a valerble slave ;" and, getting in the vehicle himself, he ordered Nace to drive on "*pretty peart*," as night would soon overtake us.

Just as we were starting I perceived Josh, one of my playmates, running after us with a small bundle, shouting,—

"Here, Ann, you've lef' yer bundle of close."

"Stop, Nace," said Mr. Peterkin, "let's git the gal's duds, or I'll be put to the 'spence of gittin' new ones for her."

Little Josh came bounding up, and, with an affectionate manner, handed me the little wallet that contained my entire wardrobe. I leaned forward, and, in a muffled tone, but with my whole heart hanging on my lip, asked Josh " how is mother ?" but a cut of Nace's whip, and a quick "gee-up," put me beyond the hearing of the reply. I strained my eyes after Josh, to interpret the motion of his lips.

In a state of hopeless agony I sat through the remainder of the journey. The coarse jokes and malignant threats of Mr. Peterkin were answered with laughing and dutiful assent by the veteran Nace. I tried to deceive my persecutors by feigning sleep, but, ah, a strong finger held my lids open, and slumber fled away to gladden lighter hearts and bless brighter eyes.

CHAPTER II.

THE young moon had risen in mild and meek serenity to bless the earth. With a strange and fluctuating light the pale rays played over the leaves and branches of the forest trees, and flickered fantastically upon the ground! Only a few stars were discernible in the highest dome of heaven! The lowing of wandering cows, or the chirp of a night-bird, had power to beguile memory back to a thousand vanished joys. I mused and wept; still the wagon jogged along. Mr. Peterkin sat half-sleeping beside old Nace, whose occasional "gee-up" to the lagging horses, was the only human sound that broke the soft serenity! Every moment seemed to me an age, for I dreaded the awakening of my cruel master. Ah, little did I dream that that horrid day's experience was but a brief foretaste of what I had yet to suffer; and well it was for me that a kind and merciful Providence veiled that dismal future from my gaze. About midnight I had fallen into a quiet sleep, gilded by the sweetest dream, a dream of the old farm-house, of mother, grandfather, and my companions.

From this vision I was aroused by the gruff voice of Peterkin, bidding me get out of the wagon. That voice was to me more frightful and fearful than the blast of the last trump. Springing suddenly up, I threw off the shackles of sleep; and consciousness, with all its direful burden, returned fully to me. Looking round, by the full light of the moon, I beheld a large country house, half hidden among trees. A white paling enclosed the ground, and the scent of dewy roses and other garden flowers filled the atmosphere.

"Now, Nace, put up the team, and git yourself to bed," said

Peterkin. Turning to me he added, " give this gal a blanket, and let her sleep on the floor in Polly's cabin; keep a good watch on her, that she don't try to run off."

"Needn't fear dat, Massa, for de bull-dog tear her to pieces if she 'tempt dat. By gar, I'd like to see her be for tryin' it ;" and the old negro gave a fiendish laugh, as though he thought it would be rare sport.

Mr. Peterkin entered the handsome house, of which he was the rich and respected owner, whilst I, conducted by Nace, repaired to a dismal cabin. After repeated knocks at the door of this most wretched hovel, an old crone of a negress muttered between her clenched teeth, " Who's dar ?"

" It's me, Polly ; what you be 'bout dar, dat you don't let me in ?"

" What for you be bangin' at my cabin ? I's got no bisness wid you."

" Yes, but I's got bisness wid you; stir yer ole stumps now."

" I shan't be for troublin' mysef and lettin' you in my cabin at dis hour ob de night-time ; and if you doesn't be off, I'll make Massa gib you a sound drubbin' in de mornin'."

" Ha, ha ! now I'm gots you sure ; for massa sends me here himsef."

This was enough for Polly ; she broke off all further colloquy, and opened the door instantly.

The pale moonlight rested as lovingly upon that dreary, unchinked, rude, and wretched hovel, as ever it played over the gilded roof and frescoed dome of ancient palaces; but ah, what squalor did it not reveal ! There, resting upon pallets of straw, like pigs in a litter, were groups of children, and upon a rickety cot the old woman reposed her aged limbs. How strange, lonely, and forbidding appeared that tenement, as the old woman stood in the doorway, her short and scanty kirtles but poorly concealing her meagre limbs. A dark, scowling countenance looked out from under a small cap of faded muslin : little bleared eyes glared upon me, like the red light of a heated furnace. Instinctively I shrank back from her, but Nace was tired, and not wishing to be longer kept from his bed, pushed me within the door, saying—

"Thar, Polly, Massa say dat gal mus' sleep in dar."

"Come 'long in, gal," said the woman, and closing the door, she pointed to a patch of straw, " sleep dar."

The moonbeams stole in through the crevices and cracks of the cabin, and cast a mystic gleam upon the surrounding objects. Without further word or comment, Polly betook herself to her cot, and was soon snoring away as though there were no such thing as care or slavery in the world. But to me sleep was a stranger. There I lay through the remaining hours of the night, wearily thinking of mother and home. "Sold," I murmured. "What is it to be sold? Why was *I* sold? Why separated from my mother and friends? Why couldn't mother come with me, or I stay with her? I never saw Mr. Peterkin before. Who gave him the right to force me from my good home and kind friends?" These questions would arise in my mind, and, alas! I had no answers for them. Young and ignorant as I was, I had yet some glimmering idea of justice. Later in life, these same questions have often come to me, as sad commentaries upon the righteousness of human laws; and, when sitting in splendid churches listening to ornate and *worldly* harangues from *holy men*, these same thoughts have tingled upon my tongue. And I have been surprised to see how strangely these men mistake the definition of servitude. Why, from the exposition of the worthy divines, one would suppose that servitude was a fair synonym for slavery! Admitting that we are the descendants of the unfortunate Ham, and endure our bondage as the penalty affixed to his crime, there can be no argument or fact adduced, whereby to justify slavery as a moral right. Serving and being a slave are very different. And why may not Ham's descendants claim a reprieve by virtue of the passion and death of Christ? Are we excluded from the grace of that atonement? No; there is no argument, no reason, to justify slavery, save that of human cupidity. But there will come a day, when each and every one who has violated that divine rule, "Do unto others as you would have them do unto you," will stand with a fearful accountability before the Supreme Judge. Then will there be loud cries and lamentations, and a wish for the mountains to hide them from the eye of Judicial Majesty.

The next morning I rose with the dawn, and sitting upright upon my pallet, surveyed the room and its tenants. There, in comfortless confusion, upon heaps of straw, slumbered five children, dirty and ragged. On the broken cot, with a remnant of a coverlet thrown over her, lay Aunt Polly. A few broken stools and one pine box, with a shelf containing a few tins, constituted the entire furniture.

"And this wretched pen is to be my home; these dirty-looking children my associates." Oh, how dismal were my thoughts; but little time had I for reflection. The shrill sound of a hunting-horn was the summons for the servants to arise, and woe unto him or her who was found missing or tardy when the muster-roll was called. Aunt Polly and the five children sprang up, and soon dressed themselves. They then appeared in the yard, where a stout, athletic man, with full beard and a dull eye, stood with whip in hand. He called over the names of all, and portioned out their daily task. With a smile more of terror than pleasure, they severally received their orders. I stood at the extremity of the range. After disposing of them in order, the overseer (for such he was) looked at me fiercely, and said:

"Come here, gal."

With a timid step, I obeyed.

"What are you fit for? Not much of anything, ha?" and catching hold of my ear he pulled me round in front of him, saying,

"Well, you are likely-looking; how much work can you do?"

I stammered out something as to my willingness to do anything that was required of me. He examined my hands, and concluding from their dimensions that I was best suited for house-work, he bade me remain in the kitchen until after breakfast. When I entered the room designated, par politesse, as the kitchen, I was surprised to find such a desolate and destitute-looking place. The apartment, which was very small, seemèd to be a sort of Pandora's Box, into which everything of household or domestic use had been crowded. The walls were hung round with saddles, bridles, horse-blankets, &c. Upon a swinging shelf in the centre of the room were ranged all the seeds, nails, ropes, dried elms, and the rest of the thousand and one little notions of domestic economy. A rude, wooden shelf contained a dark, dusty row of unclean tins; broken stools and old kegs were substituted for chairs; upon these were stationed four or five ebony children; one of them, a girl about nine years old, with a dingy face, to which soap and water seemed foreign, and with shaggy, moppy hair, twisted in short, stringy plaits, sat upon a broken keg, with a squalid baby in her lap, which she jostled upon her knee, whilst she sang in a sharp key, "hushy-by-baby." Three other wretched children, in tow-linen dresses, whose brevity of skirts made a sad appeal to the modesty of spectators, were perched round this girl, whom they called Amy. They were furiously begging Aunt Polly (the cook) to give them a piece of hoe-cake.

"Be off wid you, or I'll tell Massa, or de overseer," answered the beldame, as their solicitations became more clamorous. This threat had power to silence the most earnest demands of the stomach, for the fiend of hunger was far less dreaded than the lash of Mr. Jones, the overseer. My entrance, and the sight of a strange face, was a diversion for them. They crowded closer to Amy, and eyed me with a half doubtful, and altogether ludicrous air.

"Who's her?" "whar she come from?" "when her gwyn away?" and such like expressions, escaped them. in stifled tones.

"Come in, set down," said Aunt Polly to me, and, turning to the group of children, she levelled a poker at them.

"Keep still dar, or I'll break your pates wid dis poker."

Instantly they cowered down beside Amy, still peeping over

her shoulder, to get a better view of me. With a very uneasy
feeling I seated myself upon the broken stool, to which Aunt
Polly pointed. One of the boldest of the children came up to
me, and, slyly touching my dress, said, " tag," then darted off
to her hiding-place, with quite the air of a victress. Amy
made queer grimaces at me. Every now and then placing her
thumb to her nose, and gyrating her finger towards me, she
would drawl out, " you ka-n-t kum it." All this was perfect
jargon to me ; for at home, though we had been but imperfectly
protected by clothing from the vicissitudes of seasons, and
though our fare was simple, coarse, and frugal, had we been
kindly treated, and our manners trained into something like the
softness of humanity. There, as regularly as the Sunday
dawned, were we summoned to the house to hear the Bible
read, and join (though at a respectful distance) with the family
in prayer. But this I subsequently learned was an unusual
practice in the neighborhood, and was attributed to the fact,
that my master's wife had been born in the State of Massachusetts, where the people were crazy and fanatical enough to believe that " niggers" had souls, and were by God held to be responsible beings.

The loud blast of the horn was the signal for the " hands "
to suspend their labor and come to breakfast. Two negro men
and three women rushed in at the door, ravenous for their
rations. I looked about for the table, but, seeing none, concluded
it had yet to be arranged ; for at home we always took our
meals on a table. I was much surprised to see each one here
take a slice of fat bacon and a pone of bread in his or her hand,
and eat it standing.

" Well," said one man, " I'd like to git a bit more bread."

" You's had your sher," replied Aunt Polly. " Mister Jones
ses one slice o' meat and a pone o' bread is to be the 'lowance."

" I knows it, but if thar's any scraps left from the house table,
you wimmin folks always gits it."

" Who's got de bes' right ?   Sure, and arn't de one who cooks
it got de bes' right to it ?" asked Polly, with a triumphant voice.

"Ha, ha!" cried Nace, "here comes de breakfust leavin's, now who's smartest shall have 'em;" whereupon Nace, his comrade, and the three women, seized a waiter of fragments of biscuit, broiled ham, coffee, &c., the remains of the breakfast prepared for the white family.

"By gar," cried Nace, "I've got de coffee-pot, and I'll drink dis;" so, without further ceremony, he applied the spout to his mouth, and, sans cream or sugar, he quaffed off the grounds. Jake possessed himself of the ham, whilst the two women held a considerable contest over a biscuit. Blow and lie passed frequently between them. Aunt Polly brandished her skimmer-spoon, as though it were Neptune's trident of authority; still she could not allay the confusion which these excited cormorants raised. The children yelled out and clamored for a bit; the sight and scent of ham and biscuits so tantalized their palates, that they forgot even the terror of the whip. I stood all agape, looking on with amazement.

The two belligerent women stood with eyes blazing like comets, their arms twisted around each other in a very decided and furious rencontre. One of them, losing her balance, fell upon the floor, and, dragging the other after her, they rolled and wallowed in a cloud of dust, whilst the disputed biscuit, in the heat of the affray, had been dropped on the hearth, where, unperceived by the combatants, Nace had possessed himself of it, and was happily masticating it.

Melinda, the girl from whom the waiter had been snatched, doubtless much disappointed by the loss of the debris, returned to the house and made a report of the fracas.

Instantly and unexpectedly, Jones, flaming with rage, stood in the midst of the riotous group. Seizing hold of the women, he knocked them on their heads with his clenched fists.

"Hold, black wretches, come, I will give you a leetle fun; off now to the post."

Then such appeals for mercy, promises of amendment, entreaties, excuses, &c., as the two women made, would have touched a heart of stone; but Jones had power to resist even

2

the prayers of an angel. To him the cries of human suffering and the agony of distress were music. My heart bled when I saw the two victims led away, and I put my hands to my ears to shut out the screams of distress which rang with a strange terror on the morning air. Poor, oppressed African! thorny and rugged is your path of life! Many a secret sigh and bleeding tear attest your cruel martyrdom! Surely He, who careth alike for the high and the low, looks not unmoved upon you, wearing and groaning beneath the pressing burden and galling yoke of a most inhuman bondage. For you there is no broad rock of Hope or Peace to cast its shadow of rest in this "weary land." You must sow in tears and reap in sorrow. But He, who led the children of Israel from the house of bondage and the fetters of captivity, will, in His own inscrutable way, lead you from the condition of despair, even by the pillar of fire and the cloud. Great changes are occurring daily, old constitutions are tottering, old systems, fraught with the cruelty of darker ages, are shaking to their centres. Master minds are everywhere actively engaged. Keen eyes and vigilant hearts are open to the wrongs of the poor, the lowly and the outcast. An avenging angel sits concealed 'mid the drapery of the wasting cloud, ready to pour the vials of God's wrath upon a haughty and oppressive race. In the threatened famine, see we nothing but an accidental failure of the crops? In the exhausted coffers and empty public treasury, is there nothing taught but the lesson of national extravagance? In the virulence of disease, the increasing prevalence of fatal epidemics, what do we read? Send for the seers, the wise men of the nation, and bid them translate the "mysterious writing on the wall." Ah, well may ye shake, Kings of Mammon, shake upon your tottering throne of human bones! Give o'er your sports, suspend your orgies, dash down the jewelled cup of unhallowed joy, sparkling as it is to the very brim. You must pay, like him of old, the fearful price of sin. God hath not heard, unmoved, the anguished cries of a down-trodden and enslaved nation! And it needs no Daniel to tell, that "God hath numbered your Kingdom and it is finished."

As may be supposed, I had little appetite for my breakfast, but I managed to deceive others into the belief that I had made a hearty meal. But those screams from half-famished wretches had a fatal and terrifying fascination; never once could I forget it.

A look of fright was on the face of all. "They be gettin' awful beatin' at the post," muttered Nace, whilst a sardonic smile flitted over his hard features. Was it not sad to behold the depths of degradation into which this creature had fallen? He could smile at the anguish of a fellow-creature. Originally, his nature may have been kind and gentle; but a continuous system of brutality had so deadened his sensibilities, that he had no humanity left. *For this*, the white man is accountable.

After the breakfast was over, I received a summons to the house. Following Melinda, I passed the door-sill, and stood in the presence of the assembled household. A very strange group I thought them. Two girls were seated beside the uncleared breakfast table, "trying their fortune" (as the phrase goes) with a cup of coffee-grounds and a spoon. The elder of the two was a tall, thin girl, with sharp features, small gray eyes, and red-hair done up in frizettes; the other was a prim, dark-skinned girl, with a set of nondescript features, and hair of no particular hue, or "just any color;" but with the same harsh expression of face that characterized the elder. As she received the magic cup from her sister, she exclaimed, "La, Jane, it will only be two years until you are married," and made a significant grimace at her father (Mr. Peterkin), who sat near the window, indulging in the luxury of a cob-pipe. The taller girl turned toward me, and asked,

"Father, is that the new girl you bought at old Nelson's sale?"

"Yes, that's the gal. Does she suit you?"

"Yes, but dear me! how very light she is—almost white! I know she will be impudent."

"She has come to the wrong place for the practice of that article," suggested the other.

"Yes, gal, you has got to mind them ar' *wimmen*," said Mr. Peterkin to me, as he pointed toward his daughters.

"Father, I do wish you would quit that vulgarism; say *girl*, not gal, and *ladies*, not women."

"Oh, I was never *edicated*, like you."

"*Educated* is the word."

"Oh, confound your dictionaries! Ever since that school-marm come out from Yankee-land, these neighborhood gals talk so big, nobody can understand 'em."

CHAPTER III.

THE YANKEE SCHOOL-MISTRESS—HER PHILOSOPHY—THE
AMERICAN ABOLITIONISTS.

THE family with whom I now found a home, consisted of
Mr. Peterkin and his two daughters, Jane and Matilda, and a
son, John, much younger than the ladies.

The death of Mrs. Peterkin had occurred about three years
before I went to live with them. The girls had been very well
educated by a Miss Bradly, from Massachusetts, a spinster of
"no particular age." From her, the Misses Peterkin learned to
set a great value upon correct and elegant language. She was
the model and instructress of the country round; for, under her
jurisdiction, nearly all the farmers' daughters had been initiated into the mysteries of learning. Scattered about, over the
house, I used to frequently find odd leaves of school-books, ele-
mentary portions of natural sciences, old readers, story-books,
novels, &c. These I eagerly devoured; but I had to be very
secret about it, studying by dying embers, reading by moonlight, sun-rise, &c. Had I been discovered, a severe punishment
would have followed. Miss Jane used to say, "a literary negro
was disgusting, not to be tolerated." Though she quarrelled
with the vulgar talk and bad pronunciation of her father, he was
made of too rough material to receive a polish; and, though
Miss Bradly had improved the minds of the girls, her efforts to
soften their hearts had met with no success. They were the
same harsh, cold and selfish girls that she had found them. It
was Jane's boast that she had whipped more negroes than any
other girl of her age. Matilda, though less severe, had still a
touch of the tigress.

This family lived in something like "style." They were

famed for their wealth and social position throughout the neighborhood. The house was a low cottage structure, with large and airy apartments; an arching piazza ran the whole length of the building, and around its trellised balustrade the clematis vine twined in rich luxuriance. A primrose-walk led up to the door, and the yard blossomed like a garden, with the fairest flowers. It was a very Paradise of homes; pity, ah pity 'twas, that human fiends marred its beauty. There the sweet flowers bloomed, the young birds warbled, pure springs gushed forth with limpid joy—there truly, "All, save the spirit of man, was divine." The traveller often paused to admire the tasteful arrangements of the grounds, the neat and artistic plan of the house, and the thorough " air" of everything around. It seemed to bespeak refined minds, and delicate, noble natures; but oh, the flowers were no symbols of the graces of their hearts, for the dwellers of this highly-adorned spot were people of coarse natures, rough and cruel as barbarians. The nightly stars and the gentle moon, the deep glory of the noontide, or the blowing of twilight breezes over this chosen home, had no power to ennoble or elevate their souls. Acts of diabolical cruelty and wickedness were there perpetrated without the least pang of remorse or regret. Whilst the white portion of the family were revelling in luxury, the slaves were denied the most ordinary necessaries. The cook, who prepared the nicest dainties, the most tempting viands, had to console herself with a scanty diet, coarse enough to shock even a beggar. What wonder, then, if the craving of the stomach should allow her no escape from downright theft! Who is there that could resist? Where is the honesty that could not, under such circumstances, find an argument to justify larceny?

Every evening Miss Bradly came to spend an hour or so with them. The route from the school to her boarding-house wound by Mr. Peterkin's residence, and the temptation to talk to the young ladies, who were emphatically the belles of the neighborhood, was too great for resistance. This lady was of that class of females which we meet in every quarter of the globe,—of

perfectly kind intentions, yet without the independence necessary for their open and free expression. Bred in the North, and
having from her infancy imbibed the spirit of its free institutions,
in her secret soul she loathed the abomination of slavery, every
pulse of her heart cried out against it, yet with a strange compliance she lived in its midst, never once offering an objection
or an argument against it. It suited *her policy* to laugh with
the pro-slavery man at the fanaticism of the Northern Abolitionist. With a Judas-like hypocrisy, she sold her conscience for
silver; and for a mess of pottage, bartered the noble right of
free expression. 'Twas she, base renegade from a glorious cause,
who laughed loudest and repeated wholesale libels and foul as-
persions upon the able defenders of abolition—noble and generous men, lofty philanthropists, who are willing, for the sake of
principle, to wear upon their brows the mark of social and political ostracism! But a day is coming, a bright millennial day,
when the names of these inspired prophets shall be inscribed
proudly upon the litany of freedom; when their noble efforts
for social reform shall be told in wondering pride around the
winter's fire. Then shall their fame shine with a glory which
no Roman tradition can eclipse. Freed from calumny, the
names of Parker, Seward and Sumner, will be ranked, as they
deserve to be, with Washington, Franklin and Henry. All
glory to the American Abolitionists. Though they must now
possess their souls in patience, and bear the brand of social op-
probrium, yet will posterity accord them the meed of everlasting honor. They " who sow in dishonor shall be raised in glory."
Already the watchman upon the tower has discerned the signal.
A light beameth in the East, which no man can quench. A fire
has broken forth, which needs only a breath to fan it into a
flame. The eternal law of sovereign right will vindicate itself.
In the hour of feasting and revelry the dreadful bolt of retribu-
tion fell upon Gomorrah.

CHAPTER IV

CONVERSATION WITH MISS BRADLY—A LIGHT BREAKS THROUGH THE DARKNESS.

I HAD been living with Mr. Peterkin about three years, during which time I had frequently seen Miss Bradly. One evening when she called (as was her custom after the adjournment of school), she found, upon inquiry, that the young ladies had gone out, and would not probably be back for several hours. She looked a little disconcerted, and seemed doubtful whether she would go home or remain. I had often observed her attentively watching me, yet I could not interpret the look; sometimes I thought it was of deep, earnest pity. Then it appeared only an anxious curiosity; and as commiseration was a thing which I seldom met with, I tried to guard my heart against anything like hope or trust; but on this afternoon I was particularly struck by her strange and irresolute manner. She turned several times as if to leave, then suddenly stopped, and, looking very earnestly at me, asked, "Did you say the girls would not return for several hours?"

Upon receiving an answer in the affirmative, she hesitated a moment, and then inquired for Mr. Peterkin. He was also from home, and would probably be absent for a day or two. "Is there no white person about the place?" she asked, with some trepidation.

"No one is here but the slaves," I replied, perhaps in a sorrowful tone, for the word "slave" always grated upon my ear, yet I frequently used it, in obedience to a severe and imperative conventionality.

"Well then, Ann, come and sit down near me; I want to talk with you awhile."

This surprised me a great deal. I scarcely knew what to do. The very idea of sitting down to a conversation with a white lady seemed to me the wildest improbability. A vacant stare was the only answer I could make. Certainly, I did not dream of her being in earnest.

"Come on, Ann," she said, coaxingly; but, seeing that my amazement increased, she added, in a more persuasive tone, "Don't be afraid, I am a friend to the colored race."

This seemed to me the strangest fiction. A white lady, and yet a friend to the colored race! Oh, impossible! such condescension was unheard of! What! she a refined woman, with a snowy complexion, to stoop from her proud elevation to befriend the lowly Ethiopian! Why, she could not, she dare not! Almost stupefied with amazement, I stood, with my eyes intently fixed upon her.

"Come, child," she said, in a kind tone, and placing her hand upon my shoulder, she endeavored to seat me beside her, "look up,—be not ashamed, for I am truly your friend. Your down-cast look and melancholy manner have often struck me with sorrow."

To this I could make no reply. Utterance was denied me. My tongue clove to the roof of my mouth; a thick, filmy veil gathered before my sight; and there I stood like one turned to stone. But upon being frequently reassured by her gentle manner and kind words, I at length controlled my emotions, and, seating myself at her feet, awaited her communication.

"Ann, you are not happy here?"

I said nothing, but she understood my look.

"Were you happy at home?"

"I was;" and the words were scarcely audible.

"Did they treat you kindly there?"

"Indeed they did; and there I had a mother, and was not lonely."

"They did not beat you?"

"No, no, they did not," and large tears gushed from my burning eyes;—for I remembered with anguish, how many a smarting blow had been given to me by Mr. Jones, how many a cuff by Mr. Peterkin, and ten thousand knocks, pinches, and tortures, by the young ladies.

"Don't weep, child," said Miss Bradly, in a soothing tone, and she laid her arm caressingly around my neck. This kindness was too much for my fortitude, and bursting through all restraints I gave vent to my feelings in a violent shower of tears. She very wisely allowed me some time for the gratification of this luxury. I at length composed myself, and begged her pardon for this seeming disrespect.

"But ah, my dear lady, you have spoken so kindly to me that I forgot myself."

"No apology, my child, I tell you again that I am your friend, and with me you can be perfectly free. Look upon me as a sister; but now that your excited feelings have become allayed, let me ask you why your master sold you ?"

I explained to her that it was necessary to the equal division of the estate that some of the slaves should be sold, and that I was among the number.

"A bad institution is this one of slavery. What fearful entailments of anguish! Manage it as the most humane will, or can, still it has horrible results. Witness your separation from your mother. Did these thoughts never occur to you ?"

I looked surprised, but dared not tell her that often had vague doubts of the justice of slavery crossed my mind. Ah, too much I feared the lash, and I answered only by a mournful look of assent.

"Ann, did you never hear of the Abolition Society ?"

I shook my head. She paused, as if doubtful of the propriety of making a disclosure; but at length the better principle triumphed, and she said, "There is in the Northern States an organization which devotes its energies and very life to the cause of the slave. They wish to abolish the shameful system, and make you and all your persecuted race as free and happy as the whites."

"Does there really exist such a society ; or is it only a wild fable that you tell me, for the purpose of allaying my present agony ?"

" No, child ; I do not deceive you. This noble and beneficent society really lives ; but it does not, I regret to say, flourish as it should."

" And why ?" I asked, whilst a new wonder was fastening on my mind.

" Because," she answered, " the larger portion of the whites are mean and avaricious enough to desire, for the sake of pecuniary aggrandizement, the enslavement of a race, whom the force of education and hereditary prejudice have taught them to regard as their own property."

I did but dimly conceive her meaning. A slow light was breaking through my cloudy brain, kindling and inflaming hopes that now shine like beacons over the far waste of memory. Should I, could I, ever be *free* ? Oh, bright and glorious dream ! how it did sparkle in my soul, and cheer me through the lonely hours of bondage ! This hope, this shadow of a hope, shone like a mirage far away upon the horizon of a clouded future.

Miss Bradly looked thoughtfully at me, as if watching the effect of her words; but she could not see that the seed which she had planted, perhaps carelessly, was destined to fructify and flourish through the coming seasons. I longed to pour out my heart to her ; for she had, by this ready " sesame,"unlocked its deepest chambers. I dared not unfold even to her the wild dreams and strange hopes which I was indulging.

I spied Melinda coming up, and signified to Miss Bradly that it would be unsafe to prolong the conversation, and quickly she departed; not, however, without reassuring me of the interest which she felt in my fate.

" What was Miss Emily Bradly talking wid you 'bout ?" demanded Melinda, in a surly tone.

"Nothing that concerns you," I answered.

" Well, but you'll see that it consarns yerself, when I goes and tells Masser on you."

" What can you tell him on me ?"

"Oh, I knows, I hearn you talking wid dat ar' woman;" and she gave a significant leer of her eye, and lolled her tongue out of her mouth, à la mad dog.

I was much disturbed lest she had heard the conversation, and should make a report of it, which would redound to the disadvantage of my new friend. I went about my usual duties with a slow and heavy heart; still, sometimes, like a star shining through clouds, was that little bright hope of liberty.

CHAPTER V.

A FASHIONABLE TEA-TABLE—TABLE-TALK—AUNT POLLY'S EX-
PERIENCE—THE OVERSEER'S AUTHORITY—THE WHIPPING-
POST—TRANSFIGURING POWER OF DIVINE FAITH.

THAT evening when the family returned, I was glad to find the
young ladies in such an excellent humor. It was seldom Miss
Jane, whose peculiar property I was, ever gave me a kind word;
and I was surprised on this occasion to hear her say, in a somewhat gentle tone:

"Well, Ann, come here, I want you to look very nice to-night,
and wait on the table in style, for I am expecting company;"
and, with a sort of half good-natured smile, she tossed an old
faded neck-ribbon to me, saying,

"There is a present for you." I bowed low, and made a
respectful acknowledgment of thanks, which she received in an
unusually complacent manner.

Immediately I began to make arrangements for supper, and
to get myself in readiness, which was no small matter, as my
scanty wardrobe furnished no scope for the exercise of taste.
In looking over my trunk, I found a white cotton apron, which
could boast of many mice-bites and moth-workings; but with a
needle and thread I soon managed to make it appear decent,
and, combing my hair as neatly as possible, and tying the ribbon which Miss Jane had given me around it, I gave the finishing touch to my toilette, and then set about arranging the table.
I assorted the tea-board, spoons, cups, saucers, &c., placed a
nice damask napkin at each seat, and turned down the round
little plates of white French china. The silver forks and ivory-
handled knives were laid round the table in precise order.
This done, I surveyed my work with an air of pride. Smiling

complacently to myself, I proceeded to Miss Jane's room, to
request her to come and look at it, and express her opinion.

On reaching her apartment, I found her dressed with great
care, in a pink silk, with a rich lace berthé, and pearl ornaments. Her red hair was oiled until its fiery hue had darkened
into a becoming auburn, and the metallic polish of the French
powder had effectually concealed the huge freckles which
spotted her cheeks.

Dropping a low courtesy, I requested her to come with me to
the dining-room and inspect my work. With a smile, she followed, and upon examination, seemed well pleased.

"Now, Ann, if you do well in officiating, it will be well for
you ; but if you fail, if you make one mistake, you had better
never been born, for," and she grasped me strongly by the
shoulder, " I will flay you alive; you shall ache and smart in
every limb and nerve."

Terror-stricken at this threat, I made the most earnest
promises to exert my very best energies. Yet her angry manner and threatening words so unnerved me, that I was not able
to go on with the work in the same spirit in which I had begun,
for we all know what a paralysis fear is to exertion.

I stepped out on the balcony for some purpose, and there,
standing at the end of the gallery, but partially concealed by
the clematis blossoms, stood Miss Jane, and a tall gentleman
was leaning over the railing talking very earnestly to her. In
that uncertain light I could see the flash of her eye and the
crimson glow of her cheek. She was twirling and tearing to
pieces, petal by petal, a beautiful rose which she held in her
hand. Here, I thought here is happiness; this woman loves
and is beloved. She has tasted of that one drop which sweetens
the whole cup of existence. Oh, what a thing it is to be *free*—
free and independent, with power and privilege to go whithersoever you choose, with no cowardly fear, no dread of espionage,
with the right to hold your head proudly aloft, and return
glance for glance, not shrink and cower before the white man's
look, as we poor slaves *must* do. But not many moments could

I thus spend in thought, and well, perhaps, it was for me that
duty broke short all such unavailing regrets.

Hastening back to the dining-room, I gave another inquiring
look at the table, fearful that some article had been omitted.
Satisfying myself on this point, I moved on to the kitchen,
where Aunt Polly was busy frying a chicken.

"Here, child," she exclaimed, "look in thar at them biscuits.
See is they done. Oh, that's prime, browning beautiful-like,"
she said, as I drew from the stove a pan of nice biscuits, "and
this ar' chicken is mighty nice. Oh, but it will make the young
gemman smack his lips," and wiping the perspiration from her
sooty brow, she drew a long breath, and seated herself upon a
broken stool.

"Wal, this ar' nigger is tired. I's bin cooking now this
twelve years, and never has I had 'mission' to let my old man
come to see me, or I to go see him."

The children, with eyes wide open, gathered round Aunt
Polly to hear a recital of her wrongs. "Laws-a-marcy, sights
I's seen in my times, and often it 'pears like I's lost my senses.
I tells you, yous only got to look at this ar' back to know what
I's went through." Hereupon she exposed her back and arms,
which were frightfully scarred.

"This ar' scar," and she pointed to a very deep one on her
left shoulder, "Masser gib me kase I cried when he sold my
oldest son; poor Jim, he was sent down the river, and I've
never hearn from him since." She wiped a stray tear from her
old eyes.

"Oh me! 'tis long time since my eyes hab watered, and now
these tears do feel so quare. Poor Jim is down the river, Johnny
is dead, and Lucy is sold somewhar, so I have neither chick
nor child. What's I got to live fur?"

This brought fresh to my mind recollections of my own
mother's grief, when she was forced to give me up, and I could
not restrain my tears.

"What fur you crying, child?" she asked. "It puts me in
mind ov my poor little Luce, she used to cry this way whenever

anything happened to me. Oh, many is the time she screamed
if master struck me."

"Poor Aunt Polly," I said, as I walked up to her side, "I do
pity you. I will be kind to you; I'll be your daughter."

She looked up with a wild stare, and with a deep earnestness
seized hold of my out-stretched hand; then dropping it suddenly,
she murmured,

"No, no, you ain't my darter, you comes to me with saft
words, but you is jest like Lindy and all the rest of 'em; you'll go
to the house and tell tales to the white folks on me. No, I'll not
trust any of you."

Springing suddenly into the room, with his eyes flaming, came
Jones, and, cracking his whip right and left, he struck each of
the listening group. I retreated hastily to an extreme corner
of the kitchen, where, unobserved by him, I could watch the
affray.

"You devilish old wretch, Polly, what are you gabbling and
snubbling here about ? Up with your old hide, and git yer
supper ready. Don't you know thar is company in the house ?"
and here he gave another sharp cut of the whip, which descended upon that poor old scarred back with a cruel force, and
tore open old cicatriced wounds. The victim did not scream,
nor shrink, nor murmur; but her features resumed their wonted
hard, encrusted expression, and, rising up from her seat, she
went on with her usual work.

"Now, cut like the wind," he added, as he flourished his whip
in the direction of the young blacks, who had been the interested
auditors of Aunt Polly's hair-breadth escapes, and quick as
lightning they were off to their respective quarters, whilst I
proceeded to assist Aunt Polly in dishing up the supper.

"This chicken," said I, in a tone of encouragement, " is beautifully cooked. How brown it is, and oh, what a delightful
savory odor."

"I'll be bound the white folks will find fault wid it. Nobody
ever did please Miss Jane. Her is got some of the most per-
kuler notions 'bout cookin'. I knows she'll be kommin' out

here, makin' a fuss 'long wid me 'bout dis same supper," and
the old woman shook her head knowingly.

I made no reply, for I feared the re-appearance of Mr. Jones,
and too often and too painfully had I felt the sting of his lash,
to be guilty of any wanton provocation of its severity.

Silently, but with bitter thoughts curdling my life-blood, did
I arrange the steaming cookies upon the luxurious board, and
then, with a deferential air, sought the parlor, and bade them
walk out to tea.

I found Miss Jane seated near a fine rosewood piano, and standing beside her was a gentleman, the same whom I had observed
with her upon the verandah.   Miss Matilda was at the window,
looking out upon the western heaven.   I spoke in a soft tone,
asking them, "Please walk out to tea."   The young gentleman
rose, and offered his arm to Miss Jane, which was graciously
accepted, and Miss Matilda followed.   I swung the dining-room
door open with great pomp and ceremony, for I knew that anything showy or grand, either in the furniture of a house or the
deportment of a servant, would be acceptable to Miss Jane.
Fashion, or style, was the god of her worship, and she often declared that her principal objection to the negro, was his great
want of style in thought and action.   She was not deep enough
to see that, fathoms down below the surface, in all the crudity of
ignorance, lay a stratum of this same style, so much worshipped
by herself.   Does not the African, in his love of gaud, show, and
tinsel, his odd and grotesque decorations of his person, exhibit a
love of style ?   But she was not philosopher enough to see that
this was a symptom of the same taste, though ungarnished and
semi-barbarous.

The supper passed off very handsomely, so far as my part
was concerned.   I carried the cups round on a silver salver to
each one; served them with chicken, plied them with cakes,
confections, &c., and interspersed my performance with innumerable courtesies, bows and scrapes.

"Ah," said Miss Jane to the gentleman, "ah, Mr. Somerville,
you have visited us at the wrong season; you should be here

later in the autumn, or earlier in the summer," and she gave one of her most benign smiles.

"Any season is pleasant here," replied Mr. Somerville, as he held the wing of a chicken between his thumb and fore-finger. Miss Jane simpered and looked down ; and Miss Matilda arched her brows and gave a significant side-long glance toward her sister.

"Here, you cussed yellow gal," cried Mr. Peterkin, in a rage, "take this split spoon away and fetch me a fork what I ken use. These darned things is only made for grand folks," and he held the silver fork to me. Instantly I replaced it with a steel one.

"Now this looks something like. We only uses them ar' other ones when we has company, so I suppose, Mr. Somerville, the girl sot the table in this grand way bekase you is here."

No thunder-cloud was ever darker than Miss Jane's brow. It gathered, and deepened, and darkened like a thick-coming tempest, whilst lightnings blazed from her eye.

"Father," and she spoke through her clenched teeth, "what makes you affect this horrid vulgarity ? and how can you be so very *idiosyncratic*" (this was a favorite word with her) "as to say you never use them ? Ever since I can remember, silver forks have been used in our family ; but," and she smiled as she said it, "Mr. Somerville, father thinks it is truly a Kentucky fashion, and in keeping with the spirit of the early settlers, to rail out against fashion and style."

To this explanation Mr. Somerville bowed blandly. "Ah, yes, I do admire your father's honest independence."

"I'll jist tell you how it is, young man, my gals has bin better edicated than their pappy, and they pertends to be mighty 'shamed of me, bekase I has got no larnin' ; but I wants to ax 'em one question, whar did the money kum from that give 'em thar larning ?" and with a triumphant force he brought his hard fist down on the table, knocking off with his elbow a fine cut-glass tumbler, which was shivered to atoms.

"Thar now," he exclaimed, "another piece of yer cussed

frippery is breaked to bits. What did you put it here fur? I
wants that big tin-cup that I drinks out of when nobody's
here."

"Father, father," said Miss Matilda, who until now had kept
an austere silence, "why will you persist in this outrageous
talk? Why will you mortify and torture us in this cruel way?"
and she burst into a flood of angry tears.

"Oh, don't blubber about it, Tildy, I didn't mean to hurt
your feelin's."

Pretty soon after this, the peace of the table being broken up,
the ladies and Mr. Somerville adjourned to the parlor, whilst
Melinda, or Lindy, as she was called, and I set about clearing
off the table, washing up the dishes, and gathering and counting
over the forks and spoons.

Now, though the young ladies made great pretensions to
elegance and splendor of living, yet were they vastly economi-
cal when there was no company present. The silver was all
carefully laid away, and locked up in the lower drawer of an
old-fashioned bureau, and the family appropriated a commoner
article to their every-day use; but let a solitary guest appear,
and forthwith the napkins and silver would be displayed, and
treated by the ladies as though it was quite a usual thing.

"Now, Ann," said 'Lindy "you wash the dishes, and I'll count
the spoons and forks."

To this I readily assented, for I was anxious to get clear of
such a responsible office as counting and assorting the silver
ware.

Mr. Peterkin, or master, as we called him, sat near by, smoking his cob-pipe in none the best humor; for the recent encounter
at the supper-table was by no means calculated to improve his
temper.

"See here, gals," he cried in a tone of thunder, "if thar be
one silver spoon or fork missin', yer hides shall pay for the loss."

"Laws, master, I'll be 'tickler enough," replied Lindy, as she
smiled, more in terror than pleasure.

"Wal," he said, half aloud, "whar is the use of my darters

takin' on in the way they does ?   Jist look at the sight o' money that has bin laid out in that ar' tom-foolery."

This was a sort of soliloquy spoken in a tone audible enough to be distinct to us.

He drew his cob-pipe from his mouth, and a huge volume of smoke curled round his head, and filled the room with the aroma of tobacco.

"Now," he continued, "they does not treat me wid any per-liteness. They thinks they knows a power more than I does; but if they don't cut their cards square, I'll cut them short of a nigger or two, and make John all the richer by it."

Lindy cut her eye knowingly at this, and gave me rather a strong nudge with her elbow.

"Keep still thar, gals, and don't rattle them cups and sassers so powerful hard."

By this time Lindy had finished the assortment of the silver, and had carefully stowed it away in a willow-basket, ready to be delivered to Miss Jane, and thence consigned to the drawer, where it would remain in *statu quo* until the timely advent of another guest.

"Now," she said, "I am ready to wipe the dishes, while you wash."

Thereupon I handed her a saucer, which, in her carelessness, she let slip from her hand, and it fell upon the floor, and there, with great consternation, I beheld it lying, shattered to fragments. Mr. Peterkin sprang to his feet, glad of an excuse to vent his temper upon some one.

"Which of you cussed wretches did this ?"

"'Twas Ann, master! She let it fall afore I got my hand on it.

Ere I had time to vindicate myself from the charge, his iron arm felled me to the floor, and his hoof-like foot was placed upon my shrinking chest.

"You d—n yallow hussy, does you think I buys such expen-sive chany-ware for you to break up in this ar' way? No, you 'bominable wench, I'll have revenge out of your saffer'n hide. Here, Lindy, fetch me that cowhide."

"Mercy, master, mercy," I cried, when he had removed his foot from my breast, and my breath seemed to come again. "Oh, listen to me; it was not I who broke the saucer, it was only an accident; but oh, in God's name, have mercy on me and Lindy."

"Yes, I'll tache you what marcy is. Here, quick, some of you darkies, bring me a rope and light. I'm goin' to take this gal to the whippin'-post."

This overcame me, for, though I had often been cruelly beaten, yet had I escaped the odium of the "post;" and now for what I had not done, and for a thing which, at the worst, was but an accident, to bear the disgrace and the pain of a public whipping, seemed to me beyond endurance. I fell on my knees before him:

"Oh, master, please pardon me; spare me this time. I have got a half-dollar that Master Edward gave me when you bought me, I will give you that to pay for the saucer, but please do not beat me."

With a wild, fiendish grin, he caught me by the hair and swung me round until I half-fainted with pain.

"No, you wretch, I'll git my satisfaction out of yer body yit, and I'll be bound, afore this night's work is done, yer yallow hide will be well marked."

A deadly, cold sensation crept over me, and a feeling as of crawling adders seemed possessing my nerves. With all my soul pleading in my eyes I looked at Mr. Peterkin; but one glance of his fiendish face made my soul quail with even a newer horror. I turned my gaze from him to Jones, but the red glare of a demon lighted up his frantic eye, and the words of a profane bravo were on his lips. From him I turned to poor, hardened, obdurate old Nace, but he seemed to be linked and leagued with ny torturers.

"Oh, Lindy," I cried, as she came up with a bunch of cord in her hand, "be kind, tell the truth, maybe master will forgive you. You are an older servant, better known and valued in the family. Oh, let your heart triumph. Speak the truth, and free me from the torture that awaits me. Oh, think of me, away off here, separated from my mother, with no friend. Oh, pity me, and do acknowledge that you broke it."

"Well, you is crazy, you knows dat I never touched de sacer," and she laughed heartily.

"Come along wid you all. Now fur fun," cried Nace.

"Hold your old jaw," said Jones, and he raised his whip. Nace cowered like a criminal, and made some polite speech to "Massa Jones," and Mr. Peterkin possessed himself of the rope which Lindy had brought.

"Now hold yer hands here," he said to me.

For one moment I hesitated. I could not summon courage to offer my hands. It was the only resistance that I had ever dared to make. A severe blow from the overseer's riding-whip reminded me that I was still a slave, and dared have no will save that of my master. This blow, which struck the back of my head, laid me half-lifeless upon the floor. Whilst in this condition old Nace, at the command of his master, bound the rope tightly around my crossed arms and dragged me to the place of torment.

The motion or exertion of being pulled along over the ground, restored me to full consciousness. With a haggard eye I looked up to the still blue heaven, where the holy stars yet held their silent vigil; and the serene moon moved on in her starry track, never once heeding the dire cruelty, over which her pale beam shed its friendly light. "Oh," thought I, "is there no mercy throned on high? Are there no spirits in earth, air, or sky, to lend me their gracious influence? Does God look down with kindness upon injustice like this? Or, does He, too, curse me in my sorrow, and in His wrath turn away His glorious face from my supplication, and say 'a servant of servants shalt thou be?'" These wild, rebellious thoughts only crossed my mind; they did not linger there. No, like the breath-stain upon the polished surface of the mirror, they only soiled for a moment the shining faith which in my soul reflected the perfect goodness of that God who never forgets the humblest of His children, and who makes no distinction of color or of race. The consoling promise, "He chasteneth whom He loveth," flashed through my brain with its blessed assurance, and reconciled me to a heroic endurance. Far away I strained my gaze to the starry heaven, and I could almost fancy the sky breaking asunder and disclosing the wondrous splendors which were beheld by the rapt Apostle on the isle of Patmos! Oh, transfiguring power of faith! Thou hast a wand more potent than that of fancy, and a vision brighter than the dreams of enchantment! What was it that reconciled me to the horrible tortures which were awaiting me? Surely, 'twas faith alone that sustained me. The present scene faded away from my vision, and, in fancy, I stood in the lonely garden of Gethsemane. I saw the darkness and gloom that overshadowed the earth, when, deserted by His disciples, our blessed Lord prayed alone. I heard the sighs and groans that burst from his tortured breast. I saw the bloody sweat, as prostrate on the earth he lay in the tribulation of mortal agony. I saw the inhuman captors, headed by one of His chosen twelve, come to seize his sacred person. I saw his face uplifted to the mournful heavens, as He prayed to His Father to remove the cup of sorrow. I saw Him bound and led away to death, without a friend to solace Him. Through the various stages of His awful passion, even to the Mount of Crucifixion, to the bloody and sacred Calvary, I followed my Master. I saw Him nailed to the cross, spit upon, vilified and abused, with the thorny crown pressed upon His brow. I heard the rabble shout; then I saw the solemn mystery of Nature, that did attestation to the awful fact that a fiendish work had been done and the prophecy fulfilled. The vail of the great temple was rent, the sun overcast, and the moon turned to blood; and in my ecstasy of passion, I could have shouted, Great is Jesus of Nazareth!! Then I beheld Him triumphing over the powers of darkness and death, when, robed in the white garments of the grave, He broke through the rocky sepulchre, and stood before the affrighted guards. His work was done, the propitiation had been made, and He went to His Father. This same Jesus, whom the civilized world now worship as their Lord, was once lowly, outcast,

and despised; born of the most hated people of the world, belonging to a race despised alike by Jew and Gentile; laid in
the manger of a stable at Bethlehem, with no earthly possessions,
having not whereon to lay His weary head; buffetted, spit
upon; condemned by the high priests and the doctors of law;
branded as an impostor, and put to an ignominious death, with
every demonstration of public contempt; crucified between two
thieves; this Jesus is worshipped now by those who wear purple
and fine linen.   The class which once scorned Him, now offer
at His shrine frankincense and myrrh; but, in their adoration
of the despised Nazarene, they never remember that He has declared, not once, but many times, that the poor and the lowly
are His people.   "Forasmuch as you did it unto one of these
you did it unto me."   Then let the African trust and hope on—
let him still weep and pray in Gethsemane, for a cloud hangs
round about him, and when he prays for the removal of this
cup of bondage, let him remember to ask, as his blessed Master
did, "Thy will, oh Father, and not our own, be done;" still
trust in Him who calmed the raging tempest: trust in Jesus of
Nazareth!   Look beyond the cross, to Christ.

These thoughts had power to cheer; and, fortified by faith
and religion, the trial seemed to me easy to bear.   One prayer
I murmured, and my soul said to my body, "pass under the
rod;" and the cup which my Father has given me to drink
must be drained, even to the dregs.

In this state of mind, with a moveless eye I looked upon the
whipping-post, which loomed up before me like an ogre.

This was a quadri-lateral post, about eight feet in height,
having iron clasps on two opposing sides, in which the wrists
and ankles were tightly secured.

"Now, Lindy," cried Jones, "jerk off that gal's rigging, I am
anxious to put some marks on her yellow skin."

I knew that resistance was vain; so I submitted to have my
clothes torn from my body; for modesty, so much commended
in a white woman, is in a negro pronounced affectation.

Jones drew down a huge cow-hide, which he dipped in a barrel of brine that stood near the post.

" I guess this will sting," he said, as he flourished the whip toward me.

" Leave that thin slip on me, Lindy," I ventured to ask; for I dreaded the exposure of my person even more than the whipping.

" None of your cussed impedence; strip off naked. What is a nigger's hide more than a hog's ?" cried Jones. Lindy and Nace tore the last article of clothing from my back. I felt my soul shiver and shudder at this; but what could I do ? *I could pray*—thank God, I could pray !

I then submitted to have Nace clasp the iron cuffs around my hands and ankles, and there I stood, a revolting spectacle. With what misery I listened to obscene and ribald jests from my master and his overseer !

" Now, Jones," said Mr. Peterkin, " I want to give that gal the first lick, which will lay the flesh open to the bone."

" Well, Mr. Peterkin, here is the whip; now you can lay on."

" No, confound your whip; I wants that cow-hide, and here, let me dip it well into the brine. I want to give her a real good warmin'; one that she'll 'member for a long time."

During this time I had remained motionless. My heart was lifted to God in silent prayer. Oh, shall I, can I, ever forget that scene ? There, in the saintly stillness of the summer night, where the deep, o'ershadowing heavens preached a sermon of peace, there I was loaded with contumely, bound hand and foot in irons, with jeering faces around, vulgar eyes glaring on my uncovered body, and two inhuman men about to lash me to the bone.

The first lick from Mr. Peterkin laid my back open. I writhed, I wrestled ; but blow after blow descended, each harder than the preceding one. I shrieked, I screamed, I pleaded, I prayed, but there was no mercy shown me. Mr. Peterkin having fully gratified and quenched his spleen, turned to Mr. Jones, and said, "Now is yer turn; you can beat her as much as you please, only jist leave a bit o' life in her, is all I cares for."

"Yes; I'll not spile her for the market; but I does want to take a little of the d——d pride out of her."

"Now, boys"—for by this time all the slaves on the place, save Aunt Polly, had assembled round the post—"you will see what a true stroke I ken make; but darn my buttons if I doesn't think Mr. Peterkin has drawn all the blood."

So saying, Jones drew back the cow-hide at arm's length, and, making a few evolutions with his body, took what he called "sure aim." I closed my eyes in terror. More from the terrible pain, than from the frantic shoutings of the crowd, I knew that Mr. Jones had given a lick that he called "true blue." The exultation of the negroes in Master Jones' triumph was scarcely audible to my ears; for a cold, clammy sensation was stealing over my frame; my breath was growing feebler and feebler, and a soft melody, as of lulling summer fountains, was gently sounding in my ears; and, as if gliding away on a moonbeam, I passed from all consciousness of pain. A sweet oblivion, like that sleep which announces to the wearied, fever-sick patient, that his hour of rest has come, fell upon me! It was not a dreamful sensibility, filled with the chaos of fragmentary visions, but a rest where the mind, nay, the very soul, seemed to sleep with the body.

How long this stupor lasted I am unable to say; but when I awoke, I was lying on a rough bed, a face dark, haggard, scarred and worn, was bending over me. Disfigured as was that visage, it was pleasant to me, for it was human. I opened my eyes, then closed them languidly, re-opened them, then closed them again.

"Now, chile, I thinks you is a leetle better," said the dark-faced woman, whom I recognized as Aunt Polly; but I was too weak, too wandering in mind, to talk, and I closed my eyes and slept again.

CHAPTER VI.

RESTORED CONSCIOUSNESS—AUNT POLLY'S ACCOUNT OF MY MIRACULOUS RETURN TO LIFE—THE MASTER'S AFFRAY WITH THE OVERSEER.

WHEN I awoke (for I was afterwards told by my good nurse that I had slept four days), I was lying on the same rude bed; but a cool, clear sensation overspread my system. I had full and active possession of my mental faculties. I rose and sat upright in the bed, and looked around me. It was the deep hour of night. A little iron lamp was upon the hearth, and, for want of a supply of oil, the wick was burning low, flinging a red glare through the dismal room. Upon a broken stool sat Aunt Polly, her head resting upon her breast, in what nurses call a "stolen nap." Amy and three other children were sleeping in a bed opposite me.

In a few moments I was able to recall the whole of the scenes through which I had passed, while consciousness remained; and I raised my eyes to God in gratitude for my partial deliverance from pain and suffering. Very softly I stole from my bed, and, wrapping an old coverlet round my shoulders, opened the door, and looked out upon the clear, star-light night. Of the vague thoughts that passed through my mind I will not now speak, though they were far from pleasant or consolatory.

The fresh night air, which began to have a touch of the frost of the advancing autumn, blew cheerily in the room, and it fell with an awakening power upon the brow of Aunt Polly.

"Law, chile, is dat you stannin' in de dor? What for you git up out en yer warm bed, and go stand in the night-ar?"

"Because I feel so well, and this pleasant air seems to brace my frame, and encourage my mind."

"But sure you had better take to your bed again; you hab had a mighty bad time ob it."

"How long have I been sick? It all seems to me like a horrible dream, from which I have been suddenly and pleasantly aroused."

As I said this, Aunt Polly drew me from the door, and closing it, she bade me go to bed.

"No, indeed, I cannot sleep. I feel wide awake, and if I only had some one to talk to me, I could sit up all night."

"Well, bress your heart, I'll talk wid you smack, till de rise ob day," she said, in such a kind, good-natured tone, that I was surprised, for I had regarded her only as an ill-natured, miserable beldame.

Seating myself on a ricketty stool beside her, I prepared for a long conversation.

"Tell me what has happened since I have been sick?" I said. "Where are Miss Jane and Matilda? and where is the young gentleman who supped with them on that awful night?"

"Bress you, honey, but 'twas an awful night. Dis ole nigger will neber forget it long as she libs;" and she bent her head upon her poor old worn hands, and by the pale, blue flicker of the lamp, I could discern the rapidly-falling tears.

"What," thought I, "and this hardened, wretched old woman can weep for me! Her heart is not all ossified if she can forget her own bitter troubles, and weep for mine."

This knowledge was painful, and yet joyful to me. Who of us can refuse sympathy? Who does not want it, no matter at what costly price? Does it not seem like dividing the burden, when we know that there is another who will weep for us? I threw my arms round Aunt Polly. I tightly strained that decayed and revolting form to my breast, and I inly prayed that some young heart might thus rapturously go forth, in blessings to my mother. This evidence of affection did not surprise Aunt Polly, nor did she return my embrace; but a deep, hollow sigh, burst from her full heart, and I knew that memory was far away—that, in fancy, she was with her children, her loved and lost.

"Come, now," said I, soothingly, "tell me all about it. How did I suffer? What was done for me? Where is master?" and I shuddered, as I mentioned the name of my horrible persecutor.

"Oh, chile, when Masser Jones was done a-beatin' ob yer, dey all ob 'em tought you was dead; den Masser got orful skeard. He cussed and swore, and shook his fist in de oberseer's face, and sed he had kilt you, and dat he was gwine to law wid him 'bout de 'struction ob his property. Den Masser Jones he swar a mighty heap, and tell Masser he dar' him to go to law 'bout it. Den Miss Jane and Tilda kum out, and commenced cryin', and fell to 'busin' Masser Jones, kase Miss Jane say she want to go to de big town, and take you long wid her fur lady's maid. Den Mr. Jones fell to busen ob her, and den Masser and him clinched, and fought, and fought like two big black dogs. Den Masser Jones sticked his great big knife in Masser's side, and Masser fell down, and den we all tought he was clar gone. Den away Maser Jones did run, and nobody dared take arter him, for he had a loaded pistol and a big knife. Den we all on us, de men and wimmin folks both, grabbed up Masser, and lifted him in de house, and put him on de bed. Den Jake, he started off fur de doctor, while Miss Jane and Tilda 'gan to fix Masser's cut side. Law, bress your heart, but thar he laid wid his big form stretched out just as helpless as a baby. His face was as white as a ghost, and his eyes shot right tight up. Law bress you, but I tought his time hab kum den. Well, Lindy and de oder wimmin was a helpin' ob Miss Jane and Tildy, so I jist tought I would go and look arter yer body. Thar you was, still tied to de post, all kivered with blood. I was mighty feared ob you; but den I tought you had been so perlite, and speaked so kind to me, dat I would take kare ob yer body; so I tuck you down. and went wid you to de horse-trough, and dere I poured some cold water ober yer, so as to wash away de clotted blood. Den de

cold water sorter 'vived you, and yer cried out 'oh, me!' Wal
dat did skeer me, and I let you drap right down in de trough,
and de way dis nigger did run, fur de life ob her. Well, as I
git back I met Jake, who had kum back wid de doctor, and I
cried out, 'Oh Jake, de spirit ob Ann done speaked to me!'
'Now, Polly,' says he, 'do hush your nonsense, you does
know dat Ann is done cold dead.' 'Well Jake,' says I, 'I tuck
her down frum de post, and tuck her to the trough to wash her,
and tought I'd fix de body out right nice, in de best close dat
she had. Well, jist as I got de water on it, somping hollowed
out, 'oh me!' so mournful like, dat it 'peared to me it kum out
ob de ground.

"'What fur den you do?' says Jake. 'Why, to be sure, I lef
it right dar, and run as fas' as my feet would carry me.'

" By dis time de house was full ob de neighbors ; all hab collected in de house, fur de news dat Masser was kilt jist fly
trough de neighborhood. Miss Bradly hearn in de house 'bout
de 'raculous 'pearance ob de sperit, and she kum up to me, and
say ' Polly, whar is de body of Ann?' ' Laws, Miss Bradly, it
is out in de trough, I won't go agin nigh to it.'

"'Well,' say she, 'where is Jake? let him kum along wid me.'

"'What, you ain't gwine nigh it?' I asked.

"'Yes I is gwine right up to it,' she say, 'kase I knows thar
is life in it.' Well this sorter holpd me up, so I said, 'well I'll
go too.' So we tuck Jake, and Miss Bradly walked long wid
us to de berry spot, and dar you wus a settin up in de water ob
de trough where I seed you; it skeered me worse den eber, so
I fell right down on de ground, and began to pray to de Lord to
hab marcy on us all; but Miss Bradly (she is a quare woman)
walked right up to you, and spoke to you.

" ' Laws,' says Jake, ' jist hear dat ar' woman talking wid a
sperit,' and down he fell, and went to callin on de Angel Ga-
briel to kum and holp him.

" Fust ting I knowed, Miss Bradly was a rollin' her shawl round
yer body, and axed you to walk out ob de trough.

" Well, tinks I, dese am quare times when a stone-dead nigger gits up and walks agin like a live one. Well, widout any help from us, Miss Bradly led you 'long into dis cabin. I followed arter. After while she kind o' 'suaded me you was a livin'. Den I helped her wash you, and got her some goose-greese, and we rubbed you all ober, from your head to yer feet, and den you kind ob fainted away, and I began to run off; but Miss Bradly say you only swoon, and she tuck a little glass vial out ob her pocket, and held it to yer nose, and dis bring you to agin. After while you fell off to sleep, and Miss Bradly bringed de Doctor out ob de house to look at you. Well, he feel ob yer wrist, put his ear down to yer breast, den say, 'may be wid care she will git well, but she hab been powerful bad treated.' He shuck his head, and I knowed what he was tinkin' 'bout, but I neber say one word. Den Miss Bradly wiped her eyes, and de Doctor fetch anoder sigh, and say, dis is very 'stressing,' and Miss Bradly say somepin agin ' slavery,' and de Doctor open ob his eyes right wide and say, ' 'tis worth your head, Miss, for to say dat in dis here country.' Den she kind of 'splained it to him, and tings just seemed square 'twixt 'em, for she was monstrous skeered like, and turned white as a sheet. Den I hearn de Doctor say sompin' 'bout ridin' on a rail, and tar and feaders, and abolutionist. So arter dat, Miss Bradly went into de house, arter she had bin a tellin' ob me to nurse you well; dat you was way off hare from yer mammy, so eber sence den you has bin a lying right dar on dat bed, and I hab nursed you as if you war my own child."

I threw my arms around her again, and imprinted kisses upon her rugged brow; for, though her skin was sooty and her face worn with care, I believed that somewhere in a silent corner of her tried heart there was a ray of warm, loving, human feeling.

" Oh, child," she begun, " can you wid yer pretty yellow face kiss an old pitch-black nigger like me ?"

" Why, yes, Aunt Polly, and love you too ; if your face is dark I am sure your heart is fair."

" Well, I doesn't know 'bout dat, chile ; once 'twas far, but I tink all de white man done made it black as my face."

"Oh no, I can't believe that, Aunt Polly," I replied.

"Wal, I always hab said dat if dey would cut my finger and cut a white woman's, dey would find de blood ob de very same color," and the old woman laughed exultingly.

"Yes, but, Aunt Polly, if you were to go before a magistrate with a case to be decided, he would give it against you, no matter how just were your claims."

"To be sartin, de white folks allers gwine to do every ting in favor ob dar own color."

"But, Aunt Polly," interposed I, "there is a God above, who disregards color."

"Sure dare is, and dar we will all ob us git our dues, and den de white folks will roast in de flames ob old Nick."

I saw, from a furtive flash of her eye, that all the malignity and revenge of her outraged nature were becoming excited, and I endeavored to change the conversation.

"Is master getting well?"

"Why, yes, chile, de debbil can't kill him. He is 'termined to live jist as long as dare is a nigger to torment. All de time he was crazy wid de fever, he was fightin' wid de niggers— 'pears like he don't dream 'bout nothin' else."

"Does he sit up now?" I asked this question with trepidation, for I really dreaded to see him.

"No, he can't set up none. De doctor say he lost a power o' blood, and he won't let him eat meat or anyting strong, and I tells you, honey, Masser does swar a heap. He wants to smoke his pipe, and to hab his reglar grog, and dey won't gib it to him. It do take Jim and Jake bofe to hold him in de bed, when his tantarums comes on. He fights dem, he calls for de oberseer, he orders dat ebery nigger on de place shall be tuck to de post. I tells you now, I makes haste to git out ob his way. He struck Jake a lick dat kum mighty nigh puttin' out his eye. It's all bunged up now."

"Where did Mr. Somerville go?" I asked.

"Oh, de young gemman dat dey say is a courtin' Miss Jane, he hab gone back to de big town what he kum from; but Lindy say Miss Jane got a great long letter from him, and Lindy say she tink Miss Jane gwine to marry him."

"Well, I belong to Miss Jane; I wonder if she will take me with her to the town."

"Why, yes, chile, she will, for she do believe in niggers. She wants 'em all de time right by her side, a waitin' on her."

This thought set me to speculating. Here, then, was the prospect of another change in my home. The change might be auspicious; but it would take me away from Aunt Polly, and remove me from Miss Bradly's influence; and this I dreaded, for she had planted hopes in my breast, which must blossom, though at a distant season, and I wished to be often in her company, so that I might gain many important items from her.

Aunt Polly, observing me unusually thoughtful, argued that I was sleepy, and insisted upon my returning to bed. In order to avoid further conversation, and preserve, unbroken, the thread of my reflections, I obeyed her.

Throwing myself carelessly upon the rough pallet, I wandered in fancy until leaden-winged sleep overcame me.

CHAPTER VII.

AMY'S NARRATIVE, AND HER PHILOSOPHY OF A FUTURE STATE.

WHEN the golden sun had begun to tinge with light the distant tree-tops, and the young birds to chant their matin hymn, I awoke from my profound sleep. Wearily I moved upon my pillow, for though my slumber had been deep and sweet, yet now, upon awaking, I experienced no refreshment.

Rising up in the bed, and supporting myself upon my elbow, I looked round in quest of Aunt Polly; but then I remembered that she had to be about the breakfast. Amy was sitting on the floor, endeavoring to arrange the clothes on a little toddler, her orphan brother, over whom she exercised a sort of maternal care. She, her two sisters, and infant brother, were the orphans of a woman who had once belonged to a brother of Mr. Peterkin. Their orphanage had not fallen upon them from the ghastly fingers of death, but from the far more cruel and cold mandate of human cupidity. A fair, even liberal price had been offered their owner for their mother, Dilsy, and such a speculation was not to be resigned upon the score of philanthropy. No, the man who would refuse nine hundred dollars for a negro woman, upon the plea that she had three young children and a helpless infant, from whom she must not be separated, would, in Kentucky, be pronounced insane; and I can assure you that, on this subject, the brave Kentuckians had good right to decide, according to their code, that Elijah Peterkin was *compos mentis.*

"Amy," said I, as I rubbed my eyes, to dissipate the film and mists of sleep, "is it very late? have you heard the horn blow for the hands to come in from work?"

"No, me hab not hearn it yet, but laws, Ann, me did tink you would neber talk no more."

"But you see I am talking now," and 1 could not resist a smile; "have you been nursing me?"

"No, indeed, Aunt Polly wouldn't let me come nigh yer bed, and she keep all de time washing your body and den rubbin' it wid a feader an' goose-greese. Oh, you did lay here so still, jist like somebody dead. Aunt Polly, she wouldn't let one ob us speak one word, sed it would 'sturb you; but I knowed you wasn't gwine to kere, so ebery time she went out, I jist laughed and talked as much as I want."

"But did you not want me to get well, Amy?"

"Why, sartin I did; but my laughin' want gwine to kill you. was it?" She looked up with a queer, roguish smile.

"No, but it might have increased my fever."

"Well, if you had died, I would hab got yer close, now you knows you promised 'em to me. So when I hearn Jake say you was dead, I run and got yer new calico dress, and dat ribbon what Miss Jane gib you, an' put dem in my box; den arter while Aunt Polly say you done kum back to life; so I neber say notin' more, I jist tuck de close and put dem back in yer box, and tink to myself, well, maybe I will git 'em some oder time."

It amused me not a little to find that upon mere suspicion of my demise, this little negro had levied upon my wardrobe, which was scanty indeed; but so it is, be we ever so humble or poor, there is always some one to regard us with a covetous eye. My little paraphernalia was, to this half-savage child, a rich and wondrous possession.

"Here, hold up yer foot, Ben, or you shan't hab any meat fur breakus." This threat was addressed to her young brother, whom she nursed like a baby, and whose tiny foot seemed to resist the restraint of a shoe.

I looked long at them, and mused with a strange sorrow upon their probable destiny. Bitter I knew it must be. For, where is there, beneath the broad sweep of the majestic heavens, a single one of the dusky tribe of Ethiopia who has not felt that existence was to him far more a curse than a blessing? You, oh, my tawny brothers, who read these tear-stained pages, ask your own hearts, which, perhaps, now ache almost to bursting, ask, I say, your own vulture-torn hearts, if life is not a hard, hard burden? Have you not oftentimes prayed to the All-Merciful to sever the mystic tie that bound you here, to loosen your chains and set you, soul and body, free? Have you not, from the broken chinks of your lonely cabins at night, looked forth upon the free heavens, and murmured at your fate? Is there, oh! slave, in your heart a single pleasant memory? Do you not, captive-husband, recollect with choking pride how the wife of your bosom has been cruelly lashed while you dared not say one word in her defence? Have you not seen your children, precious pledges of undying love, ruthlessly torn from you, bound hand and foot and sold like dogs in the slave market, while you dared not offer a single remonstrance? Has not every social and moral feeling been outraged? Is it not the white man's policy to degrade your race, thereby finding an argument to favor the perpetuation of Slavery? Is there for us one thing to sweeten bondage? Free African! in the brave old States of the North, where the shackles of slavery exist not, to you I call. Noble defenders of Abolition, you whose earnest eyes may scan these pages, I call to you with a *tearful voice;* I pray you to go on in your glorious cause; flag not, faint not, prosecute it before heaven and against man. Fling out your banners and march on to the defence of the suffering ones at the South. And you, oh my heart-broken sisters, toiling beneath a tropic sun, wearing out your lives in the service of tyrants, to you I say, hope and pray still! Trust in God! He is mighty and willing to save, and, in an hour that you know not of, he will roll the stone away from the portal of your hearts. My prayers are with you and for you, I have come up from the same tribulation, and I vow, by the scars and wounds upon my flesh, never to forget your cause. Would that

my tears, which freely flow for you, had power to dissolve the
fetters of your wasting bondage.

Thoughts like these, though with more vagueness and less
form, passed through my brain as I looked upon those poor
little outcast children, and I must be excused for thus making,
regardless of the usual etiquette of authors, an appeal to the
hearts of my free friends. Never once do I wish them to lose
sight of the noble cause to which they have lent the influence
of their names. I am but a poor, unlearned woman, whose
heart is in her cause, and I should be untrue to the motive
which induced me to chronicle the dark passages in my woe-
worn life if I did not urge and importune the Apostles of Abolition to move forward and onward in their march of reform.

"Come, Amy, near to my bed, and talk a little with me."

"I wants to git some bread fust."

"You are always hungry," I pettishly replied.

"No, I isn't, but den, Ann, I neber does git enuf to eat here.
Now, we use to hab more at Mas' Lijah's."

"Was he a good master?" I asked.

"No, he wasn't; but den mammy used to gib us nice tings
to eat. She buyed it from de store, and she let us hab plenty
ob it."

"Where is your mammy?"

"She bin sold down de ribber to a trader," and there was a
quiver in the child's voice.

"Did she want to go?" I inquired.

"No, she cried a heap, and tell Masser she wouldn't mind it
if he would let her take us chilen; but Masser say no, he
wouldn't. Den she axed him please to let her hab little Ben,
any how. Masser cussed, and said, Well, she might hab Ben,
as he was too little to be ob any sarvice; den she 'peared so
glad and got him all ready to take; but when de trader kum to
take her away, he say he wouldn't 'low her to take Ben, kase
he couldn't sell her fur as much, if she hab a baby wid her;
den, oh den, how poor mammy did cry and beg; but de trader
tuck his cowhide and whipped her so hard she hab to stop cryin'

or beggin'. Den she kum to me and make me promise to take
good care ob Ben, to nurse him and tend on him as long as I
staid whar he was. Den she knelt down in de corner of her
cabin and prayed to God to take care ob us, all de days of our
life ; den she kissed us all and squeezed us tight, and when she
tuck little Ben in her arms it 'peared like her heart would
break. De water from her eyes wet Ben's apron right ringing
wet, jist like it had come out ob a washing tub. Den de trader
called to her to come along, and den she gib dis to me, and told
me dat ebery time I looked at it, I must tink of my poor mammy dat was sold down de ribber, and 'member my promise to
her 'bout my little brudder.''

Here the child exhibited a bored five-cent piece, which sue
wore suspended by a black string around her neck.

" De chilen has tried many times to git it away frum me ; but
I's allers beat 'em off ; and whenever Miss Tildy wants me fur
to mind her, she says, ' Now, Amy, I'll jist take yer mammy's
present from yer if yer doesn't do what I bids yer ;' den de way
dis here chile does work isn't slow, I ken tell yer,'' and with
her characteristic gesture she run her tongue out at the corner
of her mouth in an oblique manner, and suddenly withdrew it,
as though it had passed over a scathing iron.

" Could anything induce you to part with it ?'' I asked.

She rolled her eyes up with a look of wonderment, and
replied, half ferociously, " Gracious ! no—why, hasn't I bin
whipped, 'bused and treed ; still I'd hold fast to this. No mortal ken take it frum me. You may kill me in welcome,'' and
the child shook her head with a philosophical air, as she said,
" and I don't kere much, so mammy's chilen dies along wid me,
fur I didn't see no use in our livin' eny how. I's done got my
full shere ob beatin' an' we haint no use on dis here airth—so I
jist wants fur to die.''

I looked upon her, so uncared for, so forlorn in her condition,
and I could not find it in my heart to blame her for the wish,
erring and rebellious as it must appear to the Christian. What
had she to live for ? To those little children, the sacred bequests

of her mother, she was no protection; for, even had she been capable of extending to them all the guidance and watchfulness, both of soul and body, which their delicate and immature natures required, there was every probability, nay, there was a certainty, that this duty would be denied her. She could not hope, at best, to live with them more than a few years. They were but cattle, chattels, property, subject to the will and pleasure of their owners. There would speedily come a time when a division must take place in the estate, and that division would necessarily cause a separation and rupture of family ties. What wonder then, that this poor ignorant child sighed for the calm, unfearing, unbroken rest of the grave? She dreamed not of a "more beyond;" she thought her soul mortal, even as her body; and had she been told that there was for her a world, even a blessed one, to succeed death, she would have shuddered and feared to cross the threshold of the grave. She thought annihilation the greatest, the only blessing awaiting her. The idea of another life would have brought with it visions of a new master and protracted slavery. Freedom and equality of souls, irrespective of *color*, was too transcendental and chimerical an idea to take root in her practical brain. Many times had she heard her master declare that "niggers were jist like dogs, laid down and died, and nothin' come of them afterwards." His philosophy could have proposed nothing more delightful to her ease-coveting mind.

Some weeks afterwards, when I was trying to teach her the doctrine of the immortality of the soul, she broke forth in an idiotic laugh, as she said, "oh, no, dat gold city what dey sings 'bout in hymns, will do fur de white folks; but nothin' eber comes of niggers; dey jist dies and rots."

"Who do you think made negroes?" I inquired.

Looking up with a meaning grin, she said, "White folks made 'em fur der own use, I 'spect."

"Why do you think that?"

"Kase white folks ken kill 'em when dey pleases; so I 'spose dey make 'em."

This was a species of reasoning which, for a moment, confounded my logic. Seeing that I lacked a ready reply, she went on :

"Yes, you see, Ann, we hab no use wid a soul. De white folks won't hab any work to hab done up dere, and so dey won't hab no use fur niggers."

"Doesn't this make you miserable ?"

"What ?" she asked, with amazement.

"This thought of dying, and rotting like the vilest worm."

"No, indeed, it makes me glad ; fur den I'll not hab anybody to beat me ; knock, kick, and cuff me 'bout, like dey does now."

"Poor child, happier far," I thought, "in your ignorance, than I, with all the weight of fearful responsibility that my little knowledge entails upon me. On you, God will look with a more pitying eye than upon me, to whom he has delegated the stewardship of two talents."

CHAPTER VIII.

TALK AT THE FARM-HOUSE—THREATS—THE NEW BEAU—LINDY.

SEVERAL days had elapsed since the morning conversation with Amy; meanwhile matters were jogging along in their usually dull way. Of late, since the flight of Mr. Jones, and the illness of Mr. Peterkin, there had been considerably less fighting; but the ladies made innumerable threats of what they would do, when their father should be well enough to allow a suspension of nursing duties.

My wounds had rapidly healed, and I had resumed my former position in the discharge of household duties. Lindy, my old assistant, still held her place. I always had an aversion to her. There was that about her entire physique which made her odious to me. A certain laxity of the muscles and joints of her frame, which produced a floundering, shuffling sort of gait that was peculiarly disagreeable, a narrow, soulless countenance, an oblique leer of the eye where an ambushed fiend seemed to lurk, full, voluptuous lips, lengthy chin, and expanded nostril, combined to prove her very low in the scale of animals. She had a kind of dare-devil courage, which seemed to brave a great deal, and yet she shrank from everything like punishment. There was a union of degrading passions in her character. I doubt if the lowest realm of hades contained a baser spirit. This girl, I felt assured from the first time I beheld her, was destined to be my evil genius. I felt that the baleful comet that presided over her birth, would in his reckless and maddening course, rush too near the little star which, through cloud and shadow, beamed on my destiny.

She was not without a certain kind of sprightliness that passed for intelligence; and she could by her adroitness of manœuvre amble out of any difficulty. With a good education she would have made an excellent female pettifogger. She had all of the quickness and diablerie usually summed up in that most expressive American word, "*smartness.*"

I was a good deal vexed and grieved to find myself again a partner of hers in the discharge of my duties. It seemed to open my wounds afresh; for I remembered that her falsehood had gained me the severe castigation that had almost deprived me of life; and her laugh and jibe had rendered my suffering at the accursed post even more humiliating. Yet I knew better than to offer a demurrer to any arrangement that my mistress had made.

One day as I was preparing to set the table for the noon meal, Lindy came to me and whispered, in an under-tone, "You finish the table, I am going out; and if Miss Jane or Tildy axes where I is, say dat I went to de kitchen to wash a dish."

"Very well," I replied in my usual laconic style, and went on about my work. It was well for her that she had observed this precaution; for in a few moments Miss Tildy came in, and her first question was for Lindy. I answered as I had been desired to do. The reply appeared to satisfy her, and with the injunction (one she never failed to give), that I should do my work well and briskly, she left the room.

After I had arranged the table to my satisfaction, I went to the kitchen to assist Aunt Polly in dishing up dinner.

When I reached the kitchen I found Aunt Polly in a great quandary. The fire was not brisk enough to brown her bread, and she dared not send it to the table without its being as beautifully brown as a student's meditations.

"Oh, child," she began, "do run somewhar' and git me a scrap or so of dry wood, so as to raise a smart little blaze to brown dis bread."

"Indeed I will," and off I bounded in quest of the combustible material. Of late Aunt Polly and I had become as devoted as mother and child. 'Tis true there was a deep yearning in my heart, a thirst for intercommunion of soul, which this untutored negress could not supply. She did not answer, with a thrilling response, to the deep cry which my spirit sent out; yet she was kind, and even affectionate, to me. Usually harsh to others, with me she was gentle as a lamb. With a thousand little motherly acts she won my heart, and I strove, by assiduous kindness, to make her forget that I was not her daughter. I started off with great alacrity in search of the dry wood, and remembered that on the day previous I had seen some barrel staves lying near an out-house, and these I knew would quickly ignite. When rapidly turning the corner of the stable, I was surprised to see Lindy standing in close and apparently free conversation with a strange-looking white man. The sound of my rapid footsteps startled them; and upon seeing me, the man walked off hastily. With a fluttering, excited manner, Lindy came up and said:

"Don't say nothing 'bout haven' seed me wid dat ar' gemman; fur he used to be my mars'er, and a good one he was too."

I promised that I would say nothing about the matter, but first I inquired what was the nature of the private interview.

"Oh, he jist wanted fur to see me, and know how I was gitten' long.

I said no more; but I was not satisfied with her explanation. I resolved to watch her narrowly, and ferret out, if possible, this seeming mystery. Upon my return to the kitchen, with my bundle of dry sticks, I related what I had seen to Aunt Polly.

"Dat gal is arter sompen not very good, you mark my words fur it."

"Oh, maybe not, Aunt Polly," I answered, though with a conviction that I was speaking at variance with the strong probabilities of the case.

I hurried in the viands and meats for the table, and was not surprised to find Lindy unusually obliging, for I understood the object. There was an abashed air and manner which argued guilt, or at least, that she was the mistress of a secret, for the entire possession of which she trembled. Sundry little acts of unaccustomed kindness she offered me, but I quietly declined them. I did not desire that she should insult my honor by the offer of a tacit bribe.

In the evening, when I was arranging Miss Jane's hair (this was my especial duty), she surprised me by asking, in a careless and incautious manner :

"Ann, what is the matter with Lindy ? she has such an excited manner."

"I really don't know, Miss Jane ; I have not observed anything very unusual in her."

"Well, I have, and I shall speak to her about it.   Oh, there! slow, girl, slow ; you pulled my hair.   Don't do it again.   You niggers have become so unruly since pa's sickness, that if we don't soon get another overseer, there will be no living for you. There is Lindy in the sulks, simply because she wants a whipping, and old Polly hasn't given us a meal fit to eat."

"Have I done anything, Miss Jane?" I asked with a misgiving.

"No, nothing in particular, except showing a general and continued sullenness.   Now, I do despise to see a nigger always sour-looking ; and I can tell you, Ann, you must change your ways, or it will be worse for you."

"I try to be cheerful, Miss Jane, but—" here I wisely checked myself."

"*Try to be*," she echoed with a satirical tone.   "What do you mean by *trying* ?   You don't dare to say you are not happy *here* ?"

Finding that I made no reply, she said, "If you don't cut your cards squarely, you will find yourself down the river before long, and there you are only half-clad and half-fed, and flogged every day."   Still I made no reply.   I knew that if I spoke truthfully, and as my heart prompted, it would only redound to my misery.   What right had I to speak of my mother. ·She was no more than an animal, and as destitute of the refinement of common human feeling—so I forbore to allude to her, or my great desire to see her.   I dared not speak of the horrible manner in which my body had been cut and slashed, the half-lifeless condition in which I had been taken from the accursed post, and all for a fault which was not mine. These were things which, as they were done by my master's commands, were nothing more than right; so with an effort, I controlled my emotion, and checked the big tears which I felt were rushing up to my eyes.

When I had put the finishing stroke to Miss Jane's hair, and whilst she was surveying herself in a large French mirror, Miss Bradly came in. Tossing her bonnet off, she kissed Miss Jane very affectionately, nodded to me, and asked,

"Where is Tildy?"

"I don't know, somewhere about the house, I suppose," replied Miss Jane.

"Well, I have a new beau for her; now it will be a fine chance for Tildy. I would have recommended you; but, knowing of your previous engagement, I thought it best to refer him to the fair Matilda."

Miss Jane laughed, and answered, that "though she was engaged, she would have no objections to trying her charms upon another beau."

There was a strange expression upon Miss Bradly's face, and a flurried, excited manner, very different from her usually quiet demeanor.

Miss Jane went about the room collecting, here and there, a stray pocket handkerchief, under-sleeve, or chemisette; and, dashing them toward me, she said,

"Put these in wash, and do, pray, Ann, try to look more cheerful. Now, Miss Emily," she added, addressing Miss Bradly, "we have the worst servants in the world. There is Lindy, I believe the d——l is in her. She is so strange in her actions. I have to repeat a thing three or four times before she will understand me; and, as for Ann, she looks so sullen that it gives one the horrors to see her. I've a notion to bring Amy into the house. In the kitchen she is of no earthly service, and doesn't earn her salt. I think I'll persuade pa to sell some of these worthless niggers. They are no profit, and a terrible expense." Thereupon she was interrupted by the entrance of Miss Tildy, whose face was unusually excited. She did not perceive Miss Bradly, and so broke forth in a torrent of invectives against " niggers."

" I hate them. I wish this place were rid of every black face. Now we can't find that wretched Lindy anywhere, high nor low. Let me once get hold of her, and I'll be bound she shall remember it to the day of her death. Oh! Miss Bradly, is that you ? pray excuse me for not recognizing you sooner; but since pa's sickness, these wretched negroes have half-taken the place, and I shouldn't be surprised if I were to forget myself," and with a kiss she seemed to think she had atoned to Miss Bradly for her forgetfulness.

To all of this Miss B. made no reply, I fancied (perhaps it was only fancy) that there was a shade of discontent upon her face ; but she still preserved her silence, and Miss Tildy waxed warmer and warmer in her denunciation of ungrateful " niggers."

" Now, here, ours have every wish gratified ; are treated well, fed well, clothed well, and yet we can't get work enough out of them to justify us in retaining our present number. As soon as pa gets well I intend to urge upon him the necessity of selling some of them. It is really too outrageous for us to be keeping such a number of the worthless wretches ; actually eating us out of house and home. Besides, our family expenses are rapidly increasing. Brother must be sent off to college. It will not do to have his education neglected. I really am becoming quite ashamed of his want of preparation for a profession. I wish him sent to Yale, after first receiving a preparatory course in some less noted seminary,—then he will require a handsome outfit of books, and a wardrobe inferior to none at the institution ; for, Miss Emily, I am determined our family shall have a position in every circle." As Miss Tildy pronounced these words, she stamped her foot in the most emphatic way, as if to confirm and ratify her determination.

"Yes," said Miss Jane, "I was just telling Miss Emily of our plans; and I think we may as well bring Amy in the house. She is of no account in the kitchen, and Lindy, Ginsy, and those brats, can be sold for a very pretty sum if taken to the city of L———, and put upon the block, or disposed of to some wealthy trader."

"What children?" asked Miss Bradly.

"Why, Amy's two sisters and brother, and Ginsy's child, and Ginsy too, if pa will let her go."

My heart ached well-nigh to bursting, when I heard this. Poor, poor Amy, child-sufferer! another drop of gall added to thy draught of wormwood—another thorn added to thy wearing crown. Oh, God! how I shuddered for the victim.

Miss Jane went on in her usual heartless tone. "It is expensive to keep them; they are no account, no profit to us; and young niggers are my 'special aversion. I have, for a long time, intended separating Amy from her two little sisters; she doesn't do anything but nurse that sickly child, Ben, and it is scandalous. You see, Miss Emily, we want an arbor erected in the yard, and a conservatory, and some new-style table furniture."

"Yes, and I want a set of jewels, and a good many additions to my wardrobe, and Jane wishes to spend a winter in the city. She will be forced to have a suitable outfit."

"Yes, and I am going to have everything I want, if the farm is to be sold," said Miss Jane, in a voice that no one dared to gainsay.

"But come, let me tell you, Tildy, about the new beau I have for you," said Miss Bradly.

Instantly Miss Tildy's eyes began to glisten. The word "beau" was the ready "sesame" to her good humor.

"Oh, now, dear, good Miss Emily, tell me something about him. Who is he? where from?" &c.

Miss Bradly smiled, coaxingly and lovingly, as she answered:

"Well, Tildy, darling, I have a friend from the North, who is travelling for pleasure through the valley of the Mississippi;

and I promised to introduce him to some of the pretty ladies of the West; so, of course, I feel pride in introducing my two pupils to him."

This was a most agreeable sedative to their ill-nature; and both sisters came close to Miss Bradly, fairly covering her with caresses, and addressing to her words of flattery.

As soon as my services were dispensed with I, repaired to the kitchen, where I found Aunt Polly in no very good or amiable mood. Something had gone wrong about the arrangements for supper. The chicken was not brown enough, or the cakes were heavy; something troubled her, and as a necessary consequence her temper was suffering.

" I's in an orful humor, Ann, so jist don't come nigh me."

" Well, but, Aunt Polly, we should learn to control these humors. They are not the dictates of a pure spirit; they are unchristian."

" Oh, laws, chile, what hab us to do do wid der Christians? We are like dem poor headens what de preachers prays 'bout. We haint got no 'sponsibility, no more den de dogs."

" I don't think that way, Aunt Polly; I think I am as much bound to do my duty, and expect a reward at the hands of my Maker, as any white person."

" Oh, 'taint no use of talkin' dat ar' way, kase ebery body knows niggers ain't gwine to de same place whar dar massers goes."

I dared not confront her obstinacy with any argument; for I knew she was unwilling to believe. Poor, apathetic creature! she was happier in yielding up her soul to the keeping of her owner, than she would have been in guiding it herself. This to me would have been enslavement indeed; such as I could not have endured. He, my Creator, who gave me this heritage of thought, and the bounty of Hope, gave me, likewise, a strong, unbridled will, which nothing can conquer. The whip may bring my body into subjection, but the free, free spirit soars where it lists, and no man can check it. God is with the soul! aye, in it, animating and encouraging it, sustaining it amid the crash, conflict, and the elemental war of passion! The poor, weak flesh may yield; but, thanks to God! the soul, well-girded and heaven-poised, will never shrink.

Many and long have been the unslumbering nights when I have lain upon my heap of straw, gazing at the pallid moon, and the sorrowful stars; weaving mystic fancies as the wailing night-wind seemed to bring me a message from the distant and the lost! I have felt whole vials of heavenly unction poured upon my bruised soul; rich gifts have descended, like the manna of old, upon my famishing spirit; and I have felt that God was nearer to me in the night time. I have imagined that the very atmosphere grew luminous with the presence of angelic hosts; and a strange music, audible alone to my ears, has lulled me to the gentlest of dreams! God be thanked for the night, the stars, and the spirit's vision! Joy came not to me with the breaking of the morn; but peace, undefined, enwrapped me when the mantle of darkness and the crown of stars attested the reign of Night!

I grieved to think that my poor friend, this old, lonely negress, had nothing to soothe and charm her wearied heart. There was not a single flower blooming up amid the rank weeds of her nature. Hard and rocky it seemed; yet had I found the prophet's wand, whereby to strike the flinty heart, and draw forth living waters! pure, genial draughts of kindliness, sweet honey-drops, hived away in the lonely cells of her caverned soul! I would have loved to give her a portion of that peace which radiated with its divine light the depths of my inmost spirit. I had come to her now for the purpose of giving her the sad intelligence that awaited poor Amy; but I did not find her in a suitable mood. I felt assured that her harshness would, in some way or other, jar the finer and more sensitive harmonies of my nature. Perhaps she would say that she did not care for the sufferings of the poor, lonely child; and that her bereavement would be nothing more than just; yet I knew that she did not feel thus. Deep in her secret soul there lay folded a white-winged angel, even as the uncomely bulb envelopes the fair petals of the lily; and I longed for the summer warmth of kindness to bid it come forth and bloom in beauty.

But now I turned away from her, murmuring, " 'Tis not the time." She would not open her heart, and my own must likewise be closed and silent; but when I met poor little Amy, looking so neglected, with scarcely apparel sufficient to cover her nudity, my heart failed me utterly. There she held upon her hip little Ben, her only joy; every now and then she addressed some admonitory words to him, such as " Hush, baby, love," "you's my baby," "sissy loves it," and similar expressions of coaxing and endearment. And this, her only comfort, was about to be wrenched from her. The only link of love that bound her to a weary existence, was to be severed by the harsh mandate of another. Just God! is this right? Oh, my soul, be thou still! Look on in patience! The cloud deepens above! The day of God's wrath is at hand! They who have coldly forbidden our indulging the sweet humanities of life, who have destroyed every social relation, severed kith and kin, ruptured the ties of blood, and left us more lonely than the beasts of the forest, may tremble when the avenger comes!

I ventured to speak with Amy, and I employed the kindest tone; but ever and anon little Ben would send forth such a piteous wail, that I feared he was in physical pain. Amy, however, very earnestly assured me that she had administered catnip tea in plentiful quantities, and had examined his person very carefully to discover if a pin or needle had punctured his flesh; but everything seemed perfectly right.

I attempted to take him in my arms; but he clung so vigorously to Amy's shoulder, that it required strength to unfasten his grasp.

"Oh, don'tee take him; he doesn't like fur to leab me. Him usen to me," cried Amy, as in a motherly way she caressed him. "Now, pretty little boy donee cry any more. Ann shan't hab you;—now be a good nice boy;" and thus she expended upon him her whole vocabulary of endearing epithets.

"Who could," I asked myself, " have the heart to untie this

sweet fraternal bond ?- Who could dry up the only fountain in this benighted soul ? Oh, I have often marvelled how the white mother, who knows, in such perfection, the binding beauty of maternal love, can look unsympathizingly on, and see the poor black parent torn away from her children. I once saw a white lady, of conceded *refinement*, sitting in the portico of her own house, with her youngest born, a babe of some seven months, dallying on her knee, and she toying with the pretty gold-threads of its silken hair, whilst her husband was in the kitchen, with a whip in his hand, severely lashing a negro woman, whom he had sold to a trader—lashing her because she refused to go *cheerfully* and leave her infant behind. The poor wretch, as a last resource, fled to her Mistress, and, on her knees, begged her to have her child. "Oh, Mistress," cried the frantic black woman, "ask Master to let me take my baby with me." What think you was the answer of this white mother?

"Go away, you impudent wretch, you don't deserve to have your child. It will be better off away from you!" Aye, this was the answer which, accompanied by a derisive sneer, she gave to the heart-stricken black mother. Thus she felt, spoke, and acted, even whilst caressing her own helpless infant! Who would think it injustice to "commend the poison-chalice to her own lips"? She, this fine lady, was known to weep violently, because an Irish woman was unable to save a sufficiency of money from her earnings to bring her son from Ireland to America; but, for the African mother, who was parting eternally from her helpless babe, she had not so much as a consolatory word. Oh, ye of the proud Caucasian race, would that your hearts were as fair and spotless as your complexions! Truly can the Saviour say of you, "Oh, Jerusalem, Jerusalem, I would have gathered you together as a hen gathereth her chickens, but ye would not!" Oh, perverse generation of vipers, how long will you abuse the Divine forbearance !

CHAPTER IX.

IN about an hour Lindy came in, looking very much excited,
yet attempting to conceal it beneath the mask of calmness. I
affected not to notice it, yet was it evident, from various little
attentions and manifold kind words, that she sought to divert
suspicion, and avoid all questioning as to her absence.

"Where," she asked me, "are the young ladies ? have they
company ?"

"Yes," I replied, "Miss Bradly is with them, and they are
expecting a young gentleman, an acquaintance of Miss B.'s." ·

"Who is he ?"

"Why, Lindy, how should I know ?"

"I thought maybe you hearn his name."

"No, I did not, and, even if I had, it would have been so un-
important to me that I should have forgotten it."

She opened her eyes with a vacant stare, but it was perceptible that she wandered in thought.

"Now, Lindy," I began, "Miss Jane has missed you from the
house, and both she and Miss Tildy have sworn vengeance
against you."

"So have I sworn it agin' them."

"What ! what did you say, Lindy ?"

Really I was surprised at the girl's hardihood and boldness.
She had been thrown from her guard, and now, upon regaining
her composure, was alarmed.

"Oh, I was only joking, Ann ; you knows we allers jokes."

"I never do," I said, with emphasis.

"Yes, but den, Ann, you see you is one ob de quare uns."

"What do you mean by quare?" I asked.

"Oh, psha, 'taint no use ob talkin wid you, for you is good; but kum, tell me, is dey mad wid me in de house, and did dey say dey would beat me?"

"Well, they threatened something of the kind."

Her face grew ashen pale; it took that peculiar kind of pallor which the negro's face often assumes under the influence of fear or disease, and which is so disagreeable to look upon. Enemy of mine as she had deeply proven herself to be, I could not be guilty of the meanness of exulting in her trouble.

"But," she said, in an imploring tone, "you will not repeat what I jist said in fun."

"Of course I will not; but don't you remember that it was your falsehood that gained for me the only post-whipping that I ever had?"

"Yes; but den I is berry sorry fur dat, and will not do it any more."

This was enough for me. An acknowledgment of contrition, and a determination to do better, are all God requires of the offender; and shall poor, erring mortals demand more? No; my resentment was fully satisfied. Besides, I felt that this poor creature was not altogether blamable. None of her better feelings had been cultivated; they were strangled in their incipiency, whilst her savage instincts were left to run riot. Thus the bad had ripened into a full and noxious development, whilst the noble had been crushed in the bud. Who is to be answerable for the short-comings of such a soul? Surely he who has cut it off from all moral and mental culture, and has said to the glimmerings of its faint intellect, "Back, back to the depths of darkness!" Surely he will and must take upon himself the burden of accountability. The sin is at his door, and woe-worth the day, when the great Judge shall come to pass sentence upon him. I have often thought that the master of slaves must, for consistency's sake, be an infidel—or doubt man's exact accountability to God for the deeds done in the body;

for how can he willingly assume the sins of some hundreds of souls? In the eye of human law, the slave has no responsibility; the master assumes all for him. If the slave is found guilty of a capital offence, punishable with death, the master is indemnified by a paid valuation, for yielding up the person of the slave to the demands of offended justice? If a slave earns money by his labors at night or holidays, or if he is the successful holder of a prize ticket in a lottery, his master can legally claim the money, and there is no power to gainsay him? If, then, human law recognizes a negro as irresponsible, how much more lenient and just will be the divine statute? Thus, I hold (and I cannot think there is just logician, theologian, or metaphysician, who will dissent), that the owner of slaves becomes sponsor to God for the sins of his slave; and I cannot, then, think that one who accredits the existence of a just God, a Supreme Ruler, to whom we are all responsible for our deeds and words, would willingly take upon himself the burden of other people's faults and transgressions.

Whilst I stood talking with Lindy, the sound of merry laughter reached our ears.

"Oh, dat is Miss Tildy, now is my time to go in, and see what dey will say to me; maybe while dey is in a good humor, dey will not beat me."

And, thus saying, Lindy hurried away. Sad thoughts were crowding in my mind. Dark misgivings were stirring in my brain. Again I thought of the blessed society, with its humanitarian hope and aim, that dwelt afar off in the north. I longed to ask Miss Bradly more about it. I longed to hear of those holy men, blessed prophets foretelling a millennial era for my poor, down-trodden and despised race. I longed to ask questions of her; but of late she had shunned me; she scarcely spoke to me; and when she did speak, it was with indifference, and a degree of coldness that she had never before assumed.

With these thoughts in my mind I stole along through the yard, until I stood almost directly under the window of the parlor. Something in the tone of a strange voice that reached

my ear, riveted my attention.   It was a low, manly tone, lute-
like, yet swelling on the breeze, and charming the soul!   It
refreshed my senses like a draught of cooling water.   I caught
the tone, and could not move from the spot.   I was transfixed.

"I do not see why Fred Douglas is not equal to the best
man in the land.   What constitutes worth of character?   What
makes the man?   What gives elevation to him?"   These were
the words I first distinctly heard, spoken in a deep, earnest tone,
which I have never forgotten.   I then heard a silly laugh, which
I readily recognized as Miss Jane's, as she answered, "You
can't pretend to say that you would be willing for a sister of
yours to marry Fred Douglas, accomplished as you consider
him?"

"I did not speak of marrying at all; and might I not be an
advocate of universal liberty, without believing in amalgamation?
Yet, it is a question whether even amalgamation should be forbidden by law.   The negro is a different race; but I do not
know that they have other than human feelings and emotions.
The negroes are, with us, the direct descendants from the great
progenitor of the human family, old Adam.   They may, when
fitted by education, even transcend us in the refinements and
graces which adorn civilized character.   In loftiness of purpose,
in mental culture, in genius, in urbanity, in the exercise of
manly virtues, such as fortitude, courage, and philanthropy, where
will you show me a man that excels Fred Douglas?   And must
the mere fact of his tawny complexion exclude him from the pale
of that society which he is so eminently fitted to grace?   Might
I not (if it were made a question) prefer uniting my sister's fate
with such a man, even though partially black, to seeing her
tied to a low fellow, a wine-bibber, a swearer, a villain,
who possessed not one cubit of the stature of true manhood, yet
had a complexion white as snow?   Ah, Miss, it is not the skin
which gives us true value as men and women; 'tis the mo-
mentum of mind and the purity of morals, the integrity of purpose and nobility of soul, that make our place in the scale of
being.   I care not if the skin be black as Erebus or fair and

smooth as satin, so the heart and mind be right. I do not deal-
in externals or care for surfaces."

These words were as the bread of life to me. I could
scarcely resist the temptation to leave my hiding-place and look
in at the open window, to get sight of the speaker; surely, I
thought, he must wear the robes of a prophet. I could not
very distinctly hear what Miss Jane said in reply. I could catch
many words, such as "nigger" and "marry" "white lady," and
other expressions used in an expostulatory voice; but the plati-
tudes which she employed would not have answered the demand
of my higher reason. Old perversions and misinterpretations of
portions of the Bible, such as the story of Hagar, and the curse
pronounced upon Ham, were adduced by Miss Jane and Miss
Tildy in a tone of triumph.

"Oh, I sicken over these stories," said the same winning
voice. "How long will Christians willingly resist the known
truth? How long will they bay at heaven with their cruel
blasphemies? For I hold it to be blasphemy when a body of
Christians, professing to be followers of Him who came from
heaven to earth, and assumed the substance of humanity to
teach us a lesson, argue thus. Our Great Model declares that
'He came not to be ministered unto but to minister.' He inculcated practically the lesson of humility in the washing of the
disciples'. feet; yet, these His modern disciples, the followers
of to-day, preach, even from the sacred desk, the right of men to
hold their fellow-creatures in bondage through endless generations, to sell them for gold, to beat them, to keep them in a heathen-
ish ignorance; and yet declare that it all has the divine sanction.
Verily, oh night of Judaism, thou wast brighter than this our
noon-day of Christianity! Black and bitter is the account, oh
Church of God, that thou art gathering to thyself! I could pray
for a tongue of inspiration, wherewith to denounce this foul
crime. I could pray for the power to show to my country the
terrible stain she has painted upon the banner of freedom.
How dare we, as Americans, boast of this as the home and
temple of liberty? Where are the 'inalienable rights' of

which our Constitution talks in such trumpet-tones? Does not our Declaration of Independence aver, that all men are born free and equal? Now, do we not make this a practical falsehood? Let the poor slave come up to the tribunal of justice, and ask the wise judge upon the bench to interpret this piece of plain English to him ! How would the man of ermine blush at his own quibbles ?"

I could tell from the speaker's voice that he had risen from his seat, and I knew, from the sound of footsteps, that he was approaching the window. I crouched down lower and lower, in order to conceal myself from observation, but gazed up to behold one whose noble sentiments and bold expression of them had so entranced me.

Very noble looked he, standing there, with the silver moon-light beaming upon his broad, white brow, and his deep, blue eye uplifted to the star-written skies. His features were calm and classic in their mould, and a mystic light seemed to idealize and spiritualize his face and form. Kneeling down upon the earth, I looked reverently to him, as the children of old looked upon their prophets. He did not perceive me, and even if he had, what should I have been to him—a pale-browed student, whose thought, large and expansive, was filled with the noble, the philanthropic, and the great. Yet, there I crouched in fear and trembling, lest a breath should betray my secret place. But, would not his extended pity have embraced me, even me, a poor, insignificant, uncared-for thing in the great world —one who bore upon her face the impress of the hated nation ? Ay, I felt that he would not have condemned me as one devoid of the noble impulse of a heroic humanity. If the African has not heroism, pray where will you find it ? Are there in the high endurance of the heroes of old Sparta, sufferings such as the unchronicled life of many a slave can furnish forth ? Martyrs have gone to the stake ; but amid the pomp and sound-ing psaltery of a choir, and above the flame, the fagot and the scaffold, they descried the immortal crown, and even the worldly and sensuous desire of canonization may not have been

4*

dead with them. The patriot braves the battle, and dies amid
the thickest of the carnage, whilst the jubilant strains of
music herald him away. The soldier perishes amid the proud
acclaim of his countrymen; but the poor negro dies a martyr,
unknown, unsung, and uncheered. Many expire at the whipping-post, with the gleesome shouts of their inhuman tormentors,
as their only cheering. Yet few pity us. We are valuable
only as property. Our lives are nothing, and our souls—why
they scarcely think we have any. In reflecting upon these
things, in looking calmly back over my past life, and in review-
ing the lives of many who are familiar to me, I have felt that
the Lord's forbearance must indeed be great; and when thoughts
of revenge have curdled my blood, the prayer of my suffering
Saviour: "Father forgive them, for they know not what they
do," has flashed through my mind, and I have repelled them
as angry and unchristian. Jesus drank the wormwood and the
gall; and we, oh, brethren and sisters of the banned race,
must "tread the wine-press alone." We must bear firmly upon
the burning ploughshare, and pass manfully through the ordeal,
for vengeance is His and He will repay.

But there, in the sweet moonlight, as I looked upon this young
apostle of reform, a whole troop of thoughts less bitter than
these swept over my mind. There were gentle dreamings of a
home, a quiet home, in that Northland, where, at least, we are
countenanced as human beings. "Who," I asked myself, "is this
mysterious Fred Douglas?" A black man he evidently was;
but how had I heard him spoken of? As one devoted to self-culture in its noblest form, who ornamented society by his imposing and graceful bearing, who electrified audiences with the
splendor of his rhetoric, and lured scholars to his presence by
the fame of his acquirements; and this man, this oracle of lore,
was of my race, of my blood. What he had done, others
might achieve. What a high determination then fired my
breast! Give, give me but the opportunity, and my chief ambition will be to prove that we, though wronged and despised,
are not inferior to the proud Caucasians. I will strive to redeem

from unjust aspersion the name of my people. He, this illustrious stranger, gave the first impetus to my ambition ; from him my thoughts assumed a form, and one visible aim now possessed my soul.

How long I remained there listening I do not remember, for soon the subject of conversation was changed, and I noted not the particular words ; but that mournfully musical voice had a siren-charm for my ear, and I could not tear myself away. Whilst listening to it, sweet sleep, like a shielding mantle, fell upon me.

CHAPTER X.

THE CONVERSATION IN WHICH FEAR AND SUSPICION ARE AROUSED—THE YOUNG MASTER.

It must have been long after midnight when I awoke. I do not remember whether I had dreamed or not, but the slumber had brought refreshment to my body and peace to my heart.

I was aroused by the sound of voices, in a suppressed whisper, or rather in a tone slightly above a whisper. I thought I detected the voice of Lindy, and, as I rose from my recumbent posture, I caught sight of a figure flitting round the gable of the house. I followed, but there was nothing visible. The pale moonlight slept lovingly upon the dwelling and the roofs of the out-buildings. Whither could the figure have fled? There was no sign of any one having been there. Slowly and sadly I directed my steps toward Aunt Polly's cabin. I opened the door cautiously, not wishing to disturb her; but easy and noiseless as were my motions, they roused that faithful creature. She sprang from the bed, exclaiming:

"La, Ann, whar has yer bin? I has bin so oneasy 'bout yer."

With my native honesty I explained to her that I had been beguiled by the melody of a human voice, and had lingered long out in the autumn moonlight.

"Yes; but, chile, you'll be sick. Sleepin' out a doors is berry onwholesome like."

"Yes; but, Aunt Polly, there is an interior heat which no autumnal frost has power to chill."

"Yes, chile, you does talk so pretty, like dem ar' great white scholards. Many times I has wondered how a poor darkie could larn so much. Now it 'pears to me as if you knowed

[84]

much as any ob 'em. I don't tink Miss Bradly hersef talks any better dan you does."

"Oh, Aunt Polly, your praise is sweet to me; but then, you must remember not to do me more than justice. I am a poor, illiterate mulatto girl, who has indeed improved the modicum of time allowed her for self-culture; yet, when I hear such ladies as Miss Bradly talk, I feel how far inferior I am to the queens of the white tribe Often I ask myself why is this? Is it because my face is colored? But then there is a voice, deep down in my soul, that rejects such a conclusion as slanderous. Oh, give me but opportunity, and I will strive to equal them in learning."

"I don't see no use in yer wanting to larn, when you is nothing but a poor slave. But I does think the gift of fine speech mighty valable."

And here is another thing upon which I would generalize. Does it not argue the possession of native mind—the immense value the African places upon words—the high-flown and broad-sounding words that he usually employs? The ludicrous attempts which the most untutored make at grandiloquence, should not so much provoke mirth as admiration in the more reflective of the white race. Through what barriers and obstacles do not their minds struggle to force a way up to the light. I have often been astonished at the quickness with which they seized upon expressions, and the accuracy with which they would apply them. Every crude attempt which they make toward self-culture is laughed at and scorned by the master, or treated as the most puerile folly. No encouragement is given them. If, by almost superhuman effort, they gain knowledge, why they may; but, unaided and alone, they must work, as I have done. Moreover, I have been wonder-stricken at the facility with which the negro-boy acquires learning. 'Tis as though the rudiments of the school came to him by flashes of intuition. He is allowed only a couple of hours on Sunday afternoons for recitations, and such odd moments during the week as he can catch to prepare his lessons; for, a servant-boy often caught with his book in hand, would be pronounced indolent, and punished as such. Then, how unjust it is for the proud statesman—prouder of his snowy complexion than of his stores of knowledge—how unjust, I say, is it in him to assert, in the halls of legislation, that the colored race are to the white far inferior in native mind! Has he weighed the advantages and disadvantages of both? Has he remembered that the whites, through countless generations, have been cultivated and refined—familiarized with the arts and sciences and ele. gancies of a graceful age, whilst the blacks are bound down in ignorance; unschooled in lore; untrained in virtue; taught to look upon themselves as degraded—the mere drudges of their masters; debarred the privileges of social life; excluded from books, with the products of their labor going toward the enrichment of others? When, as in some solitary instance, a single mind dares to break through the restraints and impediments imposed upon it, does not the fact show of what strength the race, when properly cared for, is capable? Is not the bulb, which enshrouds the snowy leaves of the fragrant lily, an unsightly thing? Does the uncut diamond show any of the polish and brilliancy which the lapidary's hand can give it? Thus is it with the African mind. Let but the schoolmen breathe upon it, let the architect of learning fashion it, and no diamond ever glittered with more resplendence. With a more than prismatic light, it will refract the beams of the sun of knowledge; and the heart, the most noble African's heart, that now slumbers in the bulb of ignorance, will burst forth, pure and lovely as the white-petaled lily!

I hope, kind reader, you will pardon these digressions, as I write my inner as well as outer life, and I should be unfaithful to my most earnest thoughts were I not to chronicle such reflections as these. This book is not a wild romance to beguile your tears and cheat your fancy. No; it is the truthful autobiography of one who has suffered long, long, the pains and trials of slavery. And she is committing her story, with her own calm deductions, to the consideration of every thoughtful and truth-loving mind.

"Where," I asked Aunt Polly, "is Lindy?"

"Oh, chile, I doesn't know whar dat gal is. Sompen is de matter wid her. She bin flyin' round here like somebody out ob dar head. All's not right wid her, now you mark my words fur it."

I then related to her the circumstance which had occurred whilst I was under the window.

"I does jist know dat was Lindy! You didn't see who she was talkin' wid?"

"No; and I did not distinctly discern her form; but the voice I am confident was her's."

"Well, sompen is gwine to happen; kase Lindy is berry great coward, and I well knows 'twas sompen great dat would make her be out dar at midnight."

"What do you think it means?" I asked.

"Why, lean up close to me, chile, while I jist whisper it low like to you. I believe Lindy is gwine to run off."

I started back in terror. I felt the blood grow cold in my veins. Why, if she made such an attempt as this, the whole country would be scoured for her. Hot pursuers would be out in every direction. And then her flight would render slavery ten times more severe for us. Master would believe that we were cognizant of it, and we should be put to torture for the purpose of wringing from us something in regard to her. Then, apprehension of our following her example would cause the reins of authority to be even more tightly drawn. What wonder, then, that fright possessed our minds, as the horrid suspicion began to assume something like reality. We regarded each other in silent horror. The dread workings of the fiend of fear were visible in the livid hue which overspread my companion's face and shone in the glare of her aged eye. She clasped her skinny hands together, and cried,

"Oh, my chile, orful times is comin' fur us. While Lindy will be off in that 'lightful Canady, we will be here sufferin' all sorts of trouble. Oh, de Lord, if dar be any, hab marcy on us!"

"Oh, Aunt Polly, don't say 'if there be any;' for, so certain as we both sit here, there is a Lord who made us, and who cares for us, too.   We are as much the children of His love as are the whites."

" Oh Lord, chile, I kan't belieb it; fur, if he loves us, why docs he make us suffer so, an' let de white folks hab such an easy time ?"

" He has some wise purpose in it. And then in that Eternity which succeeds the grave, He will render us blest and happy."

The clouds of ignorance hung too thick and close around her mind; and the poor old woman did not see the justice of such a decree.   She was not to blame if, in her woeful ignorance, she yielded to unbelief; and, with a profanity which knowledge would have rebuked, dared to boldly question the Divine Purpose.   This sin, also, is at the white man's door.

I did not strive further to enlighten her; for, be it confessed, I was myself possessed by physical fear to an unwonted degree. I did not think of courting sleep.   The brief dream which had fallen upon me as I slept beneath the parlor window, had given me sufficient refreshment.   And as for Aunt Polly, she was too much frightened to think of sleep.   Talk we did, long and earnestly.   I mentioned to her what I had heard Misses Tildy and Jane say in regard to Amy.

" Poor thing," exclaimed Aunt Polly, " she'll not be able to stand it, for her heart is wrapped up in dat ar' chile's.   She 'pears like its mother."

" I hope they may change their intentions," I ventured to say.

" No ; neber.   When wonst Miss Jane gets de notion ob finery in her head, she is gwine to hab it.   Lord lûb you, Ann, I does wish dey would sell you and me."

" So do I," was my fervent reply.

" But dey will neber sell you, kase Miss Jane tinks you is good-lookin', an' I hearn her say she would like to hab a nice-lookin' maid.   You see she tinks it is 'spectable."

" I suppose I must bear my cross and crown of thorns with patience."

Just then little Ben groaned in his sleep, and quickly his ever-watchful guardian was aroused; she bent over him, soothing his perturbed sleep with a low song. Many were the endearing epithets which she employed, such as, "Pretty little Benny, nothing shall hurt you." "Bless your little heart," and "here I is by yer side," "I'll keep de bars way frum yer."

"Poor child," burst involuntarily from my lips, as I reflected that even that one only treasure would soon be taken from her; then in what a hopeless eclipse would sink every ray of mind. Hearing my exclamation, she sprung up, and eagerly asked,

"What is de matter, Ann? Why is you and Aunt Polly sittin' up at dis time ob of de night? It's most day; say, is anything gwine on?"

"Nothing at all," I answered, "only Aunt Polly does not feel very well, and I am sitting up talking with her."

Thus appeased, she returned to her bed (if such a miserable thing could be called a bed), and was soon sleeping soundly.

Aunt Polly wiped her eyes as she said to me,

"Ann, doesn't we niggers hab to bar a heap? We works hard, and gits nothing but scanty vittels, de scraps dat de white folks leabes, and den dese miserable old rags dat only half kevers our nakedness. I declare it is too hard to bar."

"Yes," I answered, "it is hard, very hard, and enough to shake the endurance of the most determined martyr; yet, often do I repeat to myself those divine words, 'The cap which my Father has given me will I drink;' and then I feel calmed, strong, and heroic."

"Oh, Ann, chile, you does talk so beautiful, an' you has got de rale sort ob religion."

"Oh, would that I could think so. Would that my soul were more patient. I am not sufficiently hungered and athirst after righteousness. I pant too much for the joys of earth. I crave worldly inheritance, whilst the Christian's true aim should be for the mansions of the blest."

Thus wore on the night in social conversation, and I forgot, in that free intercourse, that there was a difference between us. The heart takes not into consideration the distinction of mind.

Love banishes all thought of rank or inequality. By her kindness and confidence, this old woman made me forget her ignorance.

When the first red streak of day began to announce the slow coming of the sun, Aunt Polly was out, and about her breakfast arrangements.

Since the illness of Master, and the departure of Mr. Jones, things had not gone on with the same precision as before. There was a few minutes difference in the blowing of the horn; and, for offences like these, Master had sworn deeply that "every nigger's hide" should be striped, as soon as he was able to preside at the "post." During his sickness he had not allowed one of us to enter his room; "for," as he said to the doctor, " a cussed nigger made him feel worse, he wanted to be up and beatin' them. They needed the cowhide every breath they drew." And, as the sapient doctor decided that our presence had an exciting effect upon him, we were banished from his room. "Banished!—what's banished but set free!"

Now, when I rose from my seat, and bent over the form of Amy, and watched her as she lay wrapt in a profound sleep, with one arm encircling little Ben, and the two sisters, Jane and Luce, lying close to her—so dependent looked the three, as they thus huddled round their young protectress, so loving and trustful in that deep repose, that I felt now would be a good time for the angel Death to come—now, before the fatal fall of the Damoclesian sword, whose hair thread was about to snap : but no— Death comes not at our bidding; he obeys a higher appointment. The boy moaned again in his sleep, and Amy's faithful arm was tightened round him. Closer she drew him to her maternal heart, and in a low, gurgling, songful voice, lulled him to a sweeter rest. I turned away from the sight, and, sinking on my knees, offered up a prayer to Him our common Father. I prayed that strength might be furnished me to endure the torture which I feared would come with the labors of the day. I asked, in an especial way, for grace to be given to the child, Amy. God is merciful! He moves in a mysterious manner. All power comes direct from Him; and, oh, did I not feel that this young creature had need of grace to bear the burden that others were preparing for her !

My business was to clean the house and set to rights the young ladies' apartment, and then assist Lindy in the breakfast-room; but I dared not venture in the ladies' chamber until half-past six o'clock, as the slightest foot-fall would arouse Miss Jane, who, I think, was too nervous to sleep. Thus I was left some little time to myself; and these few moments I generally devoted to reading some simple story-book or chapters in the New Testament. Of course, the mighty mysteries of the sacred volume were but imperfectly appreciated by me. I read the book more as a duty than a pleasure; but this morning I could not read. Christ's beautiful parable of the Ten Virgins, which has such a wondrous significance even to the most childish mind, failed to impart interest, and the blessed page fell from my hands unread.

I then thought I would go to the kitchen and assist Aunt Polly. I found her very much excited, and in close conversation with our master's son John, whom the servants familiarly addressed as "young master."

I have, as yet, forborne all direct and special mention of him, though he was by no means a person lacking interest. Unlike his father and sisters, he was gentle in disposition, full of loving kindness; yet he was so taciturn, that we had seldom an indication of that generosity that burned so intensely in the very centre of his soul, and which subsequent events called forth. His sisters pronounced him stupid; and, in the choice phraseology of his father, he was "poke-easy;" but the poor, undiscriminating black people, called him gentle. To me he said but little; yet that little was always kindly spoken, and I knew it to be the dictate of a soft, humane spirit.

Fair-haired, with deep blue eyes, a snowy complexion and pensive manners, he glided by us, ever recalling to my mind the thought of seraphs. He was now fifteen years of age, but small of stature and slight of sinew, with a mournful expression and dejected eye, as though the burden of a great sorrow had been early laid upon him. During all my residence there, I had never heard him laugh loud or seen him run. He had none of that exhilaration and buoyancy which are so captivating in childhood. If he asked a favor of even a servant, he always expressed a hope that he had given no trouble. When a slave was to be whipped, he would go off and conceal himself some-where, and never was he a spectator of any cruelty; yet he did not remonstrate with his father or intercede for the victims. No one had ever heard him speak against the diabolical acts of his father; yet all felt that he condemned them, for there was a silent expression of reproof in the earnest gaze which he sometimes gave him. I always fancied when the boy came near me, that there was about him a religion, which, like the wondrous virtue of the Saviour's garment, was manifest only when you approached near enough to touch it. It was not expressed in any open word, or made evident by any signal act, but, like the life-sustaining air which we daily breathe, we knew it only through its beneficent though invisible influence.

CHAPTER XI.

I was not a little surprised to find young master now in an apparently earnest colloquy with Aunt Polly. A deep carnation spot burned upon his cheeks, and his soft eye was purple in its intensity.

" What is the matter ?" I asked.

" Lor, chile," replied Aunt Polly, " Lindy can't be found no-whar."

" Has every place been searched ?" I inquired.

" Yes," said little John, " and she is nowhere to be found."

" Does master know it ?"

" Not yet, and I hope it may be kept from him for some time, at least two or three hours," he replied, with a mournful earnest-ness of tone.

" Why ? Is he not well enough to bear the excitement of it ?" I inquired.

The boy fixed his large and wondering eyes upon me. His gaze lingered for a minute or two; it was enough; I read his inmost thoughts, and in my secret soul I revered him, for I bowed to the majesty of a heaven-born soul. Such spirits are indeed few. God lends them to earth for but a short time; and we should entertain them well, for, though they come in forms un-recognized, yet must we, despite the guise of humanity, do rev-erence to the shrined seraph. This boy now became to me an object of more intense interest. I felt assured, by the power of that magnetic glance, that he was not unacquainted with the facts of Lindy's flight.

"How far is it from here to the river?" he said, as if speaking with himself, "nine miles—let me see—the Ohio once gained, and crossed, they are comparatively safe."

He started suddenly, as if he had been betrayed or beguiled of his secret, and starting up quickly, walked away. I followed him to the door, and watched his delicate form and golden head, until he disappeared in a curve of the path which led to the spring. That was a favorite walk with him. Early in the morning (for he rose before the lark) and late in the twilight, alike in winter or summer, he pursued his walk. Never once did I see him with a book in his hand. With his eye upturned to the heavens or bent upon the earth, he seemed to be reading Nature's page. He had made no great proficiency in book-knowledge; and, indeed, as he subsequently told me, he had read nothing but the Bible. The stories of the Old Testament he had committed to memory, and could repeat with great accuracy. That of Joseph possessed a peculiar fascination for him. As I closed the kitchen door and rejoined Aunt Polly, she remarked,

"Jist as I sed, Lindy is off, and we is left here to hab trouble; oh, laws, look for sights now!"

I made no reply, but silently set about assisting her in getting breakfast. Shortly after old Nace came in, with a strange expression lighting up his fiendish face.

"Has you hearn de news?" And without waiting for a reply, he went on, "Lindy is off fur Kanaday! ha, ha, ha!" and he broke out in a wild laugh; "I guess dat dose 'ere hounds will scent her path sure enoff; I looks out for fun in rale arnest. I jist hopes I'll be sint fur her, and I'll scour dis airth but what I finds her."

And thus he rambled on, in a diabolical way, neither of us heeding him. He seemed to take no notice of our silence, being too deeply interested in the subject of his thoughts.

"I'd like to know at what hour she started off. Now, she was a smart one to git off so slick, widout lettin' anybody know ob it. She had no close worth takin' wid her, so she ken run de faster. I wish Masser would git wake, kase I wants to be de fust one to tell him ob it."

Just then the two field-hands, Jake and Dan, came in.

"Wal," cried the former, "dis am news indeed. Lindy's off fur sartin. Now she tinks she is some, I reckon."

"And why shouldn't she?" asked Dan, a big, burly negro, good-natured, but very weak in mind; of a rather low and sensuous nature, yet of a good and careless humor—the best worker upon the farm. I looked round at him as he said this, for I thought there was reason as well as feeling in the speech. Why shouldn't she be both proud and happy at the success of her bold plan, if it gains her liberty and enables her to reach that land where the law would recognize her as possessed of rights? I could almost envy her such a lot.

"I guess she'll find her Kanady down de river, by de time de dogs gits arter her," said Nace, with another of his ha, ha's.

"I wonder who Masser will send fur her? I bound, Nace, you'll be sent," said Jake.

"Yes, if dar is any fun, I is sure to be dar; but hurry up yer hoe-cakes, old 'ooman, ɛ lat de breakfust will be ober, and we can hab an airly start."

The latter part of this speech was addressed to Aunt Polly, who turned round and brandished the poker toward him, saying,

"Go 'bout yer business, Nace; kase you is got cause fur joy, it is not wort my while to be glad. You is an old fool, dat nobody keres 'bout, no how. I spects you would be glad to run off, too, if yer old legs was young enuff fur to carry you."

"Me, Poll, I wouldn't be free if I could, kase, you see, I has done sarved my time at de 'post,' and now I is Masser's head-man, and I gits none ob de beatings. It is fun fur me to see de oders."

I turned my eyes upon him, and he looked so like a beast that I shut out any feeling of resentment I might otherwise have entertained. Amy came in, bearing little Ben in her arms, followed by her two sisters, Jinny and Lucy.

"La, Aunt Polly, is Lindy gone?" and her blank eyes opened to an unusual width, as she half-asked, half-asserted this fact.

" Yes, but what's it to you, Amy ?"

" I jist hear 'em say so, as I was comin' along."

" Whar she be gone to ?" asked Lucy.

" None ob yer bisness," replied Aunt Polly, with her usual gruffness.

Strange it was, that, when she was alone with me, she appeared to wax soft and gentle in her nature; but, when with others, she was " wolfish." It seemed as if she had two natures. Now, with Nace, she was as vile and almost as inhuman as he; but I, who knew her heart truly, felt that she was doing herself injustice. I did not laugh or join in their talk, but silently worked on.

" Now, you see, Ann is one ob de proud sort, kase she ken read, and her face is yaller; she tinks to hold herself 'bove us; but I 'members de time when Masser buyed her at de sale. Lor' lub yer, but she did cry when she lef her mammy ; and de way old Kais flung herself on de ground, ha ! ha ! it makes me laf now."

I turned my eyes upon him, and, I fear, there was anything but a Christian spirit beaming therefrom. He had touched a chord in my heart which was sacred to memory, love, and silence. My mother ! Could I bear to have her name and her sorrow thus rudely spoken of ? Oh, God, what fierce and fiendish feelings did the recollection of her agony arouse ? With burning head and thorn-pierced heart, I turned back a blotted page in life. Again, with horror stirring my blood, did I see her in that sweat of mortal agony, and hear that shriek that rung from her soul ! Oh, God, these memories are a living torture to me, even now. But though Nace had touched the tenderest, sorest part of my heart, I said nothing to him. The strange workings of my countenance attracted Amy's attention, and, coming up to me, with an innocent air, she asked :

" What is the matter, Ann ? Has anything happened to you ?"

These questions, put by a simple child, one, too, whose own young life had been deeply acquainted with grief, were too much for my assumed stolidity   Tears were the only reply I could make. The child regarded me curiously, and the expression, " poor thing," burst from her lips. I felt grateful for even her sympathy, and put my hand out to her.

She grasped it, and, leaning close to me, said :

"Don't cry, Ann; me is sorry fur you. Don't cry any more."

Poor thing, she could feel sympathy ; she, who was so loaded with trouble, whose existence had none of the freshness and vernal beauty of youth, but was seared and blighted like age, held in the depths of her heart a pure drop of genuine sympathy, which she freely offered me. Oh, did not my selfishness stand rebuked.

Looking out of the window, far down the path that wound to the spring, I descried the fair form of the young John, advancing toward the house. Pale and pure, with his blue eyes pensively looking up to heaven, an air of peaceful thought and subdued emotion was breathing from his very form. When I looked at him, he suggested the idea of serenity. There was that about him which, like the moonlight, inspired calm. He was walking more rapidly than I had ever seen him ; but the pallor of his cheek, and the clear, cold blue of his heaven-lit eye, harmonized but poorly with the jarring discords of life. I thought of the pure, passionless apostle John, whom Christ so loved ? And did I not dream that this youth, too, had on earth a mission of love to perform ? Was he not one of the sacred chosen ? He came walking slowly, as if he were communing with some invisible presence,

" Thar comes young Masser, and I is glad, kase he looks so good like. I does lub him," said Amy.

" Now, I is gwine fur to tell Masser, and he will gib you a beatin', nigger-gal, for sayin' you lub a white gemman," replied the sardonic Nace.

"Oh, please don't tell on me. I did not mean any harm," and she burst into tears, well-knowing that a severe whipping would be the reward of her construed impertinence.

Before I had time to offer her any consolation, the subject

of conversation himself stood among us. With a low, tuneful voice, he spoke to Amy, inquiring the cause of her tears.

"Oh, young Masser, I did not mean any harm. Please don't hab me beat." Little Ben joined in her tears, whilst the two girls clung fondly to her dress.

"Beaten for what?" asked young master, in a most encouraging manner.

"She say she lub you—jist as if a black wench hab any right to lub a beautiful white gemman," put in Nace.

"I am glad she does, and wish that I could do something that would make her love me more." And a *beatific* smile overspread his peaceful face. "Come, poor Amy, let me see if I haven't some little present for you," and he drew from his pocket a picayune, which he handed her. With a wild and singular contortion of her body, she made an acknowledgment of thanks, and kissing the hem of his robe, she darted off from the kitchen, with little Ben in her arms.

Without saying one word, young master walked away from the kitchen, but not without first casting a sorrowful look upon Nace. Strange it seemed to me, that this noble youth never administered a word of reproof to any one. He conveyed all rebukes by means of looks. Upon me this would have produced a greater impression, for those mild, reproachful eyes spoke with a power which no language could equal; but on one of Nace's obtuseness, it had no effect whatever.

Shortly after, I left the kitchen, and went to the breakfast-room, where, with the utmost expedition, I arranged the table, and then repaired to the chamber of the young ladies. I found that they had already risen from their bed. Miss Bradly (who had spent the night with them) was standing at the mirror, braiding her long hair. Miss Jane was seated in a large chair, with an elegant dressing-wrapper, waiting for me to comb her "auburn hair," as she termed it. Miss Tildy, in a lazy attitude, was talking about the events of the previous evening.

"Now, Miss Emily, I do think him very handsome; but I cannot forgive his gross Abolition sentiments."

"How horribly vulgar and low he is in his notions," said Miss Jane.

"Oh, but, girls, he was reared in the North, with those fanatical Abolitionists, and we can scarcely blame him."

"What a horrible set of men those Abolitionists must be. They have no sense," said Miss Jane, with quite a Minerva air.

"Oh, sense they assuredly have, but judgment they lack. They are a set of brain-sick dreamers, filled with Utopian schemes. They know nothing of Slavery as it exists at the South; and the word, which, I confess, has no very pleasant sound, has terrified them." This remark was made by Miss Bradly, and so astonished me that I fixed my eyes upon her, and, with one look, strove to express the concentrated contempt and bitterness of my nature. This look she did not seem to heed. With strange feelings of distrust in the integrity of human nature, I went on about my work, which was to arrange and deck Miss Jane's hair, but I would have given worlds not to have felt toward Miss Bradly as I did. I remembered with what a different spirit she had spoken to me of those Abolitionists, whom she now contemned so much, and referred to as vain dreamers. Where was the exalted philanthropy that I had thought dwelt in her soul? Was she not, now, the weakest and most sordid of mortals? Where was that far and heaven-reaching love, that had seemed to encircle her as a living, burning zone? Gone! dissipated, like a golden mist! and now, before my sight she stood, poor and a beggar, upon the great highway of life.

"I can tell you," said Miss Tildy, "I read the other day in a newspaper that the reason these northern men are so strongly in favor of the abolition of slavery is, that they entertain a prejudice against the South, and that all this political warfare originated in the base feeling of envy."

"And that is true," put in Miss Jane; "they know that cotton, rice and sugar are the great staples of the South, and where can you find any laborers but negroes to produce them?"

"Could not the poor class of whites go there and work for

wages ?" pertinently asked Miss Tildy, who had a good deal of
the spirit of altercation in her.

"No, of course not ; because they are free and could not be
made to work at all times.   They would consent to be employed
only at certain periods.   They would not work when they were
in the least sick, and they would, because of their liberty, claim
certain hours as their own ; whereas the slave has no right to
interpose any word against the overseer's order.   Sick or well,
he *must* work at busy seasons of the year.   The whip has a
terribly sanitary power, and has been proven to be a more
efficient remedy than rhubarb or senna."   After delivering herself of this wonderful argument, Miss Jane seemed to experience
great relief.   Miss Bradly turned from the mirror, and, smiling
sycophantically upon her, said : "Why, my dear, how well
you argue!   You are a very Cicero in debate."

That was enough.   This compliment took ready root in the
shallow mind of the receiver, and her love for Miss B. became
greater than ever.

"But I do think him so handsome," broke from Miss Tildy's
lips, in a half audible voice.

"Whom ?" asked Miss Bradly,

"Why, the stranger of last evening; the fair-browed Robert
Worth."

"Handsome, indeed, is he !" was the reply.

"I hope, Matilda Peterkin, you would not be so disloyal to
the South, and to the very honorable institution under which
your father accumulated his wealth, as to even admire a low-
flung northern Abolitionist;" and Miss Jane reddened with all
a Southron's ire.

Miss Bradly was about to speak, but to what purpose the
world to this day remains ignorant, for oath after oath, and
blasphemy by the volley, so horrible that I will spare myself
and the reader the repetition, proceeded from the room of Mr.
Peterkin.

The ladies sprang to their feet, and, in terror, rushed from
the apartment.

CHAPTER XII.

MR. PETERKIN'S RAGE—ITS ESCAPE—CHAT AT THE BREAKFAST TABLE—CHANGE OF VIEWS—POWER OF THE FLESH POTS.

IT was as I had expected; the news of Lindy's flight had been communicated by Nace to Mr. Peterkin, and his rage knew no limits. It was dangerous to go near him. Raving like a madman, he tore the covering of the bed to shreds, brandished his cowhide in every direction, took down his gun, and swore he would "shoot every d——d nigger on the place." His daughters had no influence over him. Out of bed he would get, declaring that "all this devilment" would not have been perpetrated if he had not been detained there by the order of that d——d doctor, who had no reason for keeping him there but a desire to get his money. Fearing that his hyena rage might vent some of its gall on them, the ladies made no further opposition to his intention.

Standing just without the door, I heard Miss Jane ask him if he would not first take some breakfast.

"No; cuss your breakfast. I want none of it; I want to be among them ar' niggers, and give 'em a taste of this cowhide, that they have been sufferin' fur."

In affright I fled to the kitchen, and told Aunt Polly that the storm had at length broken in all its fury. Each one of the negroes eyed the others in silent dismay.

Pale with rage and debility, hot fury flashing from his eye, and white froth gathering upon his lips, Mr. Peterkin dashed into the kitchen. "In the name of h—ll and its fires, niggers, what does this mean? Tell me whar that d——d gal is, or I'll cut every mother's child of you to death."

Not one spoke. Lash after lash he dealt in every direction.

" Speak, h——ll hounds, or I'll throttle you!" he cried, as he caught Jake and Dan by the throat, with each hand, and half strangled them. With their eyes rolling, and their tongues hanging from their mouths, they had not power to answer. As soon as he loosened his grasp, and their voices were sufficiently their own to speak, they attempted a denial; but a blow from each of Mr. Peterkin's fists levelled them to the floor. In this dreadful state, and with a hope of getting a moment's respite, Jake (poor fellow, I forgive him for it) pointed to me, saying:

" She knows all 'bout it."

This had the desired effect; finding one upon whom he could vent his whole wrath, Peterkin rushed up to me, and Oh, such a blow as descended upon my head ! Fifty stars blazed around me. My brain burned and ached; a choking rush of tears filled my eyes and throat. " Mercy ! mercy !" broke from my agonized lips ; but, alas! I besought it from a tribunal where it was not to be found. Blow after blow he dealt me. I strove not to parry them, but stood and received them, as, right and left, they fell like a hail-storm. Tears and blood bathed my face and blinded my sight. " You cussed fool, I'll make you rue the day you was born, if you hide from me what you knows 'bout it."

I asseverated, in the most solemn way, that I knew nothing of Lindy's flight.

" You are a liar," he cried out, and enforced his words with another blow.

" She is not," cried Aunt Polly, whose forbearance had now given out. This unexpected boldness in one of the most humble and timid of his slaves, enraged him still farther, and he dealt her such a blow that my heart aches even now, as I think of it.

A summons from one of the ladies recalled him to the house. Before leaving he pronounced a desperate threat against us, which amounted to this—that we should all be tied to the " post," and beaten until confession was wrung from us, and then taken to L——, and sold to a trader, for the southern market. But I did not share, with the others, that wondrous dread of the fabled horror of "down the river." I did not believe that anywhere slavery existed in a more brutal and cruel form than in the section of Kentucky where I lived. Solitary instances of kind and indulgent masters there were; but they were the few exceptions to the almost universal rule.

Now, when Mr. Peterkin withdrew, I, forgetful of my own wounds, lifted Aunt Polly in my arms, and bore her, half senseless, to the cabin, and laid her upon her ragged bed. "Great God!" I exclaimed, as I bent above her, "can this thing last long? How much longer will thy divine patience endure? How much longer must we bear this scourge, this crown of thorns, this sweat of blood? Where and with what Calvary shall this martyrdom terminate? Oh, give me patience, give me fortitude to bow to Thy will! Sustain me, Jesus, Thou who dost know, hast tasted of humanity's bitterest cup, give me grace to bear yet a little longer!"

With this prayer upon my lips I rose from the bedside where I had been kneeling, and, taking Aunt Polly's horny hands within my own, I commenced chafing them tenderly. I bathed her temples with cold water. She opened her eyes languidly, looked round the room slowly, and then fixed them upon me, with a bewildered expression. I spoke to her in a gentle tone; she pushed me some distance from her, eyed me with a vacant glance, then, shaking her head, turned over on her side and closed her eyes. Believing that she was stunned and faint from the blow she had received, I thought it best that she should sleep awhile. Gently spreading the coverlet over her, I returned to the kitchen, where the affrighted group of negroes yet remained. Stricken by a panic they had not power of volition.

Casting one look of reproach upon Jake, I turned away, intending to go and see if the ladies required my attention in the breakfast-room; but in the entry, which separated the house from the kitchen, I encountered Amy, with little Ben seated upon her hip. This is the usual mode with nurses in Kentucky of carrying children. I have seen girls actually deformed from the practice. An enlargement of the right hip is caused by it, and Amy was an example of this. Had I been in a different mood, her position and appearance would have provoked laughter. There she stood, with her broad eyes wide open, and glaring upon me ; her unwashed face and uncombed hair were adorned by the odd ends of broken straws and bits of hay that clung to the naps of wool ; her mouth was opened to its utmost capacity ; her very ears were erect with curiosity ; and her form bent eagerly forward, whilst little Ben was coiled up on her hip, with his sharp eyes peering like those of a mouse over her shoulder.

"Ann," she cried out, "tell me what's de matter ? What's Masser goin' to do wid us all ?"

"I don't know, Amy," I answered in a faltering tone, for I feared much for her.

"I hopes de child'en will go 'long wid me, an' I'd likes for you to go too, Ann."

I did not trust myself to reply ; but, passing hastily on, entered the breakfast-room, where Jane, Tildy, and Miss Bradly were seated at the table, with their breakfast scarcely tasted. They were bending over their plates in an intensity of interest which made them forget everything, save their subject of conversation.

"How she could have gotten off without creating ny alarm, is to me a mystery," said Miss Jane, as she toyed with her spoon and cup.

"Well, old Nick is in them. Negroes, I believe, are possessed by some demon. They have the witch's power of slipping through an auger-hole," said Miss Tildy.

"They are singular creatures," replied Miss Bradly ; "and I fear a great deal of useless sympathy is expended upon them."

"You may depend there is," said Miss Jane. "I only wish these Northern abolitionists had our servants to deal with. I think it would drive the philanthropy out of them."

"Indeed would it," answered Miss Bradly, as she took a warm roll, and busied herself spreading butter thereon; "they have no idea of the trials attending the duty of a master; the patience required in the management of so many different dispositions. I think a residence in the South or South-west would soon change their notions. The fact is, I think those fanatical abolitionists agitate the question only for political purposes. Now, it is a clearly-ascertained thing, that slavery would be prejudicial to the advancement of Northern enterprise. The negro is an exotic from a tropical region, hence lives longer, and is capable of more work in a warm climate. They have no need of black labor at the North; and thus, I think, the whole affair resolves itself into a matter of sectional gain and interest."

Here she helped herself to the wing of a fried chicken. It seemed that the argument had considerably whetted her appetite. Astonishing, is it not, how the loaves and fishes of this goodly life will change and sway our opinions? Even sober-minded, educated people, cannot repress their pinings after the flesh-pots of Egypt.

Miss Jane seemed delighted to find that her good friend and instructress held the Abolition party in such contempt. Just then young master entered. With quiet, saintly manner, taking his seat at the table, he said,

" Is not the abolition power strong at the North, Miss Emily ?"

" Oh, no, Johnny, 'tis comparatively small; confined, I assure you, to a few fanatical spirits. The merchants of New York, Boston, and the other Northern cities, carry on a too extensive commerce with the South to adopt such dangerous sentiments. There is a comity of men as well as States; and the clever rule of 'let alone' is pretty well observed."

Young master made no reply in words, but fixed his large, mysterious eyes steadfastly upon her. Was it mournfulness that streamed, with a purple light, from them, or was it a sublimated contempt? He said nothing, but quietly ate his breakfast. His fare was as homely as that of an ascetic : he never used meat, and always took bread without butter. A simple crust and glass of milk, three times a day, was his diet. Miss Jane gave him a careless and indifferent glance, then proceeded with the conversation, totally unconscious of his presence; but again and again he cast furtive, anxious glances toward her, and I thought I noticed him sighing.

"What will father do with Lindy, if she should be caught?" asked Miss Tildy.

"Send her down the river, of course," was Miss Jane's response.

"She deserves it," said Miss Tildy.

"Does she?" asked the deep, earnest voice of young master.

Was it because he was unused to asking questions, or was there something in the strange earnestness of his tone, that made those three ladies start so suddenly, and regard him with such an astonished air? Yet none of them replied, and thus for a few moments conversation ceased, until he rose from the table and left the room.

"He is a strange youth," said Miss Bradly, "and how wondrously handsome! He always suggests romantic notions."

"Yes, but I think him very stupid. He never talks to any of us—is always alone, seeks old and unfrequented spots; neither in the winter nor summer will he remain within doors. Something seems to lure him to the wood, even when despoiled of its foliage. He must be slightly crazed—ma's health was feeble for some time previous to his birth, which the doctors say has injured his constitution, and I should not be surprised if his intellect had likewise suffered." This speech was pronounced by Miss Tildy in quite an oracular tone.

Miss Bradly made no answer, and I marvelled not at her changing color. Had she not power to read, in that noble youth's voice and manner, the high enduring truth and singleness of purpose that dwelt in his nature? Though he had never spoken one word in relation to slavery, I knew that all his instincts were against it; and that opposition to it was the principle deeply ingrained in his heart.

CHAPTER XIII.

RECOLLECTIONS—CONSOLING INFLUENCE OF SYMPATHY—AMY'S DOCTRINE OF THE SOUL—TALK AT THE SPRING.

As Mr. Peterkin was passing through the vestibule of the front door, he met young master standing there. Now, this was Mr. Peterkin's favorite child, for, though he did not altogether like that quietude of manner, which he called "poke-easy," the boy had never offered him any affront about his incorrect language, or treated him with indignity in any way. And then he was so beautiful! True, his father could not appreciate the spiritual nobility of his face; yet the symmetry of his features and the spotless purity of his complexion, answered even to Mr. Peterkin's idea of beauty. The coarsest and most vulgar soul is keenly alive to the beauty of the rose and lily; though that concealed loveliness, which is only hinted at by the rare fragrance, may be known only to the cultivated and poetic heart. Often I have heard him say, " John is pretty enoff to be a gal."

Now as he met him in the vestibule, he said, " John, I'm in a peck o' trouble."

" I am sorry you are in trouble father."

" That cussed black wench, Lindy, is off, and I'm 'fraid the neighborhood kant be waked up soon enough to go arter and ketch her. Let me git her once more in my clutches, and I'll make her pay for it. I'll give her one good bastin' that she'll 'member, and then I'll send her down the river fur enough."

The boy made no reply ; but, with his eyes cast down on the earth, he seemed to be unconscious of all that was going on around him. When he raised his head his eyes were burning, his breath came thick and short, and a deep scarlet spot shone

on the whiteness of his cheek; the veins in his forehead lay
like heavy cords, and his very hair seemed to sparkle. He
looked as one inspired. This was unobserved by his parent,
who hastily strode away to find more willing listeners. I tar-
ried in a place where, unnoticed by others, I commanded a good
out-look. I saw young master clasp his hands fervently, and
heard him passionately exclaim — "How much longer, oh,
how much longer shall this be?" Then slowly walking down
his favorite path, he was lost to my vision. "Blessed youth,
heaven-missioned, if thou wouldst only speak to me! One
word of consolation from God-anointed lips like thine, would
soothe even the sting of bondage; but no," I added, "that
earnest look, that gentle tone, tell perhaps as much as it is necessary for me to know. This silence proceeds from some
noble motive. Soon enough he will make himself known to
us."

In a little while the news of Lindy's departure had spread
through the neighborhood like a flame. Our yard and house
were filled with men come to offer their services to their neighbor, who, from his wealth, was considered a sort of magnate
among them.

Pretty soon they were mounted on horses, and armed to the
teeth, each one with a horn fastened to his belt, galloping off in
quest of the poor fugitive. And is this thing done beneath the
influence of civilized laws, and by men calling themselves
Christians? What has armed those twelve men with pistols,
and sent them on an excusion like this? Is it to redeem a
brother from a band of lawless robbers, who hold him in captivity? Is it to right some individual wrong? Is it to take part
with the weak and oppressed against the strong and the overbearing? No, no, my friends, on no such noble mission as this
have they gone. No purpose of high emprise has made them
buckle on the sword and prime the pistol. A poor, lone female,
who, through years, has been beaten, tyrannized over, and abused,
has ventured out to seek what this constitution professes to secure
to every one—liberty. Barefoot and alone, she has gone forth;

and 'tis to bring her back to a vile and brutal slavery that these men have sallied out, regardless of her sex, her destitution, and her misery. They have set out either to recapture her or to shoot her down in her tracks like a dog. And this is a system which Christian men speak of as heaven-ordained ! This is a thing countenanced by freemen, whose highest national boast is, that theirs is the land of liberty, equality, and free-rights ! These are the people who yearly send large sums to Ireland ; who pray for the liberation of Hungary ; who wish to transmit armed forces across the Atlantic to aid vassal States in securing their liberty ! These are they who talk so largely of Cuba, expend so much sympathy upon the oppressed of other lands, and predict the downfall of England for her oppressive form of government ! Oh, America ! "first pluck the beam out of thine own eye, then shalt thou see more clearly the mote that is in thy brother's."

When I watched those armed men ride away, in such high courage and eagerness for the hunt, I thought of Lindy, poor, lone girl, fatigued, worn and jaded, suffering from thirst and hunger ; her feet torn and bruised with toil, hiding away in bogs and marshes, with an ear painfully acute to every sound. I thought of this, and all the resentment I had ever felt toward her faded away as a vapor.

All that day the house was in a state of intense excitement. The servants could not work with their usual assiduity. Indeed, such was the excitement, even of the white family, that we were not strictly required to labor.

Miss Jane gave me some fancy-sewing to do for her. Taking it with me to Aunt Polly's cabin, intending to talk with her whilst time was allowed me, I was surprised and pleased to find the old woman still asleep. "It will do her good," I thought, "she needs rest, poor creature ! And that blow was given to her on my account ! How much I would rather have received it myself." I then examined her head, and was glad to find no mark or bruise ; so I hoped that with a good sleep she would wake up quite well. I seated myself on an old stool, near the door, which, notwithstanding the rawness of the day, I was obliged to leave open to admit light. It was a cool, windy morning, such as makes a woollen shawl necessary. My young mistresses had betaken themselves to cashmere wrappers and capes; but I still wore my thin and "seedy" calico. As I sewed on, upon Miss Jane's embroidery, many *fancies* came in troops through my brain, defiling like a band of ghosts through each private gallery and hidden nook of memory, and even to the very inmost compartment of secret thought! My mother, with her sad, sorrow-stricken face, my old companions and play-fellows in the long-gone years, all arose with vividness to my eye! Where were they all? Where had they been during the lapse of years? Of my mother I had never heard a word. Was she dead? At that suggestion I started, and felt my heart grow chill, as though an icy hand had clenched it; yet why felt I so? Did I not know that the grave would be to her as a bed of ease? What torture could await her beyond the pass of the valley of shadows? She, who had been faithful over a little, would certainly share in those blessed rewards promised by Christ; yet it seemed to me that my heart yearned to look upon her again in this life. I could not, without pain, think of her as *one who had been.* There was something selfish in this, yet was it intensely human, and to feel otherwise I should have had to be less loving, less filial in my nature. "Oh, mother!" I said, "if ever we meet again, will it be a meeting that shall know no separation? Mother, are you changed? Have you, by the white man's coarse brutality, learned to forget your absent child? Do not thoughts of her often come to your lonely soul with the sighing of the midnight wind? Do not the high and merciful stars, that nightly burn above you, recall me to your heart? Does not the child-loved moon speak to you of times when, as a little thing, I nestled close to your bosom? Or, mother, have other ties grown around your heart? Have other children supplanted your eldest-born? Do chirruping lips and bright eyes claim all your thoughts? Or do you toil alone, broken in soul and bent in body, beneath the drudgery of human labor, without one soft voice to lull you to repose? Oh, not this, not this, kind Heaven! Let her forget me, in her joy; give her but peace, and on me multiply misfortunes, rain down evils, only spare, shield and protect *her*." This tide of thought, as it rolled rapidly through my mind, sent the hot tears, in gushes, from my eyes. As I bent my head to wipe them away, without exactly seeing it, I became aware of a blessed presence; and, lifting my moist eyes, I beheld young master standing before me, with that calm, spiritual glance which had so often charmed and soothed me.

"What is the matter, Ann? Why are you weeping?" he asked me in a gentle voice.

"Nothing, young Master, only I was thinking of my mother."

"How long since you saw her?"

"Oh, years, young Master; I have not seen her since my childhood—not since Master bought me."

He heaved a deep sigh, but said nothing.; those eyes, with a soft, shadowed light, as though they were shining through misty tears, were bent upon me.

"Where is your mother now, Ann?"

"I don't know, young Master, I've never heard from her since I came here."

Again he sighed, and now he passed his thin white hand across his eyes, as if to dissipate the mist.

"You think she was sold when you were, don't you?"

"I expect she was. I'm almost sure she was, for I don't think either my young Masters or Mistresses wished or expected to retain the servants."

"I wish I could find out something about her for you; but, at present, it is out of my power. You must do the best you can. You are a good girl, Ann; I have noticed how patiently you bear hard trouble. Do you pray?"

"Oh, yes, young Master, and that is all the pleasure I have. What would be my situation without prayer? Thanks to God, the slave has this privilege!"

"Yes, Ann, and in God's eyes you are equal to a white per-

son. He makes no distinction; your soul is as precious and
dear to Him as is that of the fine lady clad in silk and gems."

I opened my eyes to gaze upon him, as he stood there,
with his beautiful face beaming with good feeling and love
for the humblest and lowest of God's creatures. This was
religion ! This was the spirit which Christ commended. This
was the love which He daily preached and practiced.

"But how is Aunt Polly ? I heard that she was suffering
much."

"She is sleeping easily now," I replied.

"Well, then, don't disturb her. It is better that she should
sleep;" and he walked away, leaving me more peaceful and
happy than before. Blessed youth !—why have we not more
such among us ! They would render the thongs and fetters of
slavery less galling.

The day was unusually quiet; but the frostiness of the atmosphere kept the ladies pretty close within doors; and Mr.
Peterkin had, contrary to the wishes of his family, and the
injunctions of his physician, gone out with the others upon the
search; besides, he had taken Nace and the other men with
him, and, as Aunt Polly was sick, Ginsy had been appointed
in her place to prepare dinner. After sewing very diligently
for some time, I wandered out through the poultry lot, lost in a
labyrinth of strange reflection. As I neared the path leading down
toward the spring, young master's favorite walk, I could not
resist the temptation to follow it to its delightful terminus,
where he was wont to linger all the sunny summer day, and
frequently passed many hours in the winter time ? I was su-
perstitious enough to think that some of his deep and rich
philanthropy had been caught, as by inspiration, from this
lovely natural retreat; for how could the child of such a low,
beastly parent, inherit a disposition so heavenly, and a soul so
spotless ? He had been bred amid scenes of the most revolting cruelty ; had lived with people of the harshest and most
brutal dispositions ; yet had he contracted from them no moral
stain. Were they not hideous to look upon, and was he not

lovely as a seraph ? Were they not low and vulgar, and he lofty and celestial-minded ? Why and how was this ? Ah, did I not believe him to be one of God's blessed angels, lent us for a brief season ?

The path was well-trodden, and wound and curved through the woods, down to a clear, natural spring of water. There had been made, by the order of young master, a turfetted seat, overgrown by soft velvet moss, and here this youth would sit for hours to ponder, and, perhaps, to weave golden fancies which were destined to ripen into rich fruition in that land beyond the shores of time. As I drew near the spring, I imagined that a calm and holy influence was settling over me. The spirit of the place had power upon me, and I yielded myself to the spell. It was no disease of fancy, or dream of enchantment, that thus possessed me; for there, half-reclining on the mossy bench, I beheld young master, and, seated at his feet, with her little, odd, wondering face uplifted to his, was Amy ; and, crawling along, playing with the moss, and looking down into the mirror of the spring, peered the bright eyes of little Ben. It was a scene of such beauty that I paused to take a full view of it, before making my presence known. Young master, with his pale, intellectual face, his classic head, his sun-bright curls, and his earnest blue eyes, sat in a half-lounging attitude, making no inappropriate picture of an angel of light, whilst the two little black faces seemed emblems of fallen, degraded humanity, listening to his pleading voice.

" Wherever you go, or in whatever condition you may be, Amy, never forget to pray to the good Lord." As he said this, he bent his eyes compassionately on her.

" Oh, laws, Masser, how ken I pray! de good Lord wouldn't hear me. I is too black and dirty."

" God does not care for that. You are as dear to Him as the finest lady of the land."

" Oh, now, Masser, you doesn't tink me is equal to you, a fine, nice, pretty white gemman—dress so fine."

" God cares not, my child, for clothes, or the color of the skin.

He values the heart alone; and if your heart is clear, it matters not whether your face be black or your clothes mean."

"Laws, now, young Masser," and the child laughed heartily at the idea, "you doesn't 'spect a nigger's heart am clean. I tells you 'tis black and dirty as dere faces."

"My poor child, I would that I had power to scatter the gloomy mist that beclouds your mind, and let you see and know that our dying Saviour embraced all your unfortunate race in the merits of his divine atonement."

This speech was not comprehended by Amy. She sat looking vacantly at him; marvelling all the while at his pretty talk, yet never once believing that Jesus prized a negro's soul. Young master's eyes were, as usual, elevated to the clear, majestic heavens. Not a cloud floated in the still, serene expanse, and the air was chill. One moment longer I waited, before revealing myself. Stepping forward, I addressed young master in an humble tone.

"Well, Ann, what do you want?" This was not said in a petulant voice, but with so much gentleness that it invited the burdened heart to make its fearful disclosure.

"Oh, young Master, I know that you will pardon me for what I am going to ask. I cannot longer restrain myself. Tell me what is to become of us? When shall we be sold? Into whose hands shall I fall?"

"Alas, poor Ann, I am as ignorant of father's intentions as you are. I would that I could relieve your anxiety, but I am as uneasy about it as you or any one can be. Oh, I am powerless to do anything to better your unfortunate condition. I am weak as the weakest of you."

"I know, young Master, that we have your kindest sympathy, and this knowledge softens my trouble."

He did not reply, but sat with a perplexed expression, looking on the ground.

"Oh, Ann, you has done gin young Masser some trouble. What fur you do dat? We niggers ain't no 'count any how, and you hab no sort ob bisiness be troublin' young Masser 'bout it," said Amy.

"Be still, Amy, let Ann speak her troubles freely. It will relieve her mind. You may tell me of yours too."

Sitting down upon the sward, close to his feet, I relieved my oppressed bosom by a copious flood of tears. Still he spoke not, but sat silent, looking down. Amy was awed into stillness, and even little Ben became calm and quiet as a lamb. No one broke the spell. No one seemed anxious to do so. There are some feelings for which silence is the best expression.

At length he said mildly, "Now, my good friends, it might be made the subject of ungenerous remarks, if you were to be seen talking with me long. You had better return to the house."

As Amy and I, with little Ben, rose to depart, he looked after us, and sighing, exclaimed, " poor creatures, my heart bleeds for you!"

CHAPTER XIV.

Upon my return to the house I hastened on to the cabin,
hoping to find Aunt Polly almost entirely recovered. Passing
hastily through the yard I entered the cabin with a light step,
and to my surprise found her sitting up in a chair, playing with
some old faded artificial flowers, the dilapidated decorations of
Miss Tildy's summer bonnet, which had been swept from the
house with the litter on the day before. I had never seen her
engaged in a pastime so childish and sportive, and was not a
little astonished, for her aversion to flowers had often been to
me the subject of remark.

"What have you there that is pretty, Aunt Polly?" I asked
with tenderness.

With a wondering, childish smile, she held the crushed blossoms up, and turning them over and over in her hands, said:

"Putty things! ye is berry putty!" then pressing them to
her bosom, she stroked the leaves as kindly as though she had
been smoothing the truant locks of a well-beloved child. I could
not understand this freak, for she was one to whose uncultured
soul all sweet and pretty fancies seemed alien. Looking up to
me with that vacant glance which at once explained all, she
said:

"Who's dar? Who is you? Oh, dat is my darter," and addressing me by the remembered name of her own long-lost child,
she traversed, in thought, the whole waste-field of memory. Not
a single wild-flower in the wayside of the heart was neglected or
forgotten. She spoke of times when she had toyed and dandled

her infant darling upon her knee; then, shudderingly, she would wave me off, with terror written all over her furrowed face, and cry, "Get you away, Masser is comin': thar, thar he is; see him wid de ropes; he is comin' to tar you 'way frum me. Here, here child, git under de bed, hide frum 'em, dey is all gwine to take you 'way—'way down de river, whar you'll never more see yer poor old mammy." Then sinking upon her knees, with her hands outstretched, and her eyes eagerly strained forward, and bent on vacancy, she frantically cried:

"Masser, please, please Masser, don't take my poor chile from me. It's all I is got on dis ar' airth; Masser, jist let me hab it and I'll work fur you, I'll sarve you all de days ob my life. You may beat my ole back as much as you please; you may make me work all de day and all de night, jist, so I ken keep my chile. Oh, God, oh, God! see, dere dey goes, wid my poor chile screaming and crying for its mammy! See, see it holds its arms to me! Oh, dat big hard man struck it sich a blow. Now, now dey is out ob sight." And crawling on her knees, with arms outspread, she seemed to be following some imaginary object, until, reaching the door, I feared in her transport of agony she would do herself some injury, and, catching her strongly in my arms, I attempted to hold her back; but she was endowed with a superhuman strength, and pushed me violently against the wall.

"Thar, you wretch, you miserble wretch, dat would keep me from my chile, take dat blow, and I wish it would send yer to yer grave."

Recoiling a few steps, I looked at her. A wild and lurid light gathered in her eye, and a fiendish expression played over her face. She clenched her hands, and pressed her old broken teeth hard upon her lips, until the blood gushed from them; frothing at the mouth, and wild with excitement, she made an attempt to bound forward and fell upon the floor. I screamed for help, and sprang to lift her up. Blood oozed from her mouth and nose; her eyes rolled languidly, and her under-jaw fell as though it were broken.

In terror I bore her to the bed, and, laying her down, I went to get a bowl of water to wash the blood and foam from her face. Meeting Amy at the door, I told her Aunt Polly was very sick, and requested her to remain there until my return.

I fled to the kitchen, and seizing a pan of water that stood upon the shelf, returned to the cabin. There I found young master bending over Aunt Polly, and wiping the blood-stains from her mouth and nose with his own handkerchief. This was, indeed, the ministration of the high to the lowly. This generous boy never remembered the distinctions of color, but with that true spirit of human brotherhood which Christ inculcated by many memorable examples, he ministered to the humble, the lowly, and the despised. Indeed, such seemed to take a firmer hold upon his heart. Here, in this lowly cabin, like the good Samaritan of old, he paused to bind up the wounds of a poor outcast upon the dreary wayside of existence.

Bending tenderly over Aunt Polly, until his luxuriant golden curls swept her withered face, he pressed his linen handkerchief to her mouth and nose to staunch the rapid flow of blood.

"Oh, Ann, have you come with the water? I fear she is almost gone; throw it in her face with a slight force, it may revive her," he said in a calm tone.

I obeyed, but there was no sign of consciousness. After one or two repetitions she moved a little, young master drew a bottle of sal volatile from his pocket, and applied it to her nose. The effect was sudden; she started up spasmodically, and looking round the room laughed wildly, frightfully; then, shaking her head, her face resumed its look of pitiful imbecility.

"The light is quenched, and forever," said young master, and the tears came to his eyes and rolled slowly down his cheeks. Amy, with Ben in her arms, stood by in anxious wonder; creeping up to young master's side, she looked earnestly in his face, saying—

"Don't cry, Masser, Aunt Polly will soon be well; she jist sick for little while. De lick Masser gib her only hurt her little time,—she 'most well now, but her does look mighty wild."

"Oh, Lord, how much longer must these poor people be tried in the furnace of affliction? How much longer wilt thou permit a suffering race to endure this harsh warfare? Oh, Divine Father, look pityingly down on this thy humble servant, who is so sorely tried." The latter part of the speech was uttered as he sank upon his knees; and down there upon the coarse puncheon floor we all knelt, young master forming the central figure of the group, whilst little Amy, the baby-boy Ben, and the poor lunatic, as if in mimicry, joined us. We surrounded him, and surely that beautiful heart-prayer must have reached the ear of God. When such purity asks for grace and mercy upon the poor and unfortunate, the ear of Divine grace listens.

"What fur you pray?" asked the poor lunatic.

"I ask mercy for sore souls like thine."

"Oh, dat is funny; but say, sir, whar is my chile? Whar is she? Why don't she come to me? She war here a minnit ago; but now she does be gone away."

"Oh, what a mystery is the human frame! Lyre of the spirit, how soon is thy music jarred into discord." Young master uttered this rhapsody in a manner scarcely audible, but to my ear no sound of his was lost, not a word, syllable, or tone!

"Poor Luce—is dat Luce?" and the poor, crazed creature stared at me with a bewildered gaze! "and my baby-boy, whar is he, and my oldest sons? Dey is all gone from me and for-ever." She began to weep piteously.

"Watch with her kindly till I send Jake for the doctor," he said to me; then rallying himself, he added, "but they are all gone—gone upon that accursed hunt;" and, seating himself in a chair, he pressed his fingers hard upon his closed eye-lids. "Stay, I will go myself for the doctor—she must not be neglected."

And rising from his chair he buttoned his coat, and, charging me to take good care of her, was about starting, but

Aunt Polly sprang forward and caught him by the arms, exclaiming,

"Oh, putty, far angel, don't leab me. I kan't let you leab me—stay here. I has no peace when you is gone. Dey will come and beat me agin, and dey will take my chil'en frum me. Oh, please now, you stay wid me."

And she held on to him with such a pitiful fondness, and there was so much anxiety in her face, such an infantile look of tenderness, with the hopeless vacancy of idiocy in the eye, that to refuse her would have been harsh; and of this young master was incapable. So, turning to me, he said,

"You go, Ann, for the doctor, and I will stay with her—poor old creature I have never done anything for her, and now I will gratify her."

As the horses had all been taken by the pursuers of Lindy, I was forced to walk to Dr. Mandy's farm, which was about two miles distant from Mr. Peterkin's. I was glad of this, for of late it was indeed but seldom that I had been allowed to indulge in a walk through the woods. All through the leafy glory of the summer season I had looked toward the old sequestered forest with a longing eye. Each little bird seemed wooing me away, yet my occupations confined me closely to the house; and a pleasure-walk, even on Sunday, was a luxury which a negro might dream of but never indulge. Now, though it was the lonely autumn time, yet loved I still the woods, dismantled as they were. There is something in the grandeur of the venerable forests, that always lifts the soul to devotion! The patriarchal trees and the delicate sward, the wind-music and the almost ceaseless miserere of the grove, elevate the heart, and to the cultivated mind speak with a power to which that of books is but poor and tame.

CHAPTER XV.

THE freshening breeze, tempered with the keen chill of the coming winter, made a lively music through the woods, as, floating along, it toyed with the fallen leaves that lay dried and sere upon the earth. There stood the giant trees, rearing their bald and lofty heads to the heavens, whilst at their feet was spread their splendid summer livery. Like the philosophers of old, in their calm serenity they looked away from earth and its troubles to the "bright above."

I wandered on, with a quick step, in the direction of the doctor's. The recent painful events were not calculated to color my thoughts very pleasingly; yet I had taught myself to live so entirely *within*, to be so little affected by what was *without*, that I could be happy in imagination, notwithstanding what was going on in the external world. 'Tis well that the negro is of an imaginative cast. Suppose he were by nature strongly practical and matter-of-fact; life could not endure with him. His dreaminess, his fancy, makes him happy in spite of the dreary reality which surrounds him. The poor slave, with not a sixpence in his pocket, dreams of the time when he shall be able to buy himself, and revels in this most delightful Utopia.

I had walked on for some distance, without meeting any object of special interest, when, passing through a large "*deadening*," I was surprised to see a gentleman seated upon a fragment of what had once been a noble tree. He was engaged at that occupation which is commonly considered to denote want of thought, viz., *whittling a stick.*

I stopped suddenly, and looked at him very eagerly, for now, with the broad day-light streaming over him, I recognized the one whom I had watched in the dubious moonbeams! This was Mr. Robert Worth, the man who held those dangerous Abolition principles—the fanatic, who was rash enough to express, south of Mason and Dixon's line, the opinion that negroes are human beings and entitled to consideration. Here now he was, and I could look at him. How I longed to speak to him, to talk with him, hear him tell all his generous views; to ask questions as to those free Africans at the North who had achieved name and fame, and learn more of the distinguished orator, Frederick Douglass! So great was my desire, that I was almost ready to break through restraint, and, forgetful of my own position, fling myself at his feet, and beg him to comfort me. Then came the memory of Miss Bradly's treachery, and I sheathed my heart. "No, no, I will not again trust to white people. They have no sympathy with us, our natures are too simple for their cunning;" and, reflecting thus, I walked on, yet I felt as if I could not pass him. He had spoken so nobly in behalf of the slave, had uttered such lofty sentiments, that my whole soul bowed down to him in worship. I longed to pay homage to him. There is a principle in the slave's nature to reverence, to look upward; hence, he makes the most devout Christian, and were it not for this same spirit, he would be but a poor servant.

So it was with difficulty I could let pass this opportunity of speaking with one whom I held in such veneration : but I governed myself and went on. All the distance I was pondering upon what I had heard in relation to those of my brethren who had found an asylum in the North. Oh, once there, I could achieve so much! I felt, within myself, a latent power, that, under more fortunate circumstances, might be turned to advantage. When I reached Doctor Mandy's residence I found that he had gone out to visit a patient. His wife came out to see me, and asked,

"Who is sick at Mr. Peterkin's?"

I told her, "Aunt Polly, the cook."

" Is much the matter ?"

" Yes, Madam ; young master thinks she has lost her reason."

" Lost her reason !" exclaimed Mrs. Mandy.

" Yes, Madam ; she doesn't seem to know any of us, and evidently wanders in her thoughts." I could not repress the evidence of emotion when I remembered how kind to me the old creature had been, nay, that for me she had received the blow which had deprived her of reason.

" Poor girl, don't cry," said Mrs. Mandy. This lady was of a warm, good heart, and was naturally touched at the sight of human suffering ; she was one of that quiet sort of beings who feel a great deal and say but little. Fearful of giving offence, she usually kept silence, lest the open expression of her sympathy should defeat the purpose. A weak, though a good person, she now felt annoyed because she had been beguiled into even pity for a servant. She did not believe in slavery, yet she dared not speak against the " peculiar institution " of the South. It would injure the doctor's practice, a matter about which she must be careful.

I knew my place too well to say much ; therefore I observed a respectful silence.

" Now, Ann, you had better hurry home. I expect there is great excitement at your house, and the ladies will need your services to-day, particularly ; to remain out too long might excite suspicion, and be of no service to you."

My looks plainly showed how entire was my acquiescence. She must have known this, and then, as if self-interest suggested it, she said,

" You have a good home, Ann, I hope you will never do as Lindy has done. Homes like yours are rare, and should be appreciated. Where will you ever again find such kind mistresses and such a good master ?"

" Homes such as mine are rare !" I would that they were ; but, alas! they are too common, as many farms in Kentucky can show ! Oh, what a terrible institution this one must be, which originates and involves so many crimes! Now, here was a kind, honest-hearted woman, who felt assured of the criminality of slavery; yet, as it is recognized and approved by law, she could not, save at the risk of social position, pecuniary loss and private inconvenience, even express an opinion against it. I was the oppressed slave of one of her wealthy neighbors; she dared not offer me even a word of pity, but needs must outrage all my nature by telling me that I had a "good home, kind mistresses and a good master!" Oh, bitter mockery of torn and lacerated feelings! My blood curdled as I listened. How much I longed to fling aside the servility at which my whole soul revolted, and tell her, with a proud voice, how poorly I thought she supported the dignity of a true womanhood, when thus, for the poor reward of gold, she could smile at, and even encourage, a system which is at war with the best interest of human nature; which aims a deadly blow at the very machinery of society; aye, attacks the noble and venerable institution of marriage, and breaks asunder ties which God has commanded us to reverence! This is the policy of that institution, which Southern people swear they will support even with their life-blood! I have ransacked my brain to find out a clue to the wondrous infatuation. I have known, during the years of my servitude, men who had invested more than half of their wealth in slaves: and he is generally accounted the greatest gentleman, who owns the most negroes. Now, there is a reason for the Louisiana or Mississippi planter's investing largely in this sort of property; but why the Kentucky farmer should wish to own slaves, is a mystery: surely it cannot be for the petty ambition of holding human beings in bondage, lording it over immortal souls! Oh, perverse and strange human nature! Thoughts like these, with a lightning-like power, drove through my brain and influenced my mind against Mrs. Mandy, who, I doubt not, was, at heart, a kind, well-meaning woman. How can the slave be a philanthropist?

Without saying anything whereby my safety could be imperilled, I left Mrs. Mandy's residence. When I had walked about a hundred yards from the house, I turned and looked back, and was surprised to see her looking after me. "Oh, white woman," I inwardly exclaimed, "nursed in luxury, reared in the lap of bounty, with friends, home and kindred, that mortal power cannot tear you from, how can *you* pity the poor, oppressed slave, who has no liberty, no right, no father, no brother, or friend, only as the white man chooses he shall have!" Who could expect these children of wealth, fostered by prosperity, and protected by the law, to feel for the ignorant negro, who through ages and generations has been crushed and kept in ignorance? We are told to love our masters! Why should we? Are we dogs to lick the hand that strikes us? Or are we men and women with never-dying souls—men and women unprotected in the very land they have toiled to beautify and adorn! Oh, little, little do ye know, my proud, free brothers and sisters in the North, of all the misery we endure, or of the throes of soul that we have! The humblest of us feel that we are deprived of something that we are entitled to by the law of God and nature.

I rambled on through the woods, wrapped in the shadows of gloom and misanthropy. "Why," I asked myself, "can't I be a hog or dog to come at the call of my owner? Would it not be better for me if I could repress all the lofty emotions and generous impulses of my soul, and become a spiritless thing? I would swap natures with the lowest insect, the basest serpent that crawls upon the earth. Oh, that I could quench this thirsty spirit, satisfy this hungry heart, that craveth so madly the food and drink of knowledge! Is it right to conquer the spirit, which God has given us? Is it best for a high-souled being to sit supinely down and bear the vile trammels of an unnatural and immoral bondage? Are these aspirings sent us from above? Are they wings lent the spirit from an angel? Or must they be clipped and crushed as belonging to the evil spirit?" As I walked on, in this state of mind, I neared the spot where I had beheld the interesting stranger.

To my surprise and joy I found him still there, occupied as

before, in whittling, perhaps the same stick. You, my free friends, who, from the fortunate accident of birth, are entitled to the heritage of liberty, can but poorly understand how very humble and degraded American slavery makes the victim. Now, though I knew this man possessed the very information for which I so longed, I dared not presume to address him on a subject even of such vital import. I dare say, and indeed after-times proved, this young apostle of reform would have applauded as heroism what then seemed to me as audacity.

With many a lingering look toward him, I pursued the "noise-less tenor of my way."

CHAPTER XVI.

A REFLECTION — AMERICAN ABOLITIONISTS — DISAFFECTION IN KENTUCKY — THE YOUNG MASTER — HIS REMONSTRANCE.

UPON my arrival home I found that the doctor, lured by curiosity, and not by business, had called. The news of Lindy's flight had reached him in many garbled and exaggerated forms; so he had come to assure himself of the truth. Of course, with all a Southern patriot's ire, he pronounced Lindy's conduct an atrocious crime, for which she should answer with life, or that far worse penalty (as some thought), banishment " down the river." Thought I not strangely, severely, of those persons, the doctor and the ladies, as they sat there, luxuriating over a bottle of wine, denouncing vengeance against a poor, forlorn girl, who was trying to achieve her liberty;—heroically contending for that on which Americans pride themselves ? Had she been a Hungarian or an Irish maid, seeking an asylum from the tyranny of a King, she would have been applauded as one whose name was worthy to be enrolled in the litany of heroes; but she was a poor, ignorant African, with a sooty face, and because of this all sympathy was denied her, and she was pronounced nothing but a "runaway negro," who deserved a terrible punishment ; and the hand outstretched to relieve her, would have been called guilty of treason. Oh, wise and boastful Americans, see ye no oppression in all this, or do ye exult in that odious spot, which will blacken the fairest page of your history " to the last syllable of recorded time" ? Does not a blush stain your cheeks when you make vaunting speeches about the character of your government? Ye cannot, I know ye cannot, be easy in your consciences ; I know that a secret, unspoken trouble gnaws like

6*

a canker in your breasts! Many of you veil your eyes, and grope through the darkness of this domestic oppression; you will not listen to the cries of the helpless, but sit supinely down and argue upon the "right" of the thing. There were kind and tender-hearted Jews, who felt that the crucifixion of the Messiah was a fearful crime, yet fear sealed their lips. And are there not now time-serving men, who are worthy and capable of better things, but from motives of policy will offer no word against this barbarous system of slavery? Oh, show me the men, like that little handful at the North, who are willing to forfeit everything for the maintenance of human justice and mercy. Blessed apostles, near to the mount of God! your lips have been touched with the flame of a new Pentecost, and ye speak as never men spake before! Who that listens to the words of Parker, Sumner, and Seward, can believe them other than inspired? Theirs is no ordinary gift of speech; it burns and blazes with a mighty power! Cold must be the ear that hears them unmoved; and hard the heart that throbs not in unison with their noble and earnest expressions! Often have I paused in this little book, to render a feeble tribute to these great reformers. It may be thought out of place, yet I cannot repress the desire to speak my voluntary gratitude, and, in the name of all my scattered race, thank them for the noble efforts they have made in our behalf!

All the malginity of my nature was aroused against Miss Bradly, when I heard her voice loudest in denunciation against Lindy.

As I was passing through the room, I could catch fragments of conversation anything but pleasing to the ear of a slave; but I had to listen in meekness, letting not even a working muscle betray my dissent. They were orthodox, and would not tolerate even from an equal a word contrary to their views.

I did not venture to ask the doctor what he thought of Aunt Polly, for that would have been called impudent familiarity, punishable with whipping at the " post ;" but when I met young master in the entry, I learned from him that the case was one of hopeless insanity. Blood-letting, &c., had been resorted to, but with no effect. The doctor gave it as his opinion that the case was "without remedy." Not knowing that young master differed from his father and sisters, the doctor had, in his jocose and unfeeling way, suggested that it was not much difference; the old thing was of but little value; she was old and worn-out. To all this young master made no other reply than a fixed look from his meek eyes—a look which the doctor could not understand; for the idea of sympathy with or pity for a slave would have struck him as being a thing existing only in the bosom of a fanatical abolitionist, whose conviction would not permit him to cross the line of Mason and Dixon. Ah! little knew he (the coarse doctor) what a large heart full of human charities had grown within; nay, was indigenous to this south-western latitude. I believe, yes have reason to know, that the pure sentiment of abolition is one that is near and dear to the heart of many a Kentuckian; even those who are themselves the hereditary holders of slaves are, in many instances, the most opposed to the system. This sentiment is, perhaps, more largely developed in, and more openly expressed by, the females of the State; and this is accounted for from the fact that to be suspected of abolition tendencies is at once the plague-mark whereby a man is ever after considered unfit for public trust or political honor. It is the great question, the strong conservative element of society. To some extent it likewise taboos, in social circles, the woman who openly expresses such sentiments; though as she has no popular interests to stake, in many cases her voice will be on the side of right, not might.

In later years I remember to have overheard a colloquy between a lady and gentleman (both slaveholders) in Kentucky. The gentleman had vast possessions, about one-third of which consisted of slaves. The lady's entire wealth was in six negroes, some of them under the age of ten. They were hired out at the highest market prices, and by the proceeds she was supported. She had been raised in a strongly conservative community; nay, her own family were (to use a Kentuckyism) the

"pick and choose" of the pro-slavery party. Some of them
had been considered the able vindicators of the "system;" yet
she, despite the force of education and the influence of domestic
training, had broken away from old trammels and leash-strings,
and was, both in thought and expression, a bold, ingrain abolitionist. She defied the lions in their chosen dens. On the occasion of this conversation, I heard her say that she could not
remain happy whilst she detained in bondage those creatures
who could. claim, under the Constitution, alike with her, their
freedom; and so soon as she attained her majority, she intended
to liberate them. "But," said she—and I shall never forget
the mournful look of her dark eye—"the statute of the State
will not allow them to remain here ten days after liberation;
and one of these men has a wife (to whom he is much attached),
who is a slave to a master that will neither free her nor sell her·
Now, this poor captive husband would rather remain in slavery
to me, than be parted from his wife; and here is the point upon
which I always stand. I wish to be humane and just to him;
and yet rid myself from the horrid crime to which, from the accident of inheritance, I have become accessory." The gentleman, who seemed touched by the heroism of the girl, was
beguiled into a candid acknowledgment of his own sentiments;
and freely declared to her that, if it were not for his political
aspirations, he would openly free every slave he owned, and
relieve his conscience from the weight of the "perilous stuff" that
so oppressed it. "But," said he, "were I to do it in Kentucky,
I should be politically dead. It would, besides, strike a blow
at my legal practice, and then what could I do? 'Othello's
occupation would be gone.' Of what avail, then, would be my
'quiddits, quillets; my cases, tenures and my tricks?' I, who
am high in political favor, should live to read my shame. I,
who now 'tower in my pride of place, should, by some mousing
owl, be hawked at and killed.' No, I must burden my conscience yet a little longer."

The lady, with all a young girl's naïve and beautiful enthusiasm, besought him to disregard popular praise and worldly

distinction. "Seek first," said she, "the kingdom of heaven, and all things else shall be given you;" but the gentleman had grown hard in this world's devious wiles. He preferred throwing off his allegiance to Providence, and, single-handed and alone, making his fate. Talk to me of your thrifty men, your popular characters, and I instantly know that you mean a cringing, parasitical server of the populace; one who sinks soul, spirit and manly independence for the mere garments that cover his perishable body, and to whom the empty plaudits of the unthinking crowd are better music than the thankful prayer of suffering humanity. Let such an one, I say, have his full measure of the "clapping of hands," let him hear it all the while; for he cannot see the frown that darkens the brow of the guardian angel, who, with a sigh, records his guilt. Go on, thou worldly Pharisee, but the day *will come*, when the lowly shall be exalted. Trust and wait we longer. Oh, ye who "know the right, and yet the wrong pursue," a fearful reckoning will be yours.

But young master was not of this sort; I felt that his lips were closed from other and higher motives. If it had been of any avail, no matter what the cost to himself, he would have spoken. His soul knew but one sentiment, and that was "love to God and good will to men on earth." And now, as he entered the room where the doctor and the ladies were seated, and listened to their heartless conversation, he planted himself firmly in their midst, saying:

"Sisters, the time has come when I *must* speak. Patiently have I lived beneath this my father's roof, and witnessed, without uttering one word, scenes at which my whole soul revolted; I have heard that which has driven me from your side. On my bare knees, in the gloom of the forest, I have besought God to soften your hearts. I have asked that the dew of mercy might descend upon the hoary head of my father, and that womanly gentleness might visit your obdurate hearts. I have felt that I could give my life up a sacrifice to obtain this; but my unworthy prayers have not yet been answered. In vain, in vain,

I have hoped to see a change in you. Are you women or
fiends? How can you persecute, to the death, poor, ignorant
creatures, whose only fault is a black skin? How can you in-
humanly beat those who have no protectors but you? Reverse
the case, and take upon yourselves their condition; how would
you act? Could you bear silently the constant "wear and
tear" of body, the perpetual imprisonment of the soul? Could
you surrender yourselves entirely to the keeping of another,
and that other your primal foe—one who for ages has had his
arm uplifted against your race? Suppose you every day
witnessed a board groaning with luxuries (the result of your
labor) devoured by your persecutors, whilst you barely got the
crumbs; your owners dressed in purple and fine linen, whilst
you wore the coarsest material, though all their luxury was the
product of your exertion; what think you would be right for
you to do? Or suppose I, whilst lingering at the little spring,
should be stolen off, gagged and taken to Algiers, kept there in
servitude, compelled to the most drudging labor; poorly clad
and scantily fed whilst my master lived like a prince; kept in
constant terror of the lash; punished severely for every venial
offence, and my poor heart more lacerated than my body;—
what would you think of me, if a man were to tell me that,
with his assistance, I could make my escape to a land of liberty,
where my rights would be recognized, and my person safe from
violence; I say what would you think, if I were to decline,
and to say I preferred to remain with the Algerines?" He
paused, but none replied. With eyes wonderingly fixed upon
him, the group remained silent.

    "You are silent all," he continued, "for conviction, like a
swift arrow, has struck your souls. Oh, God!" and he raised
his eyes upward, "out of the mouths of babes and sucklings let
wisdom, holiness and truth proceed. Touch their flinty hearts,
and let the spark of grace be emitted! Oh, sisters, know ye
not that this Algerine captivity that I have painted, is but a
poor picture of the daily martyrdom which our slaves endure?
Look on that old woman, who, by a brutal blow from our father,

has been deprived of her reason. Look at that little haggard orphan, Amy, who is the kicked football of you all. Look at the poor men whom we have brutalized and degraded. Think of Lindy, driven by frenzy to brave the passage to an unknown country rather than longer endure what we have put upon her. Gaze, till your eyes are bleared, upon that whipping-post, which rises upon our plantation; it is wet, even now, with the blood that has gushed from innocent flesh. Look at the ill-fed, ill-clothed creatures that live among us; and think they have immortal souls, which we have tried to put out. Oh, ponder well upon these things, and let this poor, wretched girl, who has sallied forth, let her go, I say, to whatever land she wishes, and strive to forget the horrors that haunted her here."

Again he paused, but none of them durst reply. Inspired by their silence, he went on:

"And from you, Miss Bradly, I had expected better things. You were reared in a State where the brutality of the slave system is not tolerated. Your early education, your home influences, were all against it. Why and how can your womanly heart turn away from its true instincts? Is it for you, a Northerner and a woman, to put up your voice in defence of slavery? Oh, shame! triple-dyed shame, should stain your cheeks! Well may my sisters argue for slavery, when you, their teacher, aid and abet them. Could you not have instilled better things into their minds? I know full well that your heart and mind are against slavery; but for the ease of living in our midst, enjoying our bounty, and receiving our money, you will silence your soul and forfeit your principles. Yea, for a salary, you will pander to this horrid crime. Judas, for thirty pieces of silver, sold the Redeemer of the world; but what remorse followed the dastard act! You will yet live to curse the hour of your infamy. You might have done good. Upon the waxen minds of these girls you might have written noble things, but you would not."

I watched Miss Bradly closely whilst he was speaking. She turned white as a sheet. Her countenance bespoke the convicted woman. Not an eye rested upon her but read the truth. Starting up at length from her chair, Miss Jane shouted out, in a theatrical way,

'Treason! treason in our own household, and from one of our own number! And so, Mr. John, you are the abolitionist that has sown dissension and discontent among our domestics. We have thought you simple; but I discover, sir, you are more knave than fool. Father shall know of this, and take steps to arrest this treason."

" As you please, sister Jane ; you can make what report you please, only speak the truth "

At this she flew toward him, and, catching him by the collar, slapped his cheeks severely.

" Right well done," said a clear, manly voice; and, looking up, I saw Mr. Worth standing in the open door. " I have been knocking," said he, " for full five minutes; but I am not surprised that you did not hear me, for the strong speech to which I have listened had force enough to overpower the sound of a thunder-storm."

Miss Jane recoiled a few steps, and the deepest crimson dyed her cheeks. She made great pretensions to refinement, and could not bear, now, that a gentleman (even though an abolitionist) should see her striking her brother. Miss Tildy assumed the look of injured innocence, and smilingly invited Mr. Worth to take a seat.

" Do not be annoyed by what you have seen. Jane is not passionate; but the boy was rude to her, and deserved a reproof."

Without making a reply, but, with his eye fixed on young master, Mr. Worth took the offered seat. Miss Bradly, with her face buried in her hands, moved not; and the doctor sat playing with his half-filled glass of wine; but young master remained standing, his eye flashing strangely, and a bright crimson spot glowing on either cheek. He seemed to take no note of the entrance of Mr. Worth, or in fact any of the group. There he stood, with his golden locks falling over his white brow; and calm serenity resting like a sunbeam on his face. Very majestic and imposing was that youthful presence. High determination and everlasting truth were written upon his face. With one look and a murmured "Father forgive them, for they know not what they do," he turned away.

"Stop, stop, my brave boy," cried Mr. Worth, "stop, and let me look upon you. Had the South but one voice, and that one yours, this country would soon be clear of its great dishonor."

To this young master made no spoken reply; but the clear smile that lit his countenance expressed his thanks; and seeing that Mr. Worth was resolved to detain him, he said,

"Let me go, good sir, for now I feel that I need the woods," and soon his figure was gliding along his well-beloved path, in the direction of the spring. Who shall say that solitary communing with Nature unfits the soul for active life? True, indeed, it does unfit it for baseness, sordid dealings, and low detraction, by lifting it from its low condition, and sending it out in a broad excursiveness.

Here, in the case of young master, was a sweet and glowing flower that had blossomed in the wilds, and been nursed by nature only. The country air had fanned into bloom the bud of virtue and the beauty of highest truth.

CHAPTER XVII.

As young Master strode away, Misses Jane and Tildy regarded each other in silent wonder. At length the latter, who caught the cue from her sister, burst forth in a violent laugh, that I can define only by calling it a romping laugh, so full of forced mirth. Miss Jane took up the echo, and the house resounded with their assumed merriment. No one else, however, seemed to take the infection; and they had the fun all to themselves.

"Well, Ann," said Miss Tildy, putting on a quizzical air, "I suppose you have been very much edified by your young master's explosion of philanthropy and good-will toward you darkies."

Too well I knew my position to make an answer; so there I stood, silent and submissive.

"Oh, yes, I suppose this young renegade has delivered abolition lectures in the kitchen hall, to his ' dearly belubed' bredderen ob de colored race," added Miss Matilda, intending to be vastly witty.

"I think we had better send him on to an Anti-slavery convention, and give him a seat 'twixt Lucy Stone and Fred Douglas. Wouldn't his white complexion contrast well with that of the sable orator?" and this Miss Jane designed should be exceedingly pungent.

Still no one answered. Mr. Worth's face wore a troubled expression; the doctor still played with his wine-glass; and Miss Bradly's face was buried deeper in her hands.

"Suppose father had been here; what do you think he would have said?" asked Miss Jane.

This, no doubt, recalled Dr. Mandy to the fact that Mr. Peterkin's patronage was well worth retaining, so he must speak *now*.

"Oh, your father, Miss Jane, is such a sensible man, that he would consider it only the freak of an imprudent beardless boy."

"Is, then," I asked myself, "all expressed humanity but idle gibberish? Is it only beardless boys who can feel for suffering slaves? Is all noble philanthropy voted vapid by sober, serious, reflecting manhood? If so, farewell hope, and welcome despair!" I looked at Mr. Worth; but his face was rigid, and a snowy pallor overspread his gentle features. He was young, and this was his first visit to Kentucky. In his home at the North he had heard many stories of the manner in which slavery was conducted in the West and South; but the stories, softened by distance, had reached him in a mild form, consequently he was unprepared for what he had witnessed since his arrival in Kentucky. He had, though desiring liberty alike for all, both white and black, looked upon the system as an unjust and oppressive one, but he had no thought that it existed in the atrocious and cruel form which fact, not report, had now revealed to him. His whole soul shuddered and shrivelled at what he saw. He marvelled how the skies could be so blue and beautiful; how the flowers could spring so lavishly, and the rivers roll so majestically, and the stars burn so brightly over a land dyed with such horrible crimes.

"Father will not deal very leniently with this boy's follies; he will teach Johnny that there's more virtue in honoring a father, than in equalizing himself with negroes." Here Miss Jane tossed her head defiantly.

Just then a loud noise was heard from the avenue, and, looking out the window, we descried the hunters returning crowned with exultation, for, alas! poor Lindy had been found, and there, handcuffed, she marched between a guard of Jake on

the one side, and Dan on the other. There were marks of
blood on her brow, and her dress was here and there stained.
Cool as was the day, great drops of perspiration rolled off her
face. With her head bowed low on her breast, she walked on
amid the ribald jests of her persecutors.

"Well, we has cotch dis 'ere runaway gal, and de way we
did chase her down is nuffen to nobody," said old Nace, who
had led the troop. "I tells you it jist takes dis here nigger
and his hounds to tree the runaway. I reckons, Miss Lindy,
you'll not be fur trying ob it agin."

"No, dat hab fixed her," replied the obsequious Jake. Dan
laughed heartily, showing his stout teeth.

"Now, Masser," said Nace, as taking off his remnant of a
hat he scraped his foot back, and grinned terribly, "dis ar'
nigger, if you pleases, sar, would like to hab a leetle drap ob
de critter dat you promise to him."

"Oh, yes, you black rascal, you wants some ob my fust-rate
whiskey, does you? Wal, I 'spects, as you treed dat ar'
d——d nigger-wench, you desarves a drap or so."

"Why, yes, Masser, you see as how I did do my best for to
ketch her, and I is right much tired wid de run. You sees dese
old legs is gettin' right stiff; dese jints ain't limber like Jake
and Dan's dar, yet I tink, Masser, I did de bestest, an' I ought
to hab a leetle drap de most, please, sar."

"Come, 'long, come 'long, boys, arter we stores dis gal away
I'll gib you yer dram."

There had stood poor Lindy, never once looking up, crest-
fallen, broken in heart, and bruised in body, awaiting a painful
punishment, scarce hoping to escape with life and limb. Striking her a blow with his huge riding-whip, Mr. Peterkin shouted,
"off with you to the lock-up!"

Now, that which was technically termed the "lock-up," was
an old, strong building, which had once been used as a smoke-
house, but since the erection of a new one, was employed for the very noble purpose of confining negroes. It was
a dark, damp place, without a window, and but one low door,

through which to enter. In this wretched place, bound and manacled, the poor fugitive was thrust.

"There, you may run off if you ken," said Mr. Peterkin, as he drew the rough door to, and fastened on the padlock with the dignified air of a regularly-installed jailer. "Now, boys, come 'long and git the liquor."

This pleasing announcement seemed to give an additional impetus to the spirits of the servants, and, with many a "ha, ha, ha," they followed their master.

"Well, father," said Miss Jane, whilst she stood beside Mr. Peterkin, who was accurately measuring out a certain quantity of whiskey to the three smiling slaves, who stood holding their tin cups to receive it, "I am glad you succeeded in arresting that audacious runaway. Where did you find her? Who was with her? How did she behave? Oh, tell me all about the adventure; it really does seem funny that such a thing should have occurred in our family; and now that the wretch has been caught, I can afford to laugh at it."

"Wal," answered Mr. Peterkin, as he replaced the cork in the brown jug, and proceeded to lock it up in his private closet, "you does ax the most questions in one breath of any gal I ever seed in all my life. Why, I haint bin in the house five minutes, and you has put more questions to me than a Philadelphy lawyer could answer. 'Pon my soul, Jane, you is a fast 'un."

"Never mind my fastness, father, but tell me what I asked."

"Wal, whar is I to begin? You axed whar Lindy was found? These dogs hunted her to Mr. Farland's barn. Thar they 'gan to smell and snort round and cut up all sorts of capers, and old Nace clumb up to the hay loft, and sung out, in a loud voice, 'Here she am, here she am.' Then I hearn a mighty scrambling and skufflin' up dar, so I jist springed up arter Nace, and thar was the gal, actually fightin' with Nace, who wanted to fetch her right down to the ground whar we was a waitin'. I tells you, now, one right good lick from my powder-horn fetched her all right. She soon seen it was no kind of use to be opposin' of us, and so she jist sot down right willin'. I then fetched several good licks, and she knowed how to do, kase, when I seed I had drawed the blood, I didn't kere to beat her any more. So I ordered her to git down out-en that ar' loft quicker than she got up. Then we bound her hands, and driv her long through the woods like a bull. I tells you she was mighty-much 'umbled and shamed; every now and thin she'd blubber out a cryin', but my whup soon shot up her howlin'."

"I've a great notion to go," said Jane, "and torment her a little more, the impudent hussy! I wonder if she thinks we will ever take her back to live with us. She has lost a good home, for she shall not come here any more. I want you to sell her, father, and at the highest price, to a regular trader."

" That will I do, and there is a trader in this very neighbor-hood now. I'll ride over this arternoon and make 'rangements with him fur her sale. But come, Jane, I is powerful hungry; can't you git me something to eat?"

" But, father, I have a word to say with you in private, draw near me."

" What ails you now, gals?" he said, as Miss Tildy joined them, with a perplexed expression of countenance. As he drew close to them I heard Miss Jane say, through her clenched teeth, in a hissing tone :

" Old Polly is insane ; lost her reason from that blow which you gave her. Do you think they could indict you ?"

" Who, in the name of h—l, can say that I struck her? Who saw it? No, I'd like fur to see the white man that would dar present Jeems Peterkin afore the Grand Jury, and a nigger darn't think of sich a thing, kase as how thar testimony ain't no count."

" Then we are safe," both of the ladies simultaneously cried.

" But whar is that d——d old hussy? She ain't crazy, only 'possuming so as to shuffle outen the work. Let me git to her once, and I'll be bound she will step as smart as ever. One shake of the old cowhide will make her jump and talk as sensible as iver she did."

"'Tisn't worth while, father, going near her. I tell you, Doctor Mandy says she is a confirmed lunatic."

"I tells yer I knows her constitution better 'an any of yer, doctors, and all; and this here cowhide is allers the best medicine fur niggers; they ain't like the white folks, no how nor ways."

So saying he, followed by his daughters, went to the cabin where poor Aunt Polly was sitting, in all the touching simplicity of second childhood, playing with some bits of ribbon, bright-colored calico, and flashy artificial flowers. Looking up with a vacant stare at the group she spoke not, but, slowly shaking her head in an imbecile way, murmured:

"These are putty, but yer mustn't take 'em frum me; dese am all dat dis ole nigger hab got, dese here am fadder, mudder, hustbund, an chile. Lit me keep 'em.

"You old fool, what's you 'bout, gwine on at this here rate? Don't you know I is yer master, and will beat the very life outen yer, if yer don't git up right at once?"

"Now who is yer? Sure now, an' dis old nigger doesn't know yer. Yer is a great big man, dat looks so cross and bad at me. I wish yer would go on 'bout yer own bisness, and be a lettin' me 'lone. I ain't a troublin' of yer, no way."

"You ain't, arnt yer, you old fool? but I'll give yer a drap of medicine that'll take the craze outen yer, and make yer know who yer master is. How does you like that, and this, and this?" and, suiting the action to the word, he dealt her blow after blow, in the most ferocious manner. Her shoulders were covered with blood that gushed from the torn flesh. A low howl (it could only be called a howl) burst from her throat, and flinging up her withered hands, she cried, "Oh, good Lord Jesus, come and help thy poor old servant, now in dis her sore time ob trouble."

"The Lord Jesus won't hear sich old nigger wretches as you," said Mr. Peterkin.

"Oh, yes, de Lord Jesus will. He 'peared to me but a leetle bit ago, and he was all dressed in white, wid a gold crown upon His head, and His face war far and putty like young Masser's, only it seemed to be heap brighter, and he smiled at dis poor old sufferin' nigger; and den 'peared like a low, little voice 'way down to de bottom ob my heart say, Polly, be ob good cheer, de Lord Jesus is comin' to take you home. He no care weder yer skin is white or black. He is gwine fur to make yer happy in de next world. Oh, den me feel so good, me no more care for anything."

"All of this is a crazy fancy," said Dr. Mandy, who stepped into the cabin; but taking hold of Polly's wrist, and holding his fingers over her pulse, his countenance changed. "She has excessive fever, and a strong flow of blood to the brain. She cannot live long. Put her instantly to bed, and let me apply leeches."

"Do yer charge extry for leeching, doctor?" asked Mr. Peterkin.

"Oh, yes, sir, but it is not much consideration, as you are one of my best customers."

"I don't want to run any useless expense 'bout the old 'oman. You see she has served my family a good many years."

"And you are for that reason much attached to her," interposed the doctor.

"Not a bit of it, sir. I never was 'tached to a nigger. Even when I was a lad I had no fancy fur 'em, not even yer bright yellow wenches; and I ain't gwine fur to spend money on that old nigger, unless you cure her, and make her able to work and pay fur the money that's bin laid out fur her."

"I can't promise to do that; neither am I certain that the leeches will do her any material good, but they will assuredly serve to mitigate her sufferings, by decreasing the fever, which now rages so high."

"I don' care a cuss for that. Taint no use then of trying the leeches. If she be gwine to die, why let her do it in the cheapest way."

Saying this, he went off with the young ladies, the doctor following in the wake. As he was passing through the door-way, I caught him by the skirts of his coat. Turning suddenly round, he saw who it was, and drew within the cabin.

"Doctor," and I spoke with great timidity, "is she so ill? Will she, must she die? Please try the leeches. Here," and I drew from an old hiding-place in the wall the blessed half-dollar which Master Eddy had given me as a keepsake. For years it had lain silently there, treasured more fondly than Egyptian amulet or Orient gem. On some rare holiday I had drawn it from its concealment to gloat over it with all a miser's pride. I did not value it for the simple worth of the coin, for I had sense enough to know that its actual value was but slight; yet what a wealth of memories it called up! It brought *back* the times when *I had a mother;* when, as a happy, careless child (though a slave), I wandered through the wild greenwood; where I ranged free as a bird, ere the burden of a blow had been laid upon my shoulders; and when my young master and mistress sometimes bestowed kind words upon me. The fair locks and mild eyes of the latter gleamed upon me with dream-like beauty. The kind, tearful face of Master Eddy, his gentle words on that last most dreadful day that bounded and closed the last chapter of happy childhood—all these things were recalled by the sight of this simple little half-dollar! And now I was going to part with it. What a struggle it was! I couldn't do it. No, I couldn't do it. It was the one *silver* link between me and remembered joy. To part with it would be to wipe out the *bright* days of my life. It would be sacrilege, in justice, a wrong; no, I replaced it in the old faded rag (in which it had been wrapped for years), and closed my hand convulsively over it. There stood the doctor! He had caught sight of the gleaming coin, and (small as it was) his cupidity was excited, and when he saw my hand closed over the shining treasure, the smile fled from his face, and he said:

"Girl, for what purpose did you detain me? My time is

precious. I have other patients to visit this morning, and cannot be kept here longer!"

"Oh, doctor, try the leeches."

"Your Master says he won't pay for them."

"But for the sake of charity, for the value of human life, you will do it without pay."

"Will I, though? Trust me for that—and who will feed my wife and children in the meantime. I can't be doctoring every old sick nigger gratuitously. Her old fagged-out frame ain't worth the waste of my leeches. I thought you were going to pay for it; but you see a nigger is a nigger the world over. They are too stingy to do anything for one of their own tribe."

"But this money is a keepsake, a parting-gift from my young Master, who gave it to me years ago, when I was sold. I prize it because of the recollections which it calls up."

"A sentimental nigger! Well, *that is* something new; but if you cared for that old woman's life you wouldn't hesitate," and, so saying, he walked away. I looked upon poor Aunt Polly, and I fancied there was a rebuking light in her feeble eye; and her withered hands seemed stretched out to ask the help which I cruelly withheld.

And shall I desert her who has suffered so deeply for me? Well may she reproach me with that "piteous action"—me, who for a romantic and fanciful feeling withhold the means of saving her life. Oh, how I blamed myself! How wicked and selfish I thought my heart.

"Doctor! come back, doctor! here is the money," I cried.

He had stood but a few steps without the cabin door, doubtless expecting this change in my sentiments.

"You have done well, Ann, to deny yourself, and make some effort to save the life of the old woman. You see I would have done it for nothing; but the leeches cost me money. It is inconvenient to get them, and I have a family, a very helpless one, to support, and you know it won't do to neglect them, lest I be worse than a heathen and infidel. In your case, my good girl, the case is quite different, for *niggers* are taken care of and supported by their Masters, and any little change that you may have is an extra, for which you have no particular need."

An "extra" indeed it was, and a very rare one. One that had come but once in my life, and, God be praised, it afforded me an opportunity of doing the good Samaritan's work! I had seen how the Levite and the priest had neglected the wounded woman, and with this little coin I could do a noble deed ; but as to my being well-cared and provided for, I thought the doctor had shot wide of his mark. I was surprised at the tone of easy familiarity which he assumed toward me ; but this was explained by the fact that he was what is commonly called a jolly fellow, and had been pretty freely indulging in the "joyful glass." Besides, I was going to pay him ; then, maybe, he felt a little ashamed of his avarice, and sought by familiar tone and manner to beguile me, and satisfy his conscience.

His "medical bags" had been left in the entry, for Miss Jane, who delighted in the Lubin-perfumed extracts, would tolerate nothing less sweet-scented, and by her prohibitory fiat, the "bags" were denied admittance to the house. Once, when the doctor was suddenly called to see a white member of the family, he, either through forgetfulness or obstinacy, violated the order, and Miss Jane had every carpet taken up and shaken, and the floor scoured, for the odor seemed to haunt her for weeks. Since then he had rigidly adhered to the rule ; I suspect, with many secret maledictions upon the acuteness of her olfactories.

Now he requested me to bring the bags to him, I found them, as I had expected, sitting in the very spot where he usually placed them.

"There they are, doctor, now be quick. Cure her, help her, do anything, but let her not die whilst this money can purchase her life, or afford her ease."

He took the coin from my hand, surveyed it for a moment, a thing that I considered very cruel, for, all the while, the victim was suffering uncared for, unattended to.

"It is but a small piece, doctor, but it is my all ; if I had
7

more, you should have it, but now please be quick in the application of your remedy."

"This money will pay but for a few leeches, not enough to do the contusion much good. You see there is a great deal of diseased blood collected at the left temple ; but I'll be charitable and throw in a few leeches, for which you can pay me at some other time, when you happen to have money."

"Certainly, doctor, I will give you *all* that you demand as fast as I get it."

After a little scarification he applied the leeches, twelve in number, little, sleek, sharp, needle-pointed, oily-looking things. Quickly, as if starved, the tiny vampires commenced their work of blood-sucking.

"She bore to be scarified better than any subject I ever saw. Not a writhe or wince," remarked the doctor.

Ah, thought I, she has endured too much pain to tremble at a needle prick like that. She, whose body had bled at every pore, whose skin had been torn and mangled until it bore a thousand scars, could surely bear, without writhing, a pain so delicate as that. Though I thought thus, I said not a word; for (to me) the worst part of our slavery is that we are not allowed to speak our opinion on any subject. We are to be mutes, save when it suits our owners to let us answer in words obsequious enough to please their greedy love of authority.

Silently I stood watching the leeches. From the loss of blood, Aunt Polly seemed somewhat exhausted, and was soon soundly, sweetly sleeping.

"Let her sleep," said the doctor, as he removed the leeches and replaced them in a little stone vase, "when she wakes she will probably be better, and you will then owe me one dollar and a half, as the bill is two dollars. It would have been more, but I allow part to go for charity." So saying he left the cabin and returned to the house. Oh, most noble Christian "charity"! Is this the blessed quality that is destined to "cover a multitude of sins"? He would not even leech a half-dying woman without a pecuniary reward. Oh, far advanced whites, fast growing in grace and ripening in holiness !

CHAPTER XVIII.

AFTER wiping the fresh blood-stains (produced by the severe beating of Mr. Peterkin) from Aunt Polly's shoulders, and binding up her brow to conceal the wounds made by the leeching process, I tenderly spread the old coverlet over her form, and then turned away from her to go about my usual avocations.

The doctor was just making his adieux, and the ladies had gathered round him in quite a social and sportive way. Misses Jane and Tildy were playfully disputing which one should take possession of his heart and hand, in the event of Mrs. Mandy's sudden demise. All this merriment and light-heartedness was exhibited, when but a few rods from them a poor, old, faithful creature lay in the agonies of a torturing death, and a young girl, who had striven for her liberty, and tried to achieve it at a perilous risk, had just been bound, hand and foot, and cast into outer darkness! Oh, this was a strange meeting of the extremes. What varied colors the glass of life can show!

At length, with many funny speeches, and promises very ridiculous, the doctor tore himself away from the chatty group.

Passing in and out of the house, through the hall or in the parlor, as my business required, I saw Mr. Worth and Miss Bradly sitting quietly and moodily apart, whilst, occasionally, Miss Tildy would flash out with a coarse joke, or Miss Jane would speculate upon the feelings of Lindy, in her present helpless and gloomy confinement.

" I reckon she does not relish Canada about this time."

"No; let us ask her *candid* opinion of it," said Miss Tildy,

who considered herself *the wit* of the family, and this last speech
she regarded as quite an extraordinary flash.

"That's very good, Till," said her patronizing sister, "but
you are always witty."

"Now, sister, ain't you ashamed to flatter me so?" and with
the most Laura Matilda-ish air, she turned her head aside and
tried to blush.

I could read, from his clear, manly glance, that Mr. Worth
was sick at heart and goaded to anguish by what he saw and
heard; yet, like many another noble man, he sat in silent endurance. Miss Jane caught the idea of his gloom, and, with a
good deal of sly, vulpine malice, determined to annoy him. She
had not for him, as Miss Tildy had, a personal admiration; so,
by way of vexing him, as well as showing off her smartness,
she asked:

"Till, is there much Worth in Abolitionism?"

"I don't know, but there is a *Robin* in it." This she thought
a capital repartee.

"Bravo! bravo, Till! who can equal you? You are the wit-
tiest girl in town or country."

"Wit is a precious gift," said Mr. Worth, as he satirically
elevated his brows.

"Indeed is it," replied Miss Tildy, "but I am not conscious
of its possession." Of course she expected he would gainsay
her; but, as he was silent, her cheeks blazed like a peony.

"What makes Miss Bradly so quiet and seemingly lachry-
mose? I do believe Johnny's Abolition lecture has given her the
blues."

"Not the lecture, but the necessity for the lecture," put in
Mr. Worth.

"What's that? what's that 'bout Aberlitionists?" exclaimed
Mr. Peterkin, as he rushed into the room. "Is there one of
'em here? Let me know it, and my roof shan't shelter the
rascal. Whar is he?"

I looked toward Mr. Worth, for I feared that, on an occasion
like this, his principles would fail as Miss Bradly's had;

but the fear was quickly dissipated, as he replied in a manly tone:

"I, a vindicator of the anti-slavery policy, and a denouncer of the slave system, stand before you, and declare myself proud of my sentiments."

"You? ha! ha! ha! ha! that's too ridiculous; a mere boy; a stripling. no bigger than my arm. I'd not disgrace my manhood with a fight with the like of yer."

"So thought Goliath when David met him in warfare; but witness the sequel, and then say if the battle is always to the strong, or the victory with the proud. Might is not always right. I ask to be heard for my cause. Stripling as you call me, I am yet able to vindicate my abolition principles upon other and higher ground than mere brute force."

"Oh, yes; you has larnt, I s'pose. to talk. That's all them windy Aberlitionists ken do; they berate and talk. but they can't act."

A contemptuous smile played over the face of Mr. Worth, but he did not deign to answer with words.

"Do you know, pa, that Johnny is an Abolitionist?" asked Miss Jane.

"What! John Peterkin? my son John?"

"The same," and Miss Jane bowed most significantly.

"Well, that's funny enuff; but I'll soon bring it outen him. He's a quiet lad; not much sperrit, and I guess he's hearn some 'cock and bull story' 'bout freedom and equality. All smart boys of his age is apt to feel that way, but he'll come outen it. It's all bekase he has hearn too many Fourth of July speeches; but I don't fear fur him, he is sure to come outen it. The very idee of my son's being an Aberlitionist is too funny."

"Funny is it, father, for your child to love mercy, and deal justly, even with the lowliest?" As he said this, young master stood in the doorway. He looked paler and even more spiritual than was his wont.

Mr. Peterkin sat for full five minutes, gazing at the boy;

and, strange to say, made no reply, but strode away from the room.

Miss Jane and Tildy regarded each other with evident surprise. They had expected a violent outburst, and thus to see their father tamed and subdued by the word and glance of their boy-brother, astonished them not a little.

Miss Tildy turned toward young master, and said, in what was meant for a most caustic tone,

"You are an embryo Van Amburgh, thus to tame the lion's rage."

"But you, Tilly, are too vulpine to be fascinated even by the glance of Van Amburgh himself."

"Well, now, Johnny, you are getting impertinent as well as spicy."

"Pertinent, you mean," said Mr. Worth. Miss Tildy would not look angry at *him*; for she was besieging the fortress of his affections, and she deemed kind measures the most advantageous.

Were I to narrate most accurately the conversation that followed, the repartees that flashed from the lips of some, and the anger that burned blue in the faces of others, I should only amuse the reader, or what is more likely, weary him.

I will simply mention that, after a few hours' sojourn, Mr. Worth took his departure, not without first having a long conversation, in a private part of the garden, with young master. Miss Bradly retired to the young ladies' room (for they would not allow her to leave the house), under pretext of headache. Often, as I passed in and out to ask her if she needed anything, I found her weeping bitterly. Late in the evening, about eight o'clock, Mr. Peterkin returned; throwing the reins of his horse to Nace, he exclaimed:

"Well, I've made a good bargain of it; I've sold Lindy to a trader for one thousand dollars—that is, if she answers the description which I gave of her. He is comin' in the mornin' to look at her; and, with a little riggin' up, I think she'll 'pear a rale good-lookin' wench."

When I went into the house to prepare some supper for Mr. Peterkin (the family tea had been despatched two hours before), he was in an excellent humor, well pleased, no doubt, with his good trade.

"Now, Ann, be brisk and smart, or you might find yourself in the trader's hands afore long. Likely yellow gals like you sells mighty well; and if you doesn't behave well you is a goner."

"Down the river" was not terrible to me, nor did I dread being "sold;" yet one thing I did fear, and that was separation from young master. In the last few days he had become to me everything I could respect; nay, I loved him. Not that it was in his power to do me any signal act of good. He could not soften the severity of his father and sisters toward me; yet one thing he could and did do, he spoke an occasional kind, hopeful word to me. Those whose hearts are fed upon kindness and love, can little understand how dear to the lonely, destitute soul, is one word of friendliness. We, to whom the husks are flung with an unfeeling tone, appreciate as manna from heaven the word of gentleness; and now I thought if I were to leave young master *my soul would die.* Had not his blessed smile elevated and inspired my sinking spirit, and his sweet tone softened my over-taxed heart? Oh, blessed one! even now I think of thee, and with a full heart thank God that such beings have lived!

I watched master dispatch his supper in a most summary manner. At length he settled himself back in his chair, and, taking his tooth-pick from his waistcoat pocket, began picking his teeth.

"Wal, Ann," he said, as he swung himself back in his chair, how's ole Poll?"

"She is still asleep."

"Yes, I said she was possuming; but by to-morrow, if she ain't up outen that ar' bunk of hers, I'll know the reason; and I'll sell her to the trader that's comin' for Lindy."

"I wish you would sell her, father, and buy a new cook;

she prepares everything in such an old-fashioned manner—can't make a single French dish," said Miss Jane.

"I don't care a cuss 'bout yer French dishes, or yer fashionable cooks; I's gwine to sell her, becase the craps didn't yield me much this year, and I wants money, so I must make it by sellin' off niggers."

"You must not sell Aunt Polly, and you shall not," said young master, with a fearful emphasis.

"What do you mean, lad?" cried the infuriated father, and he sprang from his seat, and was in the very act of rushing upon the offender; but suddenly he quailed before the fixed, determined gaze of that eye. He looked again, then cowered, reeled, and staggered like a drunken man, and, falling back in his chair, he covered his face with his hands, and uttered a fearful groan. The ladies were frightened; they had never seen their father thus fearfully excited. They dared not speak one word. The finger of an awful silence seemed laid upon each and every one present. At length young master, with a slow step, approached his father, and, taking the large hand, which swung listlessly, within his own, said, "Fath—;" but before he had finished the syllable, Mr. Peterkin sprang up, exclaiming,

"Off, I say! off! off! she sent you here; she told you to speak so to me." Then gazing wildly at Johnny, he cried, "Those are her eyes, that is her face. I say, away! away! leave me! you torment me with the sight of that face! It's her's it's hers. Blood will have blood, and now you comes to git mine!" and the strong man fell prostrate upon the floor, in a paroxysm of agony. He foamed at the mouth, and rolled his great vacant eyes around the room in a wildness fearful to behold.

"Oh Lor'," said old Nace, who appeared in the doorway, "oh Lor', him's got a fit."

The ladies shrieked and screamed in a frightful manner. Young master was almost preternaturally calm. He and Miss Bradly (after Nace and Jake had placed master on the bed) rendered him every attention. Miss Bradly chafed his temples with camphor, and moistened the lips and palms of the hands with it. When he began to revive, he turned his face to the wall and wept like a child. Then he fell off into a quiet sleep.

Young master and Miss Bradly watched beside that restless sleeper long and faithfully. And from that night there grew up between them a fervent friendship, which endured to the last of their mortal days.

Upon frequently going into Aunt Polly's cabin, I was surprised to find her still sleeping. At length when my duties were all discharged in the house, and I went to prepare for the night's rest, I thought I would arouse her from her torpor and administer a little nourishment that might benefit her.

To my surprise her arm felt rigid, and oh, so cold! What if she is dead! thought I; and a cold thrill passed over my frame. The big drops burst from my brow and stood in chilly dew upon my temples. Oh God! can it be that she is dead! One look, one more touch, and the dreadful question would be answered; yet, when I attempted to stretch forth my hand, it was stiff and powerless. In a moment the very atmosphere seemed to grow heavy; 'twas peopled with a strange, charnel gloom. My breath was thick and broken, coming only at intervals and with choking gaspings. One more desperate effort! I commanded myself, gathered all my courage, and, seizing hold of the body with a power which was stronger than my own, I turned it over—when, oh God of mercy, such a spectacle! the question was answered with a fearful affirmation. There, rigid, still and ghastly, she lay in death. The evident marks of a violent struggle were stamped upon those features, which, despite their tough hard-favoredness, and their gaunt gloom, were dear to me; for had she not been my best of friends, nay proved her friendship by a martyrdom which, if slower, was no less heroic than that which adorns the columns of historical renown? Gently I closed those wide-staring, blank eyes, and pressed tenderly together the distended jaws; and, taking from a box a slipet of white muslin, bound up her cheeks. Slowly, and not without a feeling of terror, I unwound the bandage from her brow, which concealed the wound made by the leeches ; this I replaced with my only handkerchief. I then endeavored to straighten the contracted limbs, for she had died lying upon her side, with her body drawn nearly double. I found this a rather difficult task ; yet was it a melancholy pleasure, a duty that I performed irresolutely but with tenderness.

After all was done, and before getting the water to wash the body (for I wished to enrobe her decently for the burial), I gave way to the luxury of expressed grief, and, sinking down upon my knees beside that lifeless form, thanked God for having taken her from this scene of trouble and trial. "You are gone, my poor old friend ; but that hereafter of which we all entertain so much dread, cannot be to you so bad as this wretched present ; and though I am lonely without you, I rejoice that you have left this land of bondage. And I believe that at this moment your tried soul is free and happy !"

So saying, I stepped without the door of the cabin, and, looking up to the clear, cold moon and the way-off stars, I smiled, even in my bitterness, for I imagined I could see her emancipated soul soaring away on its new-made wings, to the land forever flowing with milk and honey. She had often in her earth-pilgrimage, as many tried martyrs had done before her, fainted by the wayside ; but then was she not sorely tempted, and did not a life of captivity and seven-fold agony, atone for all her short-comings ? Besides, we are divinely informed that where little is given, little is required. In view of this sacred assurance, let not the sceptic reader think that my faith was stretched to an unwarranted degree. Yes, I did and *do* think that she was at that moment and is now happy. If not, how am I to account for the strange feeling of peace that settled over my mind and heart, when I thought of her ! For a holy, heavenly calm, like the dropping of a prophet's mantle, overspread my heart ; a cool sense of ease, refreshing as the night dew, and sustaining as the high stars, seemed to gird me round!

I did not heed the cold air, but walked out a few rods in the direction of the out-house, where Lindy was confined. "Yonder,"

I soliloquized, "perishing for a kind word, lies a poor outcast, wretched being. I will go to her, bury all thoughts of the past, and speak one kind word of encouragement."

As I drew near to the "lock-up," the moon that had been sailing swift and high through the heaven, passed beneath the screen of a dark cloud. I paused in my steps and looked up to the sky. "Such," I thought, "is the transit of a human soul across the vault of life; beneath clouds and shadows the serene face is often hidden, and the spirit's mellow light is often, by affliction, obscured from view.

Just then a sob of anguish fell upon my ear. I knew it was Lindy, and moved hastily forward; but, light as was my footfall, it aroused the sentinel-dog, and, with a loud bark, he sprang toward me. "Down, Cuff! down!" said I, addressing the dog, who, as soon as he recognized me, crouched lovingly at my feet. Just then the moon glided with a queenly air from behind the clouds. "So," I said, "passeth the soul, with the same Diana-like sweep, from the heavy fold and curtain of human sorrow." Another moan, deeper and more fearful than the first! I was close beside the door of the "lock-up," and, cowering down, with my mouth close to the crevice, I called Lindy. "Who's dar? who's dar? For de love of heaven somebody come to me," said Lindy, in a half-frantic tone.

"'Tis I, Lindy, don't you know my voice?"

"Yes, it's Ann! Oh, please, Ann, help me outen here. I's seen such orful sights and hearn sich dreful sounds, I'd be a slave all my born days jist to git way frum here. Oh, Ann, I's seed a *speerit*," and then she gave such a fearful shriek, that I felt my flesh grow cold and stony as death. Yet I knew it was my duty to appear calm, and try to persuade her that it was not true or real.

"Oh, no, Lindy, you must not be frightened; only hope and trust in God, and pray to Him. He will take you away from all this trouble. He loves you. He cares for you, for 'twas He who made you. Your soul is precious to Him. Oh, try to pray."

"Oh, but, Ann, I doesn't know how to pray. I never seed God, and I is afraid of Him. He might be like master."

This was fearful ignorance, and how to begin to teach her the way to believe was above my ability; yet I knew that every soul was precious to God; so I made an endeavor to do all I could in the way of instruction.

"Say, Our Father, who art in heaven," Lindy.

"Our Father, who art in heaven," she repeated in a slow, nervous manner.

"Hallowed be Thy name." Again she repeated, and so on we prayed, she following accurately after me, though the heavy door separated us. Think ye not, oh, gentle reader, that this prayer was heard above? Never did words come more truly from my heart; and with a low moan, they rung plaintively upon the still, moonlit air! I could tell, from the fervent tone in which Lindy followed, that her whole soul was engaged. When the final amen had been said, she asked, "Ann, what's to become of me?"

I evaded her by saying, "how can I know what master will do?"

"Yes, but haven't you heard? Oh, don't fool me, Ann, but tell me all."

For a moment I hesitated, then said: "Yes, Lindy, I'll deal fairly with you. I have heard that master intends selling you to-morrow to a trader, whom he went to see to-day; and, if the trader is satisfied with you to-morrow, the bargain will be closed."

"Oh, Lord! oh, Lord!" she groaned forth, "oh, is I gwine down de ribber? Oh, Lord, kill me right now; but don't send me to dat dreful place, down de ribber, down de ribber!"

"Oh, trust in the Lord, and He will protect you. Down the river can't be much worse than here, maybe not so bad. For my part, Lindy, I would rather be sold and run the risk of getting a good master, than remain here where we are treated worse than dogs."

"Oh, dar isn't no sort ob hope ob my gitten any better home

den dis here one; den I knows you all, and way off dar 'mong strange black folks, oh, no, I never can go; de Lord hab marcy on me."

This begging of the poor negroes to the Lord to have mercy on them, though frequent, has no particular significance. It is more a plaint of agony than a cry for actual mercy; and, in Lindy's case, it most assuredly only expressed her grief, for she had no ripe faith in the power and willingness of Our Father to send mercy to her. Religion she believed consisted in going to church every Sunday twice; consequently it was a luxury, which, like all luxuries, must be monopolized by the whites. From the very depths of my heart I prayed that the light of Divine grace might shine in upon her darkened intellect. Soul of Faith, verily art thou soul of beauty! And though, as a special gift, faith is not withheld from the lowliest, the most ignorant, yet does its possession give to the poorest and most degraded Ethiopian a divine consciousness, an inspiration, that as to what is grandest in the soul exalts him above the noblest of poets.

Whilst talking to Lindy, I was surprised to hear the muffled sound of an approaching footstep. Noiselessly I was trying to creep away, when young master said in a low voice:

"Is this you, Ann? Wait a moment. Have you spoken to Lindy? Have you told her—"

He did not finish the sentence, and I answered,

"Yes, I have told her that she is to be sold, and to a trader."

"Is she willing?"

"No, sir, she has a great terror of down the river."

"That is the way with them all, yet her condition, so far as treatment is concerned, may be bettered, certainly it cannot be made worse."

"Will you speak to her, young Master, and reconcile her to her situation?"

"Yes, I will do all I can."

"And now I will go and stay with the corpse of dear Aunt Polly;" here I found it impossible to restrain my tears, and convulsed with emotion, I seated myself upon the ground with my back against the door of the lock-up.

"Dead? dead? Aunt Polly dead?" he asked in a bewildered tone.

"Yes, young Master, I found her dead, and with every appearance of having had a severe struggle."

I then told him about the leeching process, how the doctor had acted, &c.

"Murdered! She was most cruelly murdered!" he murmured to himself.

In the excitement of conversation he had elevated his tone a good deal, and the fearful news reached the ears of Lindy, and she shrieked out,

"Is Aunt Polly dead? Oh, tell me, for I thinks I sees her sperit now."

Then such entreaties as she made to get out were agonizing to hear.

"Oh, if you can't let me out, don't leave me! Oh, don't leave me, Ann! I is so orful skeered. I do see such terrible sights, and it 'pears like when you is here talking, dem orful things don't come arter me."

"You go, Ann, and watch with Aunt Polly's body; I will stay here with this poor creature."

"What, you, young master; no, no, you shall not, it will kill you. Your cough will increase, and it might prove fatal. No, I will stay here."

"But who will watch with Aunt Polly?"

"I will awaken Amy, and make her keep guard."

"No, she is too young, lacks nerve, will be frightened; besides, you must not be found here in the morning. You would be severely punished for it. Go now, good Ann, and leave me here."

"No, young master, I cannot leave you to what I am sure will be certain death."

"That would be no misfortune to me."

And I shall never forget the calm and half-glorified expression of his face, as he pronounced these words.

" Go, Ann," he continued, "leave me to watch and pray beside this forlorn creature, and, if the Angel of Death spreads his wings on this midnight blast, I think I should welcome him; for life, with its broken promises and its cold humanity, sickens me—oh so much."

And his beautiful head fell languidly on his breast; and again I listened to that low, husky cough. To-night it had an unusual sound, and, forgetful of the humble relation in which I stood to him, I grasped his arm firmly but lovingly, saying,

" Hark to that cough ! Now you *must* go in."

' No, I cannot. I know best; besides, since nothing less gentle will do, I needs must use authority, and command you to go."

" I would that you did not exercise your authority against yourself."

But he waved me off. Reluctantly I obeyed him. Again I entered the cabin and roused Amy, who slept on a pallet or heap of straw at the foot of the bed, where the still, unbreathing form of my old friend lay. It was difficult to awake her, for she was always wearied at night, and slept with that deep soundness peculiar to healthful childhood; but, after various shakes, I contrived to make her open her eyes and speak to me.

" Come Amy," I said, "rouse, I want you to help me."

"-In what way and what fur you wake me up ?" she said as she sat upright on the straw, and began rubbing her eyes.

" Never mind, but you get up and I will tell you."

When she was fairly awake, she assisted me in lifting in a large tub of water.

" Oh, is Aunt Polly any sicker ?" she inquired.

" Amy, she is dead."

" Oh, Lord, den I ain't gwine to hope you, bekase I's afeared ob a dead body."

" It can't harm you."

"Yes it ken ; anyhow, I is feared ob it, and I ain't gwine to hope you."

"Well, you need not touch her, only sit up with me whilst I wash her and dress her nicely."

"Well, I'll do dat much."

Accordingly, she crouched down in the corner and concealed her face with her hands, whilst I proceeded to wash the body thoroughly and dress it out in an old faded calico, which, in life, had constituted her finest robe. Bare and undecked, but clean, appeared that tabernacle of flesh, which had once enshrined a tried but immortal spirit. When all was finished, I seated myself near the partly-opened door, and waited for the coming of day. Ah, when was the morn of glad freedom to break f r me ?

CHAPTER XIX.

MORN did break, bright and clear, over the face of tne sleeping earth! It was a still and blessed hour. Man, hushed from his rushing activity, lay reposeful in the arms of "Death's counterfeit—sleep." All animated nature was quiet and calm, till, suddenly, a gush of melody broke from the clear throats of the wildwood birds and made the air vocal. Another day was dawning; another day born to witness sins and cruelties the most direful. Do we not often wonder why the sky can smile so blue and lovingly, when such outrages are enacted beneath it? But I must not anticipate.

As soon as the sun had fairly risen I knocked at the housedoor, which was opened by Miss Bradly, whose languid face and crumpled dress, proved that she had taken no rest during the night. Bidding her a polite good-morning, I inquired if the ladies had risen? She answered that they were still asleep, and had rested well during the night. I next inquired for mas ter's health.

"Oh," said she, "I think he is well, quite well again. He slept soundly. I think he only suffered from a violent and sudden mental excitement. A good night's rest, and a sedative that I administered, have restored him; but *to-day*, oh, *to-day*, how I do dread to-day."

To the latter part of this speech I made no answer; for, of late, I had learned to distrust her. Even if her belief was right, I could not recognize her as one heroic enough to promulgate it from the house-tops. I saw in her only a weak, servile soul, drawn down from the lofty purpose of philanthropy, seduced by the charm of "vile lucre." Therefore I observed a rigid silence. Feeling a little embarrassed, I began playing with the strings of my apron, for I was fearful that the expression of my face might betray what was working in my mind.

"What is the matter, Ann?"

This recalled the tragedy that had occurred in the cabin, and I said, in a faltering tone,

"Death has been among us. Poor Aunt Polly is gone."

"Is it possible? When did she die? Poor old creature!"

"She died some time before midnight. When I left the house I was surprised to find her still sleeping, so I thought perhaps she was too sluggish, and, upon attempting to arouse her, I discovered that she was dead!"

"Why did you not come and inform me? I would have assisted you in the last sad offices."

"Oh, I did not like to disturb you. I did everything very well myself."

"Johnny and I sat up all night; that is, I suppose he was up, though he left the room a little after midnight, and has not since returned. I should not wonder if he has been walking the better part of the night. He so loves solitude and the night-time— but then," she added, musingly "he has a bad cough, and it may be dangerous. The night was chilly, the atmosphere heavy. What if this imprudence should rapidly develop a fearful disease?" she seemed much concerned.

"I will go," said she, "and search for him;" but ere these words had fairly died upon her lips, we were startled by a cough, and, looking up, we beheld the subject of our conversation within a few steps of us. Oh, how wretchedly he was changed! It appeared as if the wreck of years had been accomplished in the brief space of a night. Haggard and pale, with his eyes roving listlessly, dark purple lines of unusual depth surrounding them, and with his bright, gold hair, heavy with the dew, and hanging neglected around his noble head, even his clear, pearl-like complexion appeared dark and discolored.

"Where have you been, Johnny?" asked Miss Bradly.

"To commune with the lonely and comfort the bound; at the door of the 'lock-up,' our miniature Bastile, I have spent the night." Here commenced a paroxysm of coughing, so violent that he was obliged to seat himself upon the door-sill

"Oh, Johnny," exclaimed the terrified lady.

But as he attempted to check her fears, another paroxysm, still more frightful, took place, and this time the blood gushed copiously from his mouth. Miss Bradly threw her arms tenderly around him, and, after a succession of rapid gushes of blood, his head fell languidly on her shoulder, like a pale, broken lily!

I instantly ran to call up the ladies, when master approached from his chamber; seeing young master lying so pale, cold, and insensible in the arms of Miss Bradly, he concluded he was dead, and, crying out in a frantic tone, he asked,

"In h—l's name, what has happened to my boy?"

"He has had a violent hemorrhage," replied Miss Bradly, with an ill-disguised composure.

The sight of the blood, which lay in puddles and clots over the steps, increased the terror of the father, and, frantically seizing his boy in his arms, he covered the still, pale face with kisses.

"Oh, my boy! my boy! how much you are like *her!* This is her mouth, eyes, and nose, and now you 'pears jist like she did when I seed her last. These limbs are stiff and frozen. It can't be death; no, it can't be. I haven't killed you, too— say, Miss Bradly, is he dead?"

"No, sir, only exhausted from the violence of the paroxysm, and the copious hemorrhage, but he requires immediate medical treatment; send, promptly, for Dr. Mandy."

Master turned to me, saying,

"Gal, go order Jake to mount the swiftest horse, and ride

for life and death to Dr. Mandy; tell him to come instantly,
my son is dying."

I obeyed, and, with all possible promptitude, the message
was dispatched. Oh, how different when *his* son was ill. Then
you could see that human life was valuable; had it been a
negro, he would have waited until after breakfast before sending for a doctor.

Mr. Peterkin bore his son into the house, placed him on the
bed, and, seating himself beside him, watched with a tenderness that I did not think belonged to his harsh nature.

In a very short time Jake returned with Dr. Mandy, who,
after feeling young master's pulse, sounding his chest, and applying the stethescope, said that he feared it was an incipient
form of lung-fever. We had much cause for apprehension.
There was a perplexed expression upon the face of the doctor,
a tremulousness in his motions, which indicated that he was in
great fear and doubt as to the case. He left some powders, to
be administered every hour, and, after various and repeated injunctions to Miss Bradly, who volunteered to nurse the patient,
he left the house.

After taking the first powder, young master lay in a deep,
unbroken sleep As I stood by his bedside I saw how
altered he was. The cheek, which, when he was walking, had
seemed round and full, was now shrunk and hollow, and a fiery
spot burned there like a living coal; and the dark, purple ring
that encircled the eyes, and the sharp contraction of the thin
nostril, were to me convincing omens of the grave. Then, too,
the anxious, care-written face of Miss Bradly tended to deepen
my apprehension. How my friends were falling around me !
Now, just when I was beginning to live, came the fell destroyer
of my happiness. Happiness ? Oh, does it not seem a mockery
for the slave to employ that word ? As if he had anything to do
with it ! The slave, who owns nothing, ay, literally nothing.
His wife and children are all his master's. His very wearing
apparel becomes another's. He has no right to use it, save as
he is advised by his owner. Go, my kind reader, to the hotels

of the South and South-west, look at the worn and dejected countenances of the slaves, and tell me if you do not read misery there. Look in at the saloons of the restaurants, coffee-houses, &c., at late hours of the night; there you will see them, tired, worn and weary, with their aching heads bandaged up, sighing for a few moments' sleep. There the proud, luxurious, idle whites sip their sherbets, drink wine, and crack their ever-lasting jokes, but there must stand your obsequious slave, with a smile on his face, waiter in hand, ready to attend to " Master's slightest wish." No matter if his tooth is aching, or his child dying, he must smile, or be flogged for gruffness. This " chattel personal," though he bear the erect form of a man, has no right to any privileges or emotions. Oh, nation of the free, how long shall this be ? Poor, suffering Africa, country of my sires, how much longer upon thy bleeding shoulders must the cross be pressed! Is there no tomb where, for a short space, thou shalt lie, and then, bursting the bonds of night and death, spring up free, redeemed and regenerate ?"

" Oh, will he die ?" I murmured, " he who reconciles me to my bondage, who is my only friend ? Another affliction I cannot bear; I've been so tried in the furnace, that I have not strength to meet another."

Those thoughts passed through my brain as I stood beside young master; but the entrance of Mr. Peterkin diverted them, and, stepping up to him, I said, " Master, Aunt Polly is dead."

" You lie !" he thundered out.

" No, Mr. Peterkin, the old woman is really dead," said Miss Bradly, in a kind but mournful tone.

" Who killed her ?" again he thundered.

Ay, who did kill her ? Could I not have answered, " Thou art the man "? But I did not. Silently I stood before him, never daring to trust myself with a word.

" What time did she kick the bucket ?" asked Mr. Peterkin, in one of the favorite Kentucky vulgarisms, whereby the most solemn and awful debt of nature is ridiculed by the unthinking.

I told him how I had found her, what I had done, &c., all of which is known to the reader.

"I believe h—l is loose among the niggers. Now, here's Poll had to die bekase she couldn't cut any other caper. I might have made a sight o' money by her sale; and she, old fool, had to cut me outen it. Wal, I'll only have to sell some of the others, fur I's bound to make up a sartin sum of money to pay to some of my creditors in L——."

This speech was addressed to Miss Bradly, upon whom it made not half the impression that it did upon me. How I hoped I should be one, for if young master, as I began to believe, should die soon, the place would become to me more horrible than a tiger's den. Any change was desirable.

When the young ladies rose from their beds I went in to attend on them, and communicated the news of young master's illness and Aunt Polly's death. For their brother they expressed much concern, but the faithful old domestic, who had served them so long, was of no more consequence than a dog. Miss Jane did seem provoked to think that she "had died on their hands," as she expressed it. "If pa had sold her months ago, we might have had the money, or something valuable, but now we must go to the expense of furnishing her with a coffin."

"Coffin! hoity-toity! Father's not going to give her a coffin, an old store-box is good enough to put her old carcass in." And thus they spoke of one of God's dead.

Usually persons respect those upon whom death has set his ghastly signet; but these barbarians (for such I think they must have been) spoke with an irreverence of one whose body lay still and cold, only few steps from them. To some people no thing or person is sacred.

After breakfast I waited in great anxiety to hear how and when master intended to have Aunt Polly buried.

I had gone into the little desolate cabin, which was now consecrated by the presence of the dead. There *she* lay, cold and ashen; and the long white strip that I had thrown over her was too thin to conceal the face. It was an old muslin curtain that

I had found in looking over the boxes of the deceased, and out of respect had flung it over the remains. So rigid and hard-set seemed her features in that last, deep sleep, so tightly locked were those bony fingers, so mournful looked the straightened, stiffened form, so devoid of speculation the half-closed eyes, that I turned away with a shudder, saying inwardly:

"Oh, death, thou art revolting!" Yet when I bethought me of the peace passing human understanding into which she had gone, the safe bourne that she had attained, "where the wicked cease from troubling and the weary are at rest;" when I thought of this, death lost its horror, and the grave its gloom. Oh, Eternity, problem that the living can never solve. Oh, death, full of victory to the Christian! wast thou not, to my old and weary friend, a messenger of sweet peace; and was not the tomb a gateway to new and undreamed-of happiness? Yes, so will I believe; for so believing am I made joyful.

Relieved thus by faith from the burden of grief, I moved gently about the room, trying to bring something like order to its ragged appearance; for Jake, who had been dispatched for Doctor Mandy to come and see young master, had met on the way a colored preacher, to whom he announced Aunt Polly's death, and who had promised to come and preach a funeral sermon, and attend the burial. This was to the other negroes a great treat; they regarded a funeral as quite a gala occasion, inasmuch as we had never had such a thing upon the farm. I had my own doubts, though I did not express them, whether master would permit it.

Young master still slept, from the strong effects of the sleeping potion which had been administered to him. Miss Bradly, overcome by the night's watching, dozed in a large chair beside the bed, and an open Bible, in which she had been reading, lay upon her lap. The blinds were closed, but the dim light of a small fire that blazed on the hearth gave some appearance of life to the room. Every one who passed in and out, stepped on tip-toe, as if fearful of arousing the sleeper.

Oh, the comfort of a white skin! No darkened room, no

comfortable air, marked the place where she my friend had died.
No hushed dread nor whispered voice paid respect to the cabin-
room where lay her dead body; but, thanks to God, in the
morning of the resurrection we shall come forth alike, regardless
of the distinctions of color or race, each one to render a faithful
account of the deeds done in the body.

Mr. Peterkin came to the kitchen-door, and called Nace,
saying:

"Where is that old store-box that the goods and domestics
for the house was fetched home in, from L——, last fall?"

"It's in de smoke-house, Masser."

"Wal, go git it, and bury ole Poll in it."

"It's right dirty and greasy, Master," I ventured to say.

"Who keres if 'tis? What right has you to speak, slut?"
and he gave me a violent kick in the side with his rough brogan.

"Take that for yer imperdence. Who tole you to put yer
mouth in?"

Nace and Dan soon produced the box, which had no top, and
was dirty and greasy, as it well might be from its year's lodgment in the meat-house.

"Now, go dig a hole and put Poll in it."

As master was turning away, he was met by a neatly-dressed
black man, who wore a white muslin cravat and white cotton
gloves, and carried two books in his hand. He had an humble,
reverent expression, and I readily recognized him as the free
colored preacher of the neighborhood—a good, religious man,
God-fearing and God-serving. No one knew or could say aught
against him. How I did long to speak to him; to sit at his
feet as a disciple, and learn from him heavenly truths.

As master turned round, the preacher, with a polite air, took
off his hat, saying:

"Your servant, Master."

"What do you want, nigger?"

"Why, Master, I heard that one of your servants was dead,
and I come to ask your leave to convene the friends in a short
prayer-meeting, if you will please let us."

"No, I be d——d if you shall, you rascally free nigger; if you don't git yourself off my place, I'll git my cowhide to you. I wants none of yer tom-foolery here."

"I beg Master's pardon, but I meant no harm. I generally go to see the sick, and hold prayer over the dead."

"You doesn't do it here; and now take your dirty black hide away, or it will be the worse for you."

Without saying one word, the mortified preacher, who had meant well, turned away. I trust he did as the apostles of old were bidden by their Divine Master to do, "shook the dust from his feet against that house." Oh, coarse and sense-bound man, you refused entertainment to an "angel, unawares."

"Well, I sent that prayin' rascal a flyin' quick enough;" and with this self-gratulatory remark, he entered the house.

Nace and Jake carried the box into the cabin, preceded by me.

Most reverently I laid away the muslin from the face and form; and lifting the head, while Nace assisted at the feet, we attempted to place the body in the box, but found it impossible, as the box was much too short. Upon Nace's representing this difficulty to Mr. Peterkin, he only replied:

"Wal, bury her on a board, without any more foolin' 'bout it."

This harsh mandate was obeyed to the letter. With great expedition, Nace and Jake dug a hole in the earth, and laid a few planks at the bottom, upon which I threw an old quilt, and on that hard bed they laid her. Good and faithful servant, even in death thou wast not allowed a bed! Over the form I spread a covering, and the men laid a few planks, box-fashion, over that, and then began roughly throwing on the fresh earth. "Dust to dust," I murmured, and, with a secret prayer, turned from her unmarked resting-place. Mr. Peterkin expressly ordered that it should not have a grave shape, and so it was patted and smoothed down, until, save for the moisture and fresh color of the earth, you could not have known that the ground had ever been broken.

8

CHAPTER XX.

ABOUT noon a gaudily-dressed and rough-looking man rode up to the gate, and alighted from a fine bay horse. With that free and easy sort of way so peculiar to a *certain class* of mankind, he walked up the avenue to the front door.

"Gal," he said, addressing me, "whar's yer master?"

"In the house. Will you walk in?"

"No, it is skersely worth while; jist tell him that me, Bill Tompkins, wants to see him; but stay," he added, as I was turning to seek my master, "is you the gal he sold to me yesterday?"

"I don't know, sir."

"Wal, you is devilish likely. Put out yer foot. Wal, it is nice enuff to belong to a white 'ooman. You is a bright-colored mulatto. I *must* have you."

"Heavens! I hope not," was my half-uttered expression, as I turned away, for I had caught the meaning of that lascivious eye, and shrank from the threatened danger. Though I had been cruelly treated, yet had I been allowed to retain my person inviolate; and I would rather, a thousand-fold, have endured the brutality of Mr. Peterkin, than those loathsome looks which I felt betokened ruin.

"Master, a man, calling himself Bill Tompkins, wishes to see you," said I, as I entered his private apartment.

"Can't yer say Mr. Tompkins?"

"He told me to tell you Bill Tompkins; I only repeat his words."

"Whar is he?"

"At the front door."

"Didn't yer ax him in, hussy?"

"Yes, sir, but he refused, saying it was not worth while."

"Oh," thought I, when left alone, "am I sold to that monster? Am I to become so utterly degraded? No, no; rather than yield my purity I will give up my life, and trust to God to pardon the suicide."

In this state of mind I wandered up and down the yard, into the kitchen, into the cabin, into the room where young master lay sleeping, into the presence of the young ladies, and out again into the air; yet my curious, feverish restlessness, could not be allayed. A trader was in the house—a bold, obscene man, and into his possession I might fall! Oh, happy indeed must be those who feel that he or they have the exclusive cus tody of their own persons; but the poor negro has nothing, not even—save in rare cases—the liberty of choosing a home.

I had not dared, since daylight, to go near the "lock-up," for a fearful punishment would have been due the one whom Mr. Peterkin found loitering there.

I was so tortured by apprehension, that my eyes burned and my head ached. I had heard master say that the unlooked-for death of Aunt Polly would force him to sell some of the other slaves, in order to realize a certain sum of money, and Tompkins had expressed a desire for me. It was likely that he would offer a good price; then should I be lost. Oh, heavenly Virtue! do not desert me! Let me bear up under the fiercest trials!

I had wandered about, in this half-crazed manner, never daring to venture within "ear-shot" of master and Mr. Tompkins, fearing that the latter might, upon a second sight of me, have the fire of his wicked passions aroused, and then my fate would be sealed.

I determined to hide in the cabin, to pray there, in the room that had been hallowed by the presence of God's angel of Death; but there, cowering on the old brick hearth, like a hen with her brood of chickens, I found, to my surprise, Amy, with little Ben in her arms, and the two girls crouched close to her side, evidently feeling that her presence was sufficient to protect them.

"Lor', Ann," said Amy, her wide eyes stretched to their utmost tension, "thar is a trader talkin' wid Masser; I won'er whose gwine to be sole. I hope tain't us."

I didn't dare reply to her. I feared for myself, and I feared for her.

Kneeling down in the corner of the cabin, I besought mercy of the All-merciful; but somehow, my prayers fell back cold upon my heart. God seemed a great way off, and I could not realize the presence of angels. "Oh," I cried, "for the uplifting faith that hath so often blest me! oh for the hopefulness, the trustingness of times past! Why, why is the gate of heaven shut against me? Why am I thus self-bound? Oh, for a wider, broader and more liberal view! But I could not pray. Great God! had that last and only soul-stay been taken from me? With a black hopelessness gathering at my heart, I arose from my knees, and looked round upon those desolate orphans, shrinking terror-stricken, hiding away from the merciless pursuit of a giant; and then I bethought me of my own desolation, and I almost arraigned the justice of Heaven. Most wise Father! pardon me! Thou, who wast tempted by Satan, and to whom the cup of mortality was bitter, pity me and forgive!

Turning away from the presence of those pleading children I entered the kitchen, and there were Jake and Dan, terror written on their strong, hard faces; for, no matter how hard is the negro's present master, he always regards a change of owners as entailing new dangers; and no wonder that, from education and experience, he is thus suspicious, for so many troubles have come and do come upon him, that he cannot imagine a change whereby he is to be benefited.

"Has you hearn anything, Ann?" asked Dan, with his great flabby lips hanging loosely open, and his eyes considerably distended.

"Nothing."

"Who's gwine to be sole?" asked Jake.

" I don't know?"

" Hope tisn't me."

" And hope tisn't me," burst from the lips of both of them, and to this my heart gave a fervent though silent echo.

" He is de one dat's bought Lindy," said old Nace, who now entered, " and Masser's gwine to sell some de rest ob yer."

"Why do yer say de rest ob yer? Why mayn't it be you?" asked Dan.

" Bekase he ain't gwine to sell me, ha! ha! I sarved him too long fur dat."

Ginsy and Sally came rushing in, frightened, like all the rest, exclaiming,

" Oh, we's in danger; a nigger-trader is talkin' wid master."

We had no time for prolonged speculation, for the voice of Mr. Peterkin was heard in the entry, and, throwing open the door, he entered, followed by Tompkins.

" Here's the gang, and a devilish good-lookin' set they is."

" Yes, but let me fust see the one I have bought."

" Here, Nace," said master, "take this key, and tell Lindy to dress herself and come here." The last part of this sentence was said in an under-tone.

In terror I fled from the kitchen. Scarcely knowing what I did, I rushed into the young ladies' room, into which Nace had conducted Lindy, upon whom they were placing some of their old finery. A half-worn calico dress, gingham apron and white collar, completed the costume. I never shall forget the expression of Lindy's face, as she looked vacantly around her, hunting for sympathy, yet finding none, from the cold, haughty faces that gazed upon her.

" Now go," said Miss Jane, " and try to behave yourself in your new home."

" Good-bye, Miss Jane," said the humbled, weeping negro.

" Good-bye," was coldly answered; but no hand was extended to her.

" Good-bye, Miss Tildy."

Miss Tildy, who was standing at the glass arranging her hair, never turned round to look upon the poor wretch, but carelessly said,

"Good-bye."

She looked toward me; her lip was quivering and tears were rolling down her cheeks. I turned my head away, and she walked off with the farewell unspoken.

Quickly I heard Jake calling for me. Then I knew that my worst fears were on the point of realization. With a timid, hesitating step, I walked to the kitchen. There, ranged in single file, stood the servants, with anxious faces, where a variety of contending feelings were written. I nerved myself for what I knew was to follow, and stepping firmly up, joined the phalanx.

"That's the one," said Tompkins, as he eyed me with that *same* look. There he stood, twirling a heavy bunch of seals which depended from a large, curiously-wrought chain. He looked more like a fiend than a *man*.

"This here one is your'n," said Mr. Peterkin, pointing to Lindy; "and, gal, that gentleman is yer master"

Lindy dropped a courtesy to him, and tried to wipe away her tears; for experience had taught her that the only safe course was to stifle emotions.

"Here, gal, open yer mouth," Tompkins said to Lindy. She obeyed.

"Now let me feel yer arms."

He then examined her feet, ankles, legs, passed his hands over various parts of her body, made her walk and move her limbs in different ways, and then, seemingly satisfied with the bargain, said,

"Wal, that trade is closed."

Looking toward me, his dissolute eyes began to glare furiously. Again my soul quailed; but I tried to govern myself, and threw upon him a glance as cold as ice itself.

"What will you take for this yellow gal?" he said, as he laid his hand upon my shoulder. I shrank beneath his touch; yet resistance would only have made the case worse, and I was compelled to submit.

" I ain't much anxious to sell her; she is my darter Jane's waitin' 'ooman, and, you see, my darters are putty much stuck up. They thinks they must have a waitin'-maid ; but, if you offer a far price, maybe we will close in."

" Wal, as she is a fancy article, I'll jist say take twelve hundred dollars, and that's more an' she's actilly worth; but I wants her fur my *own use ;* a sorter private gal like, you knows," and he gave a lascivious blink, which Mr. Peterkin seemed to understand. I felt a deep crimson suffuse my face. Oh, God! this was the heaviest of all afflictions. *Sold !* and for *such a purpose !*

" I reckon the bargain is closed, then," said Mr. Peterkin.

I felt despair coiling around my heart. Yet I knew that to make an appeal to their humanity would be worse than idle.

" Who, which of them have you sold, father ?" asked Miss Jane, who entered the kitchen, doubtless for the humane object of witnessing the distress of the poor creatures.

" Wal, Lindy's sold, and we are 'bout closing the bargain for Ann."

" Why, Ann belongs to me."

" Yes, but Tompkins offers twelve hundred dollars; and six hundred of it you shill have to git new furniture."

" She shan't go for six thousand. I want an accomplished maid when I go up to the city, and she just suits me. Remember I have your deed of gift."

This relieved me greatly, for I understood her determination; and, though I knew all sorts of severity would be exercised over me in my present home, I felt assured that my honor would remain unstained.

The trader tried to persuade and coax Miss Jane ; but she remained impervious to all of his importunities.

" Wal, then," he said, after finding she would yield to no argument, " haven't you none others you can let me have ? I am 'bliged to fill up my lot."

"Wal, since my darter won't trade nohow, I must try and let you have some of the others, though I don't care much 'bout sellin'."

Mr. Peterkin was what was called tight on a trade; now, though he was anxious enough to sell, he affected to be perfectly indifferent. This was what would be termed an excellent ruse de guerre.

"If you want children, I think we can supply you," said Miss Jane, and, looking round, she asked,

"Where are Amy and her sisters?"

My heart sank within me, and, though I knew full well where they were, I would not speak.

Little Jim, the son of Ginsy, cried out,

"Yes, I know where dey is. I seed em in dar."

"Well, run you young rascal, and tell 'em to come here in a minnit," said Mr. Peterkin; and away the boy scampered. In a few moments he returned, followed by Amy, who was bearing Ben in her arms; and, holding on to her skirts, were the two girls, terror limned on their dark, shining faces.

"Step up here to this gentleman, Amy, and say how would you like him for a master?" said Mr. Peterkin.

"Please, sir," replied Amy, "I don't kere whar I goes, so I takes these chillen wid me."

"I do not want Amy to be sold. Sell the children, father; but let us keep Amy for a house-girl." Cold and unfeeling looked the lady as she pronounced these words; but could you have seen the expression of Amy's face! There is no human language, no painter's power, to show forth the eye of frantic madness with which the girl glared around on all. Clutching little Ben tightly, savagely to her bosom, she said no word, and all seemed struck by the extreme wildness of her manner.

"Let's look at that boy," said the trader, as he attempted to unfasten Amy's arms but were locked round her treasure.

"Dont'ee, dont'ee," shrieked the child.

"Yes, but he will," said Mr. Peterkin, as, with a giant's

force, he broke asunder the slight arms, " you imperdent hussy, arn't you my property? mine to do what I pleases with; and do you dar' to oppose me?"

The girl said nothing; but the wild expression began to grow wilder, fiercer, and more frightful. Little Ben, who was not accustomed to any kind of notice, and felt at home nowhere except in Amy's arms, set up a furious scream; but this the trader did not mind, and proceeded to examine the limbs.

" Something is the matter with this boy, he's got hip-disease; I knows from his teeth he is older than you says."

" Yes," said Amy seizing the idea, " he is weakly, he won't do no good widout me; buy me too, please, Masser," and she crouched down at the trader's feet, with her hands thrown up in an air of touching supplication; but she had gone to the wrong tribunal for mercy. Who can hope to find so fair a flower blooming amid the dreary brambles of a negro-trader's breast?

Tompkins took no other notice of her than to give her a contemptuous kick, as much as to say, " thing, get out of my way."

Turning to Mr. Peterkin he said,

" This boy is not sound. I won't have him at any price," and he handed him back to Amy, who exclaimed, in a thrilling tone,

" Thank God! Bless you, Masser!" and she clasped the shy little Ben warmly to her breast.

Ben, whose intellect seemed clouded, looked wonderingly around on the group; then, as if slowly realizing that he had escaped a mighty trouble, clung closer to Amy.

" Look here, nigger-wench, does you think to spile the sale of property in that ar' way? Wal, I'll let you see I'll have things my way. No nigger that ever was born, shall dictate to me."

" No, father, I'd punish her well, even if I had to give Ben away; he is no account here, merely an expense; and do sell those other two girls, Amy's sisters."

Mr. Peterkin then called up Lucy and Janey. I have mentioned these two but rarely in the progress of this book, and for

8*

the reason that their little lives were not much interwoven with the thread of mine. I saw them often, but observed nothing particular about them. They were quiet, taciturn, and what is usually called stupid children. They, like little Ben, never ventured far away from Amy's protecting wing. Now, with a shy step and furtive glance toward the trader, they obeyed their master's summons. Poor Amy, with Ben clasped to her heart, strained her body forward, and looked with stretched eyes and suspended breath toward Tompkins, who was examining them.

"Wal, I'll give you three hundred and fifty a-piece for 'em. Now, come, that's the highest I'll give, Peterkin, and you mustn't try to git any more out of me. You are a hard customer; but I am in a hurry, so I makes my largest offer right away: I ain't got the time to waste. That's more 'an anybody else would give for 'em; but I sees that they has good fingers fur to pick cotton, therefore I gives a big price."

"It's a bargain, then. They is yourn;" and no doubt Mr. Peterkin thought he had a good bargain, or he never would have chewed his tobacco in that peculiarly self-satisfied manner.

"Stand aside, then," said the trader, pushing his new purchases, as if they were a bundle of dry goods. Running up to Amy, they began to hold to her skirts and tremble violently, scarcely knowing what the words of Tompkins implied.

"Dey ain't sold?" asked Amy, turning first from one to the other; yet no one answered. Mr. Peterkin and Tompkins were too busy with their trade, and the negroes too much absorbed in their own fate, to attend to her. For my part I had not strength to confirm her half-formed doubt. There she stood, gathering them to her side with a motherly love.

"What will you give fur this one?" and Mr. Peterkin pointed to Ginsy, who stood with an humble countenance. When called up she made a low courtesy, and went through the examination. Name and age were given; a fair price was offered for her and her child, and was accepted.

"Take this boy for a hundred dollars," said Mr. Peterkin, as he jerked Ben from the arms of the half-petrified Amy.

"Wal, he isn't much 'count ; but, rather then seem contrary, I'll give that fur him."

And thus the trade was closed. Human beings were disposed of with as little feeling as if they had been wild animals.

"I'm sorry you won't, young Miss, let me have that maid of yourn ; but I'll be 'long next fall, and, fur a good price, I'spect you'll be willin' to trade. I wants that yellow wench," and he clicked his fingers at me.

"Say, Peterkin, ken you lend me a wagen to take 'em over to my pen ?"

"Oh, yes ; and Nace can drive 'em over."

Conscious of having got a good price, Mr. Peterkin was in a capital humor.

"Come, go with me, Peterkin, and we'll draw up the papers, and I'll pay you your money."

This was an agreeable sound to master. He ordered Nace to bring out the wagon, and the order was hardly given before it was obeyed. Dismal looked that red wagon, the same which years before had carried me away from the insensible form of my broken-hearted mother. It appeared more dark and dreary, to me, than a coffin or hearse.

"Say, Peterkin, don't let 'em take many close ; jist a change. It tires 'em too much if they have big bundles to carry."

"They shan't be troubled with that."

"Now, niggers, git your bundles and come 'long," said master.

"Oh," cried Lindy, "can I git to see young master before I start ? I wants to thank him for de comfort he gib me last night," and she wiped the tears from her eyes, and was starting toward the door of the house, when Miss Jane intercepted her.

"No, you runaway hussy, you shan't go in to disturb him, and have a scene here."

" Please, Miss Jane, I only wants to say good-bye."

" You shan't do it."

Mournfully, and with the tears streaming far down her cheeks, she turned to me, saying, " Please, you, Ann, tell him good-bye fur me, and good-bye to you. I hope you will forgive me for all de harm I has done to you."

I took her hand, but could not speak a word. Silently I pressed it.

" Whar's your close, gal ?" asked Tompkins.

" I'm gwine to git 'em."

" Well, be in a hurry 'bout it."

She went off to gather up a few articles, scarcely sufficient to cover her; for we were barely allowed a change of clothing, and that not very decent.

Ginsy, leading her child with one hand, while she held in the other a small bundle, walked up to Miss Jane, and dropping a low courtesy, said,

" Farewell, Miss Jane; can I see Miss Tildy and young master ?"

" No, John is sick, and Tildy can't be troubled just now."

" Yes, ma'm; please tell 'em good-bye fur me; and I hopes young Masser will soon be well agin. I'd like to see him afore I went, but I don't want to 'sturb him."

" Well, that will do, go on now."

" Tell young Masser good-bye," Ginsy said, addressing her child.

" Good-bye," repeated Miss Jane very carelessly, scarcely looking toward them, and they moved away, and shaking hands with the servants, they marched on to the wagon.

All this time Amy had remained like one transfixed ; little Ben held one of her hands, whilst Jancy and Luce grasped her skirts firmly. These children had no clothes, for, as they performed no regular labor, they were not allowed a change of apparel. On a Saturday night, whilst they slept, Amy washed out the articles which they had worn during the week ; and now, poor things, they had no bundles to be made up.

"Come 'long wid yer, young ones," and Tompkins took Ben by the hand; but he stoutly refused to go, crying out:

"Go 'way, and let me 'lone."

"Come on, I'll give you a lump of sugar."

"I won't, I won't."

All of them held tightly to Amy, whose vacant face was so stony in its deep despair, that it struck terror to my soul.

"No more fuss," said Mr. Peterkin, and he raised his large whip to strike the screaming Ben a blow; but that motherly instinct that had taught Amy to protect them thus long, was not now dead, and upon her outstretched arm the blow descended. A great, fearful gash was made, from which the fresh blood streamed rapidly; but she minded it not. What, to that lightning-burnt soul, were the wounds of the body? Nothing, aye nothing!

"Oh, don't mark 'em, Peterkin, it will spile the· sale," said Tompkins.

"Come 'long now, niggers, I has no more time to wait;" and, with a strong wrench, he broke Ben's arms loose from Amy's form, and, holding him firmly, despite his piteous cries, he ordered Jake to bring the other two also. This order was executed, and quickly Luce and Janey were in the grasp of Jake, and borne shrieking to the cart, in which all three of them were bound and laid.

Speechless, stony, petrified, stood Amy. At length, as if gifted with a supernatural energy, she leaped forward, as the cart drove off, and fell across the path, almost under the feet of the advancing horses. But not yet for thee, poor suffering child, will come the Angel of Death! It has been decreed that you shall endure and wait a while longer.

By an adroit check upon the rein, Nace stopped the wagon suddenly, and Jake, who was standing near by, lifted Amy up.

"Take her to the house, and see that she does herself no harm," said Mr. Peterkin.

Yes, Masser, I will," was the reply of the obsequious Jake.

And so the cart drove on. I shall never forget the sight!

Those poor, down-cast creatures, tied hand and foot, were conveyed they knew not whither. The shrieks and screams of those children ring now in my ears. Oh, doleful, most doleful! Why came there no swift execution of that Divine threat, "Whoso causeth harm to one of these little ones, it were better for him that a mill-stone were hung about his neck and that he were drowned in the sea."

CHAPTER XXI.

TOUCHING FAREWELL FULL OF PATHOS—THE PARTING—MY GRIEF.

THE half insensible form of Amy was borne by Jake into the cabin, and laid upon the cot which had been Aunt Polly's. He then closed and secured the door after him.

Where, all this time, was Miss Bradly? She, in her terror, had buried her head upon the bed, on which young master still slept. She tried to drown the sound of those frantic cries that reached her, despite the closed door and barred shutter. Oh, did they not reach the ear of Almighty love?

"Well, I am glad," exclaimed Miss Tildy, "that it is all over. Somehow, Jane, I did not like the sound of those young children's cries. Might it not have been well to let Amy go too?"

"No, of course not. Now that Lindy has been sold, we need a house-girl, and Amy may be made a very good one; besides, she enraged me so by attempting to spoil the sale of Ben."

"Did she do that? Oh, well, I have no pity for her."

"It would be something very new, Till, for you to pity a nigger."

"So it would—yet I was weak enough to feel badly when I heard the children scream."

"Oh, you are only nervous."

"I believe I am, and think I will take some medicine."

"Take medicine," to stifle human pity!

"What rhubarb, senna, or what purgative drug would scour" the slaveholder's nature of harshness and brutality? Could

6*

this be found, " I would applaud to the very echo, that should applaud again ;" but, alas! there is no remedy for it.   Education has taught many of them to guard their " beloved institution " with a sort of patriotic fervor and religious zeal.

When master returned that evening, he was elated to a wonderful degree.   Tompkins had paid him a large sum in ready cash, and this put him in a good humor with himself and everybody else.   He almost felt kindly toward the negroes.   But I looked upon him with more than my usual horror.   That great, bloated face, blazing now with joy and the effect of strong drink, was revolting to me.   Every expression of delight from his lips brought to my mind the horrid troubles he had caused by the simple exercise of his tyrannic will upon helpless women and children.   The humble appearance of Ginsy, the touching innocence of her child, the unnoticed silent grief of Lindy, the fearful, heart-rending distraction of Amy, the agony of her helpless sisters and brother, all rose to my mind when I heard Mr. Peterkin's mirthful laugh ringing through the house.

Late in the evening young master roused up.   The effect of the somnolent draught had died out, and he woke in full possession of his faculties.   Miss Bradly and I were with him when he woke.   Raising himself quickly in the bed, he asked,

" What hour is it ?"

" About half-past six," said Miss Bradly.

" So late ?   Then am I afraid that all is over !   Where is Lindy ?"

" Try and rest a little more ; then we can talk !"

" No, I must know *now*."

" Wait a while longer."

" Tell me instantly," he said with a nervous impatience very unusual to him.

" Drink this, and I will then talk to you," said Miss Bradly, as she held a cordial to his lips.

Obediently he swallowed it, and, as he returned the glass, he asked,

"How has this wretched matter terminated? What has become of that unfortunate girl?"

"She has been sold."

"To the trader?"

"Yes, but don't talk about it; perhaps she is better off than we think."

"Is it wise for us thus to silence our sympathies?"

"Yes, it is, when we are powerless to act."

"But have we not, each of us, an influence?"

"Yes, but in such a dubious way, that in cases like the present, we had better not openly manifest it."

"Offensive we should never be; but surely we ought to assume a defensive position."

"Yes, but you must not excite yourself."

"Don't think of me. Already I fear I am too self-indulged. Too much time I have wasted in inaction."

"What could you have done? And now what can you do?"

"That is the very question that agitates me. Oh, that I knew my mission, and had the power to fulfil it!"

"Who of the others are sold?" he asked, turning to me.

"Amy's sisters and brother," and I could not avoid tears.

"Amy, too?"

"No, sir."

"Oh, God, this is too bad! and is she not half-distracted?"

I made no reply, for an admonitory look from Miss Bradly warned me to be careful as to what I said.

"Where is father?"

"In his chamber."

"Ann, go tell him I wish to speak with him."

Before obeying I looked toward Miss Bradly, and, finding nothing adverse in her expression, I went to do as he bade.

"Is he any worse?" master asked, when I had delivered the message.

"No, sir; he does not appear to be worse, yet I think he is very feeble."

"What right has you to think anything 'bout it?" he said, as he took from the mantle a large, black bottle and drank from it.

I made no reply, but followed him into young master's room, and pretended to busy myself about some trifling matter.

" What is it you want, Johnny ?"

" Father, you have done a wicked thing !"

" What do you mean, boy ?"

" You have sold Amy's sisters and brothers away from her."

" And what's wicked in selling a nigger ?"

" Hasn't a negro human feeling ?"

" Why, they don't feel like white people ; of course not."

" That must be proved, father."

" Oh, now, my boy, 'taint no use for yer to be wastin' of yer good feelin's on them miserable, ongrateful niggers."

" They are not ungrateful ; miserable they are, for they have had much misery imposed upon them."

" Oh, 'taint no use of talking 'bout it, child, go to sleep."

" Yes, father, I shall soon sleep soundly enough, in our grave-yard."

Mr. Peterkin moved nervously in his chair, and young master continued,

" I do not wish to live longer. I can do no good here, and the sight of so much misery only makes me more wretched. Father, draw close to me, I have lost a great deal of blood. My chest and throat are very sore. I feel that the tide of life ebbs low. I am going fast. My little hour upon earth is almost spent. Ere long, the great mystery of existence will be known to me. A cold shadow, with death-dews on its form, hovers round me. I know, by many signs unknown to others, that death is now upon me. This difficult and labored speech, this failing breath and filmy eye, these heavy night-sweats—all tell me that the golden bowl is about to be broken : the silver cord is tightened to its utmost tension. I am young, father ; I have forborne to speak to you upon a subject that has lain near, near, very near my heart." A violent paroxysm of coughing here interrupted him. Instantly Miss Bradly was beside him with a cordial, which he drank mechanically. "There," he continued, as he poised himself upon his elbow, "there, good Miss Emily, cordials are of no avail. I do not wish to stay. Father, do you not want me to rest quietly in my grave?"

"I don't want you to go to the grave at all, my boy, my boy," and Mr. Peterkin burst into tears.

"Yes, but, father, I am going there fast, and no human power can stay me. I shall be happy and resigned, if I can elicit from you one promise."

"What promise is that?"

"Liberate your slaves."

"Never!"

"Look at me, father."

"Good God!" cried Mr. Peterkin, as his eye met the calm, clear, fixed gaze of his son, "where did you get that look? heaven and h—l! it will kill me;" and, rushing from the room, he sought his own apartment, where he drank long and deeply from the black bottle that graced his mantel-shelf. This was his drop of comfort. Always after lashing a negro, he drank plentifully, as if to drown his conscience. Alas! many another man has sought relief from memory by such libations! Yet these are the voters, the noblesse, the lords so superior to the lowly African. These are the men who vote for a perpetuation of our captivity. Can we hope for a mitigation of our wrongs when such men are our sovereigns? Cool, clear-visioned men are few, noble philanthropic ones are fewer. What then have we to hope for? Our interests are at war with old established usages. The prejudices of society are against us. The pride of the many is adverse to us. All this we have to fight against; and strong must be the moral force that can overcome it.

Mr. Peterkin did not venture in young master's room for several hours after; and not without having been sent for repeatedly. Meanwhile I sought Amy, and found her lying on the floor of the cabin, with her face downwards. She did not move when I entered, nor did she answer me when I spoke. I lifted her up, but the hard, stony expression of her face, frightened me.

"Amy, I will be your friend."

"I don't want any friend."

"Yes you do, you like me."

"No I don't, I doesn't like anybody."

"Amy, God loves you."

"I doesn't love Him."

"Don't talk that way, child."

"Well, you go off, and let me 'lone."

"I wish to comfort you."

"I doesn't want no comfort."

"Come," said I, "talk freely to me. It will do you good."

"I tells you I doesn't want no good for to happen to me. I'd rather be like I is."

"Amy," and it was with reluctance I ventured to allude to a subject so painful; but I deemed it necessary to excite her painfully rather than leave her in that granite-like despair, "you may yet have your sisters and little brother restored to you."

"How? how? and when?" she screamed with joy, and started up, her wild eyes beaming with exultation.

"Don't be so wild," I said, softly, as I took her little, hard hand, and pressed it tenderly.

"But, say, Ann, ken I iver git de chilen back? Has Masser said anything 'bout it? Oh, it 'pears like too much joy fur me to iver know any more. Poor little Ben, it 'pears like I kan't do nothin' but hear him cry. And maybe dey is a beatin' of him now. Oh, Lor' a marcy! what shill I do?" and she rocked her body back and forward in a transport of grief.

There are some sorrows for which human sympathy is unavailing. What to that broken heart were words of condolence? Did she care to know that others felt for her? that another heart wept for her grief? No, like Rachel of old, she would not be comforted.

"Oh, Ann!" she added, "please leave me by myself. It 'pears like I kan't get my breath when anybody is by me. I wants to be by myself. Jist let me 'lone for a little while, then I'll talk to you."

I understood the feeling, and complied with her request.

The slave is so distrustful of sympathy, he is so accustomed to deception, that he feels secure in the indulgence of his grief only when he is alone. The petted white, who has friends to cluster round him in the hour of affliction, cannot understand the loneliness and solitude which the slave covets as a boon.

For several days young master lingered on, declining visibly. The hectic flush deepened upon his cheek, and the glitter of his eye grew fearfully bright, and there was that sharp contraction of his features that denoted the certain approach of death. His cough became low and even harder, and those dreadful night-sweats increased. He lay in a stupid state, half insensible from the effects of sedatives. Dr. Mandy, who visited him three times a day, did not conceal from Mr. Peterkin the fact of his son's near dissolution.

"Save his life, doctor, and you shall have all I own."

"If my art could do it, sir, I would, without fee, exert myself for his restoration."

Yet for a poor old negro his art could do nothing unfeed. Do ye wonder that we are goaded on to acts of desperation, when every day, nay, every moment, brings to our eyes some injustice that is done us—and all because our faces are dark?

> "Mislike us not for our complexion,
>   The shadow'd livery of the burnish'd sun,
>   To whom we are as neighbors, and near bred ;
>   Bring us the fairest creature Northward born,
>   Where Phœbus' fire scarce thaws the icicles,
>   And let us make incision for your love
>   To prove whose blood is reddest, his or ours."

During young master's illness I had but little communication with Amy. By Miss Jane's order she had been brought into the house to assist in the dining-room. I gave her all the instruction in my power. She appeared to listen to me, and learned well; yet everything was done with that vacant, unmeaning manner, that showed she felt no interest in what she was doing. I had never heard her allude to "the children' since the conversation just recorded. Indeed, she appeared to eschew all talk. At night I had attempted to draw her into conversation, but she always silenced me by saying,

"I'm tired, Ann, and wants to sleep."

This was singular in one so young, who had been reared in such a reckless manner. I should have been better satisfied if she had talked more freely of her sorrows; that stony, silent agony that seemed frozen upon her face, terrified me more than the most volcanic grief; that sorrow is deeply-rooted and hopeless, that denies itself the relief of speech. Heaven help the soul thus cut off from the usual sources of comfort. Oh, young Miss, spoiled daughter of wealth, you whose earliest breath opened to the splendors of home in its most luxurious form; you who have early and long known the watchful blessing of maternal love, and whose soft cheek has flushed to the praises of a proud and happy father, whose lip has thrilled beneath the pressure of a brother's kiss; you who have slept upon the sunny slope of life, have strayed 'mid the flowers, and reposed beneath the myrtles, and beside the fountains, where fairy fingers have garlanded flowers for your brow, oh, bethink you of some poor little negro girl, whom you often meet in your daily walks, whose sad face and dejected air you have often condemned as sullen, and I ask you now, in the name of sweet humanity, to judge her kindly. Look, with a pitying eye, upon that face which trouble has soured and abuse contracted. Repress the harsh word; give her kindness; 'tis this that she longs for. Be you the giver of the cup of cold water in His name.

CHAPTER XXII.

A CONVERSATION—HOPE BLOSSOMS OUT, BUT CHARLESTOWN IS
FULL OF EXCITABILITY.

ONE evening, during young master's illness, when he was
able to sit up beside the fire, Dr. Mandy came to see him, and,
as I sat in his room, sewing on some fancy work for Miss Jane,
I heard the conversation that passed between them.

"Have you coughed much?" the doctor asked.

"A great deal last night."

"Do the night-sweats continue?"

"Yes, sir, and are violent."

"Let me feel your pulse. Here—it is very quick—face is
flushed—high fever."

"Yes, doctor, I am sinking fast."

"Oh, keep up your spirits. I have been thinking that the
best thing for you would be to take a trip to Havana. This
climate is too variable for your complaint."

Young master shook his head mournfully.

"The change of scene," the doctor went on, "would be of service to you. A healthful excitement of the imagination, and a
different train of thought, would, undoubtedly, benefit you."

"What in the South could induce a different train of
thought? Oh, doctor, the horrid system, that there flourishes
with such rank power, would only deepen my train of thought,
and make me more wretched than I am; I would not go near
New Orleans, or pass those dreadful plantations, even to secure
the precious boon of health."

"You will not see anything of the kind. You will only see
life at hotels; and there the slaves are all happy and well used.
Besides, my good boy, the negroes on the plantations are much
better used than you think; and I assure you they are very

happy. If you could overhear them laughing and singing of an evening, you would be convinced that they are well cared for."

"Ah, disguise thee as thou wilt, yet, Slavery, thou art horrid and revolting."

"You are morbid on the subject."

"No, only humane; but have I not seen enough to make me morbid?"

"These are subjects upon which I deem it best to say nothing."

"That is the invariable argument of self-interest."

"No, of prudence, Mr. John; I have no right to quarrel with and rail out against an institution that has the sanction of the law, and which is acceptable to the interests of my best friends and patrons.

"Exactly so; the whole matter, so vital to the happiness of others, so fraught with great humanitarian interests, must be quietly laid on the shelf, because it may lose you or me a few hundred dollars."

"Not precisely that either; but, granting, for the sake of hypothesis only, that slavery is a wrong, what good would all my arguments do? None, but rather an injury to the very cause they sought to benefit. You must not exasperate the slaveholders. Leave them to time and their own reflections. I believe many of the Western States—yes, Kentucky herself—would at this moment be free from slavery, if it had not been for the officious interference of the North. The people of the West and South are hot, fiery and impetuous. They may be persuaded and coaxed into a measure, but never driven. All this talk and gasconade of Abolitionists have but the tighter bound the negroes."

"I am sorry to hear you thus express yourself, for you give me a more contemptible opinion of the Southern and Western men, or rather the slave-holding class, than I had before. And so they are but children, who must be coaxed, begged, and be-sugar-plumed into doing a simple act of justice. Have they not the manhood to come out boldly, and say this thing is wrong, and that they will no longer countenance it in their midst; that they will, for the sake of justice and sympathy with humanity, liberate these creatures, whom they have held in an unjust and wicked bondage? Were they to act thus, then might they claim for themselves the title of chevaliers."

"Yes; but they take a different view of the subject; they look upon slavery as just and right—a dispensation of Providence, and feel that they are as much entitled to their slaves as another man is to his house, carriage, or horse."

"Oh, how they shut their hearts against the voice of misery, and close their eyes to the rueful sigh of human grief. I never heard a pro-slavery man who could, upon any reasonable ground, defend his position. The slavery argument is not only a wicked, but an absurd one. How wise men can be deluded by it I am at a loss to understand. Infatuated they must be, else they could not uphold a system as tyrannous as it is base."

"Well, we will say no more upon this subject," said the doctor, as Mr. Peterkin entered.

"What's the matter?" the latter inquired, as he listlessly threw himself into a chair.

"Nothing, only Mr. John is not all right on the 'goose,'" replied Dr. Mandy, with a facetious smile.

"And not likely to be," said Mr. Peterkin; "Johnny has given me a great deal of trouble 'bout this matter; but I hope he will outgrow it. 'Tis only a foolish notion. He was 'lowed to gad 'bout too much with them ar' devilish niggers, an' so 'bibed their quare ideas agin slavery. Now, in my 'pinion, my niggers is a darned sight better off than many of them poor whites at the North."

"But are they as free?" asked young master.

"No, to be sure they is not," and here Mr. Peterkin ejected from his mouth an amount of tobacco-juice that nearly extinguished the fire.

"Woe be unto the man who takes from a fellow-being the

9

priceless right of personal liberty!" exclaimed young master, with his fine eyes fervently raised.

"Yes, but everybody don't desarve liberty. Niggers ain't fit for to govern 'emselves nohow. They has bin too long 'customed to havin' masters. Them that's went to Libory has bin of no 'count to 'emselves nor nobody else. I tell yer, niggers was made to be slaves, and yer kan't change their Creator's design. Why, you see, doctor, a nigger's mind is never half as good as a white man's;" and Mr. Peterkin conceived this speech to be the very best extract of lore and sapience.

"Why is not the African mind equal to the Caucasian?" inquired young master, with that pointed naivete for which he was so remarkable.

"Oh, it tain't no use, Johnny, fur you to be talkin' that ar' way. It's all fine enoff in newspapers, but it won't do to bring it into practice, 'specially out here in the West."

"No, father, I begin to fear that it is of no avail to talk common sense and preach humanity in a community like this."

"Don't talk any more on this subject," said the doctor; "I am afraid it does Mr. John no particular good to be so painfully excited. I was going to propose to you, Mr. Peterkin, to send him South, either on a little coasting trip, or to Havana *via* New Orleans. I think this climate is too rigorous and uncertain for one of his frail constitution to remain in it during the winter."

"Well, doctor, I am perfectly willin' fur him to go, if I had anybody to go with him; but you see it wouldn't be safe to trust him by himself. Now an idee has jist struck me, which, if you'll agree to, will 'zackly suit me. 'Tis for you to go 'long; then he'd have a doctor to rinder him any sarvice he might need. Now Doct. if you'll go, I'll foot the bill, and pay you a good bonus in the bargain."

"Well, it will be a great professional sacrifice; but I'm willing to make it for a friend like you, and for a patient in whose recovery or improvement I feel so deeply interested."

"Make no sacrifices for me, dear doctor; my poor wreck of life is not worth a sacrifice; I can weather it out a little longer in this region. It requires a stronger air than that of the tropics to restore strength to my poor decayed lungs."

"Yes, but you must not despond," said the doctor.

"No, my boy, you musn't give up. You are too young to die. You are my only son, and I can't spare you." Again Mr. Peterkin turned uneasily in his chair.

"But tell me, doctor," he added, "don't you think he is growin' stronger?"

"Why, yes I do; and if he will consent to go South, I shall have strong hope of him."

"He must consent," exclaimed Mr. Peterkin, with a decided emphasis.

"You know my objection, doctor, yet I cannot oppose my wish against father's judgment; so I will go, but 'twill be without the least expectation of ever again seeing home."

"Oh, don't, don't, my boy," and Mr. Peterkin's voice faltered, and his eyes were very moist.

"Idols of clay!" I thought, "how frail ye are; albeit ye are manufactured out of humanity's finest porcelain, yet a rude touch, a slight jar, and the beautiful fabric is destroyed forever!"

Mr. Peterkin's treasure, his only son, was wasting slowly, inch by inch, before his eyes—dying with slow and silent certainty. The virus was in his blood, and no human aid could check its strides. The father looked on in speechless dread. He saw the insidious marks of the incurable malady. He read its ravages upon the broad white brow of his son, where the pulsing veins lay like tightly-drawn cords; and on the hueless lip, that was shrivelled like an autumn leaf; in the dilated pupil of that prophet-like eye; in the fiery spot that blazed upon each hollow cheek; and in the short, disturbed breathing that seemed to come from a brazen tube; in all these he traced the omens of that stealthy disease that robs us, like a thief in the night-time, of our riches, treasures.

"Well, my boy," began Mr. Peterkin, "you must prepare to start in the course of a few days."

"I am ready to leave at any moment, father; and, if we do

not start very soon, I am thinking you will have to consign me to the earth, rather than send me on a voyage pleasure-hunting."

A bright smile, though mournful as twilight's shadows, flitted over the pale face of young master as he said this.

"Why, Johnny, you are better this evening," said Miss Bradly, as she entered the room, rushed up to him, and began patting him affectionately on either cheek.

"Yes, I am better, good Miss Emily; but still feeble, oh so feeble! My spirits are better, but the restless fire that burns eternally here will give me no rest," and he placed his hand over his breast.

"Yes, but you must quench that fire."

"Where is the draught clear and pure enough to quench a flame so consuming?"

"The dew of divine grace can do it."

"Yes, but it descends not upon my dried and burnt spirit."

Mr. Peterkin turned off, and affected to take no note of this little colloquy, whilst Doctor Mandy began to chew furiously.

The fact is, the Peterkin family had begun to distrust Miss Bradly's principles ever since the day young master administered such a reproof to her muffled conscience; and in truth, I believe she had half-declared her opposition to the slave system; and they began to abate the fervor of their friendship for her. The young ladies, indeed, kept up their friendly intercourse with her, though with a modification of their former warmth.

I fancied that Miss Bradly looked happier, now that she had cast off disguise and stood forth in her true character. That cloud of faltering distrust that once hung round her like a filmy web, had been dissipated and she stood out, in full relief, with the beautiful robe of truth draping and dignifying her nature. Woman, when once she interests herself in the great cause of humanity, goes to work with an ability and ardor that put to shame the colder and slower action of man. The heart and mind co-work, and thus a woman, as if by the dictate of inspiration, will achieve with a single effort the mighty deed, for the attainment of which men spend years in idle planning. Women

have done much, and may yet achieve more toward the emancipation and enfranchisement of the world. The historic pages
glitter with the noble acts of heroic womanhood, and histories
yet unwritten will, I believe, proclaim the good which they
shall yet do. Who but the Maid of Orleans rescued her country?
Whose hand but woman's dealt the merited death-blow to one
of France's bloodiest tyrants? In all times, she has been
most loyal to the highest good. Woman has ever been brave!
She was the instrument of our redemption, and the early watcher
at the tomb of our Lord. To her heart the Saviour's doctrine came with a special welcome message. And I now believe
that through her agency will yet come the political ransom of
the slaves! God grant it, and speed on the blessed day!

I now looked upon Miss Bradly with the admiring interest
with which I used to regard her; and though I had never had
from her an explanation of the change or changes through
which she had passed since that memorable conversation recorded in the earlier pages of this book, I felt assured from the
fact that young master had learned to love her, that all was
right at the core of her heart; and I was willing to forgive her
for the timidity and vacillation that had caused her to play the
dissembler. The memorable example of the loving but weak
Apostle Peter should teach us to look leniently upon all those
who cannot pass safely through the ordeal of human contempt,
without having their principles, or at least actions, a little
warped. Of course there are higher natures, from whose fortitude the rack and the stake can provoke nothing but smiles;
but neither good St. Peter nor Miss Bradly were of such material.

"I am going to leave you very soon, Miss Emily."

"And where are you going, John?"

"They will send me to the South. As the poor slaves say,
I'm going down the river;" and a sweet smile flitted over that
gentle face.

"Who will accompany you?"

" Father wishes Doctor Mandy to go; but I fear it will be too great a professional sacrifice."

" Oh, some one must go with you. You shall not go alone."

" I do not wish to go at all. I shall see nothing in the South to please me. Those magnificent plantations of rice, sugar, and cotton, those lordly palaces, embowered in orange trees, those queenly magnolia groves, and all the thousand splendors that cover the coast with loveliness, will but recall to my mind the melancholy fact that slave-labor produces the whole. I shall fancy that some poor heart-broken negro man, or some hopeless mother or lonely wife watered those fields with tears. Oh, that the dropping of those sad eyes had, like the sowing of the dragon's teeth, produced a band of armed, bristling warriors, strong enough to conquer all the tyrants and liberate the captives !"

" This can never be accomplished suddenly. It must be the slow and gradual work of years. Like all schemes of reformation, it moves but by inches. Wise legislators have proposed means for the final abolition of slavery; but, though none have been deemed practicable, I look still for the advent of the day when the great sun shall look goldenly down upon the emancipation of this dusky tribe, and when the word slave shall nowhere find expression upon the lips of Christian men."

" When do you predict the advent of that millennial day ?"

" I fear it is far distant; yet is it pleasant to think that it will come, no matter at how remote an epoch."

" Distant is it only because men are not thoroughly Christianized. No man that will willingly hold his brother in bondage is a Christian. Moreover, the day is far off in the future, because of the ignorant pride of men. They wish to send the poor negro away to the unknown land from whence his ancestors were stolen. We virtually say to the Africans, now you have cultivated and made beautiful our continent, we have no further use for you. You have grown up, it is true, beneath the shadow of our trees, you were born upon our soil, your early associations are here. Your ignorance precludes you from the knowledge of the excellence of any other land : yet for all this we take no care, it is our business to drive you hence. Cross the ocean you must. Find a home in a strange country ; lay your broad shoulder to the work, and make for yourself an interest there. What wonder is it, if the poor, ignorant negro shakes his head mournfully, and says : " No, I would rather stay here ; I am a slave, it is true, but then I was born here, and here I will be buried. I am tightly kept, have a master and a mistress, but then I know what this is. Hard to endure, I grant it—but then it is known to me. I can bear on a little longer, till death sets me free. No, this is my native shore ; here let me stay." Their very ignorance begets a kind of philosophy that

> "Makes them rather bear those ills they have,
> Than fly to others that they know not of."

Now, why, I ask, have they not as much right to remain here as we have ? This is their birthplace as well as ours. We are, likewise, descendants of foreigners. If we drive them hence, what excuse have we for it ? Our forefathers were not the aborigines of this country. As well might the native red men say to us : " Fly, leave the Western continent, 'tis our home ; we will not let you stay here. You have cultivated it, now *we* will enjoy it. Go and labor elsewhere." What would we think of this ? Yet such is our line of conduct toward those poor creatures, who have toiled to adorn our homes Then again, we allow the Irish, Germans, and Hungarians, to dwell among us. Why ban the African ?"

" These, my young friend, are questions that have puzzled the wisest brains."

" If it entered more into the hearts, and disturbed the brains less, it would be better for them and for the slaves."

" Now, come, Miss Emily, I'm tired of hearing you and that boy talk all that nonsense. It's time you were both thinking of something else. You are too old to be indulgin' of him in

that ar' stuff. It will never come to any good. Them ar' niggers is allers gwine to be slaves, and white folks had better be
tendin' to what consarns 'emselves."

Such arguments as the foregoing were carried on every day.
Meanwhile we, who formed the subject of them, still went on in
our usual way, half-fed and half-clad, knocked and kicked like
dogs.

Amy went about her assigned work, with the same hard-set
composure with which she had begun. Talking little to any
one, she tried to discharge her duties with a docility and faith-
fulness very remarkable. Yet she sternly rebuked all conversation. I made many efforts to draw her out into a free, sociable
talk, and was always told that it was not agreeable to her.

I now had no companionship among those of my own color.
Aunt Polly was in the grave; Amy wrapped in the silence of
her own grief; and Sally (the successor of Aunt Polly in the
culinary department) was a sulky, ignorant woman, who did
not like to be sociable; and the men, with their beastly instincts, were objects of aversion to me. So my days and nights
passed in even deeper gloom than I had ever before known.

CHAPTER XXIII.

THE winter was now drawing to a close. The heavy, dreary winter, that had hung like an incubus upon my hours, was fast drawing to an end. Many a little, tuneful bird came chirping with the sunny days of the waning February. Already the sunbeam had begun to give us a hint of the spring-warmth; the ice had melted away, and the moistened roofs of the houses began to smoke with the drying breath of the sun, and little green pods were noticeable upon the dried branches of the forest trees. It was on such a day, when the eye begins to look round upon Nature, and almost expects to solve the wondrous phenomenon of vegetation, that I was engaged arranging Miss Jane's wardrobe. I had just done up some laces for her, and finished off a nice silk morning-dress. She was making extensive preparations for a visit to the city of L. The protracted rigors of the winter and her own fancied ill-health had induced her to postpone the trip until the opening of spring.

It was decided that I should accompany her as lady's maid; and the fact is, I was desirous of any change from the wearying monotony of my life.

Young master had been absent during the whole winter. Frequent letters from Dr. Mandy (who had accompanied him) informed the family of his slowly-improving health; yet the doctor stated in each communication that he was not strong enough to write a letter himself. This alarmed me, for I knew that he must be excessively weak, if he denied himself the gratification of writing to his family. Miss Bradly came to

the house but seldom ; and then only to inquire the news from
young master. Her principles upon the slavery question had
become pretty well known in the neighborhood; so her residence there was not the most pleasant. Inuendoes, of a most
insulting character, had been thrown out, highly prejudicial to
her situation. Foul slanders were in busy circulation about
her, and she began to be a taboed person. So I was not surprised to hear her tell Miss Jane that she thought of returning
to the North early in the spring. I had never held any private
conversation with her since that memorable one ; for now that
her principles were known, she was too much marked for a
slave to be allowed to speak with her alone. Her sorrowful
face struck me with pity. I knew her to be one of that time-
serving kind, by whom the loss of caste and social position is
regarded as the most fell disaster.

As I turned the key of Miss Jane's wardrobe, she came into
the room, with an unusually excited manner, exclaiming,

" Ann, where is your Miss Tildy ?"

Upon my answering that I did not know, she bade me go
and seek her instantly, and say that she wished to speak with
her. As I left the room, I observed Miss Jane draw a letter
from the folds of her dress. This was hint enough. My
mother-wit told me the rest.

Finding Miss Tildy with a book, in a quiet corner of the
parlor, I delivered Miss Jane's message, and withdrew. The
contents of Miss Jane's letter soon became known ; for it was,
to her, of such an exciting nature, that it could not be held in
secrecy. The letter was from Mr. Sommerville, and announced
that he would pay her a visit in the course of a few days.

And, for the next " few days," the whole house was in a
perfect consternation. All hands were at work. Carpets were
taken up, shaken, and put down again with the " clean side"
up. Paint was scoured, windows were washed ; the spare bed-
room was re-arranged, and adjusted in style ; the French couch
was overspread with Miss Tildy's silk quilt, that had taken the
prize at the Agricultural Fair ; and fresh bouquets were col-

lected from the green-house, and placed upon the mantel.
Everything looked very nice about the house, and in the kitch-
en all sorts of culinary preparations had gone on. Cakes,
cookies, and confections had been made in abundance. As
Amy expressed it, in her quaintly comical way, " Christmas is
comin' again." It was the first and only time since the departure of " the children," that I had heard her indulge in any of
her old drollery.

At length the "day" arrived, and with it came Mr. Summerville. Whilst he remained with us, everything went off in the
way that Miss Jane desired. There were fine dinners, with plenty
of wine, roast turkey, curry powder, desserts, &c. The silver
and best china had been brought out, and Mr. Peterkin be-
haved himself as well as he could. He even consented to use
a silver fork, which, considering his prejudice against the article, was quite a concession for him to make.

Time sped on (as it always will do), and brought the end of
the week, and with it, the end of Mr. Summerville's visit. I
thought, from a certain softening of Miss Jane's eye, and from
the length of the parting interview, that " *matters*" had been
arranged between her and Mr. Summerville. After the last
adieu had been given, and Miss Jane had rubbed her eyes
enough with her fine pocket-handkerchief (or, perhaps, in this
case, it would be well to employ the suggestion of a modern
author, and say her "lachrymal,") I say, after all was over,
and Mr. Summerville's interesting form was fairly lost in the
distance, Miss Tildy proposed that they should settle down to
their usual manner of living. Accordingly, the silver was all
rubbed brightly by Amy, whose business it was, then handed
over to Miss Tildy to be locked up in the bureau.

For a few weeks matters went on with their usual dullness.
Master was still smoking his cob-pipe, kicking negroes, and
blaspheming; and Miss Jane making up little articles for the
approaching visit to the city. She and Miss Tildy sat a great
deal in their own room, talking and speculating upon the coming
joys. Passing in and out, I frequently caught fragments of

conversation that let me into many of their secrets. Thus I
learned that Miss Jane's chief object in visiting the city was to
purchase a bridal trousseau, that Mr. Sommerville "had proposed," and, of course, been accepted. He lived in the city;
so it was decided that, after the celebration of the nuptial rite,
Miss Tildy should accompany the bride to her new home, and
remain with her for several weeks.

Sundry little lace caps were manufactured; handkerchiefs
embroidered; dresses made and altered; collars cut, and an im-
mence deal of "transfering" was done by the sisters Peterkin.

We, of the "colored population," were stinted even more
than formerly; for they deemed it expedient to economize, in
order to be the better able to meet the pecuniary exigencies of
the marriage. Thus time wore along, heavily enough for the
slaves; but doubtless delightful to the white family. The enjoyment of pleasure, like all other prerogatives, they considered as exclusively their own.

Time, in its rugged course, had brought no change to Amy.
If her heart had learned to bear its bereavement better, or had
grown more tender in its anxious waiting, we knew it not from
her word or manner. The same settled, rocky look, the same
abstracted air, marked her deportment. Never once had I heard
her laugh, or seen her weep. She still avoided conversation,
and was assiduous in the discharge of her domestic duties. If
she did a piece of work well, and was praised for it, she received the praise with the same indifferent air; or if, as was
most frequently the case, she was harshly chided and severely
punished, 'twas all the same. No tone or word could move
those rigid features.

One evening Miss Bradly came over to see the young ladies,
and inquire the latest news from young master. Miss Jane
gave orders that the table should be set with great care, and
all the silver displayed. They had long since lost their olden
familiarity, and, out of respect to the present coldness that existed between them, they (the Misses Peterkin) desired to show

off "before the discredited school-mistress." I heard Miss Bradly ask Mr. Peterkin when he heard from young master.

"I've just got a letter from Dr. Mandy. They ar' still in New Orleans; but expected to start for home in 'bout three days. The doctor gives me very little cause for hope; says Johnny is mighty weak, and had a pretty tough cough. He says the night-sweats can't be broke; and the boy is very weak, not able to set up an hour at a time. This is very discouragin',' Miss Emily. Sometimes it 'pears like 'twould kill me, too, my heart is so sot 'pon that boy;" and here Mr. Peterkin began to smoke with great violence, a sure sign that he was laboring under intense excitement.

"He is a very noble youth," said Miss Bradly, with a quivering voice and a moist eye; "I am deeply attached to him, and the thought of his death is one fraught with pain to me. I hope Doctor Mandy is deceived in the prognostics he deems so bad. Johnny's life is a bright example, and one that is needed."

"Yes, you think it will aid the Abolition cause ; but not in this region, I can assure you," said Miss Tildy, as she tossed her head knowingly. I'd like to know where Johnny learned all the Anti-slavery cant. Do you know, Miss Emily, that your incendiary principles lost you caste in this neighborhood, where you once stood as a model?"

Miss Tildy had touched Miss Bradly in her vulnerable point. "Caste" was a thing that she valued above reputation, and reckoned more desirable than honor. Had it not been for a certain goodness of heart, from which she could not escape (though she had offten tried) she would have renounced her Anti-slavery sentiments and never again avowed them ; but young master's words had power to rescue her almost shipwrecked principles, and then, whilst smarting under the lash of his rebuke, she attempted, like many an astute politician, to "run on both sides of the question ;" but this was an equivocal position that the "out and out" Kentuckians were not going to allow. She had to be, in their distinct phraseology, "one thing or the other ;" and, accordingly, aided by young master and her sense of jus-

tice, she avowed herself "the other." And, of course, with
this avowal, came the loss of cherished friends. In troops they
fell away from her. Their averted looks and distant nods
nearly drove her mad. If young master had been by to encourage and sustain her with gracious words, she could have
better borne it; but, single-handed and alone, she could not battle against adversity. And now this speech of Miss Tildy's
was very untimely. She winced under it, yet dared not reply.
What a contemptible character, to the brave mind, seems one
lacking moral courage!

"I want to see Johnny once again, and then I shall leave for
the North," said Miss Bradly, in a pitiful tone.

"See Naples and die, eh?" laughed Miss Tildy.

"Always and ever ready with your fun," replied Miss
Bradly.

At first her wiry turnings, her open and shameless sycophan-
cy, and now her cringing and fawning upon the Peterkins,
caused me to lose all respect for her. In the hour of her
trouble, when deserted by those whom she had loved as friends,
when her pecuniary prospects were blighted, I felt deeply for
her, and even forgave the falsehood; but now when I saw her
shrink from the taunt and invective of Miss Tildy, and then
minister to her vanity, I felt that she was too little even for contempt. At tea, that evening, whilst serving the table, I was
surprised to observe Miss Jane's face very red with anger, and
her manner exceedingly irascible. I began to wonder if I had
done anything to exasperate her; but could think of no offence
of which I had been guilty. I knew from the way in which
she conversed with all at the table, that none of them were of-
fenders. I was the more surprised at her anger, as she had
been, for the last week, in such an excellent humor, getting
herself ready for the visit to the city. Oh, how I dreaded to
see Miss Bradly leave, for then, I knew the storm would break
in all its fury!

I was standing in the kitchen, alone, trying to think what
could have offended Miss Jane, when Amy came up to me, saying,

" Oh, Ann, two silver forks is lost, an' Miss Tildy done 'cuse me of stealin' 'em, an' I declar 'fore heaven, I gib ebery one of 'em to Miss Tildy de mornin' Misser Summerbille lef, an' now she done told Miss Jane dat I told a lie, and that I stole 'em. Lor' knows what dey is gwine to do 'long wid me; but I don't kere much, so dey kills me soon and sets me out my misery at once."

" When did they miss the forks ?"

" Wy, to-night, when I went to set de table, I found dat two of 'em wasn't dar ; so I axed Miss Tildy whar dey was, an' she said she didn't know. Den I axed Miss Jane ; she say, ' ax Miss Tildy.' Den when I told Miss Tildy dat, she got mad ; struck me a lick right cross my face. Den I told her bout de time Mr. Summerbille lef, when I give 'em to her. She say, ' you's a liar, an' hab stole 'em.' Den I begun to de- clar I hadn't, and she call Miss Jane, and say to her dat she knowed I hab stole 'em, and Miss Jane got mad ; kicked me, pulled my har till I screamed ; den I 'spose she did 'ant want Miss Bradly to hear me ; so she stopped, but swar she'd beat me to death if I didn't get 'em fur her right off. Now, Ann, I doesn't know whar dey is, if I was to be kilt for it."

She drew the back of her hand across her eyes, and I saw that it was moist. I was glad of this, for her silent endur- ance was more horrible to look upon than this physical soft- ness.

" Oh, God !" I exclaimed, " I would that young master were here."

" What fur, Ann ?"

" He might intercede and prevent them from using you so cruelly."

" I doesn't wish he was har ; for I lubs young Masser, an' he is good ; if he was to see me a sufferin' it wud stress him, an' make his complaint worse ; an' he couldn't do no good ; for dey will beat me, no matter who begs. Ob, it does seem so strange that black people was eber made. I is glad dat de chillen is'nt har ; for de sight ob dem cryin' round de ' post,' wud nearly kill me. I can bar anythin' fur myself, but not fur 'em. Oh, I hopes dey is dead."

And here she heaved a dreadful groan. This was the first time I had heard her allude to them, and I felt a choking rush in my throat.

"Don't cry, Ann, take kere ob yourself. It 'pears like my time has come. I don't feel 'feard, an' dis is de fust time I'se eber bin able to speak 'bout de chillen. If eber you sees 'em, (I niver will), tell 'em dat I niver did forget 'em ; dat night an' day my mind was sot on 'em, an' please, Ann, gib 'em dis."

Here she took from her neck a string that held her mother's gift, and the coin young master had given her, suspended to it. She looked at it long and wistfully, then, slowly pressing it to her lips, she said in a low, plaintive voice that went to my heart, "Poor Mammy."

I then took it from her, and hid it in my pocket. A cold horror stole over me. I had not the power to gainsay her ; for an instinctive idea that something terrible was going to occur, chained my lips.

"Ann, I thanks you for all your kindness to me. I hopes you may hab a better time den I has hab. I feel, Ann, as if I niver should come down from dat post alive.

"Trust in God, Amy."

She shook her head despairingly.

"He will save you."

"No, God don't kare for black folks."

"What did young master tell you about that ? Did he not say God loved all His creatures alike ?"

"Yes, but black folks aint God's critters."

"Yes, they are, just as much as white people."

"No dey aint."

"Oh, Amy, I wish I could make you understand how it is."

"You kant make me belieb dat ar' way, no how you can fix it. God don't kare what a comes ob niggers ; an' I is glad he don't, kase when I dies, I'll jist lay down and rot like de worms, and dere wont be no white folks to 'buse me."

"No, there will be no white folks to abuse you in heaven; but God and His angels will love you, if you will do well and try to get there."

"I don't want to go ther, for God is one of the white people, and, in course, he'd beat de niggers."

Oh, was not this fearful, fearful ignorance? Through the solid rock of her obtusity, I could, with no argument of mine, make an aperture for a ray of heavenly light to penetrate. Do Christians, who send off missionaries, realize that heathendom exists in their very midst; aye, almost at their own hearthstone? Let them enlighten those that dwell in the bonds of night on their own borders; then shall their efforts in distant lands be blest. Numberless instances, such as the one I have recorded, exist in the slave States. The masters who instruct their slaves in religion, could be numbered; and I will venture to assert that, if the census were taken in the State of Kentucky, the number would not exceed twenty. Here and there you will find an instance of a mistress who will, perhaps, on a Sunday evening, talk to a female slave about the propriety of behaving herself; but the gist of the argument, the hinge upon which it turns, is—"obey your master and mistress;" upon this one precept hang all the law and the prophets."

That night, after my house duties were discharged, I went to the cabin, where I found Amy lying on her face, weeping bitterly. I lifted her up, and tried to console her; but she exclaimed, with more energy than I had ever heard her,

"Ann, every ting seems so dark to me. I kan't see past tomorrow. I has bin thinkin' of Aunt Polly; I keeps seein' her, no matter what way I turns."

"You are frightened," I ventured to say.

"No, I isn't, but I feels curus."

"Let me teach you to pray."

"Will it do me any good?"

"Yes, if you put faith in God."

"What's faith?"

"Believe that God is strong and willing to save you; that is faith."

" Who is God ?   I never seed him."

" No, but He sees you."

" Whar is He ?" and she looked fearfully around the room, in which the scanty fire threw a feeble glare.

" Everywhere.   He is everywhere," I answered.

" Is He in dis room ?" she asked in terror, and drew near me.

" Yes, He is here."

" Oh lor !   He may tell Masser on me.

This ignorance may, to the careless reader, seem laughable; but, to me, it was most horrible, and I could not repress my tears. Here was the force of education. Master was to her the strongest thing or person in existence. Of course she could not understand a higher power than that which had governed her life. There are hundreds as ignorant ; but no missionaries come to enlighten them !

" Oh, don't speak that way ; you know God made you."

" Yes, but dat was to please Masser. He made me fur to be a slave."

Now, how would the religious slave-holder answer that ?

I strove, but with no success, to make her understand that over her soul, her temporal master had no control; but her ignorance could not see a difference between the body and soul. Whoever owned the former, she thought, was entitled to the latter. Finding I could make no impression upon her mind, I lay down and tried to sleep; but rest was an alien to me. I dreaded the breaking of the morn. Poor Amy slept, and I was glad that she did. Her overtaxed body yielded itself up to the most profound rest. In the morning, when I saw her sleeping so soundly on the pallet, I disliked to arouse her. I felt, as I fancied a human jailer must feel, whose business it is to awaken a criminal on the morning of his execution; yet I had it to do, for, if she had been tardy at her work, it would have enraged her tyrants the more, and been worse for her.

Rubbing her eyes, she sat upright on the pallet and murmured,

" Dis is de day. I's to be led to de post, and maybe kilt."

I dared not comfort her, and only bade her to make haste and attend to her work.

CHAPTER XXIV.

THE PUNISHMENT—CRUELTY—ITS FATAL CONSEQUENCE—DEATH.

At breakfast, Miss Jane shook her head at Amy, saying, "I'll settle accounts with you, presently."

I wondered if that tremulous form, that stood eyeing her in affright, did not soften her; but no, the "shaking culprit," as she styled Amy, was the very creature upon whom she desired to deal swift justice.

Pitiable was the sight in the kitchen, where Jake and Dan, great stout fellows, were making their breakfasts off of scraps of meat, old bones and corn-bread, whilst the aroma of coffee, broiled chicken, and egg-cakes was wafted to them from the house-table.

"I wish't I had somepin' more to eat," said Dan.

"You's never satisfy," replied Sally, the cook; "you gits jist as much as de balance, yit you makes de most complaints."

"No I doesn't."

"Yes, you does; don't he, Jake?"

"Why, to be sartain he does," said Jake, who of late had agreed to live with Sally as a wife. Of course no matrimonial rite was allowed, for Mr. Peterkin was consistent enough to say, that, as the law did not recognize the validity of negro marriages, he saw no use of the tomfoolery of a preacher in the case; and this is all reasonable enough.

"You allers takes Sal's part," said Dan, "now sense she has got to be your wife; you and her is allers colloged together agin' de rest ov us."

"Wal, haint I right for to 'tect my ole 'oman?"

"Now, ha, ha!" cried Nace, as he entered, "de idee ob yer 'tectin' a wife! I jist wisht Masser sell yer apart, den whar is yer 'tection ob one anoder?"

"Oh, dat am very different. Den I'd jist git me anoder ole 'oman, an' she'd git her anoder ole man."

"Sure an' I would," was Sally's reply; "hain't I done had five old men already, an' den if Jake be sole, I'de git somebody else."

"White folks don't do dat ar' way," interposed Dan, as he picked away at a bone.

"In course dey don't. Why should dey?" put in Nace. "Ain't dey our Massers, and habn't dey dar own way in ebery ting?"

"I wisht I'd bin born white," added Dan.

"Ya, ya, dat is funny!"

"Do de free colored folks live like de whites?" asked Sally.

"Why, laws, yes; once when I went with Masser to L.," Nace began, "at de tavern whar we put up, dar was a free colored man what waited on de table, and anoder one what kipt barber-shop in de tavern. Wal, dey was drest as nice as white men. Dar dey had dar standin' collar, and nice cravat, and dar broadcloth, and dar white handkersher; and de barber, he had some wool growin' on his upper lip jist like de quality men. Ya, ya, but I sed dis am funny; so when I 'gin to talk jist as dough dey was niggers same as I is, dey straighten 'emselves up and tell me dat I was a speakin' to a gemman. Wal, says I, haint your faces black as mine? Niggers aint gemmen, says I, for I thought I'd take dar airs down; but den, dey spunk up and say dey was not niggers, but colored pussons, and dey call one anoder Mr. Wal, I t'ought it was quare enoff; and more an' dat, white folks speak 'spectable to 'em, jist same as dey war white. Whole lot ob white gemmans come in de barber-shop to be shaved; and den dey'd pay de barber, and maybe like as not, set down and talk 'long wid him."

There is no telling how long the garrulous Nace would have continued the narration of what he saw in L—, had he not been suddenly interrupted by the entrance of Miss Tildy, inquiring for Amy.

Instantly all of them assumed that cheerful, smiling, sycophantic manner, which is well known to all who have ever looked in at the kitchen of a slaveholder. Amy stood out from the group to answer Miss Tildy's summons. I shall never forget the expression of subdued misery that was limned upon her face.

"Come in the house and account for the loss of those forks," said Miss Tildy, in the most peremptory manner.

Amy made no reply to this; but followed the lady into the house. There she was court-marshalled, and of course, found guilty of a high misdemeanor.

"Wal," said Mr. Peterkin, "we'll see if the 'post' can't draw from you whar you've put 'em. Come with me."

With a face the picture of despair, she followed.

Upon reaching the post, she was fastened to it by the wrist and ankle fetters; and Mr. Peterkin, foaming with rage, dipped his cowhide in the strongest brine that could be made, and drawing it up with a flourish, let it descend upon her uncovered back with a lacerating stroke. Heavens! what a shriek she gave! Another blow, another and a deeper stripe, and cry after cry came from the hapless victim!

"Whar is the forks?" thundered Mr. Peterkin, "tell me, or I'll have the worth out of yer cussed hide."

"Indeed, indeed, Masser, I doesn't know."

"You are a liar," and another and a severer blow.

"Whar is they?"

"I give 'em to Miss Jane, Masser, indeed I did."

"Take that, you liar," and again he struck her, and thus he continued until he had to stop from exhaustion. There she stood, partially naked, bleeding at every wound, yet none of us dared go near and offer her even a glass of cold water.

"Has she told where they are?" asked Miss Tildy.

"No, she says she give 'em to you."

"Well, she tells an infamous lie; and I hope you will beat

her until pain forces her to acknowledge what she has done with them."

"Oh, I'll git it out of her yet, and by blood, too."

"Yes, father, Amy needs a good whipping," said Miss Jane, "for she has been sulky ever since we took her in the house. Two or three times I've thought of asking you to have her taken to the post."

"Yes, I've noticed that she's give herself a good many ars. It does me rale good to take 'em out of her."

"Yes, father, you are a real negro-breaker. They don't dare behave badly where you are."

This, Mr. Peterkin regarded as high praise; for, whenever he related the good qualities of a favorite friend, he invariably mentioned that he was a "tight master;" so he smiled at his daughter's compliment.

"Yes," said Miss Tildy, "whenever father approaches, the darkies should set up the tune, 'See the conquering hero comes.' "

"Good, first-rate, Tildy," replied Miss Jane.

"'Till is a wit."

"Yes, you are both high-larn't gals, a-head of yer pappy."

"Oh, father, please don't speak in that way."

"It was the fashion when I was edicated."

"Just listen," they both exclaimed.

"Jake," called out Mr. Peterkin, whose wrath was getting excited by the criticisms of his daughters, "go and bring Amy here."

In a few moments Jake returned, accompanied by Amy. The blood was oozing through the body and sleeves of the frock that she had hastily thrown on.

"Whar's the spoons?" thundered out Mr. Peterkin.

"I give 'em to Miss Tildy."

"You are a liar," said Miss Tildy, as she dashed up to her, and struck her a severe blow on the temple with a heated poker. Amy dared not parry the blow; but, as she received it, she fell fainting to the floor. Mr. Peterkin ordered Jake to take her out of their presence.

She was taken to the cabin and left lying on the floor. When I went in to see her, a horrid spectacle met my view! There she lay stretched upon the floor, blood oozing from her whole body. I washed it off nicely and greased her wounds, as poor Aunt Polly had once done for me; but these attentions had to be rendered in a very secret manner. It would have been called treason, and punished as such, if I had been discovered.

I had scarcely got her cleansed, and her wounds dressed, before she was sent for again.

"Now," said Miss Tildy, "if you will tell me what you did with the forks, I will excuse you; but, if you dare to say you don't know, I'll beat you to death with this," and she held up a bunch of briery switches, that she had tied together. Now only imagine briars digging and scraping that already lacerated flesh, and you will not blame the equivocation to which the poor wretch was driven.

"Where are they?" asked Miss Jane, and her face was frightful as the Medusa's.

"I hid 'em under a barrel out in the back yard."

"Well, go and get them."

"Stay," said Miss Jane, "I'll go with you, and see if they are there."

Accordingly she went off with her, but they were not there.

"Now, where are they, liar?" she asked.

"Oh, Miss Jane, I put 'em here; but I 'spect somebody's done stole 'em."

"No, you never put them there," said Miss Tildy. "Now tell me where they are, or I'll give you this with a vengeance," and she shook the briers.

"I put 'em in my box in the cabin."

And thither they went to look for them. Not finding them there, the tortured girl then named some other place, but with as little success they looked elsewhere.

"Now," said Miss Tildy, "I have done all that the most hu-

mane or just could demand; and I find that nothing but a touch
of this can get the truth from you, so come with me." She took
her to the "lock-up," and secured the door within. Such
screams as issued thence, I pray heaven may never hear
again. It seemed as if a fury's strength endowed Miss Tildy's
arm.

When she came out she was pale from fatigue.

"I've beaten that girl till I've no strength in me, and she has
less life in her; yet she will not say what she did with the
forks."

"I'll go in and see if I can't get it out of her," said Miss Jane.

"Wait awhile, Jane, maybe she will, after a little reflection,
agree to tell the truth about it.

"Never," said Miss Jane, "a nigger will never tell the truth
till it is beat out of her." So saying she took the key from Miss
Tildy, and bade me follow her. I had rather she had told me
to hang myself.

When she unlocked the door, I dared not look in. My eyes
were riveted to the ground until I heard Miss Jane say:

"Get up, you hussy."

There, lying on the ground, more like a heap of clotted gore
than a human being, I beheld the miserable Amy.

"Why don't she get up?" inquired Miss Jane. I did not reply. Taking the cowhide, she gave her a severe lick, and the
wretch cried out, "Oh, Lord!"

"The Lord won't hear a liar," said Miss Jane.

"Oh, what will 'come of me?"

"*Death*, if you don't confess what you did with the forks."

"Oh God, hab mercy! Miss Jane, please don't beat me any
more. My poor back is so sore. It aches and smarts dreadful,"
and she lifted up her face, which was one mass of raw flesh; and
wiping or trying to wipe the blood away from her eyes with a
piece of her sleeve that had been cut from her body, she besought Miss Jane to have mercy on her; but the spirit of her
father was too strongly inherited for Jane Peterkin to know
aught of human pity.

"Where are the forks?"

"Oh, law! oh, law!" Amy cried out, "I swar I doesn't know anything 'bout 'em."

Such blows as followed I have not the heart to describe; for they descended upon flesh already horribly mangled.

The poor girl looked up to me, crying out:

"Oh, Ann, beg for me."

"Miss Jane," I ventured to say; but the tigress turned and struck me such a blow across the face, that I was blinded for full five minutes.

"There, take that! you impudent hussy. Do you dare to ask me not to punish a thief?"

I made no reply, but withdrew from her presence to cleanse my face from the blood that was flowing from the wound.

As I bathed my face and bound it up, I wondered if acts such as these had ever been reported to those clergymen, who so stoutly maintain that slavery is just, right, *and almost* available unto salvation. I cannot think that they do understand it in all its direful wrongs. They look upon the institution, doubtless, as one of domestic servitude, where a strong attachment exists between the slave and his owner; but, alas! all that is generally fabulous, worse than fictitious. I can fearlessly assert that I never knew a single case, where this sort of feeling was cherished. The very nature of slavery precludes the existence of such a feeling. Read the legal definition of it as contained in the statute books of Kentucky and Virginia, and how, I ask you, can there be, on the slave's part, a love for his owner? Oh, no, that is the strangest resort, the fag-end of argument; that most transparent fiction. Love, indeed! The slave-master love his slave! Did Cain love Abel? Did Herod love those innocents, whom, by a bloody edict, he consigned to death? In the same category of lovers will we place the slave-owner.

When Miss Jane had beaten Amy until *she* was satisfied, she came, with a face blazing, like Mars, from the "lock-up."

"Well, she confesses now, that she put the forks under the corner of a log, near the poultry coop."

10

" Its only another one of her lies," replied Miss Tildy.

" Well, if it is, I'll beat her until she tells the truth, or I'll kill her."

So saying, she started off to examine the spot. I felt that this was but another subterfuge, devised by the poor wretch to gain a few moments' respite.

The examination proved, as I had anticipated, a failure.

" What's to be done?" inquired Miss Tildy.

"Leave her a few moments longer to herself, and then if the truth is not obtained from her, kill her."   These words came hissing though her clenched teeth.

" It won't do to kill her," said Miss Tildy.

" I don't care much if I do."

" We would be tried for murder."

" Who would be our accusers?   Who the witnesses?   You forget that Jones is not here to testify."

" Ah, and so we are safe."

" Oh, I never premeditate anything without counting the cost."

" But then the loss of property !"

" I'd rather gratify my revenge than have five hundred dollars, which would be her highest market value."

Tell me, honest reader, was not she, at heart, a murderess? Did she not plan and premeditate the deed?   Who were her accusers?   That God whose first law she had outraged; that same God who asked Cain for his slain brother.

"Now," said Miss Jane, after she had given the poor creature only a few moments relief, "now let me go and see what that wretch has to say about the forks."

" More lies," added Miss Tildy.

" Then her fate is sealed," said the human hyena.

Turning to me, she added, in the most authoritative manner,

" Come with me, and mind that you obey me ; none of your impertinent tears, or I'll give you this."

And she struck me a lick across the shoulders. I can assure you I felt but little inclination to do anything whereby such a penalty might be incurred. Taking the key of the "lock up" from her pocket, she ordered me to open the door. With a trembling hand I obeyed. Slowly the old, rusty-hinged door swung open, and oh, heavens! what a sight it revealed! There, in the centre of the dismal room, suspended from a spoke, about three feet from the ground, was the body of Amy! Driven by desperation, goaded to frenzy, she had actually hung herself! Oh, God! that fearful sight is burnt in on my brain, with a power that no wave of Lethe can ever wash out! There, covered with clotted blood, bruised and mangled, hung the wretched girl! There, a bleeding, broken monument of the white man's and white woman's cruelty! God of my sires! is there for us no redress? And Miss Jane—what did she do? Why, she screamed, and almost swooned with fright! Ay, too late it was to rend the welkin with her cries of distress. She had done the deed! Upon her head rested the sin of that freshly-shed blood! She was the real murderess. Oh, frightful shall be her nights! Peopled with racks, execution-blocks, and ghastly gallows-poles, shall be her dreams! At the lone hour of midnight, a wan and bloody corse shall glide around her bed-side, and shriek into her trembling ear the horrid word "murderess!" Let me still remain in bondage, call me still by the ignoble title of slave, but leave me the unbought and priceless inheritance of a stainless conscience. I am free of murder before God and man. Still riot in your wealth; still batten on inhumanity, women of the white complexion, but of the black hearts! I envy you not. Still let me rejoice in a darker face, but a snowy, self-approving conscience.

Miss Jane's screams brought Mr. Peterkin, Miss Tildy and the servants to her side. There, in front of the open door of the lock-up, they stood, gazing upon that revolting spectacle! No word was spoken. Each regarded the others in awe. At length, Mr. Peterkin, whose heartlessness was equal to any emergency, spoke to Jake:

"Cut down that body, and bury it instantly."

With this, they all turned away from the tragical spot; but

I, though physically weak of nerve, still remained. That poor, bereaved girl had been an object of interest to me; and I could not now leave her distorted and lifeless body. Cold-hearted ones were around her; no friendly eye looked upon her mangled corse, and I shuddered when I saw Jake and Dan rudely handle the body upon which death had set its sacred seal.

> " One more unfortunate,
>   Weary of breath;
> Rashly importunate,
>   Gone to her death.
>
> * * * * *
> Swift to be hurled,
>   Anywhere, anywhere,
> Out of the world."

This I felt had been her history! This should have been her epitaph; but, alas for her, there would be reared no recording stone. All that she had achieved in life was the few inches of ground wherein they laid her, and the shovel full of dirt with which they covered her. Poor thing! I was not allowed to dress the body for the grave. Hurriedly they dug a hole and tossed her in. I was the only one who consecrated the obsequies with funeral tears. A coarse joy and ribald jests rang from the lips of the grave-diggers; but I was there to weep and water the spot with tributary tears.

> " Perishing gloomily,
>   Spurred by contumely,
> Cold inhumanity,
> Burning insanity,
>   Into her rest,
> Cross her hands humbly,
> As if praying dumbly,
>   Over her breast."

CHAPTER XXV.

CONVERSATION OF THE FATHER AND SON—THE DISCOVERY; ITS CONSEQUENCES—DEATH OF THE YOUNG AND BEAUTIFUL.

VERY lonely to me were the nights that succeeded Amy's death. I spent them alone in the cabin. A strange kind of superstition took possession of me ! The room was peopled with unearthly guests. I buried my face in the bed-covering, as if that could protect me or exclude supernatural visitors. For two weeks I scarcely slept at all; and my constitution had begun to sink under the over-taxation. This was all the worse, as Amy's death entailed upon me a double portion of work.

"What !" said Mr. Peterkin to me, one day, "are you agoin to die, too, Ann? Any time you gits in the notion, jist let me know, and I'll give you rope enough to do it."

In this taunting way he frequently alluded to that fatal tragedy which should have bowed his head with shame and remorse.

Young master had returned, but not at all benefited by his trip. A deep carnation was burnt into his shrivelled cheek, and he walked with a feeble, tottering step. The least physical exertion would bring on a violent paroxysm of coughing. The unnatural glitter of his eye, with its purple surroundings, gave me great uneasiness; but he was the same gentle, kind-spoken young master that he had ever been. His glossy, golden hair had a dead, dry appearance; whilst his chest was fearfully sunken; yet his father refused to believe that all these marks were the heralds of the great enemy's approach.

"The spring will cure you, my boy."

"No, father, the spring is coming fast; but long before its

flowers begin to scent the vernal gales, I shall have passed through the narrow gateway of the tomb."

"No, it shall not be. All my money shall go to save you."

"I am purchased, father, with a richer price than gold; the inestimable blood of the Lamb has long since paid my ransom; I go to my father in heaven."

"Oh, my son! you want to go; you want to leave me. You do not love your father."

"Yes, I do love you, father, very dearly; and I would that you were going with me to that lovely land."

"I shill never go thar."

"'Tis that fear that is killing me, father."

"What could I, now, do to be saved?"

"Believe in the Lord Jesus, and be baptized."

"Is that all?"

"Yes, that is all; but it embraces a good deal, dear father; a good deal more than most persons deserve. In order to a perfect belief in the Lord Jesus, you must act consistently with that belief. You must deal justly. Abundantly give to the poor, and, above all, you must love mercy, and do mercifully to all. Now I approach the great subject upon which I fear you will stumble. You must," and he pronounced the words very slowly, "liberate your slaves." There was a fair gleam from his eyes when he said this.

Mr. Peterkin turned uneasily in his chair. He did not wish to encourage a conversation upon this subject.

One evening, when it had been raining for two or three days, and the damp condition of the atmosphere had greatly increased young master's complaint, he called me to his bedside.

"Ann," he said, in that deep, sepulchral tone, "I wish to ask you a question, and I urge you not to deceive me. Remember I am dying, and it will be a great crime to tell me a falsehood."

I assured him that I would answer him with a faithful regard to truth.

"Then tell me what occasioned Amy's death? Did she come to it by violence?"

I shall never forget the deep, penetrating glance that he fixed upon me. It was an inquiry that went to my soul. I could not have answered him falsely.

Calmly, quietly, and without exaggeration, I told him all the circumstances of her death.

"Murder!" he exclaimed, "murder, foul and most unnatural!"

I saw him wipe the tears from his hollow eyes, and that sunken chest heaved with vivid emotion.

Mr. Peterkin came in, and was much surprised to find young master so excited.

"What is the matter, my boy?"

"The same old trouble, father, these unfortunate negroes."

"Hang 'em; let them go to the d—l, at once. They are not worth all this consarn on your part."

"Father, they possess immortal souls, and are a part of Christ's purchase."

"Oh, that kind of talk does very well for preachers and church members."

"It should do for all humanity."

"I doesn't know what pity means whar a nigger is consarned."

"And 'tis this feeling in you that has cost me my life."

"Confound thar black hides. Every one of 'em that ever growed in Afriky isn't worth that price."

"Their souls are as precious in God's eyes as ours, and the laws of man should recognize their lives as valuable."

"Oh, now, my boy! don't talk any more 'bout it. It only 'stresses you for nothing."

"No, it distresses me for a great deal. For the value of Christ-purchased souls."

Mr. Peterkin concluded the argument as he usually did, when it reached a knotty point, by leaving. All that evening I noticed that young master was unusually restless and feverish. His mournful eyes would follow me withersoever I moved about the room. From the constant and earnest movement of his lips, I knew that he was engaged in prayer.

When Miss Bradly came in and looked at him, I thought, from the frightened expression of her face, that she detected some alarming symptoms. This apprehension was confirmed by the manner of Dr. Mandy. All the rest of the evening I wandered near Miss Bradly and the doctor, trying to catch, from their conversation, what they thought of young master's condition; but they were very guarded in what they said, well knowing how acutely sensitive Mr. Peterkin was on the subject. Miss Jane and Miss Tildy did not appear in the least anxious or uneasy about him. They sewed away upon their silks and laces, never once thinking that the angel of death was hovering over their household and about to snatch from their embrace one of their most cherished idols Verily, oh, Death, thou art like a thief in the night ; with thy still, feline tread, thou enterest our chambers and stealest our very breath away without one admonition of thy coming !

But not so came he to young master. As a small-voiced angel, with blessings concealed beneath his shadowy wing, he came, the herald of better days to him ! As a well-loved bridegroom to a waiting bride, was the angel of the tombs to that expectant spirit ! 'Twas painful, yet pleasant, to watch with what patient courage he endured bodily pain. Often, unnoticed by him, did I watch, with a terrible fascination, the heroic struggle with which he wrestled with suffering and disease. Sad and piteous were the shades and inflections of severe agony that passed over his noble face ! I recall now with sorrow, the memory of that time ! How well, in fancy, can I see him, as he lay upon that downy bed, with his beautiful gold hair thrown far back from his sunken temples, his blue, upturned eyes, fringed by their lashes of fretted gold, and those pale, thin hands that toyed so fitfully with the drapery of the couch, and the restless, loving look which he so frequently cast upon each of the dear ones who drew around him. It must be that the "sun-set of life" gives us a keener, quicker sense, else why do we love the more fondly as the curtain of eternity begins to descend upon us ? Surely, there must be a deeper, undeveloped sense lying beneath the surface of general feeling, which only the tightening of life's cords can reveal! He grew gentler, if possible, as his death approached. Very heavenly seemed he in those last, most trying moments! All that had ever been earthly of him, began to recede; the fleshly taints (if there were any) grew fainter and fainter, and the glorious spiritual predominated! Angel more than mortal, seemed he. The lessons which his life taught me have sunk deep in my nature; and I can well say, " it was good for him to have been here."

It was a few weeks after the death of Amy, when Miss Tildy was overlooking the bureau that contained the silver and glass ware, she gave a sudden exclamation, that, without knowing why, startled me very strangely. A thrill passed over my frame, an icy contraction of the nerves, and I knew that something awful was about to be revealed.

"What *is* the matter with you ?" asked Miss Jane.

Still she made no reply, but buried her face in her hands, and remained thus for several minutes; when she did look up, I saw that something terrible was working in her breast. "Culprit," was written all over her face. It was visible in the downcast terror of her eye, and in the blanched contraction of the lips, and quivered in the dilating nostril, and was stamped upon the whitening brow!

"What ails you, Tildy ?" again inquired her sister.

" *Why, look here !*" and she held up, to my terror, the two missing forks !

Oh, heavens! and for her own carelessness and mistake had Amy been sacrificed ? I make no comment. I merely state the case, and leave others to draw their own conclusions. Yet, this much I will add, that there were no Caucasian witnesses to the bloody deed, therefore no legal cognizance could be taken of it ! Most noble and righteous American laws ! Who that lives beneath your shelter, would dare to say they are not wise and sacred as the laws of the Decalogue ? Thrice a day should their authors go up into the Temple, and thank our Lord that they are not like publicans and sinners.

10*

One evening—oh! I shall long remember it, as one full of sacredness, full of sorrow, and yet tinged with a hue of heaven! It was in the deep, delicious beauty of the flowering month of May. The twilight was unusually red and refulgent. The evening star shone like the full eye of love upon the dreamy earth! The flowers, each with a dew-pearl glittering on its petals, lay lulled by the calm of the hour. Young master, fair saint, lay on his bed near the open window, through which the scented gales stole sweetly, and fanned his wasted cheek! Thick and hard came his breath, and we, who stood around him, could almost see the presence of the "monster grim," whose skeleton arms were fast locking him about!

Flitting round the bed, like a guardian spirit, was Miss Bradly, whilst her tearful eye never wandered for an instant from that face now growing rigid with the kiss of death! Miss Jane stood at the head of the bed wiping the cold damps from his brow, and Miss Tildy was striving to impart some of her animal warmth to his icy feet. Mr. Peterkin sat with one of those thin hands grasped within his own, as if disputing and defying the advance of that enemy whom no man is strong enough to baffle.

Slowly the invalid turned upon his couch, and, looking out upon the setting sun, he heaved a deep sigh.

"Father," he said, as he again turned his face toward Mr. Peterkin, who still clasped his hand, "do you not know from my failing pulse, that my life is almost spent?"

"Oh, my boy, it is too, too hard to give you up."

"Yet you *must* nerve yourself for it.

"I have no nerve to meet this trouble."

"Go to God, He will give you ease."

"I want Him to give me you."

Me He lent you for a little while. Now He demands me at your hands, and His requisition you must obey."

"Oh, I won't give up; maybe you'll yet be spared to me."

"No, God's decree it is, that I should go."

"It cannot, shall not be."

"Father, father, you do but blaspheme."

"I will do anything rather than see you die."

"I am willing to die. I have only one request to make of you. Will you grant it? If you refuse me, I shall die wretched and unhappy."

"I will promise you anything."

"But will you keep your promise?"

"Yes, my boy."

"Do you promise most faithfully?"

"I do."

"Then promise me that you will instantly manumit your slaves."

Mr. Peterkin hesitated a moment.

"Father, I shall not die happy, if you refuse me."

"Then I promise faithfully to do it."

A glad smile broke over the sufferer's face, like a sunbeam over a snow-cloud.

"Now, at least I can die contentedly! God will bless your effort, and a great weight has been removed from my oppressed heart."

Dr. Mandy now entered the room; and, taking young master's hand within his own, began to count the pulsations. A very ominous change passed over his face.

"Oh, doctor," cried the patient, "I read from your countenance the thoughts that agitate your mind; but do not fear to make the disclosure to my friends even here. It will do me no harm. I know that my hours are numbered; but I am willing, nay, anxious to go. Life has been one round of pain, and now, as I am about to leave the world, I take with me a blessed assurance that I have not lived in vain. Doctor, I call upon you, and all the dear ones here present, to witness the fact that my father has most solemnly promised me to liberate each of his slaves and never again become the holder of such property? Father, do you not promise before these witnesses?"

"I do, my child, I do," said the weeping father.

"Sisters," continued young master, "will you promise to urge or offer no objection to the furtherance of this sacred wish of your dying brother ?"

" I do," " I do," they simultaneously exclaimed.

" And neither of you will ever become the owner of slaves ?"

" Never," " never," was the stifled reply.

" Come, now, Death, for I am ready for thee !"

" You have exerted yourself too much already," said the doctor, " now pray take this cordial and try to rest; you have overtaxed your power. Your strength is waning fast."

" No, doctor, I cannot be silent; whilst I've the strength, pray let me talk. I wish this death-bed to be an example. Call in the servants. Let me speak with them. I wish to devote my power, all that is left of me now, to them."

To this Mr. Peterkin and the doctor objected, alleging that his life required quiet.

" Do not think of me, kind friends, I shall soon be safe, and am now well-cared for. If I did not relieve myself by speech, the anxiety would kill me. As a kind favor, I beg that you will not interrupt me. Call the good servants."

Instantly they all, headed by Nace, came into the chamber, each weeping bitterly.

" Good friends," he began, and now I noticed that his voice was weak and trembling, " I am about to leave you. On earth you will never see me again ; but there is a better world, where I trust to meet you all. You have been faithful and attentive to me. I thank you from the bottom of my soul for it, and, if ever I have been harsh or unkind to you in any way, I now beg that you will forgive me. Do not weep," he continued, as their loud sobs began to drown his feeble voice. " Do not weep, I am going to a happy home, where trouble and pain will never harm me more. Now let me tell you, that my father has promised me that each of you shall be free immediately after my death."

This announcement was like a panic to the poor, broken-spirited wretches. They looked wonderingly at young master, and then at each other, never uttering a word.

"Come, do not look so bewildered. Ah, you do not believe me; but, good as is this news, it is true; is it not, father?"

"Yes, my son, it is true."

When Mr. Peterkin spoke, they simultaneously started. That voice had power to recall them from the wildest dream of romance. Though softened by sorrow and suffering, there was still enough of the wonted harshness to make those poor wretches know it was Mr. Peterkin who spoke, and they quaked with fear.

"In the new home and new position in life, which you will take, my friends, I hope you will not forget me; but, above all things, try to save your souls. Go to church; pray much and often. Place yourselves under God's protection, and all will be right. You, Jake, had better select as an occupation that of a farmer, or manager of a farm for some one of those wealthy but humane men of the Northern States. You, Dan, can make an excellent dray driver; and at that business, in some of the Northern cities, you would make money. Sally can get a situation as cook; and Ann, where is Ann?" he said, as he looked around.

I stepped out from a retired corner of the room, into which I had shrunk for the purpose of indulging my grief unobserved.

"Don't weep, Ann," he began; "you distress me when you do so. You ought, rather, to rejoice, because I shall so soon be set free from this unhappy condition. If you love me, prepare to meet me in heaven. This earth is not our home; 'tis but a transient abiding-place, and, to one of my sensitive temperament, it has been none the happiest. I am glad that I am going; yet a few pangs I feel, in bidding you farewell; but think of me only as one gone upon a pleasant journey from snow-clad regions to a land smiling with tropic beauty, rich in summer bloom and vocal with the melody of southern birds! Think of me as one who has exchanged the garments of a beggar for the crown of a king and the singing-robes of a prophet. I hope you will do well in life, and I would advise that you improve your education, and then become a teacher. You are fitted for that position. You could fill it with dignity. Do all you can to elevate the mind as well as manners of your most unfortunate race. And now, poor old Nace, what pursuit must I recommend to you?" After a moment's pause, he added with a smile, "I will point out none; for you are Yankee enough, Nace, to get along anywhere."

He then requested that we should all kneel, whilst he besought for us and himself the blessings of Divine grace.

I can never forget the words of that beautiful prayer. How like fairy pearls they fell from his lips! And I do not think there was a single heart present that did not send out a fervent response! It seemed as if his whole soul were thrown into that one burning appeal to heaven. His mellow eyes grew purple in their intense passionateness; his pale lip quivered; and the throbbing veins, that wandered so blue and beautifully through his temples, were swollen with the rapid tide of emotion.

As we rose from our knees, he elevated himself upon his elbow, and looking earnestly at each one of us, said solemnly,

"God bless all of you!" then sank back upon the pillow; a bright smile flitted over his face, and he held his hand out to Miss Bradly, who clasped it lovingly.

"Good-bye, kind friend," he murmured, "never forsake the noble Anti-slavery cause. Cling to it as a rock and anchor of safety. Good-bye, and God bless you."

He then gave his other hand to Dr. Mandy, but, in attempting to speak, he was checked by a violent attack of coughing, and blood gushed from his mouth. The doctor endeavored to arrest the flow, but in vain; the crimson tide, like a stream broken loose from its barrier, flowed with a stifling rush.

Soon we discovered, from the ghastly whiteness of the patient's face, and the calm, set stare of the eyes, that his life was almost gone. Oh, God! how hard, pinched and contracted appeared those once beauteous features! How terrible was the blank fixedness of those blue orbs! No motion of the hand could distract their look.

" Heavens !!" cried Miss Jane, " his eyes are set !"

" No, no," exclaimed Mr. Peterkin, and with many gestures, he attempted to draw the staring eyes away from the object upon which they were fastened; but vain were all his endeavors. He had no power to call back a parting spirit; he, who had sent others to an unblest grave, could not now breathe fresh vigor into a frame over which Death held his skeleton arm. Where was Remorse, the unsleeping fiend, in that moment ?

I was looking earnestly at young master's face, when the great change passed over it. I saw Dr. Mandy slowly press down the marble eye-lids and gently straighten the rigid limbs; then, very softly turning to the friends, whose faces were hidden by their clasped hands, he murmured,

" All is over !"

Great heaven ! what screams burst from the afflicted family.

Mr. Peterkin was crazy. His grief knew no bounds ! He raved, he tore his hair, he struck his breast violently, and then blasphemed. He did everything but pray. And that was a thing so unfamiliar to him, that he did not know how to do it. Miss Jane swooned, whilst Miss Tildy raved out against the injustice of Providence in taking her brother from her.

Miss Bradly and I laid the body out, dressed it in a suit of pure white, and filletted his golden curls with a band of white rose-buds. Like a gentle infant resting in its first, deep sleep, lay he there !

After spreading the snowy drapery over the body, Miss Bradly covered all the furniture with white napkins, giving to the room the appearance of a death-like chill. There were no warm, rosy, life-like tints. Upon entering it, the very heart grew icy and still. The family, one by one, retired to their own apartments for the indulgence of private and sacred grief!

CHAPTER XXVI.

WHEN I entered the kitchen, I found the servants still weeping violently.

"Poor soul," said Sally, "he's at rest now. If he hain't gone to heaven, 'taint no use of havin' any; fur he war de best critter I iver seed. He never gived me a cross word in all his life-time. Oh, Lord, he am gone now !"

"I 'members de time, when Mister Jones whipt me, dat young masser comed to me wid some grease and rubbed me all over, and talked so kind to me. Den he tell me not to say nothin' 'bout it, and I niver did mention it from dat day until dis."

"Wal, he was mighty good," added Jake, "and I's sorry he's dead."

"I'se glad he got us our freedom afore he died. I wonder if we'll git it?" asked Nace, who was always intent upon selfishness.

"Laws ! didn't he promise ? Den he mus' keep his word," added Jake.

I made no comment. My thoughts upon the subject I kept locked in the depths of my own bosom. I knew then, as now, that natures like Mr. Peterkin's could be changed only by the interposition of a miracle. He had now shrunk beneath the power of a sudden blow of misfortune; but this would soon pass away, and the savage nature would re-assert itself.

All that gloomy night, I watched with Miss Bradly and Dr. Mandy beside the corpse. Often whilst the others dozed, would I steal to the bed and turn down the covering, to gaze upon that still pale face! Reverently I placed my hand upon that rich golden head, with its band of flowers.

There is an angel-like calm in the repose of death; a subdued awe that impresses the coldest and most unbelieving hearts! As I looked at that still body, which had so lately been illumined by a radiant soul, and saw the noble look which the face yet wore, I inwardly exclaimed, 'Tis well for those who sleep in the Lord!

All that long night I watched and waited, hoped and prayed. The deep, mysterious midnight passed, with all its fearful power of passion and mystery; the still, small hours glided on as with silver slippers, and then came the purple glory of a spring dawn! I left the chamber of death, and went out to muse in the hazy day-break. And, as I there reflected, my soul grew sick and sore afraid. One by one my friends had been falling around me, and now I stood alone. There was no kind voice to cheer me on; no gentle, loving hand stretched forth to aid me; no smile of friendship to encourage me. In the thickest of the fight, unbucklered, I must go. Up the weary, craggy mountain I must climb. The burning sands I must tread alone! What wonder that my spirit, weak and womanly, trembled and turned away, asking for the removal of the cup of life! Only the slave can comprehend the amount of agony that I endured. He alone who clanks the chain of African bondage, can know what a cloud of sorrow swept over my heart.

I saw the great sun rise, like a blood-stained gladiator, in the East, and the diamond dew that glittered in his early light. I saw the roses unclose fragrantly to his warming call; yet my heart was chill. Through the flower-decked grounds I walked, and the aroma of rarest blooms filled my senses with delight, yet woke no answering thrill in my bosom. Must it not be wretchedness indeed, when the heart refuses to look around upon blooming, vernal Nature, and answer her with a smile of freshness?

A little after daylight I re-entered the house, and found Miss Bradly dozing in a large arm-chair, with one hand thrown upon

the cover of the bed where lay young master's body. Dr. Mandy
was outstretched upon the lounge in a profound sleep. The long
candles had burnt very low in the sockets, and every now and
then sent up that flicker, which has been so often likened to the
struggles of expiring humanity. I extinguished them, and closed
the shutters, to exclude the morning rays that would else have
stolen in to mar the rest of those who needed sleep. Then returning to the yard, I culled a fresh bouquet and placed it upon
the breast of the dead. Gently touching Miss Bradly, I roused
her and begged that she would seek some more comfortable
quarters, whilst I watched with the body. She did so, having
first imprinted a kiss upon the brow of the heavenly sleeper.

When she withdrew, I took from my apron a bundle of freshly-
gathered flowers, and set about weaving fairy chains and gar-
lands, which I scattered in fantastic profusion over and around
the body.

A beautiful custom is it to decorate the dead with fresh flowers ! There is something in the delicate, fairy-like perfume, and
in the magical shadings and formation of flowers, that make
them appropriate offerings to the dead. Strange mystical things
that they are, seemingly instinct with a new and inchoate life ;
breathing in their heavenly fragrance of a hidden blessing, telling a story which our dull ears of clay can never comprehend.
Symbols of diviner being, expressions of quickening beauty,
we understand ye not. We only *feel* that ye are God's richest
blessing to us, therefore we offer ye to our loved and holy dead!

When the broad daylight began to beam in through the crevices of the shutters, and noise of busy life sounded from without,
the family rose. Separately they entered the room, each turning
down the spread, and gazing tearfully upon the ghastly face.
Often and often they kissed the brow, cheek, and lips.

"How lovely he was in life," said Miss Jane.

"Indeed he was, and he is now an angel," replied Miss Tildy,
with a fresh gush of emotion.

"My poor, poor boy," said Mr. Peterkin, as he sank down on
the bed beside the body; "how proud I was of him. I allers

knowed he'd be tuck 'way from me. He was too putty an' smart an' good fur this world. My heart wus so sot on him! yit sometimes he almost run me crazy. I don't think it was just in Providence to take my only boy. I could have better spared one of the gals. Oh, tain't right, no how it can be fixed."

And thus he rambled on, perfectly unconscious of the bold blasphemy which he was uttering with every breath he drew. To impugn the justice of his Maker's decrees was a common practice with him. He had so long rejoiced in power, and witnessed the uncomplaining vassalage of slaves, that he began to regard himself as the very highest constituted authority! This is but one of the corrupting influences of the slave-system.

That long, wearing day, with its weight of speechless grief, passed at last. The neighbors came and went. Each praised the beauty of the corpse, and inquired who had dressed it. At length the day closed, and was succeeded by a lovely twilight. Another night, with its star-fretted canopy, its queenly, slow-moving moon, its soft aromatic air and pearly dew. And another gray, hazy day-break, yet still, as before, I watched near the dead. But on the afternoon of this day, there came a long, black coffin, with its silver plate and mountings; its interior trimmings of white satin and border of lace, and within this they laid the form of young master! His pale, fair hands were crossed prayerfully upon his breast; and a fillet of fresh white buds bound his smooth brow, whilst a large bouquet lay on his breast, and the wreaths I had woven were thrown round him and over his feet. Then the lid was placed on and tightly screwed down. Then came the friends and neighbors, and a good man who read the Bible and preached a soothing and ennobling sermon. The friends gave one more look, another, a longer and more clinging kiss, then all was over. The slow procession followed after the vehicle that carried the coffin, the servants walking behind. Poor, uncared-for slaves, as we were, we paid a heart-felt tribute to his memory, and watered his new-made grave with as sincere tears as ever flowed from eyes that had looked on happier times.

I lingered until long after the last shovel-full of dirt was thrown upon him. Others, even his kindred, had left the spot ere I turned away. That little narrow grave was dearer and nearer to me, as there it lay so fresh and damp, shapen smoothly with the sexton's spade, than when, several weeks after, a patrician obelisk reared its Parian head towards the blue sky. I have always looked upon grave-monuments as stony barriers, shutting out the world from the form that slowly moulders below. When the wild moss and verdant sward alone cover the grave, 'tis easy for us to imagine death only a sleep; but the grave-stone, with its carvings and frescoes, seems a sort of prison, cold and grim in its aristocratic splendor. For the grave of those whom I love, I ask no other decoration than the redundant grass, the enamelled mosaic of wild flowers, a stream rolling by with its dirge-like chime, a weeping willow, and a moaning dove.

The shades of evening were falling darkly ere I left the burial-ground. There, amid the graves of his ancestors, beside the tomb of his mother, I left him sleeping pleasantly. "Life's fitful fever over," his calm soul rests well.

*   *   *   *   *   *   *

In a few weeks after his death, the family settled back to their original manner of life. Mr. Peterkin grew sulky in his grief. He chewed and drank incessantly. The remonstrances of his daughters had no effect upon him. He took no notice of them, seemed almost to ignore their existence. Feeding sullenly on his own rooted sorrow, he cared nothing for those around him.

We, the servants, had been allowed a rather better time; for as he was entirely occupied with his own moody reflections, he bestowed upon us no thought. Yet we had heard no word about his compliance with the sacred promise he had made to the dead. Did he feel no touch of remorse, or was he so entirely sold to the d—l, as to be incapable of regret?

The young ladies had been busy making up their mourning, and took but little notice of domestic affairs. Miss Jane concluded to postpone her visit to the city, on account of their recent bereavement; but later in the summer, she proposed going.

One afternoon, several weeks after the burial of young master, Miss Bradly came over to see the ladies, for the purpose, as she said, of bidding them farewell, as early on the following morning she expected to start North, to rejoin her family, from whom she had been so long separated. Miss Jane received the announcement with her usual haughty smile; and Miss Tildy, who was rather more of a hypocrite, expressed some regret at parting from her old teacher.

"I fear, dear girls, that you will soon forget me. I hoped that an intimate friendship had grown up between us, which nothing could destroy; but it seems as if, in the last half-year, you have ceased to love me, or care for me."

"I can only answer for myself, dear Miss Bradly," said Miss Tildy, "and I shall ever gratefully and fondly remember you, and my interesting school-days."

"So shall I pleasantly recollect my school-hours, and Miss Bradly as our preceptress; and, had she not chosen to express and defend those awfully disgraceful and incendiary principles of the North, I should have continued to think of her with pleasure." Miss Jane said this with her freezing air of hauteur.

"But I remained silent, dear Jane, for years. I lived in your midst, in the very families where slave-labor was employed; yet I molested none. I did not inveigh against your peculiar domestic institution; though, Heaven knows, every principle of my nature cried out against it. Surely for all this I deserve some kind consideration."

"'Tis a great pity your prudence did not hold out to the last; and I can assure you 'tis well for the safety of your life and person that you were a woman, else would it have gone hard with you. Kited through the streets with a coat of tar and a plumage of hen-feathers, you would have been treated to a rail-ride, none the most complimentary." Here Miss Jane laughed heartily at the ridiculous picture she had drawn.

Miss Bradly's face reddened deeply as she replied :

"And all this would have been inflicted upon me because I dared to have an opinion upon a subject of vital import to this our proud Republic. This would have been the gracious hospitality, which, as chivalry-loving Southerners, you would have shown to a stranger from the North! If this be your mode and manner of carrying out the Comity of States, I am heartily glad that I am about returning to the other side of the border."

"And we give you joy of your swift return. Pray, tell all your Abolition friends that such will be their reception, should they dare to venture among us."

"Yet, as with tearful eyes you stood round your brother's death-bed, you solemnly promised him that his dying wish, with regard to the liberation of your father's slaves, should be carried out, and that you would never become the owner of such property."

"Stop! stop!" exclaimed Miss Jane, and her face was livid with rage, "you have no right to recur to that time. You are inhuman to introduce it at this moment. Every one of common sense knows that brother was too young to have formed a correct opinion upon a question of such momentous value to the entire government; besides, a promise made to the dying is never binding. Why should it be? We only wished to relieve him from anxiety. Father would sell every drop of his blood before he would grant a negro liberty. He is against it in principle. So am I. Negroes were made to serve the whites; for that purpose only were they created, and I am not one who is willing to thwart their Maker's wise design."

Miss Jane imagined she had spoken quite conclusively and displayed a vast amount of learning. She looked around for admiration and applause, which was readily given her by her complimentary sister.

"Ah, Jane, you should have been a man, and practiced law. The courts would have been the place for the display of your brilliant talents."

"But the halls of legislation would not, I fear," said Miss

Bradly, "have had the benefit of her wise, just, and philanthropic views."

"I should never have allowed the Abolitionists their present weight of influence, whilst the power of speech and the strength of action remained to me," answered Miss Jane, very tartly.

"Oh no, doubtless you would have met the Douglas in his hall, and the lion in his den," laughingly replied Miss Bradly.

Thus the conversation was carried on, upon no very friendly terms, until Miss Jane espied me, when she thundered out,

"Leave the room, Ann, we've no use for negro company here, unless, indeed, as I think most probable, Miss Bradly came to visit you, in which case she had better be shown to the kitchen."

This insult roused Miss Bradly's resentment, and she rose, saying,

"Young ladies, I came this evening to take a pleasant adieu, little expecting to meet with such treatment ; but be it as you wish ; I take my leave;" and, with a slight inclination of the head, she departed.

"Oh, she is insulted!" cried Miss Tildy.

"I don't care if she is, we owe her nothing. For teaching us she was well paid ; now let her take care of herself."

"I am going after her to say I did not wish to insult her; for really, notwithstanding her Abolition sentiments, I like her very much, and I wish her always to like me."

So she started off and overtook Miss Bradly at the gate. The explanation was, I presume, accepted, for they parted with kisses and tears.

That evening, when I was serving the table, Miss Jane reported the conversation to her father, who applauded her manner of argument greatly.

"Set my niggers free, indeed ! Catch me doing any such foolish thing. I'd sooner be shot. Don't you look for anything of the kind, Ann ; I'd sooner put you in my pocket."

And this was the way he kept a sacred promise to his dead son ! But cases such as this are numerous. The negro is lulled with promises by humane masters—promises such as those that led the terror-stricken Macbeth on to his fearful doom. They

> "Keep the word of promise to the ear,
> But break it to the hope."

How many of them are trifled with and lured on; buoyed up from year to year with stories, which those who tell them are resolved shall never be realized.

My memory runs back now to some such wretched recollections; and my heart shrivels and crumbles at the bare thought, like scorched paper. Oh, where is there to be found injustice like that which the American slaves daily and hourly endure, without a word of complaint? "We die daily"—die to love, to hope, to feeling, humanity, and all the high and noble gifts that make existence something more than a mere breathing span. We die to all enlargement of mind and expansion of heart. Our every energy is bound down with many bolts and bars; yet whole folios have been written by men calling themselves wise, to prove that we are by far the happiest portion of the population of this broad Union! What a commentary upon the liberality of free men!

After the conversation with Miss Bradly, the young ladies began to resume their old severity, which the death of young master had checked ; but Mr. Peterkin still seemed moody and troubled. He drank to a frightful excess. It seemed to have increased his moroseness. He slept sounder at night, and later in the morning, and was swollen and bloated to almost twice his former dimensions. His face was a dark crimson purple ; he spoke but little, and then never without an oath. His daughters remarked the change, but sought not to dissuade him. Perhaps they cared not if his excesses were followed by death. I had long known that they treated him with respect only out of apprehension that they would be cut short of patrimonial favors. But the death of young master had almost certainly insured them against this, and they were unusually insolent to their father; but this he appeared not to notice; for he was too sottishly drunk even to heed them.

The necessity of wearing black, and the custom of remaining away from places of amusement, had forced Miss Jane to decline, or at least, postpone her trip to the city.

I shall ever remember that summer as one of unusual luxuriance. It seemed to me, that the forests were more redundant of foliage than I had ever before seen them. The wild flowers were gayer and brighter, and the sky of a more glorious blue; even the little feathered songsters sang more deliciously; and oh, the moonlight nights seemed wondrously soft and silvery, and the hosts of stars seven times multiplied! I began to live again. Away through the old primeval woods I took occasionally a stolen ramble! Whole volumes of romance I drained from the ever-affluent library of Nature. I truly found—

> "Tongues in the trees; books, in the running brooks,
> Sermons in stones, and good in everything."

It is impossible to imagine how much I enjoyed those solitary walks, few and far between as they were. I used to wonder why the ladies did not more enjoy the luxury of frequent communion with Nature in her loveliest haunts! Strange, is it not, how little the privileged class value the pleasures and benefits by which they are surrounded! I would have given ten years of my life (though considering my trouble, the sacrifice would have been small) to be allowed to linger long beside the winding, murmuring brook, or recline at the fountain, looking far away into the impenetrable blue above; or to gather wild flowers at will, and toy with their tiny leaflets! but indulgences such as these would have been condemned and punished as indolence.

I cannot now, honestly, recall a single pleasure that was allowed me, during my long slavery to Mr. Peterkin. Then who can ask me, if I would not rather go back into bondage than *live*, aye *live* (that is the word), with the proud sense of freedom mine? I have often been asked if the burden of find-

1!

ing food and raiment for myself was not great enough to make me wish to resign my liberty. No, a thousand times no! Let me go half-clad, and meanly fed, but still give me the custody of my own person, without a master to spy into and question out my up-risings and down-sittings, and confine me like a leashed hound! Slavery in its mildest phases (of which I have *only* heard, for I've always seen it in its darker terrors) must be unhappy. The very knowledge that you have no control over yourself, that you are subject to the will, even whim, of another; that every privilege you enjoy is yours only by concession, not right, must depress and all but madden the victim. In no situation, with no flowery disguises, can the revolting institution be made consistent with the free-agency of man, which we all believe to be the Divine gift. We have been and are cruelly oppressed; why may we not come out with our petition of right, and declare ourselves independent? For this were the infant colonies applauded; who then shall inveigh against us for a practice of the same heroism? Every word contained in their admirable Declaration, applies to us.

CHAPTER XXVII.

TIME passed on; Mr. Peterkin drank more and more violently. He had grown immense in size, and now slept nearly all the day as well as night. Dr. Mandy had told the young ladies that there was great danger of apoplexy. I frequently saw them standing off, talking, and looking at their father with a strange expression, the meaning of which I could not divine; but sure I am there was no love in it, 'twas more like a surmise or inquiry, "How long will you be here?" I would not "set down aught in malice," I would rather "extenuate," yet am I bound in truth to say that I think their father's death was an event to which they looked with pleasure. He had not been showy enough for them, nor had he loved such display as they wished: true, he allowed them any amount of money; but he objected to conforming to certain fashions, which they considered indispensable to their own position; and this difference in ideas and tastes created much discord. They were not girls of feeling and heart. To them, a father was nothing more than an accidental guardian, whose duty it was to supply them with money.

Late one night, when I had fallen into a profound sleep, such an one as I had not known for months, almost years, I was suddenly aroused by a loud knocking at the cabin-door, and a shout of—

"Ann! Ann!"

I instantly recognized the sharp staccato notes of Miss Jane's voice; and, starting quickly up, I opened the door, but half-dressed, and inquired what was wanting?

" Are you one of the Seven Sleepers, that it requires such
knocking to arouse you ?   Here I've been beating and banging
the door, and yet you still slept on."

I stammered out something like an excuse ; and she told me
master was very ill, and I must instantly heat a large kettle of
water ; that Dr. Mandy had been sent for, and upon his arrival,
prescribed a hot bath.

As quickly as the fire, aided by mine and Sally's united
efforts, could heat the water, it was got ready.   Jake, Nace,
and Dan lifted the large bathing-tub into Mr. Peterkin's room,
filled it with the warm water, and placed him in it.   The case
was as Dr. Mandy had predicted.   Mr. P. had been seized with
a violent attack of apoplexy, and his life was despaired of.

All the efforts of the physician seemed to fail.   When Mr.
Peterkin did revive, it was frightful to listen to him.   Such
revolting oaths as he used !   Such horrid blasphemy as poured
from his lips, I shrink from the foulness of recording.

Raving like a madman, he called upon God to restore his
son, or stand condemned as unjust.   His daughters, in sheer
affright, sent for the country preacher ; but the good man
could effect nothing.   His pious words were wasted upon ears
duller than stone.

" I don't care a d—n for your religion.   None of your hypocritical prayin' round me," Mr. Peterkin would say, when the
good parson sought to beguile his attention, and lead him to
the contemplation of divine things.

Frightful it was, to me, to stand by his bed-side, and hear
him call with an oath for whiskey, which was refused.

He had drunk so long, and so deeply, that now, when he
was suddenly checked, the change was terrible to witness.   He
grew timid, and seemed haunted by terrible spectres.   Anon
he would call to some fair-haired woman, and shout out that
there was blood, clotted blood, on her ringlets ; then, rolling
himself up in the bed covering, he would shriek for the skies
and mountains to hide him from the meek reproach of those
girlish eyes !

"Something terrible is on his memory," said the doctor to Miss Jane? "Do you know aught of this?"

"Nothing," she replied with a shudder.

"Don't you remember," asked Miss Tildy, "how often Johnny's eyes seemed to recall a remorseful memory, and how father would, as now, cry for them to shut out that look which so tormented him?"

"Yes, yes," and they both fled from the room, and did not again go near their father. On the third evening of his illness, when Dr. Mandy (who had been constantly with him) sat by his bed, holding his pulse, he turned on his side, and asked in a mild tone, quite unusual to him,

"Doctor, must I die? Tell me the truth; I don't want to be deceived."

After a moment's pause, the doctor replied, "Yes, Mr. Peterkin, I will speak the truth; I don't think you can recover from this attack, and, if I am not very much mistaken, but a few hours of mortal life now remain to you."

"Then I must speak on a matter what has troubled me a good deal. If I was a good scholar I'd a writ it out, and left it fur you to read; but as I warn't much edicated, I couldn't do that, so I'll jist tell you all, and relieve my mind." Here Mr. Peterkin's face assumed a frightful expression; his eyes rolled terribly in his head, and blazed with an expression which no language can paint. His very hair seemed erect with terror.

"Don't excite yourself; be calm! Wait until another time, then tell me."

"No, no, I must speak now, I feel it 'twill do me good. Long time ago I had a good kind mother, and one lovely sister;" and here his voice sank to a whisper. "My father I can't remember; he died when I was a baby. I was a wild boy; a 'brick,' as they usin' to call me. 'Way off in old Virginny I was born and raised. My mother was a good, easy sort of woman, that never used any force with her children, jist sich a person as should raise gals, not fit to manage onruly boys like me. I jist had my own way; came and went when I pleased. Mother didn't often reprove me; whenever she did, it was in a gentle sort of way that I didn't mind at all. I'd promise far enough; but then, I'd go and do my own way. So I growed up to the age of eighteen. I'd go off on little trips; get myself in debt, and mother 'd have to pay. She an' sis had to take in sewin' to support 'emselves, and me too. Wal, they didn't make money fast enough at this; so they went out an' took in washin'. Sis, poor little thing, hired herself out by the day, to get extry money for to buy little knic-nacs fur mother, whose health had got mighty bad. Wal, their rent had fell due, and Lucy (my sister) and mother had bin savin' up money fur a good while, without sayin' anything to me 'bout it; but of nights when they thought I was asleep, I seed 'em slip the money in a drawer of an old bureau, that stood in the room whar I slept. Wal, I owed some men a parcel of money, gamblin' debts, and they had bin sorter quarrelin' with me 'bout it, and railin' of me 'bout my want of spirit, and I was allers sort of proud an' very high-tempered. So I 'gan to think mother and Luce was a saving up money fur to buy finery fur 'emselves, an' I 'greed I'd fix 'em fur it. So one night I made my brags to the boys that I'd pay the next night, with intrust. Some of 'em bet big that I wouldn't do it. So then I was bound fur it. Accordin', next night I tried to get inter the drawer; but found it fast locked. I tried agin. At length, with a wrinch, I bust it open, an' thar before me, all in bright specie, lay fifty dollars! A big sum it 'peared to me, and then I was all afired with passion, for Luce had refused me when I had axed her to lend me money. Jist as I had pocketed it, an' was 'about to drive out of the room, Lucy opened the door, an' seein' the drawer wide open, she guessed it all. She gave one loud scream, saying, ' Oh, all our hard savin's is gone.' I made a sign to her to keep silent; but she went on hallowin' and cotcht hold of me, an' by a sort of quare strength, she got her arm round me, an' her hand in my pocket, where the money was "

" You musn't have this, indeed you musn't," said she, " for it is to pay our rent."

One desperate effort I made, an' knocked her to the floor. Her head struck agin the sharp part of the bureau, and the blood gushed from it; I give one loud yell for mother, an' then fled. Give me some water," he added, in a hollow tone.

After moistening his lips, he continued :

" Reachin' my companions, I paid down every cent of the money, principal and interest, then got my bet paid, and left 'em, throwin' a few dollars toward 'em for the gineral treat.

" About midnight, soft as a cat, I crept along to our house ; and I knew from the light through the open shutter of the winder, that she was either dead or dyin' ; for it was a rule at our house to have the lights put out afore ten.

" I slipped up close to the winder, and lookin' in, saw the very wust that I had expected—Lucy in her shroud ! A long, white sheet was spread over the body ! Two long candles burnt at the head and foot of the corpse. Three neighbor-women was watchin' with her. While I still looked, the side door opened, and mother came in, looking white as a ghost. She turned down the sheet from the body. I pressed my face still closer to the winder-pane ; and saw that white, dead face; the forehead, where the wound had been given, was bandaged up. Mother knelt down, and cried out with a tone that froze my blood—

" 'My child, my murdered child !' I did not tarry another minute; but with one loud yell bounded away. This scream roused the women, who seized up the candle and run out to the door. I looked back an' saw them with candles in hand, examining round the house. For weeks I lived in the woods on herbs and nuts ; occasionally stoppin' at farm-houses, an' buyin' a leetle milk and bread, still I journeyed on toward the West, my land of promise. At last, on foot, after long travel, I reached Kaintuck. I engaged in all sorts of head-work, but did'nt succeed very well till I began to trade in niggers; then I made money fast enough. I was a hard master. It seemed like I was the same as that old Ishmael you read of in the old book;

my hand was agin every man, and every man's agin me. After while, I got mighty rich from tradin' in niggers, and married. These is my children. This is all of my story,—a bad one 'tis too ; but, doctor, that boy, my poor, dead Johnny, was so like Lucy that he almost driv' me mad. At times he had a sartin look, jist like hern, that driv' a dagger to my heart. Oh, Lord ! if I die, what will become of me ? Give me some whiskey, doctor, I mus' have some, for the devil and all his imps seem to be here."

He began raving in a frightful manner, and sprang out of bed so furiously that the doctor deemed it necessary to have him confined. Jake, Dan, and Nace were called in to assist in tying their master. It was with difficulty they accomplished their task ; but at last it was done. Panting and foaming at the mouth, this Goliath of human abominations lay ! He, who had so often bound negroes, was now by them bound down ! If he had been fully conscious, his indignation would have known no limits.

Miss Jane sent for me to come to her room. I found her in hysterics. Immediately, at her command, I set about rubbing her head, and chafing her temples and hands with cologne ; but all that I could do seemed to fall far short of affording any relief. It appeared to me that her lungs were unusually strong, for such screams I hardly ever listened to ; but her life was stout enough to stand it. The wicked are long-lived !

Miss Tildy had more self-control. She moved about the house with her usual indifference, caring for and heeding no one, except as she bestowed upon me an occasional reprimand, which, to this day, I cannot think I deserved. If she mislaid an article of apparel, she instantly accused me of having stolen it ; and persisted in the charge until it was found. She always accompanied her accusations with impressive blows. It is treatment such as this that robs the slave of all self-respect. He is constantly taught to look upon himself as an animal, devoid of all good attributes, without principle, and full of vice. If he really tries to practice virtue and integrity, he gets no credit for it. "*Honest for a nigger*," is a phrase much in use in Kentucky; the satirical significance of which is perfectly understood by the astute African. I knew that it was hard for me to hold fast to my principles amid such fierce trials. It was so common a charge—that of liar and thief—that despite my practice to the contrary, I almost began to accept the terms as deserved. In some cases, the human conscience is a flexile thing! but, thank Heaven! mine withstood the trial!

* * * * * * *

On the morning of the fifth day after Mr. Peterkin's illness, his perturbed spirit, amid imprecations and blasphemies the most horrible, took its leave of the mortal tenement. Whither went it, oh, angel of mercy? A fearful charge had his guardian-angel to render up.

This was the second time I had witnessed the death of a human master. I had no tears; and, as a veracious historian, I am bound to say that I regard it as a beneficent dispensation of Divine Providence. He, my tyrant, had gone to his Judge to render a fearful account of the dreadful deeds done in the body.

After he was laid out and appropriately dressed, and the room darkened, the young ladies came in to look at him. I believe they wept. At least, I can testify to the premonitory symptoms of weeping, viz., the fluttering of white pocket-handkerchiefs, in close proximity to the eyes! The neighbors gathered round them with bottles of sal-volatile, camphor, fans, &c., &c. There was no dearth of consolatory words, for they were rich. Though Mr. Peterkin's possessions were vast, he could carry no tithe of them to that land whither he had gone; and at that bar before which he must stand, there would flash on him the stern eye of Justice. His trial there would be equitable and rigid. His money could avail him nought; for *there* were allowed no "packed juries," bribed and suborned witnesses, no wily attorneys to turn Truth astray; no subtleties and quibbles of litigation; all is clear, straight, open, even-handed justice, and his own deeds, like a mighty cloud of evidence,

11*

would rise up against him—and so we consign him to his fate and to his mother earth.

But he was befittingly buried, even with the rites of Christianity! There was a man in a white neck-cloth, with a sombre face, who read a psalm, offered up a well-worded prayer, gave out a text, and therefrom preached an appropriate, elegiac sermon. Not one, to be sure, in which the peculiar virtues of brother Peterkin were set forth, but a sort of pious oration, wherein religion, practical and revealed, was duly encouraged, and great sympathy offered to the *lovely* and bereaved daughters, &c., &c.

The body was placed in a very fine coffin, and interred in the family burying-ground, near his wife and son! At the grave, Miss Jane, who well understood scenic effect, contrived to get up an attack of syncope, and fell prostrate beside the new-made grave. Of course "the friends" gathered round her with restoratives, and, shouting for "air," they made an opening in the crowd, through which she was borne to a carriage and driven home.

I had lingered, tenderly, beside young master's tomb, little heeding what was passing around, when this theatrical excitement roused me. Oh! does not one who has real trouble, heart-agony, sicken when he hears of these affectations of grief?

Slowly, but I suspect with right-willing hearts, the crowd turned away from the grave, each betaking himself to his own home and pursuit.

A few weeks after, a stately monument, commemorative of his good deeds, was erected to the memory of James Peterkin.

CHAPTER XXVIII.

WEEKS rolled monotonously by after the death of Mr. Peterkin. There was nothing to break the cloud of gloom that enveloped everything.

The ladies were, as ever, cruel and abusive. Existence became more painful to me than it had been before. It seemed as if every hope was dead in my breast. An iron chain bound every aspiration, and I settled down into the lethargy of despair. Even Nature, all radiant as she is, had lost her former charms. · I looked not beyond the narrow horizon of the present. The future held out to me no allurements, whilst the dark and gloomy past was an arid plain, without fountain, or flower, or sunshine, over which I dared not send my broken spirit.

In this state of dreary monotony, I passed my life for months, until an event occurred which changed my whole after-fate.

Mr. Summerville, who, it seems, had kept up a regular correspondence with Miss Jane, made us a visit, and, after much secret talking in dark parlors, long rambles through the woods, twilight and moonlight whisperings on the gallery, Miss Jane announced that there would, on the following evening, be performed a marriage ceremony of importance to all, but of very particular interest to Mr. Summerville and herself.

Accordingly, on the evening mentioned, the marriage rite was solemnized in the presence of a few social friends, among whom Dr. Mandy and wife shone conspicuously. I duly plied the guests with wine, cakes and confections.

Miss Tildy, by the advice of her bride-sister, enacted the

pathetic very perfectly. She wept, sighed, and, I do believe, fainted or tried to faint. This was at the special suggestion of her sister, who duly commended and appreciated her.

Mr. Summerville, for the several days that he remained with us, looked, and was, I suppose, the very personification of delight.

In about a week or ten days after the solemnization of the matrimonial rite, Mr. Summerville made his "better half" (or worse, I know not which), understand that very important business urged his immediate return to the city. Of course, whilst the novelty of the situation lasted, she was as obedient and complaisant as the most exacting husband could demand, and instantly consented to her lord's request. She bade me get ready to accompany her; and, as she had heard that people from the country were judged according to the wardrobe of their servants, she prepared for me quite a decent outfit.

One bright morning, I shall ever remember it, we started off with innumerable trunks, band-boxes, &c.—for the city of L——. Without one feeling of regret, I turned my face from the Peterkin farm. I never saw it after, save in dark and fearful dreams, from which I always awoke with a shudder. I felt half-emancipated, when my back was turned against it, and in the distance loomed up the city and freedom. I had a queer fancy, that if the Peterkin influence were once thrown off, the rest would speedily succeed!

If I had only been allowed, I could have shouted out like a school-boy freed from a difficult lesson; but Miss Jane's checking glance was upon me, and 'twas like winter's frozen breath over a gladsome lake.

I well remember the beautiful ride upon the boat, and how long and lingeringly I gazed over the guard, looking down at the blue, dolphin-like waves. All the day, whilst others lounged and talked, I was looking at those same curling, frothy billows, making, in my own mind, fifty fantastic comparisons, which then appeared to me very brilliant, but, since I have learned to think differently. Truly, the foam has died on the wave.

When night came on, wrapped in her sombre purple, yet glittering with a cuirass of stars and a helmet of planets, the waters sparkled and danced with a fairy-like beauty, and I thought I had never beheld anything half so ecstatic! There was none on that crowded steamer who dreamed of the glory that was nestling, like a thing of love, deep and close down in the poor slave's breast!

To those who surrounded me, this was but an ordinary sight; to me it was one of strange, unimagined loveliness. I was careful, however, to disguise my emotions. I would have given worlds (had I been their possessor) to speak my joy in one wild word, or to shout it forth in a single cry.

This pleasure, like all others, found its speedy end. The next morning, about ten o'clock, we landed in L——, a city of some commercial consequence in the West. Indeed, by old residents of the interior of Kentucky, it is regarded as "*the city*." I have often since thought of my first landing there; of its dusty, dirty coal-besmoked appearance; of its hedge of drays, its knots of garrulous and noisy drivers, and then the line of dusky warehouses, storage rooms, &c. All this instantly rises to my mind when I hear that growing city spoken of.

Mr. Summerville engaged one of the neatest-looking coaches at the wharf; and into it Miss Jane, baggage and servant were unceremoniously hurried. I had not the privilege and scarcely the wish to look out of the coach-window, yet, from my crowded and uncomfortable position, I could catch a sight of an occasional ambitious barber's pole, or myriad-tinted chemists' bottles; all these, be it remembered, were novelties to me, who had never been ten miles from Mr. Peterkin's farm. At length the driver drew a halt at the G—— House, as Mr. Summerville had directed, and, at this palatial-looking building Mr. Summerville had taken quarters. How well I recollect its wide hall, its gothic entrance and hospitable-looking vestibule! The cane-colored floor cloth, corresponding with the oaken walls, struck me as the harmonious design of an artistic mind.

For a few moments only was Miss Jane left in the neat reception-room, when a nice-looking mulatto man entered, and, in a low, gentlemanly tone, informed her that her room was ready. Taking the basket and portmanteau from me, he politely requested that we would follow him to room No. 225. Through winding corridors and interminable galleries, he conducted us, until, at last, we reached it. Drawing a key from his pocket, he applied it to the lock, and bade Miss Jane enter. She was much pleased with the arrangement of the furniture, the adjustment of the drapery, &c.

The floor was covered with a beautiful green velvet carpet, torn bouquet pattern, whilst the design of the rug was one that well harmonized with the disposition of the present tenant. It was a wild tiger reposing in his native jungle.

After Miss Jane had made an elaborate toilette, she told me, as a great favor, she would allow me to go down stairs, or walk through the halls for recreation, as she had no further use for me.

I wandered about, passing many rooms, all numbered in gilt figures. The most of them had their doors open, and I amused myself watching the different expressions of face and manners of their occupants. This had always been a habit of mine, for the indulgence of which, however, I had had but little opportunity.

I strayed on till I reached the parlors, and they burst upon me with the necromantic power of Aladdin's hall. A continuity of four apartments rolled away into a seeming mist, and the adroit position of a mirror multiplied their number and added greatly to the gorgeous effect. There were purple and golden curtains, with their many tinsel ornaments; carpets of the gayest style, from the richest looms. "Etruscan vases, quaint and old" adorned the mantel-shelf, and easy divans and lounges of mosaic-velvet were ranged tastefully around. An arcade, with its stately pillars, divided two of the rooms, and the inter-columniations were ornamented with statues and statuettes; and upon a marble table, in the centre of one of the apartments, was a blooming magnolia, the first one I had ever seen! That strange and mysterious odor, that, like a fine, inner, sub-sense, pervades the nerve with a quickening power, stole over me! I stood before the flower in a sort of delicious, delirious joy. There, with its huge fan-like leaves of green, this pure white blossom, queen of all the tribe of flowers, shed its glorious perfume and unfolded its mysterious beauty. It seemed that a new life was opening upon me. Surely, I said, this *is* fairy land. For more than an hour I lingered beside that splendid magnolia, vainly essaying to drink in its glory and its mystery.

Miss Jane and Mr. Summerville had gone out to take a drive over the city, and I was comparatively free, in their absence, to go whithersoever I pleased.

Whilst I still loitered near the flower, a very sweet but manly voice asked:

"Do you love flowers?"

I turned hastily, and to my surprise, beheld a fine-looking gentleman standing in close contiguity to me. With pleasure I think now of his broad, open face, written all over with love and kindness; his deep, fervid blue eye, that wore such a gentle expression; and the scant, yet fair hair that rolled away from his magnificent forehead! He appeared to be slightly upwards of fifty; but I am sure from his face, that those fifty years had been most nobly spent.

I trembled as I replied:

"Yes, I am very fond of flowers."

He noticed my embarrassment, and smiled most benignantly.

"Did you ever see a magnolia before?"

"Is this a magnolia?" I inquired, pointing to the luxurious flower.

"Yes, and one of the finest I ever saw. It belongs to the South. Are you sure you never saw one before?" He fixed his eyes inquiringly upon me as I answered:

"Oh, quite sure, sir; I never was ten miles from my master's farm in my life."

"You are a slave?"

"Yes, sir. I am."

He waited a moment, then said:

" Are you happy ?"

I dared not tell a falsehood, yet to have truly stated my feelings, would have been dangerous ; so I evasively replied:

" Yes, as much so as most slaves."

I thought I heard him sigh, as he slowly moved away.

My eyes followed him with inquiring wonder. Who could he be ? Certain I was that no malice had prompted the question he had asked me. The circumstance created anxiety in my mind. All that day as I walked about, or waited on Miss Jane, that stranger's faces hone like a new-risen moon upon my darkened heart. Had I found, accidentally, one of those Northern Abolitionists, about whom I had heard so much ? Often after when sent upon errands for my mistress, I met him in the halls, and he always gave me a kind smile and a friendly salutation. Once Miss Jane observed this, and instantly accused me of having a dishonorable acquaintance with him. My honor was a thing that I had always guarded with the utmost vigilance, and to such a serious charge I perhaps made some hasty reply, whereupon Miss Jane seized a riding-whip, and cut me most severely across the face, leaving an ugly mark, a trace of which I still bear, and suppose I shall carry to my grave. Mr. Summerville expostulated with his wife, saying that it was better to use gentle means at first.

" No, husband," (she always thus addressed him,) " I know more about the management of *niggers* than you do."

This gross pronunciation of the word negro has a popular use even among the upper and educated classes of Kentucky. I am at a loss to account for it, in any other way than by supposing that they use it to express their deepest contempt.

Mr. Summerville was rather disposed to be humane to his servants. He was no advocate of the rod ; he used to term it the relic of barbarism. He preferred selling a refractory servant to whipping him. This did not accord particularly well with Miss Jane's views, and the consequence was they had many a little private argument that did not promise to end well.

Miss Jane made many acquaintances among the boarders in the hotel, with whom she was much pleased. She had frequent invitations to attend the theatre, concerts, and even parties. Many of the fashionables of the city called upon her, offering, in true Kentucky style, the hospitalities of their mansions. With this she was quite delighted, and her new life became one of intense interest and gratification, as her letters to her sister proved.

She would often regret Tildy was not there to share in her delight; but it had been considered best for her to remain at the old homestead until some arrangement could be made about the division of the estate. Two of the neighbors, a gentleman and his wife, took up their abode with her; but she expected to visit the city so soon as Miss Jane went to house-keeping, which would be in a few months. Miss Jane was frequently out spending social days and evenings with her friends, thus giving me the opportunity of going about more than I had ever done through the house. In this way I formed a pleasant acquaintance with several of the chambermaids, colored girls and free. Friendships thus grew up which have lasted ever since, and will continue, I trust, until death closes over us. One of the girls, Louise, a half-breed, was an especial favorite. She had read some, and was tolerably well educated. From her I often borrowed interesting books, compends of history, bible-stories, poems, &c. I also became a furious reader of newspapers, thus picking up, occasionally, much useful information. Louise introduced me, formally, to the head steward, an intelligent mulatto man, named Henry, of most prepossessing appearance; but the shadow of a great grief lurked in the full look of his large dark eye! "I am a slave, God help me!" seemed stamped upon his face; 'twas but seldom that I saw him smile, and then it was so like the reflection of a tear, that it pained me full as much as his sigh. He had access to the gentlemen's reading-room; and through him I often had the opportunity of

reading the leading Anti-slavery journals. With what avidity
I devoured them! How full they were of the noblest philanthropy! Great exponents of real liberty! at the words of your
argument my heart leaped like a new-fledged bird! Still pour
forth your burning eloquence; it will yet blaze like a watchfire
on the Mount of Liberty! The gladness, the hope, the faith it
imparted to my long-bowed heart, would, I am sure, give joy
to those noble leaders of the great cause.

CHAPTER XXIX.

THE ARGUMENT.

ONE day, when Miss Jane and Mr. Summerville had gone out at an early hour to spend the entire day, I little knew what to do with myself as I had no books nor papers to read, and Louise had business that took her out of the house.

The day was unusually soft and pleasant. I wandered through the halls, and, drawing near a private gallery that ran along in front of the gentlemen's room, I paused to look at a large picture of an English fox-chase, that adorned the wall. Whilst examining its rare and peculiar beauties, my ear was pleasantly struck by the sound of a much-esteemed voice, saying—

"Well, very well! Let us take seats here, in this retired place, and begin the conversation we have been threatening so long."

I glanced out at the crevice of the partially open door, and distinctly recognized the gentleman who had spoken to me of the magnolia, and who (I had learned) was James Trueman, of Boston, a man of high standing and social position, and a successful practitioner of law in his native State.

The other was a gentleman from Virginia, one of the very first families (there are no second, I believe), by the name of Winston, a man reputed of very vast possessions, a land-holder, and an extensive owner of slaves. I had frequently observed him in company with Mr. Trueman, and had inquired of Henry who and what he was.

I felt a little reluctant to remain in my position and hear this conversation, not designed for me ; yet a singular impulse urged

me to remain. I felt (and I scarce know why) that it had a
bearing upon the great moral and social question that so
agitated the country. Whilst I was debating with myself
about the propriety of a retreat, I caught a few words, which
determined me to stay and hear what I believed would prove
an interesting discussion.

"Let us, my dear Mr. Winston," began Mr. Trueman, "indulge for a few moments in a conversation upon this momentous
subject. Both of us have passed that time of life when the
ardor and impetuosity of youthful blood might unfit us for such
a discussion, and we may say what we please on this vexed
question with the distinct understanding, that however offensive
our language may become, it will be regarded as *general*, neither
meant nor understood to have any application to ourselves."

" I am quite willing and ready to converse as you propose,"
replied the other, in a quick, unpleasant tone, " and I gladly
accept the terms suggested, in which you only anticipate my
design. It is well to agree upon such restraint ; for though, as
you remind me, our advancing years have taken much of the
fervor from our blood, and left us calm, sober, thoughtful men,
the agitating nature of the subject and the deep interest which
both of us feel in it, should put us on our guard. If, then,
during the progress of the conversation, either of us shall be
unduly excited, let the recollection of the conditions upon which
we engage in it, recall him to his accustomed good-humor."

" Well, we have settled the preliminaries without difficulty,
and to mutual satisfaction. And now, the way being clear, our
discussion may proceed. I assume, then, in the outset, that the
institution of slavery, as it exists in the South, is a monstrous
evil. I assume this proposition ; not alone because it is the
universal sentiment of the ' rest of mankind ;' but also, because
it is now very generally conceded by slave-holders themselves."

" Pray, where did you learn that slave-holders ever made such
a concession ? As to what may be the sentiment of the ' rest
of mankind,' I may speak by-and-bye. For the present, my
concern is with the opinion of that large slave-holding class to

which I belong. I am extensively acquainted among them, and if that is their opinion of our peculiar institution, I am entirely ignorant of it."

" Your ignorance," said Mr. Trueman, with a smile, " in that regard, while it by no means disproves my proposition, may be easily explained. With your neighbors, who feel like yourself the dread responsibility of this crying abomination, it is not pleasant, perhaps, to talk upon it, and you avoid doing so without the slightest trouble ; because you have other and more engaging topics, such as the condition of your farms, the prospect of fine crops, and all the 'changes of the varying year.' But, read the declarations of your chosen Representatives, the favorite sons of the South, in the high councils of our nation ; and you will discover, that in all the debates involving it, slavery, in itself, and in its consequences, is frankly admitted to be a tremendous evil."

"Our Representatives may have sometimes thought proper to make such an admission to appease the fanaticism of Northern Abolitionists, and to quiet the agitations of the country in the spirit of generous compromise : but *I* am not bound to make it, and *I will not make it.* Neither do I avoid conversations with my neighbors upon the subject of slavery from the motive you intimate, nor from any other motive. I have frequently talked with them upon it, boldly and candidly, as I am prepared to talk to you or any reasonable man. Your proposition I positively deny, and can quickly refute." I thought there was a little anger in the tone in which he said this ; but no excitement was discernible in the clear, calm voice with which Mr. Trueman answered—

" Independently of the admission of your Representatives, which, I think, ought to bind you (for you must have been aware of it, and since it was public and undisputed, your acquiescence might be fairly presumed), there are many considerations that establish the truth of my position. But I cannot indorse your harsh reflection upon the Representatives of your choice. I cannot believe them capable of admitting, for any purpose, a proposition which, in their opinion and that of their constituents, asserts a falsehood. The immortal Henry Clay and such men as he are responsible for the admission, and not one of them was ever so timid as to be under the dominion of fear, or so dishonest as to be hypocritical."

A moment's pause ensued, when Mr. Winston appeared to rally, and said,

"I do not understand, then, if that was their real opinion, how it was possible for them to continue to hold slaves. To say the least of it, their practice was not in accordance with their theory. Hence I said, that under certain circumstances and to serve a special purpose, they may have conceded slavery to be an evil. For my own part, if I were persuaded that this proposition is true, it would constrain me to liberate all my slaves, whatever may be my attachment to them or the loss I should necessarily suffer. Some of them have been acquired by purchase ; others by inheritance : all of them seem satisfied with their treatment upon my estate ; yet nothing could induce me to claim the property I have hitherto thought I possessed in them, when convinced of the evil which your proposition asserts."

"Nothing could be fairer, my dear Mr. Winston. Your conviction will doubtless subject you to immense sacrifices : but these will only enhance your real worth as a man, and I am sure you will make them without hesitation, though it may be, not without reluctance. Now, it is a principle of law, well settled, that no person can in any manner convey a title, even to those things which are property, greater than that which he rightfully possesses. If, for instance, I acquire, by theft or otherwise, unlawful possession of your watch or other articles of value, which is transferred, by the operation of purchase and sale, through many hands, your right never ceases; and the process of law will enable you to obtain possession. Each individual who purchased the article, may have his remedy against him from whom he procured it, however extended the series of purchasers : but, since whatever right any one of them has was derived originally from me, and since my unlawful acquisition conferred no right at all, it follows that none was transmitted. Consequently, you were not divested, and the just spirit of law, continuing to recognize your property in the article whenever found, provides the ready means whereby you may reduce it once more to possession. This principle of law is not peculiar to a single locality; it enters into the remedial code of all civilized countries. Its benefits are accessible to the free negro in this land of the dark Southern border; and, I trust, it will not be long before those who are now held in slavery may be embraced in its beneficent operation. Whether it is recognized internationally, I am not fully prepared to say; but it ought to be, if it is not, for it is the dictate of equity and common sense. But, upon the hypothesis that it is so recognized, if the property of an inhabitant of Africa were stolen from him by a citizen of the United States, he might recover it. As for those people who, in the Southern States, are held as slaves, they or their ancestors came here originally not by their own choice, but by compulsion, from distant Africa. You will hardly deny, I presume, what is, historically, so evident—that "they were captured," as the phrase is, or, in our honest vernacular, *stolen* and brought by violence from their native homes. Had they been the proper subjects of property, what could prevent the application of the principle I have quoted?"

After two or three hems and haws, Mr. Winston began:

" I have never inquired particularly into the matter; but have always entertained the impression which pervades the Southern mind, that our negroes are legitimately our slaves, in pursuance of the malediction denounced by God against Ham and his descendants, of whom they are a part. And, so thinking, I believed we were entitled to the same right to them which we exercise over the beasts of the field, the fowls of the air, and the fishes of the deep. Moreover, your principle of law, which is indeed very correct, is inapplicable to their case. There is also a principle in the law of my State, incapacitating slaves to hold property. They are property themselves; and property cannot hold property. Apart from the terrible curse, which doomed them in the beginning, they were slaves in their own country to men of their own race; slaves by right of conquest. Therefore, taking the instance you have suggested, by way of illustration, were any article of value wrested from their possession, under this additional principle, the law could not give them any redress. But, inasmuch as whatever they may acquire becomes immediately the property of their master, to him the law will furnish a remedy."

" You do not deny," and here Mr. Trueman's tone was elevated and a little excited, " that the first of those who reached this country were stolen in Africa. Now, for the sake of the argument merely, I will admit that they were slaves at home. If they were slaves at home—it matters not whether by ' right or conquest,' or ' in pursuance of *the* curse,' they must have been the property of somebody, and those who stole them and sold them into bondage in America could give no valid title to their purchasers; for by the theft they had acquired none themselves. Hence, if ever they were slaves, they are still the property of their masters in Africa; but, if your interpretation of " the curse " is correct, those masters were also slaves, and, being such, under the principle of law which you have quoted, they could not for this reason hold property. Therefore, those oppressed and outraged, though benighted people, who were first sold into slavery, to the eternal disgrace of our land, were, in sheer justice, either *free*, or the property—even after the sale—of their African masters, if they had any; in neither case could they belong to those of our citizens who were unfortunate enough to buy them. They were not slaves of African masters: for, according to your argument, all of the race are slaves, and slaves cannot own slaves any more than horses can own horses; therefore, since no other people claimed dominion over them, they were, necessarily, free. You cannot escape from this dilemma, and the choice of either horn is fatal to your cause. Being free, might they not have held property like other nations? And, had any of it been stolen from them by those who are amenable to our laws, would not consistency compel us, who recognize the just principle I have quoted, to restore it to them? This is the course pursued among ourselves; and it ceases not with restoration; but on the offender it proceeds to inflict punishment, to prevent a repetition of the offence. This is the course we should pursue toward that down-trodden race whose greatest guilt is ' a skin not colored like our own.'

"As the case stands, it is not a question of property, but of that more valuable and sacred right, the right of *personal liberty*, of which we now boast so loudly. What, in the estimation of the world, is the worth of those multitudinous orations, apostrophies to liberty, which, on each recurring Fourth of July, in whatever quarter of the globe Americans may be assembled, penetrate the public ear? What are they worth to us, if, while reminding us of early colonial and revolutionary struggles against the galling tyranny of the British crown, they fail to inculcate the easy lesson of respect for the rights of all mankind? In keeping those poor Africans in the South still enslaved, you practically ignore this lesson, and you trample with unholy feet that divine ordinance which commands you ' to do unto others as you would have others do unto you.' By the oppression to which we were subjected under the yoke of Britain, and against which we wrestled so long, so patiently, so vigorously, in so many ways, and at last so triumphantly, I adjure you to put an end, at once and forever, to this business of holding slaves. This is oppression indeed, in comparison with which, that which drew forth our angry and bitter complaints, was very freedom. Let us, instead of perpetuating this infamous institution, be true to ourselves; let us vindicate the pretensions we set up when we characterize ours as ' the land of liberty, the asylum of the oppressed,' by proclaiming to the nations of the earth that, so soon as a slave touches the soil of America, his manacles shall fall from him: let us verify the words engraven in enduring brass on the old bell which from the tower of Independence Hall rang out our glorious Declaration, and in deed and in truth

12

proclaim 'Liberty to the captives, and the opening of the prison doors to them that are bound.' As you value truth, honor, justice, consistency, aye, humanity even, wipe out the black blot which defiles the border of our escutcheon, and the country will then be in reality what is now only in name, a *free* country, loving liberty disinterestedly for its own sake, and for that of all people, and nations, and tribes, and tongues.

"You may still, if you choose, dispute and philosophize about the inequality of races, and continue to insist on the boasted superiority of *our* Caucasian blood ; but the greatest disadvantages which a comparison can indicate will not prove that one's claim to liberty is higher than another's. It may be that we of the white race, are vastly superior to our African brethren. The differences, however, are not flattering to us ; for we should remember with shame and confusion of face, that our injustice and cruelty have produced them. Having first enslaved the poor Africans and subsequently withheld from them every means of improvement, it is not strange that such differences should exist as those on which we plume ourselves. But is it not intolerable that we should now quote them with such brazen self-gratulation ?

" Despite the manifold disadvantages that encumber and clog the movements of the Africans, unfortunately for the validity of your argument their race exhibits many proud specimens to prove their capability of culture, and of the enjoyment of freedom. Give them but the same opportunities that we have, and they will rival us in learning, refinement, statesmanship, and general demeanor, as is incontestibly shown in the lives and characters of many now living. Such men as Fred Douglas and President Roberts, would honor any complexion ; or, I ought rather to say, should make us forget and despise the distinctions of color, since they reach not below the surface of the skin, nor affect, in the least, that better part that gives to man all his dignity and worth. Nor need I point to these illustrious examples to rebut the inferences you deduce from color. Every village and hamlet in your own sunny South, can furnish an abundant refutation, in its obscure but eloquent 'colored preachers'—noble patterns of industry and wisdom, who show forth, by their exemplary bearing, all the beauty of holiness,— 'allure to brighter worlds and lead the way.'"

It is impossible to furnish even the faintest description of the pleading earnestness of the speaker's tone. His full, round, rich voice, grew intense, low and silvery in its harmonious utterance. As he pronounced the last sentence, it was with difficulty I could repress a cry of applause. Oh, surely, surely, I thought, our cause, the African's cause, is not helpless, is not lost, whilst it still possesses such an advocate. My eyes overflowed with grateful tears, and I longed to kiss the hem of his garment.

"You forget," answered Mr. Winston, "or you would do well to consider, that these cases are exceptional cases, which neither preclude my inferences nor warrant your assumption."

"Exceptions, indeed, they are; but why?" inquired Mr. Trueman. "Exceptions, you know, prove the rule. Now, you infer from the sooty complexion of the Africans, a natural and necessary incapacity for the blessings of self-government and the refinements of education. I have mentioned individuals of this fatal complexion who are in the wise enjoyment of these sublime privileges: one of them has acquired an enviable celebrity as an orator, the other is the accomplished President of the infant Liberian Republic. If color incapacitated, as you seem to think, it would affect all alike; but it has not incapacitated these, therefore it does not incapacitate at all. These are exceptions not to the general *capacity* of the blacks, but only to their general opportunity. What they have done others may do—the opportunities being equal."

"I have listened to you entire argument," rejoined Mr. Winston, "very patiently, with the expectation of hearing the proposition sustained with which you so vauntingly set out. You will, perhaps, accord to me the credit of being—what in this age of ceaseless talk is rarely met—'a good listener.' But, after all my patience and attention, I am still unsatisfied—if not unshaken. You have failed to meet the argument drawn from the ' curse' pronounced on the progenitors of the unfortunate race : you have failed to present or notice what is generally considered by theologians and moralists the right of a purchaser—in your illustration from stolen goods—to something for the money with which he parts ; and here, I think, you manifested great unfairness ; and, above all, you have failed to propose any feasible remedy for the state of things against which you inveigh. What have you to say on these material points ?"

"Very much, my good sir, as you will find, if, instead of taking advantage of every momentary pause to make out such a ' failure' as you desire, you only prolong your very complimentary patience. I wish you to watch the argument narrowly ; to expose the faintest flaw you can detect in it ; and, at the end, if unsatisfied, cry out ' failure,' or let it wring from you a reluctant confession. You will, at least, before I shall have done, withdraw the illiberal imputation of unfairness. It would be an easy task for me to anticipate all you can say, and to refute it ; but such a course would leave you nothing to say, and, since I intend this discussion to be strictly a conversation, I shall leave you at liberty to present your own arguments in your own way. Now, as to the argument from ' the curse,' you must permit me to observe, that your interpretation is too free and latitudinarian. Mine is more literal, more in accordance with the character of God ; it fully satisfies the Divine vengeance, and, whether correct or not, has, at least, as much authority in its favor. Granting the dominion of the white over the black race to be in virtue of ' the curse,' it by no means conveys such power as your Southern institution seeks to justify. The word *slave* nowhere occurs in that memorable malediction ; but there is an obvious distinction between *its* import and that of the word *servant*, which it *does* employ. Surely, for the offence of looking upon the nakedness of his father, Ham could not have incurred and entailed upon his posterity a heavier punishment than they would necessarily suffer as the simple servants of their brethren. And this consideration should induce you to give them, at least, the same share of freedom as is enjoyed by the *white servants* to be found in many a household in the South Such servitude would be the utmost that a merciful God could require. Even this, however, was under the old dispensation; and the reign of its laws, customs, and punishments, should melt under the genial rays of the sun of Christianity. Many of your own patriots, headed by Washington and Jefferson, have long since thought so; and but few in these days plead ' the curse' as excuse or justification for that ' damned spot' which all will come ultimately to consider the disgrace of this enlightened age and nation. As to your next point, the right which a purchaser of stolen goods may acquire in them in consideration of the money which he pays, I grant all the benefit that even the most generous theologian or moralist can allow in the best circumstances of such a case. And what does this amount to? A return of the purchase-money, with a reasonable or very high rate of interest for the detention, would be as much as any one could demand. Applying this to the case of the stolen Africans, how many of those who were forced from their native land to this have died on their master's hands without yielding by their labor, not alone the principal, but a handsome percentage upon the money invested in their purchase ? Thus purchasers were indemnified—abundantly indemnified, against loss. The indemnity, however, should have been sought from the seller, not from the article or person sold. But, at best, purchasers of stolen goods, to entitle themselves to any indemnity, should at least be innocent; for if they buy such goods, *knowing them to be stolen*, they are guilty of a serious misdemeanor, which is everywhere punishable under the law. ' He who asks equity must do equity.' When, therefore, you of the South would realize the benefit of the concession of theologians and moralists—the benefit of justice—you should bring yourselves within the conditions they require; you should come into court with clean hands, and with the intention of acting in good faith. Have you done so ?

Did your fathers do so before you? Not at all. They were not ignorant purchasers of the poor, ravished African; they knew full well that he had been stolen and brought by violence from his distant home : consequently, they were guilty of a misdemeanor in purchasing; consequently, too, they come not within the case proposed by the theologians and moralists, which might entitle them to indemnity; nor were they in a condition to ask it. The present generation, claiming through them, find themselves in the same predicament, with the same title only, and the same unclean hands, perpetuating their foul oppression. None of them, as I have shown, had a right to claim indemnity by reason of having invested their money in that way; and, if they ever had such right, they have been richly indemnified already. Therefore, it is absurd for you to continue the slave business upon this plea. Having thus answered your only objections to my position, I might remind you of your determination, and call upon you to 'liberate your slaves,' and take sides with me in opposition to the cruel institution. You are greatly mistaken in supposing that my omission to propose a plan, by which slave-holders could *conveniently, and without pecuniary loss,* emancipate their slaves, constitutes the slightest objection to the argument I have advanced. If you defer their emancipation until such a plan is proposed; if you are unwilling to incur even a little sacrifice, what nobility will there be in the act, to entitle you to the consideration of the just and good, or to the approval of your own consciences? I sought by this discussion, to convince you that slavery is an enormous evil; the proposition was declared in all its boldness. You volunteered a pledge to release your slaves if I could sustain it, let the sacrifice be what it might. Some sacrifice, then, you must have anticipated; and, should your conviction now demand it, you have no cause to complain of me. Your pledge was altogether voluntary; I did not even ask it; nor did I design to suggest any such plan of universal emancipation as would suit the *convenience* of everybody. I am not so extravagantly silly as to hope to do that. But, after all, why wait for a *plan*?

Immediate, universal emancipation is not impracticable, and numberless methods might and would at once be devised, if the people of your States were sincere when they profess to desire its accomplishment. Their *real* wish, however, whatever it may be, need not interfere between your individual pledge, and its prompt fulfilment."

Mr. Trueman paused for full five minutes, and, as I peered out from my hiding-place, I thought there was a very quizzical sort of expression on his fine face.

" Well, what have you to say ?" he at length asked.

" It seems to me," Mr. Winston began, in an angry tone, " you speak very flippantly and very wildly about general emancipation. Consider, sir, that slavery is so woven into our society, that there is scarcely a family that would not be more or less affected by a change. Fundamental alterations in society, to be safely made, must be the slow work of years :

> ' Not the hasty product of a day,
> But the well-ripened fruit of wise delay.'

So it is only by almost imperceptible degrees that the emancipationists and impertinent Abolitionists can ever attain ' the consummation' they pretend to have so much at heart. If they would just stay at home and devote their spare time to cleansing their own garments, leaving us of the South to suffer alone what they are pleased to esteem the evil and sin and curse, the shame, burden and abomination of slavery, we should the sooner discover its blasting enormities, and strive more zealously to abolish them and the institution from which they proceed. Their super-serviceable interference, hitherto, has only riveted and tightened the bondage of those with whom they sympathize; and such a result will always attend it. Our slaves, as at present situated, are very well satisfied, as, indeed, they ought to be : for they are exempt from the anxious cares of the free, as to what they shall eat or what they shall drink, or wherewithal they shall be clothed. Many poor men of our own color would gladly exchange conditions with them, because they find life to be a hard, an incessant struggle for the scantiest comforts, with which our slaves are supplied at no cost of personal solicitude. Besides, sir, our institution of slavery is vastly more burdensome to ourselves than to the negroes for whom you affect so much fraternal love."

" One would suppose, that if you thought it burdensome, you would be making some effort to relieve yourselves," interposed Mr. Trueman, in that clear and pointed manner that was his peculiarity ; " and, if immediate emancipation were deemed impracticable in consequence of the radical hold which this institution has at the South, you might naturally be expected to be doing something toward that end by the encouragement of education among those in bondage, by the sanction of marriage ties between them, and by other efforts to ameliorate their condition. Certain inducements might be presented for the manumission of slaves by individual owners, for there are some of this class, I am happy to think, who, in tender humanity, would release their slaves, if the stringency of the laws did not deter them from it. Would it not be well to abate somewhat of this rigor, and allow all slaves, voluntarily manumitted, to remain in the several States with at least the privileges of the free negroes now resident therein, so that the olden ties, which have grown up between themselves and their owners, might not be abruptly snapped asunder ? Besides, to enforce the propriety of this alteration of the law, it would be well to reflect that the South is the native home of most of the slaves, who cherish their local attachments quite as much as ourselves ; and hence the law which now requires them, when by any means they have obtained their freedom, to remove beyond the limits of the State, is a very serious hardship and should cease to exist. This would be a long stride toward your own relief from the burden of which you complain. As to the slaves, who you think should be content with their condition, in which they have, as you say, ' no care for necessary food and raiment,' I would suggest that they have the faculty of distinguishing between slavery and bondage, and have sense enough to see that though these things, which are generally of the coarsest kind, are provided by their masters, the means by which they are furnished are but a scanty portion of their own hard earnings. Were they free, they could work in the same way, and be entitled to *all* the fruits of their labor. Then they would have the same inducements to toil that we now have, and the same ambition to lift themselves higher and higher in the social scale. Those white men whom you believe willing to exchange situations with them, are too indolent to enjoy the privileges of freedom, and would be utterly worthless as slaves. You declaim against the course which the Abolitionists have pursued, and seem disposed, in consequence, to tighten the cords of servitude. You would be let alone, forsooth, to bear this burden as long as you please, and to get rid of it at pleasure. So long as there was any hope that you would do what you ought in the matter, you were let alone, and if you were the only sufferers from your peculiar institution, you might continue undisturbed; but the yoke lies heavy and galling upon the poor slaves themselves, whose voices are stifled, and it is high time for the friends of human rights to speak in their behalf, till they make themselves heard. At this momentous period, when new States and Territories are knocking for admission at the doors of our Union—States and Territories of free and virgin soil, which you are seeking to defile by the introduction of slavery—it is fit that they should persevere in their noble efforts, that they should resist your endeavors, and strive with all their energies to confine the obnoxious institution within its already too-extended bounds; for they know, that, if they would attain their object—the ultimate and entire abolition of slavery from our land—they should oppose strenuously every movement tending to its extension; for, the broader the surface over which it spreads, the more formidable will be the difficulty of its removal. Therefore it is that they are now so zealously engaged, and they address you as men whose 'judgment has not fled to brutish beasts,' with arguments against the evil itself and the weight of anguish it entails. Thus they have ever done, and you tell me that the result has

12*

been to rivet the chains of those in whose behalf they plead. As well might the sinner, whose guilt is pointed out to him by the minister of God, resolve for that very reason to plunge more deeply into sin."

His voice became gradually calmer and calmer, until finally it sank into the low notes of a solemn half-whisper. I held my breath in intense excitement, but this transport was broken by the harsh tones of the Virginian, who said :

"All this is very ridiculous as well as unjust; for, at the South slaves are regarded as property, and, inasmuch as our territories are acquired by the common blood and treasure of the whole country, we have as much right to locate in them with our property as you have with any of those things which are recognized as property at the North. In your great love of human rights you might take some thought of us ; but the secret of your action is jealousy of our advancement by the aid of slave-labor, which you would have at the North if you needed it. We understand you well, and we are heartily tired of your insulting and impudent cant about the evils of the system of slavery. We want no more of it."

Mr. Trueman, without noticing the insolence of Winston, continued in the same impressive manner:

"We do take much thought of you at the South, and hence it is that we dislike to see you passively submitting to the continuance of an institution so fraught with evil in itself, and very burdensome, as even you have admitted. We, of the North, feel strongly bound to you by the recollection of common dangers, struggles and trials ; and, with an honorable pride, we wish our whole nation to stand fair, and, so far as possible, blameless before the world. We are doing all we can to remove the evils of every kind which exist at the North; and, as we are not sectional in our purposes, we would stimulate you to necessary action in regard to your especial system. We know its evils from sore experience, for it once prevailed amongst us ; but, fortunately, we opened our eyes, and gave ourselves a blessed riddance of it. The example is well worthy of your imitation, but, 'pleased as you are with the possession, says Blackstone, speaking of the origin and growth of property, 'you seem afraid to look back to the means by which it was acquired, as if fearful of some defect in your title ; or, at best, you rest satisfied with the decision of the laws in your favor, without examining the reason or authority upon which those laws have been built.' To the eyes of the nations, who regard us from far across the ocean, and who see us, as a body, better than we see ourselves, slavery is the great blot that obscures the disc of our Republic, dimming the effulgence of its Southern half, as a partial eclipse darkens the world's glorious luminary. It is, therefore, not alone upon the score of human rights in general, but from a personal interest in our National character, that the Abolitionists interfere. Various Congressional enactments have confirmed the justice of these views, which they are endeavoring to enforce by moral suasion (for they deprecate violence) upon the South. Those enactments assume jurisdiction, to some extent at least, upon the subject of slavery, having gone so far as to prohibit the continuance of the slave-trade, denouncing it as piracy, and punishing with death those who are in any way engaged in it. I have·yet to learn that the South has ever protested against this law, in which the Abolitionists see a strong confirmation of their own just principles. Why should they not go a step further, and forbid all traffic in slaves, such as is pursued among your people ? Why do not the States themselves interpose their power to put down at once and forever, such nefarious business? This would be productive of vastly more good than anything which Colonization societies can effect."

"Suppose, sir," began Mr. Winston, "we were to annul the present laws regulating the manumission of slaves, and to abolish the institution entirely from our midst ; where would be the safety of our own white race ? There is great cause for the apprehension generally entertained, of perpetual danger and annoyance, if they were permitted to remain among us. They are there in large numbers, and, having once obtained their

freedom, with permission to reside where they now are, they
would seek to become ' a power in the State,' which would in-
cite them, if resisted, into fearful rebellion.   These are contin-
gencies which sagacious statesmen have foreseen. and which
they would be unable to avert.   Consequently, they had rather
bear those ills they have, than fly to others that they know not
of."

"How infelicitous," Mr. Trueman suddenly retorted, "is your
quotation, for, truly, you ' know not' that these anticipated
consequences would ensue ; but ' motes they are to trouble
the mind's eye.'   Your sagacious statesmen might more wisely
employ their thoughts in contemplating the more probable results of continuing your slaves in their present abject condition.
Far more reason is there to apprehend rebellion and insurrection
now, than the distant dangers you predict.   Even this last objection is vain, unsubstantial, and, at best, only speculative,
resorted to as an unction to mollify the sores of conscience.
Some of your eminent men have expressed a hope that the
colored race might be removed from the South, and from
slavery, through the instrumentality of Colonization, by which,
it is expected, that they would eventually be transported to
Africa, and encouraged to establish governments for themselves.   This proposal is liable, and with more emphasis, to the
objection I advanced a while ago, when speaking of the laws
which practically discourage manumission, for, if it is a hardship (as I contend it is) for them to be driven from their native
State to one strange and unfamiliar to them, it is increasing
that severity to require them to seek a home in Africa, whose
climate is as uncongenial to them as to us, and with whose institutions they 'feel as little interest, or identity, as we do.
Admit, for a moment, the practicability of such a scheme.   We
should, soon after, be called upon to recognize them as one of
the nations of the earth, with whom we should treat as we do
now with the English, French, German, and other nations.   I
will suggest to your Southern sages, who delight in specula-
tions, that, in the progress of years, they might desire, in imita-

tion of some other people, to accept the invitations we extend to the oppressed and unhappy of the earth. What is there, in that case, to hinder them from immigrating in large numbers? Could you distinguish between immigrants of their class, and those who now settle upon our soil? Either you could or you could not. If you could not so distinguish, you would in all likelihood have them speedily back, in greater numbers than they come from Green Erin, or Fader-land. Thus you would be reduced to almost the same condition as general emancipation would bring about; but, if you could, and did make the distinction, is it not quite likely that deadly offence would be given to their government, which, added to their already accumulated wrongs, would light up the fires of a more frightful war than the intestine rebellion you have talked of; or than any that has ever desolated this continent? Bethink yourselves of these things amid your gloomy forebodings, and you will find them pregnant with fearful issues. You will discover, too, the folly of longer maintaining your burdensome system, and the wisdom of heeding whilst you may, the counsel of the philanthropic, which urges you to just, generous, speedy, universal emancipation. But I have fatigued you, and will stop; hoping soon to hear that you have magnanimously redeemed the promise which I had the gratification to hear at the commencement of our conversation."

When Mr. Trueman paused, Mr. Winston sprang to his feet in a rage, knocking over his chair in the excitement, and declaring that he had most patiently listened to flimsy Abolition talk, in which there was no shadow of argument, mere common cant; that he would advise Mr. Trueman to be more particular in the dissemination of his dangerous and obnoxious opinions; and, as to his own voluntary pledge, it was conditional, and those conditions had not been complied with, and he did not consider himself bound to redeem it. Mr. Trueman endeavored to calm and soothe the hot-blooded Southerner; but his words had no effect upon the illiberal man, whom he had so fairly demolished in argument.

As they passed my hiding-place, *en route* to their respective apartments, I peeped out through a crevice in the door at them. It was very easy to detect the calm, self-poised man, the thoughtful reasoner, in the still, pale face and erect form of Trueman; whilst the red, hot-flushed countenance, the quick, peering eye and audacious manner of the other, revealed his unpleasant disposition and unsystematized mind.

When the last echo of their retreating footsteps had died upon the ear, I stole from my concealment, and ventured to my own quarters. Many new thoughts sprang into existence in my mind, suggested by the conversation to which I had listened.

I venerated Mr. Trueman more than ever. No disciple ever regarded the face of his master so reverently as I watched his countenance, when I chanced to meet him in any part of the house.

CHAPTER XXX.

THE next day Miss Jane, observing my unusual thoughtfulness, said :

"Come, now, Ann, you are not quite free. From the airs that you have put on, one would think you had been made so."

"What have I done, Miss Jane ?" This was asked in a quiet tone, perhaps not so obsequiously as she thought it should be. Thereupon she took great offence.

"How dare you, Miss, speak *to me* in that tone ? Take that," and she dealt me a blow across the forehead with a long, limber whalebone, that laid the flesh open. I was so stunned by it that I reeled, and should have fallen to the floor, had I not supported myself by the bed-post.

"Don't you dare to scream."

I attempted to bind up my brow with a handkerchief This she regarded as affectation.

"Take care, Miss Ann," she often prefixed the Miss when she was mad, by way of taunting me; "give yourself none of those important airs. I'll take you down a little."

When Mr. Summerville entered, she began to cry, saying :

"Husband, this nigger-wench has given me a great deal of impertinence. Father never allowed it ; now I want to know if you will not protect me from such insults."

"Certainly, my love, I'll not allow any one, white or black, to insult you. Ann, how dare you give your mistress impudence ?"

"I did not mean it, Master William." I had thus addressed him ever since his marriage.

I attempted to relate the conversation that had occurred,

wherein Miss Jane thought I had been impudent, when she
suddenly sprang up, exclaiming :

"Do you allow a negro to give testimony against your own
wife ?"

"Certainly not."

"Now, Mr. Summerville," she was getting angry with him,
"I require you to whip that girl severely; if you don't do
it—why—" and she ground her teeth fiercely.

"I will have her whipped, my dear, but I cannot whip her."

"Why can't you ?" and the lady's eye flashed.

"Because I should be injured by it. *Gentlemen* do not correct negroes ; they hire others to do that sort of business."

"Ah, well, then, hire some one who will do it well."

"Come with me, Ann," he said to me, as I stood speechless
with fear and mortification.

"Seeing him again motion me to follow, I, forgetful of the injustice that had been done me, and the honest resentment I
should feel—forgetful of everything but the humiliation to which
they were going to subject me—fell on my knees before Miss
Jane, and besought her to excuse, to forgive me, and I would
never offend her again.

"Don't dare to ask mercy of me. You know that I am too
much like father to spare a nigger."

Ah, well I knew it! and vainly I sued to her. I might have
known that she rejoiced too much in the sport; and, had she
been in the country, would have asked no higher pleasure than
to attend to it personally. A negro's scream of agony was
music to her ears.

I governed myself as well as I could while I followed Mr.
Summerville through the halls and winding galleries. Down
flights of steps, through passages and lobbys we went, until at
last we landed in the cellar. There Mr. Summerville surrendered me to the care of a Mr. Monkton, the bar-keeper of the
establishment duly appointed and fitted for the office of slave-
whipping.

"Here," said Mr. Summerville, "give this girl a good, gen-

teel whipping; but no cruelty, Monkton, and here is your fee;"
so saying he handed him a half-dollar, then left the dismal
cellar.

I have since read long and learned accounts of the gloomy,
subterranean cells, in which the cruel ministers of the Spanish
Inquisition performed their horrible deeds; and I think this
cellar very nearly resembled them. There it was, with its low,
damp, vault-like roof; its unwholesome air, earthen floor, covered with broken wine bottles, and oyster cans, the debris of
many a wild night's revel! There stood the monster Monkton,
with his fierce, lynx eye, his profuse black beard, and frousy
brows; a great, stalwart man, of a hard face and manner, forming no bad picture of those wolfish inquisitors of cruel, Catholic
Spain!

Over this untempting scene a dim, waning lamp, threw its
blue glare, only rendering the place more hideous.

"Now, girl, I am to lick you well. You see the half-dollar.
Well, I'm to git the worth of it out of your hide. Now, what
would you think if I didn't give you a single lick?"

I looked him full in the face, and even by that equivocal
light I had power to discern his horrid purpose, and I quickly
and proudly replied,

"I should think you did your duty poorly."

"And why?"

"Because you engaged to do *the job*, and even received your
pay in advance; therefore, if you fail to comply with your bargain, you are not trustworthy."

' Wal, you're smart enough for a lawyer."

"Well, attend to your business."

"This is my business," and he held up a stout wagon-whip;
" come, strip off."

"That is not a part of the contract."

"Yes; but it's the way I always whips 'em."

"You were not told to use me so, and I am not going to remove one article of my clothing."

"Yes, but you *shall*;" and he approached me, his wild eye

glaring with a lascivious light, and the deep passion-spot blazing on his cheek.

"Girl, you've got to yield to me. I'll have you now, if its only to show you that I can."

I drew back a few steps, and, seizing a broken bottle, waited, with a deadly purpose, to see what he would do. He came so near that I almost fancied his fetid breath played with its damnable heat upon my very cheek.

"You've got to be mine. I'll give you a fine calico dress, and a pretty pair of ear-bobs!"

This was too much for further endurance. What! must I give up the angel-sealed honor of my life in traffic for trinkets? Where is the woman' that would not have hotly resented such an insult?

I turned upon him like a hungry lioness, and just as his wanton hand was about to be laid upon me, I dexterously aimed, and hurled the bottle directly against his left temple. With a low cry of pain he fell to the floor, and the blood oozed freely from the wound.

As my first impression was that I had slain him, so was it my first desperate impulse to kill myself; yet with a second thought came my better intention, and, unlocking the door, I turned and left the gloomy cell. I mounted the dust-covered steps, and rapidly threaded silent, spider-festooned halls, until I regained the upper courts. How beautiful seemed the full gush of day-light to me! But the heavy weight of a supposed crime bowed me to the earth.

My first idea was to proceed directly to Mr. Summerville's apartment and make a truthful statement of the affair. What he would do or have done to me was a matter upon which I had expended no thought. My apprehension was altogether for the safety of my soul. Homicide was so fearful a thing, that even when committed in actual self-defence, I feared for the justice of it. The Divine interrogatory made to Cain rang with painful accuracy in my mental ear! "Am I my brother's keeper?" I repeated it again and again, and I lived years in the brief space of a moment. Away over the trackless void of the future fled imagination, painting all things and scenes with a sombre color.

The first recognizable person whom I met was Mr. Winston. I knew there was but little to hope for from him, for ever since the argument between himself and Mr. Trueman, he had appeared unusually haughty; and the waiters said that he had become excessively overbearing, that he was constantly knocking them around with his gold-headed cane, and swearing that Kentucky slaves were almost as bad as Northern free negroes.

Henry (who had become a *most dear friend of mine*) told me that Mr. Winston had on one or two occasions, without the slightest provocation, struck him severely over the head; but these things were pretty generally done in the presence of Mr. Trueman, and for no higher object, I honestly believe, than to annoy that pure-souled philanthropist. So I was assured that he was not one to entrust with my secret, especially as a great intimacy had sprung up between him and Miss Jane. I, therefore, hastily passed him, and a few steps on met Mr. Trueman. How serene appeared his chaste, marble face ! Who that looked upon him, with his quiet, reflective eye, but knew that an angel sat enthroned within his bosom ? Do not such faces help to prove the perfectibility of the race ? If, as the transcendentalists believe, these noble characters are only types of what the *whole man* will be, may we not expect much from the advent of that dubious personage ?

"Mr. Trueman," I said, and my voice was clear and unfaltering, for something in his face and manner exorcised all fear, "I have done a fearful deed."

"What, child ?" he asked, and his eye was full of solicitude.

I then gave him a hurried account of what had occurred in the cellar. After a slight pause, he said :

"The best thing for you to do will be to make instant confession to Mr. Summerville. Alas ! I fear it will go hard with you, for *you are a slave*."

I thanked him for the interest he had manifested in me, and

passed on to Miss Jane's room. I paused one moment at the door, before turning the knob. What a variety of feelings were at work in my breast! Had I a fellow-creature's blood upon my hands? I trembled in every limb, but at length controlled myself sufficiently to enter.

There sat Miss Jane, engaged at her crochet-work, and Master William playing with the balls of cotton and silk in her little basket.

"Well, Ann, I trust you've got your just deserts, a good whipping," said Miss Jane, as she fixed her eyes upon me.

Very calmly I related all that had occurred. Mr. Summerville sprang to his feet and rushed from the room, whilst Miss Jane set up a series of screams loud enough to reach the most distant part of the house. All my services were required to keep her from swooning, or *affecting to swoon.*

The ladies from the adjoining room srushed in to her assistance, and were soon busy chafing her hands, rubbing her feet, and bathing her temples.

"Isn't this terrible!" ejaculated one.

"What *is* the matter?" cried another.

"Poor creature, she is hysterical," was the explanation of a third.

I endeavored to explain the cause of Miss Jane's excitement.

"You did right," said one lady, whose truly womanly spirit burst through all conventionality and restraint.

"What," said one, a genuine Southern conservative, "do you say it was right for a slave to oppose and resist the punishment which her master had directed?"

"Certainly not; but it was right for a female, no matter whether white or black, to resist, even to the shedding of blood, the lascivious advances of a bold libertine."

"Do you believe the girl's story?"

"Yes; why not?"

"I don't; it bears the impress of falsehood on its very face."

"No," added another Kentucky true-blue, "Mr Monkton

was going to whip her, and she resisted him. That's the correct version of the story, I'll bet my life on it."

To all of this aspersion upon myself, I was bound to be a silent auditor, yet ever obeying their slightest order to hand them water, cologne, &c. Is not this slavery indeed?

When Mr. Summerville left the room, he hastily repaired to the bar, where he made the story known, and getting assistance, forthwith went to the cellar, Mr. Winston forming one of the party of investigation. His Southern prejudices were instantly aroused, and he was ready " to do or die" for the propogation of the " peculiar institution."

The result of their trip was to find Monkton very feeble from the loss of blood, and suffering from the cut made by the broken bottle, but with enough life left in him for the fabrication of a falsehood, which was of course believed, as he had a *white face.* He stated that he had proceeded to the administration of the whipping, directed by my master ; that I resisted him ; and finding it necessary to bind me, he was attempting to do so, when I swore that I would kill him, and that suiting the action to the word, I hurled the broken bottle at his temples.

When Mr. Summerville repeated this to Miss Jane, in my presence, stating that it was the testimony that Monkton was prepared to give in open court, for I was to be arrested, I could not refrain from uttering a cry of surprise, and saying :

" Mr. Monkton has misrepresented the case, as ' I can show.' "

"' Yes, but you will not be allowed to give evidence," said Master William.

" Will Mr. Monkton's testimony be taken ?" I inquired.

" Certainly, but a negro cannot bear witness against a white person."

I said nothing, but many thoughts were troubling me.

" You see, Ann, what your bad conduct has brought *you to,*" said Miss Jane.

Again I attempted to tell the facts of the case, and defend myself, but she interrupted me, saying :

" Do you suppose I believe a word of that ? I can assure

you I do not, and, moreover, I'm not going to spend my money to have a lawyer employed to keep you from the punishment you so richly deserve. So you must content yourself to take the public hanging or whipping in the jail yard, which is the penalty that will be affixed to your crime." Turning to Mr. Summerville, she added, " I think it will do Ann good, for it will take down her pride, and make her a valuable nigger. She has been too proud of her character; for my part, I had rather she had had less virtue. I've always thought she was virtuous because she did not want us to increase in property, and was too proud to have her children live in bondage."

I dared not make any remark; but there I stood in dread of the approaching arrest, which came full soon.

As I was sewing for Miss Jane, Mr. Summerville opened the door, and said to a rough man, pointing to me—

" There's the girl."

" Come along with me to jail, gal."

How fearfully sounded the command. The jail-house was a place of terror, and though I had in my brief life "supped full of horrors," this was a new species of torture that I had hoped to leave untasted.

Taking with me nothing but my bonnet, I followed Constable Calcraft down stairs into the street. Upon one of the landings I met Henry, and I knew from his kindly mournful glance, that he gave me all his compassion.

" Good-bye, Ann," he said, extending his hand to me, " good-bye, and keep of good cheer; the Lord will be with you." I looked at him, and saw that his lip was quivering; and his dark eye glittered with a furtive tear. I dared not trust my voice, so, with a grateful pressure of the hand, I passed him by, keeping up my composure right stoutly. At the foot of the stair I met Louise, who was weeping.

" I believe you, Ann, we all believe you, and the Lord will make it appear on the day of your trial that you are right, only keep up your spirits, and read this," and she slipped a little pocket-Testament into my hand, which was a welcome present.

Now, I thought, the last trial is over. All the tender ones who love me have spoken their comforting words, and I may resume my pride and hauteur; but no—standing within the vestibule was the man whom I reverenced above all others, Mr. Trueman. One effort more, and then I might be calm; but before the sunshine of his kindliness the snow and ice of my pride melted and passed away in showers of tears. The first glance of his pitying countenance made me weep. I was weary and heavy-laden, and, even as to a mortal brother, I longed to pour into his ear the pent-up agony of my soul.

"Poor girl," he said kindly, as he offered me his white and finely-formed hand, "I believe you innocent; there is that in your clear, womanly look, your unaffected utterance, that proves to me you are worthy to be heard. Trust in God."

Oh, can I ever forget the diamond-like glister of his blue eyes! and *that tear* was evoked from its fountain for my sorrow; even then I felt a thrill of joy. We love to have the sympathy and confidence of the truly great. I made no reply, in words, to Mr. Trueman, but he understood me.

Conducted by the constable, I passed through a number of streets, all crowded with the busy and active, perhaps the *happy*. Ah, what a fable that word seemed to express! I used to doubt every smiling face I saw, and think it a *radiant lie !* but, since then, though in a subdued sense, I have learned that mortals may be happy.

We stopped, after a long walk, in front of a large building of Ionic architecture, and of dark brown stone, ornamented by beautiful flutings, with a tasteful slope of rich sward in front, adorned with a variety of flowers and shrubbery. Through this we passed and reached the first court, which was surrounded by a high stone-wall. Passing through a low door-way, we stood on the first pave; here I was surrendered to the keeping of the jailer, a man apparently devoid of generosity and humanity. After hearing from Constable Calcraft an account of the crime for which I was committed, he observed—

"A sassy, impudent, *on*ruly gal, I guess; we have plenty

sich; this will larn her a lessin. Come with me," he said, as he turned his besotted face toward me.

Through dirty, dark, filthy passages I went, until we reached a gloomy, loathsome apartment, in which he rudely thrust me, saying—

" Thar's your quarters."

Such a place as it was ! A small room of six by eight, with a dirty, discolored floor, over which rats and mice scampered *ad libitum.* One miserable little iron grate let in a stray ray of daylight, only revealing those loathsome things which the friendly darkness would have concealed. Cowering in the corner of this wretched pen was a poor, neglected white woman, whose face seemed unacquainted with soap and water, and her hair tagged, ragged, and unused to comb or brush. She clasped to her breast a weasly suckling, that every now and then gave a sickly cry, indicative of the cholic or a heated atmosphere.

" Poor comfort !" said the woman, as I entered, " poor comfort here, whare the starved wretches are cryin' for ar. My baby has bin a sinkin' ever sense I come here. I'd not keer much if we could both die."

" For what are you to be tried ?"

" For takin' a loaf of bread to keep myself and child from starvin'."

She then asked me for what I stood accused. I told her my story, and we grew quite talkative and sociable, thereby realizing the old axiom, " Misery loves company."

    *   *   *   *   *   *   *

For several days I lingered on thus, diversifying the time only by reading my Testament, the gift of Louise, and occasionally having a long talk with my companion, whom I learned to address by the name of Fanny. She was a woman of remarkably sensitive feelings, quick and warm in all her impulses; just such a creature as an education and kindly training would have made lovely and lovable; but she had been utterly neglected—had grown up a complete human weed.

Our meals were served round to us upon a large wooden drawer, as filthy as dirt and grease could make it. The cuisine dashed our rations, a slice of fat bacon and "pone" of corn bread to us, with as little ceremony as though we had been dogs; and we were allowed one blanket to sleep on.

One day, when I felt more than usually gloomy, I was agreeably disappointed, as the cumbersome door opened to admit my kind friend Louise. The jailer remarked:

"You may stay about a quarter of an hour, but no longer."

"Thank you, sir," she replied.

"This is very kind of you, Louise," for I was touched by the visit.

"I wanted to see you, Ann; and look what I brought you!" She held a beautiful bouquet to me.

"Thank you, thank you a thousand times, this *is* too kind," I said, as I watered the lovely flowers with my tears.

"Oh, they were sent to you," she answered, with a smile.

"And who sent them?"

"Why, Henry, of course;" and again she smiled.

I know not why, but I felt the blood rushing warmly to my face, as I bent my head very low, to conceal a confusion which I did not understand.

"But here is something that I did bring you," and, opening a basket, she drew out a nice, tempting pie, some very delicious fruit cake, and white bread.

"I suppose your fare is miserable?"

"Oh, worse than miserable."

Fanny drew near me, and without the least timidity, stretched forth her hand.

"Oh, please give me some, only a little; I'm nearly starved?"

I freely gave her the larger portion, for she could enjoy it. I had the flowers, the blessed flowers, that Henry had sent, and they were food and drink for me!

Louise informed me that, since my arrest, she had cleared up and arranged Miss Jane's room; and she thought it was Mr. Summerville's intention to sell me after the trial.

13

"Have you heard who will buy me?" I asked.

"Oh, no, I don't suppose an offer has yet been made; nor do I know that it is their positive intention to sell you; but that is what I judged from their conversation."

"If they get me a good master I am very willing to be sold; for I could not find a worse home than I have now."

"I expect if he sells you, it will be to a trader; but, keep up your heart and spirits. Remember, 'sufficient for the day is the evil thereof.' But I hear the sound of footsteps; the jailer is coming; my quarter of an hour is out."

"How came he to admit you?"

"Oh, I know Mr. Trayton very well. I've washed for his wife, and she owes me a little bill of a couple of dollars; so when I came here, I said by way of a bait, 'Now, Mrs. Trayton, I didn't come to dun you, I'll make you a present of that little bill;' then she and he were both in a mighty good humor with me. I then said, "I've got a friend here, and I'd take it as a favor if you'd let me see her for a little while.'

"Mr. Trayton said:

"'Oh, that can't be—it's against the rules.'

"So his wife set to work, and persuaded him that he owed me a favor, and he consented to let me see you for a quarter of an hour only. Before he comes, tell me what message I am to give Henry for you. I know he will be anxious to hear."

Again I felt the blood tingling in my veins, and overspreading my face. I began to play with my flowers, and muttered out something about gratitude for the welcome present, a message which, incoherent as it was, her woman's wit knew to be sincere and gracious. After a few moments the jailer came, saying:

"Louise, your time is up."

"I am ready to go," and she took up her basket. After bidding me a kind adieu she departed, carrying with her much of the sunshine which her presence had brought, but not all of it, for she left with me a ray or so to illumine the darkened cell of recollection. There on my lap lay the blooming flowers, *his* gift! Flowers are always a joy to us—they gladden and beautify our outer and every-day life; they preach us a sermon of beauty and love; but to the weary, lonely captive, in his dismal cell, they are particularly beautiful! They speak to him in a voice which nothing else can, of the glory of the sun-lit world, from which he is exiled. Thanks to God for flowers! Rude, and coarse, and vile must be the nature that can trample them with unhallowed feet!

There I sat toying with them, inhaling their mystic odor, and luxuriating upon the delicacy of their ephemeral beauty. All flowers were dear to me; but these were particularly precious, and wherefore? Is there a single female heart that will not divine "the wherefore"? You, who are clad in satin, and decked with jewels, albeit your face is as white as snow, cannot boast of emotions different from ours? Feeling, emotion, is the same in the African and the white woman? We are made of the same clay, and informed by the same spirit.

The better portion of the night I sat there, sadly wakeful, still clutching those flowers to my breast, and covering them with kisses.

The heavy breathing of my companion sounded drowsily in my ear, yet never wooed me to a like repose. Thus wore on the best part of the night, until the small, shadowy hours, when I sank to a sweet dream. I was wandering in a rich garden of tropical flowers, with Henry by my side! Through enchanted gates we passed, hand in hand, singing as we went. Long and dreamily we loitered by low-gurgling summer fountains, listening to the lulling wail of falling water. Then we journeyed on toward a fairy flower-palace, that loomed up greenly in the distance, which ever, as we approached it, seemed to recede further.

I awoke before we reached the floral palace, and I am womanly enough to confess, that I felt annoyed that the dream had been broken by the cry of Fanny's babe. I puzzled myself trying to read its import. Are there many women who would have differed from me? Yet I was distressed to find

Fanny's little boy-babe very sick, so much so as to require medical attention; but, alas! she was too poor to offer remuneration to a doctor, therefore none was sent for; and, as the child was attacked with croup, it actually died for the want of medical attention. And this occurred in a community boasting of its enlightenment and Christianity, and in a city where fifty-two churches reared their gilded domes and ornamented spires, in a God-fearing and God-serving community, proud of its benevolent societies, its hospitals, &c. In what, I ask, are these Christians better than the Pharisees of old, who prayed long, well, and much, in their splendid temples?

CHAPTER XXXI.

THE DAY OF TRIAL—ANXIETY—THE VOLUNTEER COUNSEL—VERDICT OF THE JURY.

THE day of my trial dawned as fair and bright as any that ever broke over the sinful world. It rose upon my slumber mildly, and without breaking its serenity. I slept better on the night preceding the trial, than I had done since my incarceration.

I knew that I was friendless and alone, and on the eve of a trial wherein I stood accused of a fearful crime ; that I was defenceless ; yet I rested my cause with Him, who has bidden the weary and heavy-laden to come unto Him, and He will give them rest. Strong in this consciousness, I sank to the sweetest slumber and the rosiest dreams. Through my mind gracefully flitted the phantom of Henry.

When Fanny woke me to receive my unrelished breakfast, she said :

" You've forgot that this is the day of trial ; you sleep as unconsarned as though the trial was three weeks off. For my part, now that the baby is dead, I don't kere much what becomes of me."

" My cause," I replied, " is with God. To His keeping I have confided myself ; therefore, I can sleep soundly."

" Have you got any lawyer ?"

" No ; I am a slave, and my master will not employ one."

After a few hours we heard the sound of a bell, that announced the opening of court. The jailer conducted me out of the jail yard into the Court House. It was the first time I had ever seen the interior of a court-room, when the court was in full session, and I was not very much edified by the sight.

The outside of the building was very tasteful and elegant, with most ornate decorations; but the interior was shocking. In the first place it was unfinished, and the bald, unplastered walls struck me as being exceedingly comfortless. Then the long, redundant cobwebs were gathered in festoons from rafter to rafter, whilst the floor was fairly tesselated with spots of tobacco-juice, which had been most dexterously ejected from certain *legal* orifices, commonly known as the *mouths of lawyers*, who, for want of opportunity to *speak*, resorted to chewing.

The judge, a lazy-looking old gentleman, sat in a time-worn arm-chair, ready to give his decision in the case of the Commonwealth *versus* Ann, slave of William Summerville; and seeming to me very much as though his opinion was made up without a hearing.

And there, ranged round his Honor, were the practitioners and members of the bar, all of them in seedy clothes, unshorn and unshaven. Here and there you would find a veteran of the bar, who claimed it as his especial privilege to outrage the King's or the President's English and common decency; and, as a matter of course, all the younger ones were aiming to imitate him; but, as it was impossible to do that in ability, they succeeded, to admiration, in copying his ill-manners.

Two of them I particularly noticed, as I sat in the prisoner's dock, awaiting the "coming up of my case." One of them the Court frequently addressed as Mr. Spear, and a very pointless spear he seemed;—a little, short, chunky man, with yellow, stiff, bristling hair, that stood out very straight, as if to declare its independence of the brain, and away it went on its owner's well-defined principle of "going it on your own hook." He had a little snub of a nose that possessed the good taste to turn away in disgust from its neighbor, a tobacco-stained mouth of no particular dimensions, and, I should judge from the sneer of the said nose, of no very pleasant odor; little, hard, flinty, grizzly-gray eyes, that seemed to wink as though they were afraid of seeing the truth. Altogether, it was the most disagreeably-comic phiz that I remember ever to have seen. To com-

plete the ludicrous picture, he was a self-sufficient body, quite
elate at the idea of speaking "in public on the stage." His
speech was made up of the frequent repetition of "my client
claims" so and so, and "may it please your Honor," and "I'll
call the attention of the Court to the fact," and such like phrases,
but whether his client was guilty of the charge set forth in the
indictment, he neither proved nor disproved.

The other individual whom I remarked, was a great, fat,
flabby man, whose flesh (like that of a rhinoceros) hung loosely
on the bones. He seemed to consider personal ease, rather than
taste, in the arrangement of his toilet; for he appeared
in the presence of the court in a pair of half-worn slippers,
stockings "down-gyved," a shirt-bosom much spotted with
tobacco-juice, and a neck-cloth loosely adjusted about his red,
beefish throat. His little watery blue eye reminded me
forcibly of skimmed milk; whilst his big nose, as red as a peony,
told the story that he was no advocate of the Maine liquor law,
and that he had "*voted for license.*"

He was said, by some of the bystanders, to have made an excellent speech adverse to his client, and in favor of the side
against which he was employed.

"Hurrah for litigation," said an animadverter who stood in
proximity to me. After awhile, and in due course of docket,
my case came up.

"Has she no counsel?" asked the judge.

After a moment's pause, some one answered, "No; she has
none."

I felt a chill gathering at my heart, for there was a slight
movement in the crowd; and, upon looking round, I discovered
Mr. Trueman making his way through the audience. After a
few words with several members of the bar and the judge, he
was duly sworn in, and introduced to the Court as Mr. Trueman,
a lawyer from Massachusetts, who desired to be admitted as a
practitioner at this bar. Thus duly qualified, he volunteered
his services in my defence. The look which I gave him came
directly from my overflowing heart, and I am sure spoke my

thanks more effectual than words could have done. But he gave me no other recognition than a faint smile.

As the case began, my attention was arrested. The jury was selected without difficulty; for, as none of the panel had heard of the case, the counsel waived the privilege of challenging. After the reading of the indictment, setting forth formally " an assault upon Mr. Monkton, with intent to kill, by one Ann, slave of William Summerville," the Commonwealth's attorney introduced Mr. Monkton himself as the only witness in the case

In a very minute and evidently pre-arranged story, he proceeded to detail the circumstances of a violent and deadly assault, which seemed to impress the jury greatly to my prejudice. When he had concluded, the prosecutor remarked that he had no further evidence, and proposed to submit the case, without argument, to the jury, as Mr. Trueman had no witnesses in my favor. To this proposal, however, Mr. Trueman would not accede; and so the prosecutor briefly argued upon the testimony and the law applicable to it. Then Mr. Trueman rose, and a thrill seemed to run through the audience as his tall, commanding form stood proud and erect, his mild saint-like eyes glowing with a fire that I had never seen before. He began by endeavoring to disabuse the minds of the jury of the very natural ill-feeling they might entertain against a slave, supposed to have made an attack upon the life of a white man ; reviewed at length the distinctions which are believed, at the South, to exist between the two races; and dwelt especially upon those oppressive enactments which virtually place the life of a slave at the mercy of even the basest of the white complexion. Passing from these general observations, he examined, with scrutiny the prepared story of Mr. Monkton, showing it to be a vile fabrication of defeated malice, flatly contradictory in essential particulars, and utterly unworthy of reliance under the wise maxim of the law, that "being false in one thing, it was false in all." In conclusion, he made a stirring appeal to the jury, exhorting them to rescue this feeble woman from the foul machinations which had been invented for her ruin; to rebuke, by their righteous verdict, this swift and perjured witness; and to vindicate before the world the honor of their dear old Commonwealth, which was no less threatened by this ignominious proceeding than the safety of his poor and innocent client.

The officers of the Court could scarcely repress the applause which succeeded this appeal.

"Finally, gentlemen," resumed Mr. Trueman, "permit me to take back to my Northern home the warm, personal testimony to your love of justice, which, unbiased by considerations of color, is dealt out to high and low, rich and poor, white and black, with equal and impartial hands. Disarm, by your verdict in this instance, the reproach by which Kentucky may hereafter be assailed when her enemies shall taunt her with injustice and cruelty. It has long been said, at the North, that 'the South cannot show justice to a slave.' Now, gentlemen, 'tis for you, in the character of sworn jurors, to disprove, by your verdict, this oft-repeated, and, alas! in too many instances, well-authenticated charge. And I conjure you as men, as Christians, as jurors, to deal justly, kindly, humanely with this poor uncared-for slave-woman. As you are men and fathers, slave-holders even, show her justice, and, if need be, mercy, as in like circumstances you would have these dispensed to your own daughters or slaves. She is a woman, it may be an uncultured one; this place, this Court, is strange to her. There she sits alone, and seemingly friendless, in the dock. Where was her master? Had he prepared or engaged an advocate? No, sir; he left her helpless and undefended; but that God, alike the God of the Jew and the Gentile, has, in the hour of her need, raised up for her a friend and advocate. And be ye, Gentlemen of the Jury, also the friend of the neglected female! By all the artlessness of her sex, she appeals to you to rescue her name from this undeserved aspersion, and her body from the tortures of the lash or the halter. Mark, with your strongest reprobation, that lying accuser of the powerless, who, thwarted in the attempt to violate one article in the Decalogue, has here, and in your presence, accomplished the outrage of another, in-

13*

voking upon his soul, with unholy lips, the maledictions with which God will sooner or later overwhelm the perjurer. Look at him now as he cowers beneath my words. His blanched cheek and shrivelling eye denote the detected villain. He dares not, like an honest, truth-telling man, face the charges arrayed against him. No, conscious guilt and wicked passion are bowing him now to the earth. Dare he look me full in the eye? No; for he fears lest I, with a lawyer's skill, should draw out and expose the malicious fiend that has urged him on to the persecution of the innocent and defenceless. Send him from your midst with the brand of severest condemnation, as an example of the fate which awaits a false witness in the Courts of the Commonwealth of Kentucky. Restore to this prisoner the peace of mind which has been destroyed by this prosecution. Thus you will provide for yourselves a source of consolation through all the future, and I shall thank heaven with my latest breath for the chance that threw me, a stranger, in your city to-day, and led me to this temple of justice to urge your minds to the right conclusion."

He sat down amid such thunders of applause as incurred the censure of the judge. When order was restored, the Commonwealth's attorney rose to close the case. He said "he could see no reason for doubting the veracity of his witness whom the opposition had so strenuously endeavored to impeach. For his own part, he had long known Mr. Monkton, and had always regarded him as a man of truth. The present was the first attempt at his impeachment that he had ever heard of; and he felt perfectly satisfied that Mr. Monkton would survive it. Had he been the character which his adversary had described, it might have been possible to find some witness who could invalidate his testimony. No one, however, has appeared ; and I take it that no one exists. The gentleman would do well to observe a little more caution before he attacks so recklessly the reputation of a man."

Mr. Trueman rising, requested the prosecutor to indulge him for one moment.

"Certainly," was the reply.

"I desire the jury and the Court to remember," said **Mr.** Truman, "that I made no attack upon the *reputation* of the witness in this case. Doubtless *that* is all which it is claimed to be. I freely concede it; but the earnest prosecutor must permit me to distinguish between *reputation* and *character*. I did assail the character of the man, but not hypothetically or by shrewd conjectures; 'out of his own mouth I condemned him.' This is not the first instance of crime committed by a man, who, up to the period of transgression, stood fair before the world. The gentleman's own library will supply abundant proofs of the success of strong temptation in its encounters with even *established virtue;* and I care not if this willing witness could bolster up his reputation with the voluntary affidavits of hosts of friends; his own testimony, to-day, would have still produced and riveted the conviction of his really base character. I thank the gentleman for his indulgence."

The prosecutor continuing, endeavored to show that the testimony was, upon its face, entirely credible, and ought to have its weight with the jury. He labored hard to reconcile its many and material contradictions, reiterated his own opinion of the witness as a man of truth; and, with an inflammatory warning against the *Abolition counsel*, who, he said, was perhaps now "meditating in our midst some sinister design against the peculiar institution of the South," he ended his fiery harangue.

When he had taken his seat, Mr. Trueman addressed the Court as follows:

"Before the jury retire, may it please your Honor, as the case is of a serious nature, and as we have no witness for the defence, I would ask permission merely to repeat the version of the circumstances of this case detailed to me by the prisoner at the bar. Such a statement, I am aware, is not legal evidence; but if, in your clemency, you would permit it to go to the jury simply for what it is worth, the course of justice I am sure would by no means be impeded."

The judge readily consented to this request, and **Mr.**

11

Trueman rehearsed my story, as narrated in the foregoing pages.

The Commonwealth's attorney then rejoined with a few remarks.

After a retirement of a few minutes, the jury returned with a verdict of "guilty as charged in the indictment," ordering me to receive two hundred lashes on my bare back, not exceeding fifty at a time. I was then remanded to jail to await the execution of my sentence.

Very gloomy looked that little room to me when I returned to it, with a horrid crime of which, Heaven knows, I was guiltless, affixed to my name, and the prospect of a cruel punishment awaiting me. Who may tell the silent, unexpressed agony that I there endured? Certain I am, that the nightly stars and the old pale moon looked not down upon a more wretched heart. There I sat, looking ever and again at the stolid Fanny, who had been sentenced to the work-house for a limited time. Since the death of her infant she had lost all her loquacity, and remained in a kind of dreamy, drowsy state, between waking and sleeping.

Through how many scenes of vanished days, worked the plough-share of memory, upturning the fresh earth, where lay the buried seeds of some few joys! And, sometimes, a sly, nestling thought of Henry hid itself away in the most covert folds of my heart. His melancholy bronze face had cut itself like a fine cameo, on my soul. The old, withered flowers, which he had sent, lay carefully concealed in a corner of the cell. Their beauty had departed like a dim dream; but a little of their fragrance still remained despite decay.

One day, after the trial, I was much honored and delighted by a visit from no less a personage than Mr. Trueman himself.

I was overcome, and had not power to speak the thanks with which my grateful heart ran over. He kindly pitied my embarrassment, and relieved me by saying,

"Oh, I know you are thankful to me. I only wish, my good girl, that my speech had rescued you from the punishment you have to suffer. Believe me, I deeply pity you; and. if money could avert the penalty which I know you have not merited, I would relieve you from its infliction; but nothing more can be done for you. You must bear your trouble bravely."

"Oh, my kind, noble friend!" I passionately exclaimed, "words like these would arm me with strength to brave a punishment ten times more severe than the one that awaits me. Sympathy from you can repay me for any suffering. That a noble white gentleman, of distinguished talents, should stoop from his lofty position to espouse the cause of a poor mulatto, is to me as pleasing as it is strange."

"Alas, my good girl, you and all of your wronged and injured race are objects of interest and affection to me. I would that I could give you something more available than sympathy: but these Southerners are a knotty people; their prejudices of caste and color grow out, unsightly and disgusting, like the rude excrescences upon a noble tree, eating it away, and sucking up its vital sap. These Western people are of a noble nature, were it not for their sectional blemishes. I never relied upon the many statements which I have heard at the North, taking them as natural exaggerations; but my sojourn here has proved them to be true."

I then told him of the discussion that I had overheard between him and Mr. Winston.

"Did you hear that?" he asked with a smile. "Winston has been very cool toward me ever since; yet he is a man with some fine points of character, and considerable mental cultivation. This one Southern feeling, or rather prejudice, however, has well-nigh corrupted him. He is too fiery and irritable to argue; but all Southerners are so. They cannot allow themselves to discuss these matters. Witness, for instance, the conduct of their Congressional debaters. Do they reason? Whenever a matter is reduced to argumentation, the Southerner flies off at a tangent, resents everything as personal, descends to abuse, and thus closes the debate."

I ventured to ask him some questions in relation to Fred Douglas; to all of which he returned satisfactory answers. He informed me that Douglas had once been a slave; that he was now a man of social position; of very decided talent and energy. "I know of no man," continued Mr. Trueman, "who is more deserving of public trust than Douglas. He conducts himself with extreme modesty and propriety, and a quiet dignity that inclines the most fastidious in his favor."

He then cited the case of Miss Greenfield (*the* black swan), showing that my race was susceptible of cultivation and refinement in a high degree.

Thus inspired, I poured forth my full soul to him. I told him how, in secret, I had studied; how diligently I had searched after knowledge; how I longed for the opportunity to improve my poor talents. I spoke freely, and with a degree of nervous enthusiasm that seemed to affect him.

"Ann," he said, and large tears stood in his eyes, "it is a shame for you to be kept in bondage. A proud, aspiring soul like yours, if once free to follow its impulses, might achieve much. Can you not labor to buy yourself? At odd times do extra work, and, by your savings, you may, in the course of years, be enabled to buy yourself."

"My dear sir, I've no 'odd times' for extra work, or I would gladly avail myself of them. Lazy I am not; but my mistress requires all my time and labor. If she were to discover that I was working, even at night for myself, she would punish me severely."

I said this in a mournful tone; for I felt that despair was my portion. He was silent for awhile; then said,

"Well, you must do the best you can. I would that I could advise you; but now I must leave. A longer stay would excite suspicion. You heard what they said the other day about Abolitionists."

I remembered it well, and was distressed to think that he had been abused on my account.

With many kind words he took his leave, and I felt as if the sunshine had suddenly been extinguished.

During his entire visit poor Fanny had slept. She lay like one in an opium trance. For hours after his departure she remained so, and much time was left me for reflection.

CHAPTER XXXII.

EXECUTION OF THE SENTENCE—A CHANGE—HOPE.

On the last and concluding day of the term of the court, the jailer signified to me that the constable would, on the morrow, administer the first fifty lashes : and, of course, I passed the night in great trepidation.

But the morning came bright and clear, and the jailer, accompanied by Constable Calcraft, entered.

" Come, girl, said the latter, " I have to execute the sentence upon you."

Without one word, I followed him into the jail yard.

" Strip yourself to the waist," said the constable.

I dared not hesitate, though feminine delicacy was rudely shocked. With a prayer to heaven for fortitude, I obeyed.

Then, with a strong cowhide, he inflicted fifty lashes (the first instalment of the sentence) upon my bare back; each lacerating it to the bone. I was afterwards compelled to put my clothes on over my raw, bloody back, without being allowed to wash away the clotted gore; for, upon asking for water to cleanse myself, I was harshly refused, and quickly re-conducted to the cell, where, wounded, mortified, and anguish-stricken, I was left to myself.

Oh, God of the world-forgotten Africa ! Thou dost see these things ; Thou dost hear the cries which daily and nightly we are sending up to Thee ! On that lonely, wretched night Thou wert with me, and my prison became as a radiant mansion, for angels cheered me there ! Glory to God for the cross which He sent me ; for it led me on to Him.

Poor Fanny, after her sentence was pronounced, was soon
sent to the work-house; so I was alone. The little Testament which Louise had given me, was all the company
that I desired. Its rich and varied words were as manna to my
hungry soul; and its blessed promises rescued me from a dreadful bankruptcy of faith.

Subsequently, and at three different times, I was led forth to
receive the remainder of my punishment.

After the last portion was given, I was allowed to go to the
kitchen of the jail and wash myself and dress in some clean
clothes, which Miss Jane had sent me. I was then conducted
by the constable to the hotel.

Miss Jane met me very distantly, saying—

" I trust you are somewhat humbled, Ann, and will in future
be a better nigger."

I was in but a poor mood to take rebukes and reproaches;
for my flesh was perfectly raw, the intervals between the whip-
pings having been so short as not to allow the gashes even to
close; so that upon this, the final day, my back presented one
mass of filth and clotted gore. I was then, as may be supposed, in a very irritable humor, but a slave is not allowed to
have feeling. It is a privilege denied him, because his skin is
black.

I did not go out of Miss Jane's room, except on matters of
business, about which she sent me. I would, then, go slipping
around, afraid of meeting Henry. I did not wish him to see
me in that mutilated condition. I saw Louise in Miss Jane's
room; but there she merely nodded to me. Subsequently we
met in a retired part of the hall, and there she expressed that
generous and friendly sympathy which I knew she so warmly
cherished for me.

Somehow or other she had contrived to insinuate herself
wondrously into Miss Jane's good graces; and all her influence
she endeavored to use in my favor.

In this private interview she told me that she would induce

Miss Jane to let me sleep in her room; and she thought she knew what key to take her on.

"If," added she, "I get you to my apartment, I will care for you well. I will wash and dress your wounds, and render you every attention in my power."

I watched, with admiration, her tactics in managing Miss Jane. That evening when I was seated in an obscure corner of the room, Miss Jane was lolling in a large arm-chair, playing with a bouquet that had been sent her by a gentleman. This bouquet had been delivered to her, as I afterwards learned, by Louise. Miss Jane had grown to be fashionable indeed; and had two favorite beaux, with whom she interchanged notes, and Louise had been selected as a messenger.

On this occasion, the wily mulatto came up to her, rather familiarly, I thought, and said—

"Ah, you are amusing yourself with the Captain's flowers! I must tell him of it. Dear sakes! but it will please him;" she then whispered something to her, at which both of them laughed heartily.

After this Miss Jane was in a very decided good humor, and Louise fussed about the apartment pretty much as she pleased. At length, throwing open the window, she cried out—

"How close the air is here! Why, Mrs. St. Lucian, the fashionable, dashing lady who occupied this room just before you, Mrs. Somerville, wouldn't allow three persons to be in it at a time; and her servant-girl always slept in my room. By the way, that just reminds me how impolite I've been to you; do excuse me, and I will be glad to relieve you by letting Ann go to my room of nights."

"Oh, it will trouble you, Louise."

"Don't talk or think of troubling me; but come along girl," she said, turning to me.

"Go with Louise, Ann," added Miss Jane, as she perceived me hesitate, "but come early in the morning to get me ready for breakfast."

Happy even for so small a favor as this, I followed Louise

to her room. There I found everything very comfortable and
neat. A nice, downy bed, with its snowy covering; a bright-
colored carpet, a little bureau, washstand, clock, rocking-chair,
and one or two pictures, with a few crocks of flowers, completed the tasteful furniture of this apartment.

All this, I inly said, is the arrangement and taste of a mulatto in the full enjoyment of her freedom! Do not her thrift
and industry disprove the oft-repeated charge of indolence that
is made upon the negro race ?

She seemed to read my thoughts, and remarked, " You are
surprised, Ann, to see my room so nice ! I read the wonder in
your face. I have marked it before, in the countenances of
slaves. They are taught, from their infancy up, to regard
themselves as unfit for the blessings of free, civilized life ; and
I am happy to give the lie, by my own manner of living, to this
rude charge."

" How long have you been free, Louise, and how did you obtain your freedom ?"

" It is a long story," she answered; " you must be inclined to
sleep ; you need rest. At some other time I'll tell you. Here,
take this arm-chair, it is soft ; and your back is wounded and
sore ; I am going to dress it for you."

So saying, she left the room, but quickly returned with a
basin of warm water and a little canteen of grease. She very
kindly bade me remove my dress, then gently, with a soft
linten-rag, washed my back, greased it, and made me put on
one of her linen chemises and a nice gown, and giving me a
stimulant, bade me rest myself for the night upon her bed,
which was clean, white, and tempting.

When she thought I was soundly sleeping, she removed from
a little swinging book-shelf a well-worn Bible. After reading a
chapter or so, she sank upon her knees in prayer ! There may
be those who would laugh and scoff at the piety of this woman,
because of her tawny complexion ; but the Great Judge, to
whose ear alone her supplication was made, disregards all such

distinctions. Her soul was as precious to Him, as though her complexion had been of the most spotless snow.

On the following morning, whilst I was arranging Miss Jane's toilette, she said to me, in rather a kind tone :

" Ann, Mr. Summerville wants to sell you, and purchase a smaller and cheaper girl for me. Now, if you behave yourself well, I'll allow you to choose your own home."

This was more kindness than I expected to receive from her, and I thanked her heartily.

All that day my heart was dreaming of a new home—perhaps a kind, good one ! On the gallery I met Mr. Trueman (I love to write his name). Rushing eagerly up to him, I offered my hand, all oblivious of the wide chasm that the difference of race had placed between us; but, if that thought had occurred to me, his benignant smile would have put it to flight. Ah, he was the true reformer, who illustrated, in his own deportment, the much talked-of theory of human brotherhood ! He, with all his learning, his native talent, his social position and legal prominence, could condescend to speak in a familiar spirit to the lowliest slave, and this made me, soured to harshness, feel at ease in his presence.

I told him that I was fast recovering from the effects of my whipping. I spoke of Louise's kindness, &c.

" I am to be sold, Mr. Trueman; I wish that you would buy me."

" My good girl, if I had the means I would not hesitate to make the purchase, and instantly draw up your free papers; but I am, at the present, laboring under great pecuniary embarrassments, which deny me the right of exercising that generosity which my heart prompts in this case."

I thanked him, over and over again, for his kindness. I felt not a little distressed when he told me that he should leave for Boston early on the following day. In bidding me adieu, he slipped, very modestly, into my hand a ten-dollar bill, but this I could not accept from one to whom I was already heavily indebted.

"No, my good friend, I cannot trespass so much upon you. Already I am largely your debtor. Take back this money." I offered him the bill, but his face colored deeply, as he replied:

"No, Ann, you would not wound my feelings, I am sure."

"Not for my freedom," I earnestly answered.

"Then accept this trifling gift. Let it be among the first of your savings, as my contribution, toward the purchase-money for your freedom." Seeing that I hesitated, he said, "if you persist in refusing, you will offend me."

"Anything but that," I eagerly cried, as I took the money from that blessed, charity-dispensing hand.

And this was the last I saw of him for many years; and, when we again met, the shadow of deeper sorrows was resting on my brow.

*   *   *   *   *

Several weeks had elapsed since Miss Jane's announcement that I was to be sold, and I had heard no more of it. I dared not renew the subject to her, no matter from what motive, for she would have construed it as impudence. But my time was now passing in comparative pleasure, for Miss Jane was wholly engrossed by fun, frolic, and dissipation. Her mornings were spent in making or receiving fashionable calls, and her afternoons were devoted to sleep, whilst the night-time was given up entirely to theatres, parties, concerts, and such amusements. Consequently my situation, as servant, became pretty much that of a sinecure. Oh, what delightful hours I passed in Louise's room, reading! I devoured everything in the shape of a book that fell into my hands. I began to improve astonishingly in my studies. It seemed that knowledge came to me by magic. I was surprised at the rapidity of my own advancement. In the afternoons, Henry had a good deal of leisure, and he used to steal round to Louise's room, and sit with us upon a little balcony that fronted it, and looked out upon a beautiful view. There lay the placid Ohio, and just beyond it ran the blessed Indiana shore! "Why was I not born on that side of the river?" I used to say to Henry, as I pointed across the water.

"Or why," he would answer, as his dark eye grew intensely black, "were our ancestors ever stolen from Africa?"

"These are questions," said the more philosophical Louise, "that we must not propose. They destroy the little happiness we already enjoy."

"Yes, you can afford to talk thus, Louise, for you are free; but we, poor slaves, know slavery from actual experience and endurance," said Henry.

"I have had my experience too," she answered, "and a dark one has it been."

The evening on which this conversation occurred, was unusually fair and calm. I shall ever remember it. There we three sat, with mournful memories working in our breasts; there each looking at the other, murmuring secretly, "Mine is the heaviest trouble!"

"Louise," I said, "tell us how you broke the chains of bondage."

"I was," said she, after a moment's pause, "a slave to a family of wealth, residing a few miles from New Orleans. I am, as you see, but one-third African. My mother was a bright mulatto. My father a white gentleman, the brother of my mistress. Louis De Calmo was his name. My mother was a housemaid, and only fifteen years of age at my birth. She was of a meek, quiet disposition, and bore with patience all her mistress' reproaches and harshness; but, when alone with my father, she urged him to buy me, and he promised her he would; still he put her off from time to time. She often said to him that for herself she did not care; but, for me, she was all anxiety. She could not bear the idea of her child remaining in slavery. All her bright hopes for me were suddenly brought to a close by my father's unexpected death. He was killed by the explosion of a steamboat on the lower Mississippi, and his horribly-mangled body brought home to be buried. My mother loved him; and, in her grief for his death, she had a double cause for sorrow. By it her child was debarred the privilege of freedom. I was but nine years of age at the time, but I well remember her wild lamentation. Often she would catch me to her heart, and cry out, ' if you could only die I should be so happy ;' but I did not. I lived on and grew rapidly. We had a very kind overseer, and his son took a great fancy to me. He taught me to read and write. I was remarkably quick. When I was but fifteen, I recollect mistress fancied, from my likely appearance and my delicate, gliding movements, that she would make a dining-room servant of me. I was taken into the house, and thus deprived of the instructions which the overseer's son had so faithfully rendered me. I have often read half of the night. Now I approach a melancholy part of my story. Master becoming embarrassed in his business, he must part with some of his property. Of course the slaves went. My mother was numbered among the lot. I longed and begged to be sold with her ; but to this mistress would not consent,— she considered me too valuable as a house-girl. Well, mother and I parted. None can ever know my wretchedness, unless they have suffered a similar grief, when I saw her borne weeping and screaming away from me. I have never heard from her since. Where she went or into whose hands she fell, I never knew. She was sold to the highest bidder, under the auctioneer's hammer, in the New Orleans market. I lived on as best I could, bearing an aching heart, whipped for every little offence, serving, as a bond-woman, her who was, by nature and blood, *my Aunt*. After a year or so I was sold to James Canfield, a bachelor gentleman in New Orleans, and I lived with him, as a wife, for a number of years. I had several beautiful children, though none lived to be more than a few months old. At the death of this man I was set free by his will, and three hundred dollars were bequeathed me by him. I had saved a good deal of money during his life-time, and this, with his legacy, made me independent. I remained in the South but a short time. For two years after his death I sojourned in the North, sometimes hiring myself out as chambermaid, and at others living quietly on my means ; but I must work. In activity I stifle memory, and for awhile am happy, or, at least, tranquil."

After this synopsis of her history, Louise was silent. She bent her head upon her hand, and mused abstractedly.

"I think, Henry, you are a slave," I said, as I turned my eye upon his mournful face.

"Yes, and to a hard master," was the quick reply; "but he has promised me I shall buy myself. I am to pay him one thousand dollars, in instalments of one hundred dollars each. Three of these instalments I have already paid."

"Does he receive any hire for your services at this hotel?"

"Oh yes, the proprietor pays him one hundred and fifty dollars a year for me."

"How have you made the money?"

"By working at night and on holidays, going on errands, and doing little jobs for gentlemen boarding in the house. Sometimes I get little donations from kind-hearted persons, Christmas gifts in money, &c. All of it is saved."

"You must work very hard."

"Oh yes, it's very little sleep I ever get. How old would you think me?"

"Thirty-five," I answered, as I looked at his furrowed face.

"That is what almost every one says; yet I am only twenty-five. All these wrinkles and hard spots are from work."

"You ought to rest awhile," I ventured to suggest.

"Oh, I'll wait until I am my own master; then I'll rest."

"But you may die before that time comes."

"So I may, so I may," he repeated despondingly. "All my family have died early and from over-work. Sometimes I think freedom too great a blessing for me ever to realize."

He brushed a tear from his eye with the back of his hand. I looked at him, so young and energetic, yet lonely. Noble and handsome was his face, despite the lines of care and labor. What wonder that a soft feeling took possession of my heart, particularly when I remembered how he had gladdened my imprisonment with kind messages and the gift of flowers. I did but follow an irrepressible and spontaneous impulse, when I said with earnestness.

"Do not work so hard, Henry."

He looked me full in the face. Why did my eye droop beneath that warm, inquiring gaze; and why did he ask so low, in a half whisper:

"Should I die who will grieve for me?"

And did not my uplifted glance tell him who would? We understood each other. Our hearts had spoken, and what followed may easily be guessed. Evening after evening we met upon that balcony to pledge our souls in earnest vows. Henry's eye grew brighter; he worked the harder; but his pile of money did not increase as it had done. Many a little present to me, many a rare nosegay, that was purchased at a price he was not able to afford, put off to a greater distance his day of freedom. Like a green, luxuriant spot in the wide desert of a lonely life, seems to me the memory of those hours? On Sunday evenings, when his labor was over, which was generally about eight o'clock, we walked through the city, and on moonlight nights we strayed upon the banks of the Ohio, and planned for the future.

Henry was to buy himself, then go North, and labor in some hotel, or at whatever business he could make the most money; then he would return to buy me. This was one of our plans; but as often as we talked, we made a new one.

"Oh, we shall be so happy, Ann," he would exclaim.

Then I would repeat the often-asked question, "Where shall we live?"

Sometimes we decided upon New York city; then a village in the State of New York; but I think Henry's preference was a Canadian town. Idle speculators that we were, we seldom adhered long to our preference for any one spot!

"At least, dear," he used to say, in his encouraging way, "we will hunt a home; and, no matter where we find it, we can make it a happy one if we are together."

And to this my heart gave a warm echo. I was beginning to be happy; for imagination painted joys in the future, and the present was not all mournful, for Henry was with me!

The same roof covered us. Twenty times a-day I met him in the dining-room, hall, or in the lobby, and he was always with me in the evening.

Slaves as we were, I've often thought as we wandered beneath the golden light of the stars, that, for the time being, we were as happy as mortals could be. Young first-love knit the air in a charmed silver mist around us; and, hand in hand, we trod the wave-washed shore, always with our eyes turned toward the North, the bourne whither all our thoughts inclined.

"Does not the north star point us to our future home?" Henry frequently asked. I love to recall this one sunny epoch in my life. For months, not an unpleasant thing occurred.

Immediately after my trial, Monkton left the city, and went, as I understood, south. Miss Jane was busied with fashion and gayety. Mr. Summerville was engaged at his business, and every one whom I saw was kind to me. So I may record the fact that for a while I was happy!

CHAPTER XXXIII.

WHILST the hours thus rosily slided away, and I dreamed
amid the verdure of existence, the syren charmed me wisely,
indeed, with her beautiful promises. Poor, simple-hearted,
trusting slaves! We could not see upon what a rocking bridge
our feet were resting, how slippery and unsubstantial was the
flowery declivity whereon we stood. There we reposed in the
gentle light of a happy trance; we saw not the clouds, dark
and tempest-charged, that were rising rapidly to hide the stars
from our view.

One Sunday afternoon, Henry having finished his work much
earlier than usual, and done some little act whereby the good
will of his temporary master (the keeper of the hotel) was pro-
pitiated, and Miss Jane and Mr. Summerville having gone out,
I willingly consented to his proposal to take a walk. We accordingly wandered off to a beautiful wood, just without the city
limits, a very popular resort with the negroes and poorer classes,
though it was the only pretty green woodland near the city.
Yet, because the "common people and negroes" (a Kentucky phrase) went there, it was voted vulgar, and avoided by
the rich and refined. One blessing was thus given to the poor!

Henry and I sought a retired part of the grove, and, seating
ourselves on an old, moss-grown log, we talked with as much
hope, and indulged in as rosy dreams, as happier and lordlier
lovers. For three bright hours we remained idly rambling
through the flower-realm of imagination; but, as the long
shadows began to fall among the leaves, we prepared to return
home.

That night when I assisted Miss Jane in getting ready for bed, I observed that she was unusually gloomy and petulant. I could do nothing to please her; she boxed my ears repeatedly; stuck pins in me, called me "detestable nigger," &c. Even the presence of Louise failed to restrain her, and I knew that something awful had happened.

For two or three days this cloud that hung about her deepened and darkened, until she absolutely became unendurable. I often found her eyes red and swollen, as though she had spent the entire night in weeping.

Mr. Summerville was gloomy and morose, never saying much, and always speaking harshly to his wife.

At length the explosion came. One morning he said to me, " gather up your clothes, Ann, and come with me; I have sold you."

Though I was stricken as by a thunderbolt, I dared not express my surprise, or even ask who had bought me. All that I ventured to say was,

" Master William, I have a trunk."

" Well, shoulder it yourself. I'm not going to pay for having it taken."

Though my heart was wrung I said nothing, and, lifting up my trunk, beneath the weight of which I nearly sank, I followed Master William out of the house.

" Good-bye, Miss Jane," I said.

" Good-bye, and be a good girl," she replied, kindly, and my heart almost softened toward her; for in that moment I felt as if deserted by every faculty.

"Come on, Ann, come on," urged Master William; and I mechanically obeyed.

In the cross-hall I met Louise, who exclaimed, " Why, Ann, where are you going?"

"I don't know, Louise, I'm sold."

" Sold! Who's bought you?"

" I don't know—Master William didn't tell me."

" Who's bought her, Mr. Summerville?"

"The man to whom I sold her," he answered, with a laugh.

"But who is he?" persisted Louise, without noticing the ʲoke.

"Well, Atkins, a negro-trader down here, on Second street."

"Good gracious!" she cried out; then, turning to me, said, "does Henry know it?"

"I have not seen him." She darted off from us, and we walked on. I hoped that she would not see Henry, for I could not bear to meet him. It would dispossess me of the little forced composure that I had; but, alas! for the fulfilment of my hopes! in the lower hall, with a countenance full of terror, he stood.

"What are you going to do with Ann, Mr. Summerville?" he inquired.

"I have sold her to Atkins, and am now taking her to the pen?"

Alas! though his life, his blood, his soul cried out against it, he dared not offer any objection or entreaty; but oh, that hopeless look of brokenness of heart! I see it now, and "it comes over me like the raven o'er the infected house."

"I'll take your trunk round for you, Ann, to-night. It is too heavy for you," and so saying, he kindly removed it from my shoulder. This little act of kindness was the added drop to the already full glass, and my heart overflowed. I wept heartily. His tender, "don't cry, Ann," only made me weep the more; and when I looked up and saw his own eyes full of tears, and his lip quivering with the unspoken pang, I felt (for the slave at least) how wretched a possession is life!

Master William cut short this parting interview, by saying,

"Never mind that trunk, Henry, Ann can carry it very well."

And, as I was about to re-shoulder it, Henry said,

"No, Ann, you mustn't carry it. I'll do it for you to-night, when my work is over. She is a woman, Mr. Summerville, and it's heavy for her; but it will not be anything for me."

"Well, if you have a mind to, you may do it; but I haven't any time to parley now, come on."

Henry pressed my hand affectionately, and I saw the tears roll in a stream down his bronzed cheeks. I did not trust myself to speak; I merely returned the pressure of his hand, and silently followed Master William.

Through the streets, up one and across another, we went, until suddenly we stopped in front of a two-story brick house with an iron fence in front. Covering a small portion of the front view of the main building, an office had been erected, a plain, uncarpeted room, from the door of which projected a sheet-iron sign, advertising the passers-by, "negroes bought and sold here." We walked into this room, and upon the table found a small bell, which Mr. Summerville rang. In answer to this, a neatly-dressed negro boy appeared. To Master William's interrogatory, "Is Mr. Atkins in?" he answered, most obsequiously, that he was, and instantly withdrew. In a few moments the door opened, and a heavy man about five feet ten inches entered. He was of a most forbidding appearance; a tan-colored complexion, with very black hair and whiskers, and mean, watery, milky, diseased-looking eyes. He limped as he walked, one leg being shorter than the other, and carried a huge stick to assist his ambulations.

"Good morning, Mr. Atkins."

"Good morning, sir,"

"Here is the girl we were speaking of yesterday."

"Well," replied the other, as he removed a lighted cigar from his mouth, "she is likely enough. Take off yer bonnet, girl, let me look at yer eyes. They are good; open your mouth—no decayed teeth—all sound; hold up your 'coat, legs are good, some marks on 'em—now the back—pretty much and badly scarred. Well, what's the damage?"

"Seven hundred, cash down. You can recommend her as a first-rate house and lady's maid."

"What's your name, girl?"

"Ann," I replied.

"Ann, go within," he added, pointing to the door through which he had entered.

I turned to Mr. Summerville, saying,

" Good-bye, Master William   I wish you well."

"Good-bye, Ann," and he extended his hand to me ; " I hope Mr. Atkins will get you a good home."

Dropping a courtesy and a tear, I passed through the door designated by Mr. Atkins, and stood within the pen.   Here I was met by the mulatto who had answered the bell.

" Has you bin bought, Miss ?"

" Yes, Mr. Atkins just bought me."

" Why did your Masser sell you ?"

" I don't know."

" Oh, that's what the most of 'em says.   It 'pears so quare ter me for a Masser to sell good sarvants ; but I guess you'll soon git a home ; fur you is 'bout the likeliest yaller gal I ever seed.   Now, thim rale black 'uns hardly ever goes off here· We has to send 'em down river, or let 'em go at a mighty low price."

" How often do you have sales ?"

" Oh, we don't have 'em at all.   That's we don't have public 'uns.   We sells 'em privately like ; but we buys up more ; and when we gits a large number, we ships 'em down de river."

Wishing to cut short his garrulity, I asked him to show me the room where I was to stay.

" In here, wid de rest of 'em," he said, as he opened the door of a large shed-room, where I found some ten or twelve negroes, women and men, ranged round on stools and chairs, all neatly dressed, some of them looking very happy, others with down-cast, sorrow-stricken countenances.

One bright, gold-colored man, with long, silky black hair, and raven eyes, full of subdued power, stood leaning his elbow against the mantel.   His melancholy face and pensive attitude struck a responsive feeling, and I turned with a sisterly sentiment toward him.

I have always been of a taciturn disposition, shunning company ; but this man impressed me so favorably, he seemed the very counterpart of myself, that I forgot my usual reserve, and, after a few moments' investigation of my companions, the faces of most of whom were unpleasant to me, I approached him and inquired—

"Have you been long here?"

"Only a few days," he answered, as he lifted his mournful eyes towards mine, and I could see from their misty light, that they were dimmed by tears.

"Are you sold?" I asked.

"Oh yes," and he shuddered terribly.

I did not venture to say more; but stood looking at him, when, suddenly he turned to me, saying,

"I know that you are sold."

"Yes," I replied, with that strong sort of courage that characterized me.

"You take it calmly" he said; "have you no friends?"

"You do not talk like one familiar with slavery, to speak of a slave's having friends."

"True, true; but I have—oh, God!—a wife and children, and from them I was cruelly torn, and—and—and I saw my poor wife knocked flat upon the floor, and because I had the manhood to say that it was wrong, they tied me up and slashed me. All this is right, because my skin is darker than theirs."

What a fearful groan he gave, as he struck his breast violently

"The bitterness of all this I too have tasted, and my only wonder is, that I can live on. My heart will not break."

"Mine has long since broken; but this body will not die. My poor children! I would that they were dead with their poor slave-mother."

"Why did your master sell you?"

"Because he wanted *to buy a piano for his daughter*," and his lip curled.

To gratify the taste of *his* child, that white man had separated a father from his children, had recklessly sundered the holiest ties, and broken the most solemn and loving domestic attachments; and to such heathenism the public gave its hearty approval, because his complexion was a shade or so darker than Caucasians. Oh, Church of Christ! where is thy warning voice? Is not this a matter, upon the injustice of which thy great voice should pronounce a malison?

"My name is Charles, what is yours?"

"Ann."

"Well, Ann," he resumed, "I like your face; you are the only one I've seen in this pen that I was willing to talk with. You have just come. Tell me why were you sold?"

In a few concise words I told him my story. He seemed touched with sympathy.

"Poor girl!" he murmured, "like all the rest of our tribe, you have tasted of trouble."

I talked with him all the morning, and we both, I think, learned what a relief it is to unclose the burdened heart to a congenial, listening spirit.

When we were summoned out to our dinner, I found a very bountiful and pretty good meal served up. It is the policy of the trader to feed the slaves well; for, as Mr. Atkins said, "the fat, oily, smooth, cheerful ones, always sold the best;" and, as this business is purely a speculation, they do everything, even humane things, for the furtherance of their mercenary designs. I had not much appetite, neither had Charles, as was remarked by some of the coarser and more abject of our companions; and I was pained to observe their numerous significant winks and blinks. One of them, the old gray mouse of the company, an ancient "Uncle Ned," who had taken it pretty roughly all his days, and who being of the lower order of Epicureans, was, perhaps, happier at the pen than he had ever been. And this fellow, looking at me and Charley, said,

"They's in lub;" ha! ha! ha! went round the circle. I noticed Charley's brows knitting severely. I read his thoughts. I knew that he was thinking of his poor wife and of his fatherless children, and inwardly swearing unfaltering devotion to them.

Persuasively I said to him, "Don't mind them. They are scarcely accountable."

"I know it, I know it," he bitterly replied, "but I little thought I should ever come to this. Sold to a negro-trader, and locked up in a pen with such a set! I've always had pride; tried to behave myself well, and to make money for my master, and now to be sold to a trader, away from my wife and children!" He shook his head and burst into tears. I felt that I had no words to console him, and I ventured to offer none.

I managed, by aid of conversation with Charley, to pass the day tolerably. There may be those of my readers who will ask how this could be. But let them remember that I had never been the pampered pet, the child of indulgence; but that I was born to the ignominious heritage of American slavery. My feelings had been daily, almost hourly, outraged. This evil had not fallen on me as the *first* misfortune, but as one of a series of linked troubles " long drawn out." So I was comparatively fitted for endurance, though by no means stoical; for a certain constitutional softness of temperament rendered me always susceptible of anguish to a very high degree. At length evening drew on—the beautiful twilight that was written down so pleasantly in my memory; the time that had always heralded my re-union with Henry. Now, instead of a sweet starlight or moonlight stroll, I must betake myself to a narrow, " cribbed, cabined, and confined " apartment, through which no truant ray or beam could force an entrance! How my soul sickened over the recollections of lovelier hours! Whilst I moodily sat in one corner of the room, hugging to my soul the thought of him from whom I was now forever parted, a sound broke on my ear, a sound—a music-sound, that made my nerves thrill and my blood tingle; 'twas the sound of Henry's voice. I heard him ask—

" Where is she? let me speak to her but a single word;" and how that mellow voice trembled with the burden of painful emotion! Eagerly I sprang forward; reserve and maidenly coyness all forgotten. My only wish was to lay my weary head upon that brave, protecting breast—weep, ay, and die there! " Oh, for a swift death," I frantically cried, as I felt his arms

14*

about me, while my head was pillowed just above his warm and loving heart. I felt its manly pulsations as with a soft lullaby they seemed hushing me to the deep, eternal sleep, which I so ardently craved! Better, a thousand times, for death to part us, than the white man's cruelty! So we both thought. I read his secret wish in the hopeless, vacant, but still so agonized look, that he bent upon me. For one moment, the other slaves huddled together in blank amazement. This was to them "a show," as "uncle Ned" subsequently styled it.

"I've brought your trunk, Ann; Mr. Atkins ordered me to leave it without; though you'll get it."

"Thank you, Henry; it is of small account to me now: yet there are in it some few of your gifts that I shall always value."

"Oh, Ann, don't, pray don't talk so mournfully! Is there no hope? Can't you be sold somewhere in the city? I have got about fifty dollars now in money. I'd stop buying myself, and buy you; make my instalments in fifties or hundreds, as I could raise it; but I spoke to a lawyer about it, and he read the law to me, showing that I, as a slave, couldn't be allowed to hold property; and there is no white man in whom I have sufficient confidence, or who would be willing to accommodate me in this way. Mine is a deplorable case; but I'm going to see what can be done. I'll look about among the citizens, to see if some of them will not buy you; for I cannot be separated from you. It will kill me; it will, it will!"

"Oh, don't, Henry, don't! for myself I can stand much; but when I think of *you*."

He caught me passionately to his breast; and, in that embrace, he seemed to say, "*They shall not part us!*"

He seated himself on a low stool beside me, with one of my hands clasped in his, and thus, with his tender eyes bent upon me, such is the illusion of love, I forgot the terror by which I was surrounded, and yielded myself to a fascination as absorbing as that which encircled me in the grove on that memorable Sunday evening

"Why, Henry, is this you?" and a strong hand was laid upon his shoulder. Looking up, I beheld Charley.

"And is this you, Charles Allen?" asked the other.

"*Yes, this is me.* I dare say you scarcely expected to find me here, where I never thought I should be."

At this I was reminded of the significant ejaculation that Ophelia makes in her madness, "Lord, we know what we are, but we know not what we may be!"

"I am sold, Henry," continued Charles, " sold away from my poor wife and children;" his voice faltered and the big tears rolled down his cheeks.

"I see from your manner toward Ann, that she is or was expected to be your wife."

"Yes, she was pledged to be."

"*Yes, and is,*" I added with fervor. At this, Henry only pressed my hand tightly.

"Yet," pursued Charles, " she is taken from you."

"*She is,*" was the brief and bitter reply.

"Now, Henry Graham, are we men? and do we submit to these things?"

"Alas !" and the words came through Henry's set teeth, " we are *not* men; we are only chattels, property, merchandise, *slaves.*"

"But is it right for us to be so? I feel the high and lordly instincts of manhood within me. Must I conquer them? Must I stifle the eloquent cry of Nature in my breast? Shall I see my wife and children left behind to the mercy of a hard master, and willingly desert them simply because another man says that, in exchange for this sacrifice of happiness and hope, *his daughter* shall play upon Chickering's finest piano?"

"Heavens ! can I ever forget the princely air with which he uttered these words ! His swarthy cheek glowed with a beautiful crimson, and his rich eye fairly blazed with the fire of a seven-times heated soul, whilst the thin lip curled and the fine nostril dilated, and the whole form towered supremely in the majesty of erect and perfect manhood !

" Hush, Charley, hush," I urged, "this is no place for the expression of such sentiments, just and noble as they may be."

Again Henry pressed my hand.

" It may be imprudent, Ann, but I am reckless now. They have done the worst they can do. I defy the sharpest dagger-point. My breast is open to a thousand spears. They can do no more. But how can you, Henry, thus supinely sit by and see yourself robbed of your life's treasure ? I cannot understand it. Are you lacking in manliness, in courage ? Are you a coward, a *slave* indeed?"

" Do not listen to him ; leave now, Henry, dear, dear Henry," I implored, as I observed the singular expression of his face. " Go now, dearest, without saying another word ; for my sake go. You will not refuse me ?"

"No, I will not, dear Ann ; but there is a fire raging in my veins."

"Yes, and Charley is the incendiary. Go, I beg you."

With a long, fond kiss, he left me, and it was well he did, for in a moment more Mr. Atkins came to give the order for retiring.

I found a very comfortable mattress and covering, on the floor of a good, neatly-carpeted room, which was occupied by five other women. One of them, a gay girl of about fifteen, a full-blooded African, made her pallet close to mine. I had observed her during the day as a garrulous, racketty sort of baggage, that seemed contented with her situation. She was extremely neat in her dress ; and her ebony skin had a rich, oily, shiny look, resembling the perfect polish of Nebraska blacking on an exquisite's boot. Partly from their own superiority, but chiefly from contrast with her complexion, shone white as mountain snow, a regular row of ivory teeth. Her large flabby ears were adorned by huge wagon-wheel rings of pinch-beck, and a cumbersome strand of imitation coral beads adorned her inky throat, whilst her dress was of the gaudiest colors, plaided in large bars. Thus decked out, she made quite a figure in the assemblage.

" Is yer name Ann ?" she unceremoniously asked.

" Yes," was my laconic reply.

" Mine is Lucy ; but they calls me Luce fur short."

No answer being made, she garrulously went on :

" Was that yer husband what comed to see you this evenin' ?"

" No."

" Your brother ?"

" No."

" Your cousin ?"

" Neither."

" Well, he's too young-lookin' fur yer father. Mought he be yer uncle ?"

" No."

" Laws, then he mus' be yer sweetheart !" and she chuckled with mirth.

I made no answer.

" Why don't you talk, Ann ?"

" I don't feel like it."

" You don't ? well, that's quare."

Still I made no comment. Nothing daunted, she went on :

" Is yer gwine down the river with the next lot ?"

" I don't know ;" but this time I accompanied my reply with a sigh.

" What you grunt fur ?"

I could not, though so much distressed, resist a laugh at this singular interrogatory.

" Don't yer want to go South ? I does. They say it's right nice down dar. Plenty of oranges. When Masser fust sold me, I was mightily 'stressed ; den Missis, she told me dat dar was a sight of oranges down dar, and dat we didn't work any on Sundays, and we was 'lowed to marry ; so I got mightily in de notion of gwine. You see Masser Jones never 'lowed his black folks to marry. I wanted to marry four, five men, and he wouldn't let me. Den we had to work all day Sundays ; never had any time to make anyting for ourselves ; and I does love oranges ! I never had more an' a quarter of one in my life."

Thus she wandered on until she fell off to sleep; but the leaden-winged cherub visited me not that night. My eye-lids refused to close over the parched and tear-stained orbs. I dully moved from side to side, changed and altered my position fifty times, yet there was no repose for me.

> "Not poppy nor mandragora
> Nor all the drowsy syrups of the world,
> Could then medicine me to that sweet sleep
> Which I owed yesterday."

I saw the dull gray streak of the morning beam, as coldly it played through the gratings of my room. There, scattered in dismal confusion over the floor, lay the poor human beings, for whose lives, health and happiness, save as conducing to the pecuniary advantage of the trafficker, no thought or care was taken. I rose hastily and adjusted my dress, for I had not removed it during the night. The noise of my rising aroused several of the others, and simultaneously they sprang to their feet, apprehensive that they had slept past the prescribed hour for rising. Finding that their alarm was groundless, and that they were by the clock an hour too early, they grumbled a good deal at what they thought my unnecessary awaking. I would have given much to win to my heart the easy indifference as to fate, which many of them wore like a loose glove; but there I was vulnerable at every pore, and wounded at each. What a curse to a slave's life is a sensitive nature !

That day closed as had the preceding, save that at evening Henry did not come as before. I wandered out in the yard, which was surrounded by a high brick-wall, covered at the top with sharp iron spikes, to prevent the escape of slaves. Through this barricaded ground I was allowed to take a little promenade. There was not a shrub or green blade of grass to enliven me; but my eyes lingered not upon the earth. They were turned up to the full moon, shining so round and goldenly from the purple heaven, and, scattered sparsely through the fields of azure, were a few stars, looking brighter and larger from their scarcity.

"Will my death-hour ever come?" I asked myself despairingly. "Have I not tasted of the worst of life? Is not the poisoned cup drained to its last dregs?"

I fancied that I heard a voice answer, as from the clouds, "No, there are a few bitterer drops that must yet be drunk. Press the goblet still closer to your lips."

I shuddered coldly as the last tones of the imagined voice died away upon the soft night air.

"Is that," I cried, "a prophet warning? Comes it to me now that I may gird my soul for the approaching warfare? Let me, then, put on my helmet and buckler, and, like a life-tired soldier, rush headlong into the thickest of the fight, praying that the first bullet may prove a friend and drink my blood!"

Yet I shrank, like the weakest and most fearful of my race, when the distant cotton-fields rose upon my mental view! There, beneath the heat of a "hot and copper sky," I saw myself wearily tugging at my assigned task; yet my fear was not for the physical trouble that awaited me. Had Henry been going, "down the river" would have had no terror for me; but I was to part from joy, from love, from life itself! Oh, why, why have we—poor bondsmen and bondswomen—these fine and delicate sensibilities? Why do we love? Why are we not all coarse and hard, mere human beasts of burden, with no higher mental or moral conception, than obedience to the will or caprice of our owners?

Night closed over this second weary day. And thus passed on many days and nights. I did some plain sewing by way of employment, and at the command of a mulatto woman, who was the kept mistress of Atkins, and therefore placed in authority over us. Many of the women were hired out to residents of the city on trial, and if they were found to be agreeable and good servants, perhaps they were purchased. Before sending them out, Mr. Atkins always called them to him, and, shaking his cane over their heads, said,

"Now, you d——d hussy, or rascal (as they chanced to be male or female) if you behave yourselves well, you'll find a good home ; but you dare to get sick or misbehave, and be sent back to me, and I'll thrash you in an inch of your cursed life."

With this demoniacal threat ringing in their ears, it is not likely that the poor wretches started off with any intention of bad conduct.

We constantly received accessions to our number, but never acquisitions, for the poor, ill-fed, ill-kept wretches that came in there, "sold (as Atkins said) for a mere song," were desolate and revolting to see.

Charley found one or two old books, that he seemed to read and re-read ; indifferent novels, perhaps, that served, at least, to keep down the ravening tortures of thought. I lent him my Testament, and he read a great deal in it. He said that he had one, but had left it with his wife. He was a member of the Methodist Church ; had gone on Sunday afternoons to a school that had been established for the benefit of colored people, and thus, unknown to his master, had acquired the first principles of a good education. He could read and write, and was in possession of the rudiments of arithmetic. He told me that his wife had not had the opportunities he had, and therefore she was more deficient, but he added, "she had a great thirst for knowledge, such as I have never seen excelled, and rarely equalled. I have known her, after the close of her daily labors, devote the better portion of the night to study. I gave her all the instruction I could, and she was beginning to read with considerable accuracy; but all that is over, past and gone now." And again he ground his teeth fiercely, and a wild, lurid light gathered in his eye.

This man almost made me oblivious of my own grief, in sympathy for his. I did all I could by "moral suasion," as the politicians say, to soften his resentment. I bade him turn his thoughts toward that religion which he had espoused.

"I have no religion for this," he would bitterly say.

And in truth, I fear me much if the heroism of saints would hold out on such occasions. There, fastened to that impassioned husband's heart, playing with its dearest chords, was the fang-

like hand of the white man! Oh, slow tortures! in comparison
to which that of Prometheus was very pleasure. There is no
Tartarus like that of wounded, agonized domestic love! Far
away from him, in a lonely cabin, he beheld his stricken wife
and all his "pretty chickens" pining and unprotected.

Slowly, after a few days, he relapsed into that stony sort
of despair that denies itself the gratification of speech. The
change was very painfully visible to me, and I tried, by every
artifice, to arouse him; but I had no power to wake him.

> "Give sorrow words; the grief that does not speak,
> Whispers the o'erfraught heart, and bids it break."

And soon learning this, I left him, a remorseless prey to that
"rooted sorrow" of the brain.

*   *   *   *   *   *   *

One day, as we all sat in the shed-room, engaged at our
various occupations, we were roused by a noise of violent
weeping, and something like a rude scuffle just without the
door, when suddenly Atkins entered, dragging after him, with
his hand close about his throat, a poor negro man, aged and
worn, with a head white as cotton.

"Oh, please, Masser, jist let me go back, an' tell de ole
'ooman farewell, an' I won't ax for any more."

"No, you old rascal, you wants to run away. If you say
another word about the old voman, I'll beat the life out of
you."

"Oh lor', oh lor', de poor ole 'ooman an' de boys; oh my ole
heart will bust!" and, sobbing like a child, the old man sank
down upon the floor, in the most abandoned grief.

"Here, boys, some of you git the fiddle and play, an' I warrant that old fool will be dancin' in a minnit," said Atkins in his
unfeeling way.

Of course this speech met with the most signal applause
from "de boys" addressed.

I watched the expression of Charles' face. It was frightful.

He sat in one corner, as usual, with an open book in his hand. From it he raised his eyes, and, whilst the scene between Atkins and the old negro was going on, they flashed with an expression that I could not fathom. His brows knit, and his lip curled, yet he spoke no word.

When Atkins withdrew, the old man lay there, still weeping and sobbing piteously. I went up to him, kindly saying,

"What is the matter, old uncle?"

The sound of a kind voice aroused him, and looking up through his streaming tears, he said,

"Oh, chile, I's got a poor ole 'ooman dat lives 'bout half mile in de country. Masser fotch me in town to-day, an' say he was agwine to hire me fur a few weeks. Wal, I beliebed him, bekase Masser has bin hard run fur money, an' I was willin' to hope him 'long, so I consented to be hired in town fur little while, and den go out an' see de ole 'ooman an' de boys Saturday nights. Wal, de fust thing I knowed when I got to town I was sold to a trader. Masser wouldn't tell me hisself; but, when I got here, de gemman what I thought I was hired to, tole me dat Masser Atkins had bought me; an' I wanted to go back an' ask Masser, but he laughed an' say 'twant no use, Masser done gone out home. Oh, lor'! 'peared like dere was nobody to trus' to den. I begged to go an' say good-bye; but dey 'fused me dat, an' Masser Atkins 'gan to swear, an' he struck me 'cross de head. Oh, I didn't tink Masser wud do me so in my ole age!"

I ask you, reader, if for a sorrow like this there was any word of comfort? I thought not, and did not dare try to offer any.

"Will scenes like these ever cease?" I fretfully asked, as I turned to Charles.

"Never!" was the bitter answer.

This old man talked constantly of his little woolly-headed boys. When telling of their sportive gambols, he would smile, even whilst the tears were flowing down his cheeks.

He often had a crowd of slaves around him listening to his

talk of "wife and children," but I seldom made one of the number, for it saddened me too much. I knew that he was telling of joys that could never come to him again.

On one of these occasions, when uncle Peter, as he was called, was deep in the merits of his conversation, I was sitting in the corner of the room sewing, when Luce came running breathlessly up to me, with a bunch of beautiful flowers in her hand.

"Oh, Ann," she exclaimed, "dat likely-lookin' yallow man, dat cum to see you, an' fotch yer trunk de fust night yer comed here, was passin' by, an' I was stanin' at de gate; an' he axed me to han' dis to you."

And she gave me the bouquet, which I took, breathing a thousand blessings upon the head of my devoted Henry.

I had often wondered why Louise had never been to see me. She knew very well where I was, and access to me was easy. But I was not long kept in suspense, for, on that very night she came, bringing with her a few sweetmeats, which I distributed among those of my companions who felt more inclined to eat them than I did.

"I have wondered, Louise, why you did not come sooner."

"Well, the fact is, Ann, I've been busy trying to find you a home. I couldn't bear to come without bringing you good news. Henry and I have worked hard. All of our leisure moments have been devoted to it. We have scoured this city over, but with no success; and, hearing yesterday that Mr. Atkins would start down the river to-morrow, with all of you, I could defer coming no longer. Poor Henry is too much distressed to come ! He says he'll not sleep this night, but will ransack the city till he finds somebody able and willing to rescue you."

"How does he look ?" I asked.

"Six years older than when you saw him last. He takes this very hard; has lost his appetite, and can't sleep at night."

I said nothing ; but my heart was full, full to overflowing. I longed to be alone, to fall with my face on the earth and weep. The presence of Louise restrained me, for I always shrank from exposing my feelings.

"Are we going to-morrow?" I inquired.

"Yes, Mr. Atkins told me so this evening. Did you not know of it?"

"No, indeed; am I among the lot?"

After a moment's hesitation she replied,

"Yes, he told me that you were, and, on account of your beauty, he expected you would bring a good price in the Southern market. Oh heavens, Ann, this is too dreadful to repeat; yet you will have to know of it."

"Oh yes, yes;" and I could no longer restrain myself; I fell, weeping, in her arms.

She could not remain long with me, for Mr. Atkins closed up the establishment at half-past nine. Bidding me an affectionate farewell, and assuring me that she would, with Henry, do all that could be done for my relief, she left me.

A most wretched, phantom-peopled night was that! Ten thousand horrors haunted me! Of course I slept none; but imagination seemed turned to a fiend, and tortured me in divers ways.

CHAPTER XXXIV.

SCENE IN THE PEN—STARTING "DOWN THE RIVER"—UNCLE
PETER'S TRIAL—MY RESCUE.

ON the next day, after breakfast, Mr. Atkins came in, saying,
" Well, niggers, git yourselves ready. You must all start
down the river to-day, at ten o'clock. A good boat is going out.
Huddle up your clothes as quick as possible—no fuss, now."

When he left, there was lamentation among some; silent
mourning with others; joy for a few.

Shall I ever forget the despairing look of Charley? How
passionately he compressed his lips! I went up to him, and,
laying my hand on his arm, said,

"Let us be strong to meet the trouble that is sent us!"

He looked at me, but made no reply. I thought there was
the wildness of insanity in his glance, and turned away.

It was now eight o'clock, and I had not heard from Henry or
Louise. Alas! my heart misgave me. I had been buoyed up
for some time by the flatteries and delusions of Hope! but now
I felt that I had nothing to sustain me; the last plank had
sunk!

I did not pretend to "get myself ready," as Mr. Atkins had
directed; the fact is, I was ready. The few articles of wearing
apparel that I called mine were all in my trunk, with some little presents that Henry had made me, such as a brooch, ear-
rings, &c. These were safely locked, and the key hung round
my neck. But the others were busy "getting ready." I was
standing near the door, anxiously hoping to see either Henry or
Louise, when an old negro woman, thinly clad, without any
bonnet on her head, and with a basket in her hand, came up to
me, saying,

"Please mam, is my ole man in here? De massa out here say I may speak 'long wid him, and say farewell;" and she wiped her eyes with the corner of an old torn check apron.

I was much touched, and asked her the name of her old man.

"Pete, mam."

"Oh, yes, he is within," and I stepped aside to let her pass through the door.

She went hobbling along, making her passage through the crowd, and I followed after. In a few moments Pete saw her.

"Oh dear! oh dear!" he cried out, "Judy is come;" and running up to her, he embraced her most affectionately.

"Yes," she said, "I begged Masser to let me come and see you. It was long time before he told me dat you was sole to a trader and gwine down de ribber. Oh, Lord! it 'pears like I ken never git usin to it! Dars no way for me ever to hear from you. You kan't write, neither ken I. Oh, what shill we do?"

"I doesn't know, Judy, we's in de hands ob de Lord. We mus' trus' to Him. Maybe He'll save us. Keep on prayin', Judy."

The old man's voice grew very feeble, as he asked,

"An de chillen, de boys, how is dey?"

"Oh, dey is well. Sammy wanted to come long 'wid me; but it was too fur for him to walk. Joe gib me dis, and say, take it to daddy from me."

She looked in her basket, and drew out a little painted cedar whistle. The tears rolled down the old man's cheeks as he took it, and, looking at it, he shook his head mournfully,

"Poor boy, dis is what I give him fur a Christmas gift, an' he sot a great store to it. Only played wid it of Sundays and holidays. No, take it back to him, an' tell him to play wid it, and never forget his poor ole daddy dat's sole 'way down de ribber!"

Here he fairly broke down, and, bursting into tears, wept aloud.

"Oh, God hab bin marciful to me in lettin' me see you, Judy, once agin! an' I am an ongrateful sinner not to bar up better."

Judy was weeping violently.

"Oh, if dey would but buy me! I wants to go long wid you."

" No, no, Judy, you must stay long wid de chillen, an' take kere ob 'em. Besides, you is not strong enough to do de work dey would want you to do. No, I had better go by myself," and he wiped his eyes with his old coat sleeve.

" I wish," he added, " dat I had some little present to send de boys," and, fumbling away in his pocket, he at length drew out two shining brass buttons that he had picked up in the yard.

" Give dis to 'em ; say it was all thar ole daddy had to send 'em ; but, maybe, some time I'll have some money ; and if I meet any friends down de ribber, I'll send it to 'em, and git a letter writ back to let you and 'em know whar I is sold."

Judy opened her basket, and handed him a small bundle.

" Here, Pete, is a couple of shirts and a par of trowsers I fetched you, and here's a good par of woollen socks to keep you warm in de winter ; and dis is one of Masser's ole woollen undershirts dat Missis sent you. You know how you allers suffers in cold wedder wid de rheumatiz."

" Tell Missis thankee," and his voice was choking in his throat.

There was many a tearful eye among the company, looking at this little scene. But, suddenly it was broken up by the appearance of Mr. Atkins.

" Well, ole woman," he began, addressing Uncle Pete's wife, " it is time you was agoin'. You has staid long enough. Thar's no use in makin' a fuss. Pete belongs to me, an' I am agoin' to sell him to the highest bidder I can find down the river."

" Oh, Masser, won't you please buy me ?" asked Judy.

" No, you old fool."

" Oh, hush Judy, pray hush," put in Pete ; "humor her a little Masser Atkins, she will go in a minnit. Now do go, honey," he added, addressing Judy, who stood a moment, irresolutely, regarding her old husband ; then screaming out, " Oh no, no, I can't leave you!" fell down at his feet half insensible.

" Oh, Lord Jesus, hab marcy !" groaned Pete, as he bent over his partner's body.

"Take her out, instantly," exclaimed Atkins, as one of the men dragged the body out.

"Please be kereful, don't hurt her," implored Pete.

"Behave yourself, and don't go near her," said Atkins to him, "or I'll have both you an' her flogged. I am not goin' to have these fusses in my pen."

All this time Charley's face was frightful. As Atkins passed along he looked toward Charley, and I thought he quailed before him. That regal face of the mulatto man was well calculated to awe such a sinister and small soul as Atkins.

"Yes, yes, Charles, that proud spirit of yourn will git pretty well broken down in the cotton fields," he murmured, just loud enough to be heard. Charles made no answer, though I observed that his cheek fairly blazed.

*　　*　　*　　*　　*　　*

When we were all bonneted, trunks corded down, and bundles tied up, waiting, in the shed-room, for the order to get in the omnibus, Uncle Pete suddenly spied the basket which Judy, in her insensibility, had left. Picking it up, I saw the tears glitter in his eyes when the two bright buttons rolled out on the floor.

"These puttys," he muttered to himself, "was fur de boys. Poor fellows! Now dey won't have any keepsake from dar daddy; and den here's de little cedar whistle; oh, I wish I could send it out to 'em." Looking round the room he saw Kitty, the mulatto woman, of whom I have before spoken as the mistress of Atkins.

"Oh, please, Kitty, will you have dis basket, dis whistle, and dese putty buttons, sent out to Mr. John Jones', to my ole 'ooman Judy?"

"Yes," answered the woman, "I will."

"Thankee mam, and you'll very much oblige me."

"Come 'long with you all. The omnibus is ready," cried out Atkins, and we all took up the line of march for the door, each pausing to say good-bye to Kitty, and yet none caring much for her, as she had not been agreeable to us.

"Going down the river, really," I said to myself.

"Wait a minnit," said Atkins, and calling to a sort of foreman, who did his roughest work, he bade him handcuff us.

How fiercely-proud looked the face of Charles, as they fastened the manacles on his wrists.

I made no complaint, nor offered resistance. My heart was maddened. I almost blamed Louise, and chided Henry for not forcing my deliverance. I could have broken the handcuffs, so strongly was I possessed by an unnatural power.

"Git in the 'bus," said the foreman, as he riveted on the last handcuff.

Just as I had taken my seat in the omnibus, Henry came frantically rushing up. The great beads of perspiration stood upon his brow; and his thick, hard breathing, was frightful. Sinking down upon the ground, all he could say was,

"Ann! Ann!"

I rose and stood erect in the omnibus, looking at him, but dared not move one step toward him.

"What is the matter with that nigger?" inquired Atkins, pointing toward Henry. Then addressing the driver, he bade him drive down to the wharf.

"Stop! stop!" exclaimed Henry; "in Heaven's name stop, Mr. Atkins, here's a gentleman coming to buy Ann. Wait a moment."

Just then a tall, grave-looking man, apparently past forty, walked up.

"Who the d——l is that?" gruffly asked Mr. Atkins.

"It is Mr. Moodwell," Henry replied. "He has come to buy Ann."

"Who said that I wanted to sell her?"

"You would let her go for a fair price, wouldn't you?"

"No, but I would part with her for a first-rate one."

Just then, as hope began to relume my soul, Mr. Moodwell approached Atkins, saying,

15

"I wish to buy a yellow girl of you."

" Which one ?"

" A girl by the name of Ann.   Where is she ?"

" Don't you know her by sight ?"

" Certainly not, for I have never seen her."

" You don't want to buy without first seeing her ?"

" I take her upon strong recommendation."

With a dogged, and I fancied disappointed air, Atkins bade me stand forth.   Right willingly I obeyed; and appearing before Mr. Moodwell, with a smiling, hopeful face, I am not surprised that he was pleased with me, and readily paid down the price of a thousand dollars that was demanded by Atkins. When I saw the writings drawn up, and became aware that I had passed out of the trader's possession, and could remain near Henry, I lifted my eyes to Heaven, breathing out an ardent act of adoration and gratitude.

Quickly Henry stood beside me, and clasping my yielding hand within his own, whispered,

" You are safe, dear Ann."

I had no words wherewith to express my thankfulness; but the happy tears that glistened in my eyes, and the warm pressure of the hand that I gave, assured him of the sincerity of my gratitude.

My trunk was very soon taken down from the top of the omnibus and shouldered by Henry.

Looking up at my companions, I beheld the savagely-stern face of Charles; and thinking of his troubles, I blamed myself for having given up to selfish joy, when such agony was within my sight.   I rushed up to the side of the omnibus and extended my hand to him.

" God has taken care of you," he said, with a groan, " but I am forgotten !"

" Don't despair of His mercy, Charley."   More I could not say ; for the order was given them to start, and the heavy vehicle rolled away.

As I turned toward Henry he remarked the shadow upon my brow, and tenderly inquired the cause.

"I am distressed for Charley."

"Poor fellow! I would that I had the power to relieve him."

"Come on, come on," said Mr. Moodwell, and we followed him to the G—— House, where I found Louise, anxiously waiting for me.

"You are safe, thank Heaven!" she exclaimed, and joyful tears were rolling down her smooth cheeks.

The reaction of feeling was too powerful for me, and my health sank under it. I was very ill for several weeks, with fever. Louise and Henry nursed me faithfully. Mr. Moodwell had purchased me for a maiden sister of his, who was then travelling in the Southern States, and I was left at the G—— House until I should get well, at which time, if she should not have returned, I was to be hired out until she came. I recollect well when I first opened my eyes, after an illness of weeks. I was lying on a nice bed in Louise's room. As it was a cool evening in the early October, there was a small comfort-diffusing fire burning in the grate; and on a little stand, beside my bed, was a very pretty and fragrant bouquet. Seated near me, with my hand in his, was the one being on earth whom I best loved. He was singing in a low, musical tone, the touching Ethiopian melody of "Old Folks at Home." Slowly my eyes opened upon the pleasant scene! Looking into his deep, witching eyes, I murmured low, whilst my hand returned the pressure of his,

"Is it you, dear Henry?"

"It is I, my love; I have just got through with my work, and I came to see you. Finding you asleep, I sat down beside you to hum a favorite air; but I fear, that instead of calming, I have broken your slumber, sweet."

"No, dearest, I am glad to be aroused. I feel so much better than I have felt for weeks. My head is free from fever, and except for the absence of strength, am as well as I ever was."

"Oh, it makes me really happy to hear you say so. I have been so uneasy about you. The doctor was afraid of congestion of the brain. You cannot know how I suffered in mind about you; but now your flesh feels cool and pleasant, and your strength will, I trust, soon return."

Just then Louise entered, bearing a cup of tea and a nice brown slice of toast, and a delicate piece of chicken, on a neat little salver. At sight of this dainty repast, my long-forgotten appetite returned, with a most healthful vigor. But my kind nurse, who was glad to find me so well, determined to keep me so, and would not allow me a hearty indulgence of appetite.

In a few days I was able to sit up in an easy chair, and, at every opportunity, Louise would amuse me with some piece of pleasant gossip, in relation to the boarders, &c. And Henry, my good, kind, noble Henry, spent all his spare change in buying oranges and pine-apples for me, and in sending rare bouquets, luxuries in which I took especial delight. Then, during the long, cheerful autumnal evenings, when a fire sparkled in the grate, he would, after his work was done, bring his banjo and play for me; whilst his rich, gushing voice warbled some old familiar song. Its touching plaintiveness often brought the tears to my eyes.

Thus passed a few weeks pleasantly enough for me; but like all the other rose-winged hours, they soon had a close.

My strength had been increasing rapidly, and Mr. Moodwell, the brother and agent of my mistress, concluded that I was strong enough to be hired out. Accordingly, he apprized me of his intention, saying,

"Ann, sister Nancy has written me word to hire you out until spring, when she will return and take you home. I have selected a place for you, in the capacity of house-servant. You must behave yourself well."

I assured him that I would do my best; then asked the name of the family to whom I was hired.

"To Josiah Smith, on Chestnut street, I have hired you. He has two daughters and a young niece living with him, and wishes you to wait on them."

After apprizing Henry and Louise of my new home, *pro tem.,*

I requested the former to bring my trunk out that night, which he readily promised. Bidding them a kind and cheerful adieu, I followed Mr. Moodwell out to Chestnut street.

This is one of the most retired and beautiful streets in the city of L——, and Mr. Josiah Smith's residence the very handsomest among a number of exceedingly elegant mansions.

Opening a bronze gate, we passed up a broad tesselated stone walk that led to the house, which was built of pure white stone, and three stories in height, with an observatory on the top, and the front ornamented with a richly-wrought iron verandah. Reposing in front upon the sward, were two couchant tigers of dark gray stone.

Passing through the verandah, we stopped at the mahogany door until Mr. Moodwell pulled the silver bell-knob, which was speedily answered by a neatly-dressed man-servant, who bade Mr. Moodwell walk in the parlor, and requested me to wait without the door until he could find leisure to attend to me.

I obeyed this direction, and amused myself examining what remained of a very handsome flower-garden, until he returned, when conducting me around, by a private entrance, he ushered me into the kitchen.

CHAPTER XXXV.

I BECAME domesticated very soon in Mr. Josiah Smith's
family. I learned what my work was, and did it very faithfully, and I believe to their satisfaction.

The family proper consisted of Mr. Smith, his wife, two
daughters, and a niece. Mr. Smith was a merchant, of considerable wealth and social influence, and the young ladies were
belfes par-excellence. Mrs. Smith was the domestic of the concern, who carried on the establishment, a little, busy, fussy sort
of woman, that went sailing it round the house with a huge
bunch of keys dangling at her side, an incessant scold, with a
voice sharp and clear like a steamboat bell; a managing, thrifty
sort of person, a perfect terror to negroes; up of a morning
betimes, and in the kitchen, fussing with the cook about breakfast.

I had very little to do with Mrs. Letitia. My business was
almost exclusively with the young ladies. I cleaned and arranged their rooms, set the parlors right, swept and dusted
them, and then attended to the dining-room. This part of my
work threw me under Mrs. Letitia's dynasty; but as I generally did my task well, she had not much objection to make,
though her natural fault-finding disposition sharpened her optics
a good deal, and she generally discovered something about
which to complain.

Miss Adele Smith was the elder of the two daughters, a tall,
pale girl, with dark hair, carefully banded over a smooth,
polished brow, large black eyes and a pleasing manner.

The second, Miss Nellie, was a round, plump girl of blonde complexion, fair hair and light eyes, with a rich peach-flush on her cheek, and a round, luscious, cherry-red mouth, that was always curling and curvetting with smiles.

The cousin, Lulu Carey, was a real romantic character, with a light, fragile form, milk-white skin, the faintest touch of carmine playing over the cheek, mellow gray eyes, earnest and loving, and a profusion of chestnut-brown hair fell in the richest ringlets to her waist. Her features and caste of face were perfect. She was habited in close mourning, for her mother had been dead but one year, and the half-perceptible shadow of grief that hung over her face, form and manner, rendered her glorious beauty even more attractive.

It was a real pleasure to me to serve these young ladies, for though they were the élite, the cream of the aristocracy, they were without those offensive "airs" that render the fashionable society of the West so reprehensible. Though their parlors were filled every evening with the gayest company, and they were kept up late, they always came to their rooms with pleasant smiles and gracious words, and often chided me for remaining out of bed.

"Don't wait for us, Ann," they would say. "It isn't right to keep you from your rest on our account."

I slept on a pallet in their chamber, and took great delight in remaining up until they came, and then assisted them in disrobing.

It was the first time I had ever known white ladies (and young) to be amiable, and seemingly philanthropic, and of course a very powerful interest was excited for them. They had been educated in Boston, and had imbibed some of the liberal and generous principles that are, I think, indigenous to high Northern latitudes. Indeed, I believe Miss Lulu strongly inclined toward their social and reformatory doctrines, though she did not dare give them any very open expression, for Mr. and Mrs. Josiah Smith were strong pro-slavery, conservative people, and would not have countenanced any dissent from their opinions.

Mrs. Smith used to say, " Niggers ought to be exterminated."
And Miss Lulu, in her quiet way, would reply,

" Yes, as slaves they should be exterminated."

And then how pretty and naïvely she arched her pencilled
brows.   This was always understood by the sisters, who must
have shared her liberal views.

Mr. Smith was so much absorbed in mercantile matters, that
he seldom came home, except at meals or late at night, when
the household was wrapped in sleep; and, even on Sundays,
when all the world took rest, he was locked up in his counting-
room.   This seemed singular to me, for a man of Mr. Smith's
reputed and apparent wealth might have found time, at least on
Sunday, for quiet.

The young ladies were very prompt and regular in their at
tendance at church, but I used often to hear Miss Lulu exclaim,
after returning,

" Why don't they give us something new ?   These old rags
of theology weary, not to say annoy me.   If Christianity is
marching so rapidly on, why have we still, rising up in our
very midst, institutions the vilest and most revolting !   Why
are we cursed with slavery ?   Why have we houses of prosti-
tution, where beauty is sold for a price ?   Why have we pest
and alms-houses ?   Who is the poor man's friend ?   Who is there
with enough of Christ's spirit to speak kindly to the Magdalene,
and bid her ' go and sin no more '?   Alas, for Christianity to-
day ! "

" But we must accept life as it is, and patiently wait the
coming of the millennium, when things will be as they ought,"
was Miss Adele's reply.

" Oh, now coz, don't you and sis go to speculating upon life's
troubles, but come and tell me what I shall wear to the party
to-morrow night," broke from the gay lips of the lively Nellie.

In this strain I've many times heard them talk, but it always
wound up with a smile at the suggestion of the volatile Miss
Nellie.

When I had been there but two days, I began to suspect Mrs.

Smith's disposition, for she several times declared her opinion that niggers had no business with company, and that her's shouldn't have any. This was a damper to my hopes, for my chief motive for wishing to be sold in L—— was the pleasure I expected to derive from Henry's society. Every night, as early as eight, the servants were ordered to their respective quarters, and, as I slept in the house, a stolen interview with him would have been impossible, as Mrs. Smith was too alert for me to make an unobserved exit. On the second evening of my sojourn there, Henry called to see me about half-past seven o'clock; and, just as I was beginning to yield myself up to pleasure, Mrs. Smith came to the kitchen, and, seeing him there, asked,

" Whose negro is this?"

" Henry Graham is my name, Missis," was the reply.

" Well, what business have you here?"

Henry was embarrassed ; he hung his head, and, after a moment, faltered out,

" I came to see Ann, Missis."

" Where do you belong?"

" I belong to Mr. Graham, but am hired to the G—— House."

" Well, then, go right there; and, if ever I catch you in my kitchen again, I'll send your master word, and have you well flogged. I don't allow negro men to come to see my servants. I want them to have no false notions put into their heads. A nigger has no business visiting ; let him stay at home and do his master's work. I shouldn't be surprised if I missed something out of the kitchen, and if I do, I shall know that you stole it, and you shall be whipped for it ; so shall Ann, for daring to bring strange niggers into my kitchen. Now, clear yourself, man."

With an humbled, mortified air, Henry took his leave. A thousand scorpions were writhing in my breast. That he, my love, so honest, noble, honorable, and gentlemanly in all his feelings, should be so accused almost drove me to madness. I could not bear to have his pride so bowed and his dearly-cher-

15*

ished principles outraged.   From that day I entertained no kind feeling for Mrs. Smith.

On another occasion, a Saturday afternoon, when Louise came to sit a few moments with me, she heard of it, and, rushing down stairs, ordered her to leave on the instant, adding that her great abomination was free niggers, and she wouldn't have them lurking round her kitchen, corrupting her servants, and, perhaps, purloining everything within their reach.

Louise was naturally of a quick and passionate disposition; and, to be thus wantonly and harshly treated, was more than she could bear.   So she furiously broke forth, and such a scene as occurred between them was disgraceful to humanity !   Miss Adele hearing the noise instantly came out, and in a positive tone ordered Louise to leave; which order was obeyed.   After hearing from her mother a correct statement of the case, Miss Adele burst into tears and went to her room   I afterward heard her kindly remonstrating with her mother upon the injustice of such a course of conduct toward her servants.   But Mrs. Smith was confirmed in her notions.   They had been instilled into her early in life; had grown with her growth and strengthened with her years.   So it was not possible for her young and philanthropic daughter to remove them.   Once, when Miss Adele was quite sick, and after I had been nursing her indefatigably for some time, she said to me,

" Ann, you have told me the story of your love.   I have been thinking of Henry, and pitying his condition, and trying to devise some way for you to see him."

" Thank you, Miss Adele, you are very kind."

" The plan I have resolved upon is this : I will pretend to send you out of evenings on errands for me ; you can have an understanding with Henry, and meet at some certain point ; then take a walk or go to a friend's ; but always be careful to get home before ten o'clock."

This was kindness indeed, and I felt the grateful tears gathering in my eyes !   I could not speak, but knelt down beside the bed, and reverently kissed the hem of her robe.   Goodness such as hers, charity and love to all, elicited almost my very worship!

I remember the first evening that I carried this scheme into effect. She was sitting in a large arm-chair, carefully wrapped up in the folds of an elegant velvet *robe-de-chambre*. Her mother, sister, and cousin were beside her, all engaged in a cheerful conversation, when she called me to her, and pretended to give me some errand to attend to out in the city, telling me *pointedly* that it would require my attention until near ten o'clock. How like a lovely earth-angel appeared she then!

I had previously apprized Henry of the arrangement, and named a point of meeting. Upon reaching it, I found him already waiting for me. We took a long stroll through the lamp-lit streets, talking of the blessed hopes that struggled in our bosoms; of the faint divinings of the future; told over the story of past sufferings, and renewed olden vows of devotion.

He, with the most lover-like fondness, had brought me some little gift; for this I kindly reproved him, saying that all his money should be appropriated to himself, that, by observing a rigid economy, we but hastened on the glorious day of release from bondage. Before ten I was at home, and waiting beside Miss Adele. How kindly she asked me if I had enjoyed myself; and with what pride I told her of the joy that her kindness had afforded me! Surely the sweet smile that played so luminously over her fair face was a reflex of the peace that irradiated her soul! How beautifully she illustrated, in her single life, the holy ministrations of true womanhood! Did she not, with kind words and generous acts, "strive to bind up the bruised, broken heart." At the very mention of her name, aye, at the thought of her even, I never fail to invoke a blessing upon her life!

Thus, for weeks and months, through her ingenuity, I saw Henry and Louise frequently. Otherwise, how dull and dreary would have seemed to me that long, cold winter, with its heaped snow-banks, its dull, gray sky, its faint, chill sun, and leafless trees; but the sunbeam of her kindness made the season bright, warm and grateful!

CHAPTER XXXVI.

THE NEW ASSOCIATES—DEPRAVED VIEWS—ELSY'S MISTAKE—
DEPARTURE OF THE YOUNG LADIES—LONELINESS.

IN Mr. Smith's family of servants was Emily, the cook, a
sagacious woman, but totally without education, knowledge, or
the peculiar ambition that leads to its acquisition. She was a
bold, raw, unthinking spirit ; and, from the fact that she had
been kept closely confined to the house, never allowed any
social pleasure, she resolved to be revenged, and unfortunately
in her desire for " spite " (as she termed it), had sacrificed her
character, and was the mother of two children, with unac-
knowledged fathers. Possessed of a violent temper, she would,
at periods, rave like a mad-woman ; and only the severest lashing could bring her into subjection. She was my particular
terror. Her two children, half-bloods, were little, sick, weasly
things that excited the compassion of all beholders, and though
two years of age (twins), were, from some physical derange-
ment, unable to walk.

There was also a man servant, Duke, who attended to odd
ends of housework, and served in the capacity of decorated
carriage-driver, and a girl, Elsy, a raw, green, country concern,
good-natured and foolish, with a face as black as tar. They had
hired her from a man in the country, and she being quite delighted with town and the off-cast finery of the ladies, was as
happy as *she* could be—yet the mistakes she constantly made
were truly amusing. She had formed quite an attachment for
Duke, which he did not in the slightest degree return ; yet,
with none of the bashfulness of her sex, she confessed to the
feeling, and declared that " Duke was very mean not to love

her a little." This never failed to excite the derision of the more sprightly Emily.

"Well, you is a fool," she would exclaim, with an odd shake of the head.

"I loves him, and don't kere who knows it."

"Does he love you?" asked Emily.

"*Well*, he doesn't."

"*Then I'd hate him*," replied Emily, as, with a great force, she brought her rolling-pin down on the table.

"No, I wouldn't," answered the loving Elsy.

"You ain't worth shucks."

"Wish I was worth Duke."

"Hush, fool."

"You needn't git mad, kase I don't think as you does."

"I is mad bekase you is a fool."

"Who made me one?"

"You was born it, I guess."

"Then I aren't to blame fur it. Them that made me is."

Conversations like this were of frequent occurrence, and once, when I ventured to ask Elsy if she wouldn't like to learn to read, she laughed heartily, saying:

"Does you think I wants to run off?"

"Certainly not."

"Den why did you ax me if I wanted to larn to read?"

"So you might have a higher source of enjoyment than you now have."

"Oh, yes, so as to try to git my freedom! You is jist a spy fur de white folks, and wants to know if I'll run away. Go off, now, and mind yer own business, kase I has hearn my ole Masser, in de country, say dat whenever niggers 'gan to read books dey was ob no 'count, and allers had freedom in dar heads."

Finding her thus obstinate, I gave up all attempts to persuade her, and left her to that mental obscuration in which I found her. Emily sometimes threatened to apply herself, with vigor, to the gaining of knowledge, and thus defeat and "spite" her owners; but knowledge so obtained, I think, would be of little avail, for, like religion, it must be sought after from higher motives—sought for itself *only.*

I could find but little companionship with those around me, and lived more totally within myself than I had ever done. Many times have I gone to my room, and in silence wept over the isolation in which my days were spent; but three nights out of the seven were marked with white stones, for on these I held blissful re-unions with Henry. Our appointed spot for meeting was near an old pump, painted green, which was known as the "green pump," a very favorite one, as the water, pure lime-stone, was supposed to be better, cooler, and stronger than that of others. Much has been written, by our popular authors, on the virtues and legends of old town pumps, but, to me, this one had a beauty, a charm, a glory which no other inanimate object in wide creation possessed! And of a moonlight night, when I descried, at a distance, its friendly handle, outstretched like an arm of welcome, I have rushed up and grasped it with a right hearty good feeling! Long time afterwards, when it had ceased to be a love-beacon to me, I never passed it without taking a drink from its old, rusty ladle, and the water, like the friendly draught contained in the magic cup of eastern story, transported me over the waste of time to poetry and love! Even here I pause to wipe away the fond, sad tears, which the recollection of that old "green pump" calls up to my mind, and I should love to go back and stand beside it, and drink, aye deeply, of its fresh, cool water! There are now many stately mansions in that growing city, that sits like a fairy queen upon the shore of the charmed Ohio; but away from all its lofty structures and edifices of wealth, away from her public haunts, her galleries and halls, would I turn, to pay homage to the old "green pump"!

Some quiet evenings, too, had I in Louise's room, listening to Henry sing, while he played upon his banjo. His voice was fine, full, and round, and rang out with the clearness of a bell. Though possessed of but slight cultivation, I considered it the finest one I ever heard.

But again my pleasures were brought to a speedy close. As the winter began to grow more cold, and the city more dull, the young ladies began to talk of a jaunt to New Orleans. Their first determination was to carry me with them; but, after calculating the "cost," they concluded it was better to go without a servant, and render all necessary toilette services to each other. They had no false pride—thanks to their Northern education for that!

Before their departure they gave quite a large dinner-party, served up in the most fantastic manner, consisting of six different courses. I officiated as waiter, assisted by Duke. Owing to the scarcity of servants in the family, Elsy was forced to attend the door, and render what assistance she could at the table.

Whilst they were engaged on the fourth course, a violent ring was heard at the door-bell, which Elsy was bound to obey.

In a few moments she returned, saying to one of the guests:

"Miss Allfield, a lady wishes to speak with you."

"*With me?*" interrogated the lady.

"Yes, marm."

"Who can she be?" said Miss Allfield, in surprise.

"Bid the lady be seated in the parlor, and say that Miss Allfield is at dinner," replied Mrs. Smith.

"If the company will excuse me, I will attend to this unusual visitor," said Miss Allfield, as she rose to leave.

"*It is a colored lady*, and she is waitin' fur you at the door," put in Elsy.

The blank amazement that sat upon the face of each guest, may be better imagined than described! Some of them were ready to go into convulsions of laughter. A moment of dead silence reigned around, when Miss Nellie set the example of a hearty laugh, in which all joined, except Mr. and Mrs. Smith, whose faces were black as a tempest-cloud.

But there stood the offending Elsy, all unconscious of her guilt. When she first came to town, she had been in the habit of announcing company to the ladies as "a man wants to see

you," or " a woman is in the parlor," and had, every time, been
severely reprimanded, and told that she should say "a lady or
gentleman is in the parlor." And the poor, green creature, in
her great regard for " ears polite," did not know how to make
the distinction between the races; but most certainly was she
taught it by the severe whipping that was administered to her
afterwards by Mr. Smith. No intercession or entreaty from the
ladies could be of any avail. Upon Elsy's bare back must the
atonement be made! After this public whipping, she was held
somewhat in disgrace by the other servants. Duke gave her a
very decided cut, and Emily, who had never liked her, was
now lavish in her abuse and ill-treatment. She even struck the
poor, offenceless creature many blows; and from this there was
no redemption, for she was in sad disrepute with Mr. and Mrs.
Smith; and, after the young ladies' departure, she had no friend
at all, for I was too powerless to be of use to her.

*   *   *   *   *   *   *

The remainder of the winter was dull indeed. My inter-
views with Henry had been discontinued; and I never saw
Louise. I had no time for reading. It was work, work, delve
and drudge until my health sank under it. Mrs. Smith never
allowed us any time on Sundays, and the idea of a negro's
going to church was outrageous.

" No," she replied, when I asked permission to attend church,
" stay at home and do your work. What business have negroes
going to church? They don't understand anything about the
sermon."

Very true, I thought, for the most of them; but who is to
blame for their ignorance? If opportunities for improvement
are not allowed them, assuredly they should not suffer for it.

How dead and lifeless lay upon my spirit that dull, cold winter! The snow-storm was without; and ice was within. Constant fault-finding and ten thousand different forms of domestic
persecution well-nigh crushed the life out of me. Then there
was not one break of beauty in my over-cast sky! No faint

or struggling ray of light to illume the ice-bound circle that surrounded me!

But the return of spring began to inspire me with hope; for then I expected the arrival of my unknown mistress. Henry and Louise both knew her, and they represented her as possessed of very amiable and philanthropic views. How eagerly I watched for the coming of the May blossoms, for then she, too, would come, and I be released from torture! How dull and drear seemed the howling month of March, and even the fitful, changeful April. Alternate smiles and tears were wearying to me, and sure I am, no school-girl elected queen of the virgin month, ever welcomed its advent with such delight as I!

With its first day came the young ladies. Right glad was I to see them. They returned blooming and bright as flowers, with the same gentle manners and kindly dispositions that they had carried away.

Miss Nellie had many funny anecdotes to tell of what she had seen and heard; really it was delightful to hear her talk in that mirth-provoking manner! In her accounts of Southern dandyisms and fopperies, she drew forth her father's freest applause.

" Why, Nellie, you ought to write a book, you would beat Dickens," he used to say; but her more sober sister and cousin never failed to reprove her, though gently, for her raillery.

" Well, Elsy," she cried, when she met that little-respected personage, " Have any more ' colored ladies ' called during our absence?" This was done in a kind, jocular way; but the poor negro felt it keenly, and held her head down in mortification.

* * * * * * *

At length the second week of the month of May arrived, and with it came my new mistress! A messenger, no less a person than Henry, was despatched for me. The time for which I was hired at Mr. Smith's having expired two weeks previously, I hastily got myself ready, and Henry once again shouldered my trunk.

With a feeling of delight, I said farewell to Mrs. Smith and the servants; but when I bade the young ladies good-bye, I

own to the weakness of shedding tears ! I tried to impress
upon Miss Adele's mind the sentiment of love that I cherished
for her, and I had the satisfaction of knowing that she was not
too proud to feel an interest in me.

All the way to the G—— House, Henry was trying to cheer me
up, and embolden me for the interview with Miss Nancy. I
had been looking anxiously for the time of her arrival, and now
I shrank from it. It was well for my presence of mind that
Miss Jane and her husband had returned to their homestead, for
I do not think that I could have breathed freely in the same
house with them, even though their control over me had ceased.

Arriving at the G—— House, I had not the courage to venture
instantly into Miss Nancy's presence ; but sought refuge, for a
few moments, in Louise's apartment, where she gave me a very
cordial reception, and a delightful beverage compounded of
blackberries.

CHAPTER XXXVII.

THE NEW MISTRESS—HER KINDNESS OF DISPOSITION—A PRETTY
HOME—AND LOVE-INTERVIEWS IN THE SUMMER DAYS.

At last I contrived to "screw my courage to the sticking-place," and go to Miss Nancy's room.

I paused at the closed door before knocking for admission. When I did knock, I heard a not unpleasant voice say—

"Come in."

The tone of that voice re-inspired me, and I boldly entered.

There, resting upon the bed, was one of the sweetest and most benign faces that I ever beheld. Age had touched it but to beautify. Serene and clear, from underneath the broad cap frill shone her mild gray eyes. The wide brow was calm and white as an ivory tablet, and the lip, like a faded rose-leaf, hinted the bright hue which it had worn in health. The cheek, like the lip, was blanched by the hand of disease. "Ah," she said, as with a slight cough she elevated herself upon the pillow, "it is you, Ann. You are a little tardy. I have been looking for you for the last half-hour."

"I have been in the house some time, Miss Nancy, but had not the courage to venture into your presence; and yet I have been watching for your arrival with the greatest anxiety."

"You must not be afraid of me, child, I am but a sorry invalid, who will, I fear, often weary and overtax your patience; but you must bear with me; and, if you are faithful, I will reward you for it. Henry has told me that you are pretty well educated, and have a pleasant voice for reading. This delights me much; for your principal occupation will be to read to me."

Certainly this pleased me greatly, for I saw at once that I

was removed from the stultifying influences which had so long been exercised over my mind. Now I should find literary food to supply my craving. My eyes fairly sparkled, as I answered,

"This is what I have long desired, Miss Nancy; and you have assigned to me the position I most covet."

"I am glad I have pleased you, child. It is my pleasure to gratify others. Our lives are short, at best, and he or she only lives *truly* who does the most good."

This was a style and manner of talk that charmed me. Beautiful example and type of womankind! I felt like doing reverence to her.

She reached her thin hand out to help herself to a glass of water, that stood on a stand near by. I sprang forward to relieve her.

"Ah, thank you," she said, in a most bland tone; "I am very weak; the slightest movement convinces me of the failure of my strength."

I begged that she would not exert herself, but always call on me for everything that she needed.

"I came here to serve you, and I assure you, my dear Miss Nancy, I shall be most happy in doing it. Mine will, I believe, truly be a ' labor of love.' "

Another sweet smile, with the gilded light of a sunbeam, broke over her calm, sweet face! Bless her! she and all of her class should be held as "blessed among women;" for do they not walk with meek and reverent footsteps in the path of her, the great model and prototype of all the sex?

*   *   *   *   *   *   *

When I had been with her but a few days, she informed me that, as soon as her health permitted, she intended being removed to her house on Walnut street. I was not particularly anxious for this; for my sojourn at the G—— house was perfectly delightful My frequent intercourse with Henry and Louise, was a source of intense pleasure to me. I was allowed to pass the evenings with them. Truly were those hours dear and bright Henry played upon his banjo, and sang to us the most

enrapturing songs, airs and glees ; and Louise generally supplied us with cakes and lemonade ! How exquisite was my
happiness, as there we sat upon the little balcony gazing at the
Indiana shore, and talking of the time when Henry and I should
be free.

" How much remains to be paid to your master, Henry,"
asked Louise.

" I have paid all but three hundred and fifty ; one hundred
of which I already have ; so, in point of fact, I lack only two
hundred and fifty," said Henry.

" I am very anxious to leave here this fall. I wish to go to
Montreal. Now, if you could make your arrangements to go
on with me, I should be glad. I shall require the services and
attentions of a man; and, if you have not realized the money
by that time, I think I can lend it to you," returned Louise.

A bright light shone in Henry's eye, as he returned his
thanks ; but quickly the coming shadow banished that radiance
of joy.

" But think of her," he said tenderly, laying his hand on my
shoulder; " what can she do without us, or what should I be
without her ?"

" Oh, think not of me, dearest, I have a good home, and am
well cared for. Go, and as soon as you can, make the money,
and come back for me."

" Live years away from you ? Oh, no, no !" and he wound
his arm around my waist, and, most naturally, my head rested
upon his shoulder. Loud and heavy was his breathing, and I
knew that a fierce struggle was raging in his breast.

" I will never leave her, Louise," he at length replied.
" That tyrant, the law, may part us ; but, my free will and act
—never."

" Ah, well," added she, as she looked upon us, "you will
think better of this after you give it a little reflection. This is
only love's delusion ;" and, in her own quiet, sensible way, she
turned the stream of conversation into another channel.

I think now, with pleasure, of the lovely scenes I enjoyed

on those evenings, with the fire-flies playing in the air; and
many times have I thought how beautifully and truly they
typify the illusive glancings of hope, darting here and there
with their fire-lit wings; eluding our grasp, and sparkling e'en
as they flit.

*   *   *   *   *   *   *

A few weeks after my installation in the new office, my mistress, whose health had been improving under my nursing,
began to get ready to move to her sweet little cottage residence
on Walnut street. I was not anxious for the change, notwithstanding it gave me many local advantages; for I should be
removed from Henry, and though I knew that I could see
him often, yet the same roof would not cover us. But my life,
hitherto, had been too dark and oppressed for me to pause
and mourn over the " crumpled rose-leaf;" and so, with right
hearty good will I set to work " packing Miss Nancy's trunk,"
and gathering up her little articles that had lain scattered about
the room.

An upholsterer had been sent out to get the house ready for
us. When we were on the eve of starting, Henry came to carry
the luggage, and Miss Nancy paid him seventy-five cents, at
which he took off his hat, made a low bow, and said,

"Thank you, Missis."

Miss Nancy was seated on the most comfortable cushion, and
I directly opposite, fanning her,

We drove up to the house, a neat little brick cottage, painted
white, with green shutters, and a deep yard in front, thickly
swarded, with a variety of flowers, and a few forest trees.
Beautiful exotics, in rare plaster, and stone vases, stood about
in the yard, and a fine cast-iron watch-dog slept upon the front
steps. Passing through the broad hall, you had a fine view of
the grounds beyond, which were handsomely decorated. The
out-buildings were all neatly painted or white-washed. A
thorough air of neatness presided over the place. On the right
of the hall was the parlor, furnished in the very perfection of
taste and simplicity.

The carpet was of blue, bespeckled with yellow ; a sofa of blue brocatelle, chairs, and ottomans of the same material, were scattered about.   A cabinet stood over in the left corner, filled with the collections and curiosities of many years' gathering, whilst the long blue curtains, with festoonings of lace, swept to the floor !   Adjoining the parlor was the dining-room, with its oaken walls, and cane-colored floor-cloth.   Opposite to the parlor, and fronting the street, was Miss Nancy's room, with its French bedstead, lounge, bureau, bookcase, table, and all the et ceteras of comfort.   Opening out from her room was a small apartment, just large enough to contain a bed, chair, and wardrobe, with a cheap little mirror overhanging a tasteful dresser, whereon were laid a comb, brush, soap, basin, pitcher, &c.   This room had been prepared for me by my kind mistress. Pointing it out, she said,

" That, Ann, is your *castle*."   I could not restrain my tears.

" Heaven send me grace to prove my gratitude to you, kind Miss Nancy," I sobbed out.

" Why, my poor girl, I deserve no thanks for the performance of my duty.   You are a human being, my good, attentive nurse, and I am bound to consider your comfort or prove unworthy of my avowed principles."

" This is so unlike what I have been used to, Miss Nancy, that it excites my wonder as well as gratitude."

" I fear, poor child, that you have served in a school of rough experience !   You are so thoroughly disciplined, that, at times, you excite my keenest pity."

" Yes, ma'm, I have had all sorts of trouble. The only marvel is that I am not utterly brutalized."

" Some time you must tell me your history ; but not now, my nerves are too unquiet to listen to an account so harrowing as I know your recital must be."

As I adjusted the pillow and arranged the beautiful silk-spread (her own manufacture), I observed that her eyes were filled with tears.   I said nothing, but the sight of *those tears* served to soften many a painful recollection of former years.

I am conscious, in writing these pages, that there will be few of my white readers who can enter fully into my feelings. It is impossible for them to know how deeply the slightest act of kindness impressed *me*—how even a word or tone gently spoken called up all my thankfulness! Those to whom kindness is common, a mere household article, whose ears are greeted morning, noon and night, with loving sounds and kind tones, will deem this strange and exaggerated; but, let them recollect that I was a *slave*—not a mere servant, but a perpetual slave, according to the abhorred code of Kentucky; and their wonder will cease.

The first night that I threw myself down on my bed to sleep (did I state that I had a bedstead—that I had *actually* what slaves deemed a great luxury—a *high-post bedstead?*) I felt as proud as a queen. Henry had been to see me. I entertained him in a nice, clean, carpeted kitchen, until a few minutes of ten o'clock, when he left me; for at that hour, by the city ordinance, he was obliged to be at home.

"What," I thought, "have I now to desire? Like the weary dove sent out from the ark, I have at last found land, peace and safety. Here I can rest contentedly beneath the waving of the olive branches that guard the sacred portal of *home! Home!* home this truly was! A home where the heart would always love to lurk; and how blessed seemed the word to me, now that I comprehended its practical significance! No more was it a fable, an expression merely used to adorn a song or round a verse!

That first night that I spent at home was not given up to sleep. No, I was too happy for that! Through the long, mysterious hours, I lay wakeful on my soft and pleasant pillow, weaving fairest fancies from the dim chaos of happy hopes. Adown the sloping vista of the future I descried nought but shade and flowers!

With my new mistress, I was more like a companion than a servant. My duties were light—merely to read to her, nurse her, and do her sewing; and, as she had very little of the latter,

I may as well set it down as the "extras" of my business, rather than the business itself.

I rose every morning, winter and summer, at five o'clock, and arranged Miss Nancy's room whilst she slept; and, so accustomed had she become to my light tread, that she slept as soundly as though no one had been stirring. After this was done, I placed the family Bible upon a stand beside her bed; then took my sewing and seated myself at the window, until she awoke. Then I assisted her in making her morning toilette, which was very simple; wheeled the easy chair near the bed, and helped her into it. After which she read a chapter from the holy book, followed by a beautiful, extemporaneous prayer, in which we were joined by Biddy, the Irish cook. After this, Miss Nancy's breakfast was brought in on a large silver tray,—a breakfast consisting of black tea, Graham bread, and mutton chop. In her appetite, as in her character, she was simple. After this was over, Biddy and I breakfasted in the kitchen. Our fare was scarcely so plain, for hearty constitutions made us averse to the abstemiousness of our mistress. We had hot coffee, steaming steaks, omelettes and warm biscuits.

"Ah, but she is a love of a lady!" exclaimed Biddy, as she ate away heartily at these luxuries. "Where in this city would we find such a mistress, that allows the servants better fare than she takes herself? And then she never kapes me from church. I can attend the holy mass, and even go to vespers every Sunday of my life. The Lord have her soul for it! But she is as good as a canonized saint, if she is a Protestant!"

Sometimes I used to repeat these conversations to Miss Nancy. They never failed to amuse her greatly.

"Poor Biddy," she would say, in a quiet way, with a sweet smile, "ought to know that true religion is the same in all. It is not the being a member of a particular church, or believing certain dogmas of faith, that make us religious, heirs of God, and joint heirs with Christ. It is the living religion, not the simple believing of it, that constitutes us *Christians*. We must feel that all men are our brothers, and all women our sisters;

16

for in the kingdom of heaven there will be no distinction of
race or color, and I see no reason why we should live differently
here. The Saviour of the world associated with the humblest.
His chosen twelve were the fishermen of Galilee. I want to
live in constant preparation for death; but, alas! my weak endeavor is but seldom crowned with success."

How reverently I looked upon her at such times! What a
beautiful saint she was!

One evening in the leafy month of June, when the intensity
of summer begins to make itself felt, I took my little basket,
filled with some ruffling that I was embroidering for Miss Nancy's
wrapper, and seated myself upon the little portico at the back
of the house. I had been reading to her the greater portion
of the day, and felt that it was pleasant to be left in an indolent, dreamy state of mind, that required no concentration of
thought. As my fingers moved lazily along, I was humming
an old air, that I had heard in far less happy days. Everything around me was so pleasant! The setting sun was flinging
floods of glory over the earth, and the young moon was out
upon her new wing, softening and beautifying the scene. Afar
off, the lull of pleasant waters and the music-roar of the falls
sounded dreamily in my ear! I laid my work down in the
basket, and, with closed eyes, thought over the events and incidents of my past life of suffering; and, as the dreary picture
of my troubles at Mr. Peterkin's returned to my mind, and my
subsequent imprisonment in the city, my trials at "the pen,"
and then this my safe harbor and haven of rest, so strange the
whole seemed, that I almost doubted the reality, and feared to
open my eyes, lest the kindly, illusive dream should be broken
forever. But no, it was no dream; for, upon turning my head, I
spied through the unclosed door of the dining-room the careful arrangement of the tea-table. There it stood, with its snowy cover,
upon which were placed the fresh loaf of Graham bread, the roll of
sweet butter, some parings of cheese, the glass bowl of fruit and
pitcher of cream, together with the friendly tea-urn of bright
silver, from which I, even *I*, had often been supplied with the

delightful beverage. And then, stepping through the door, with a calm smile on her face, was Miss Nancy herself ! How beautifully she looked in her white, dimity wrapper, with the pretty blue girdle, and tiny lace cap ! She gazed out upon the yard, with the blooming roses, French pinks, and Colombines that grew in luxuriance. Stepping upon the sward, she gathered a handful of flowers, clipping them nicely from the bush with a pair of scissors, that she wore suspended by a chain to her side. Seeing me on the portico, she said,

" Ann, bring me my basket and thread here, and wheel my arm-chair out ; I wish to sit with you here."

I obeyed her with pleasure, for I always liked to have her near me. She was so much more the friend than the mistress, that I never felt any reserve in her presence. All was love. As she took her seat in the arm-chair, I threw a shawl over her shoulders to protect her from any injurious influence of the evening air. She busied herself tying up the flowers ; and their arrangement of color, &c., with a view to effect, would have done credit to a florist. My admiration was so much excited, that I could not deny myself the pleasure of an expression of it.

" Ah, yes," she answered, " this was one of the amusements of my youth. Many a bouquet have I tied up in my dear old home."

I thought I detected a change in her color, and heard a sigh, as she said this.

" Of what State are you a native, Miss Nancy ?"

" Dear old Massachusetts," she answered, with a glow of enthusiasm.

"It is the State, of all others in the Union, for which I have the most respect."

"Ah, well may you say that, poor girl," she replied, " for its people treat your unfortunate race with more humanity than any of the others."

" I have read a great deal of their liberality and cultivation, of both mind and heart, which has excited my admiring interest. Then, too, I have known those born and reared beneath the shadow of its wise and beneficent laws, and the better I knew them, the more did my admiration for the State increase. Now I feel that Massachusetts is doubly dear to me, since I have learned that it is your birth-place."

She did not say anything, but her mild eyes were suffused with tears.

Just as I was about to speak to her of Mr. Trueman, Biddy came to announce tea, and, after that, Miss Nancy desired to be left alone. As was his custom, with eight o'clock came Henry. We sat out on the portico, with the moonlight shining over us, and talked of the future! I told him what Miss Nancy said of Massachusetts, and, I believe, he was seized with the idea of going thither after purchasing himself.

He was unusually cheerful. He had made a great deal in the last few months; had grown to be quite a favorite with the keeper of the hotel, and was liberally paid for his Sunday and holiday labors, and, by errands for, and donations from, the boarders, had contrived to lay up a considerable sum.

"I hope, dearest, to be able soon to accomplish my freedom; then I shall be ready to buy you. How much does Miss Nancy ask for you?"

"Oh, Henry, I cannot leave her, even if I were able to pay down every cent that she demands for me. I should dislike to go away from her. She is so kind and good; has been such a friend to me that I could not desert her. Who would nurse her? Who would feel the same interest in her that I do? No, I will stay with her as long as she lives, and do all I can to prove my gratitude."

"What do you mean, Ann? Would you refuse to make me happy? Miss Nancy has other friends who would wait upon her."

"But, Henry, that does not release me from my obligation. When she was on the eve of starting upon a journey, you went to her with the story of my danger. She promptly consented to buy me without even seeing me. I was not purchased as an article of property; with the noble liberality of a philanthropist, she ransomed, at a heavy price, a suffering sister, and shall I be such an ingrate as to leave her? No, she and Mr. Trueman of Boston, are the two beings whom I would willingly serve forever."

Just then a deep sigh burst from the full heart of some one, and I thought I heard a retreating footstep.

" Who can that have been ?" asked Henry.

We examined the hall, the dining-room, my apartment; and I knocked at Miss Nancy's door, but, receiving no answer, I judged she was asleep.

" It was but one of those peculiar voices of the night, which are the better heard from this intense silence," said Henry, and, finding that my alarm was quieted, he bade me an affectionate good-night, and so we parted.

CHAPTER XXXVIII.

I SLEPT uninterruptedly that night, and, on awaking in the morning, I was surprised to find it ten minutes past five. Hurrying on my clothes, I went to Miss Nancy's apartment, and was much surprised to find her sitting in her easy chair, her toilette made. Looking up from the Bible, which lay open on the stand before her, she said,

"I have stolen a march, Ann, and have risen before you."

"Yes, ma'm," replied I, in a mortified tone, "I am ten minutes behind the time; I am very sorry, and hope you will excuse me."

"No apologies, now; I hope you do not take me for a cruel, exacting task-mistress, who requires every inch of your time."

"No, indeed, I do not, for I know you to be the kindest mistress and best friend in the world."

"And now, Ann, I will read some from the Lamentations of Jeremiah; and we will unite in family prayer."

At the ringing of the little bell Biddy quickly appeared, and we seated ourselves near Miss Nancy, and listened to her beautiful voice as it broke forth in the plaintive eloquence of the holy prophet!

"Let us pray," she said, fervently, extending her thin, white hands upward, and we all sank upon our knees. She prayed for grace to rest on the household; for its extension over the world; that it might visit the dark land of the South; that the blood of Christ might soften the hearts of slave-holders. She asked, in a special manner, for power to carry out her good intentions; prayed that the blessing of God might be given to me, in a particular manner, to enable me to meet the trials of life, and invoked benedictions upon Biddy.

When we rose, both Biddy and I were weeping; and as we left her, Biddy broke forth in all her Irish enthusiasm, "The Lord love her heart! but she is sanctified! I never heard a prettier *prayer said in the Cathedral !*"

*   *   *   *   *

Miss Nancy's health improved a great deal. She began to walk of evenings through the yard, and a little in the city. I always attended her. Of mornings we rode in a carriage that she hired for the occasion, and of evenings Henry came, and always brought with him his banjo.

One evening he and Louise came round to sit with me, and after we had been out upon the portico listening to Henry's songs, Miss Nancy bade me go to the sideboard and get some cake and wine. Placing it on the table in the dining-room, I invited them, in Miss Nancy's name, to come in and partake of it. After proposing the health of my kind Mistress, to which we all drank, Biddy joining in, Louise pledged a glass to the speedy ransom of Henry. Just then Miss Nancy entered, saying :

" My good Henry, when you buy yourself, and find a home in the North, write us word where you have established yourself, and I will immediately make out Ann's free papers, and remove thither; but I cannot think of losing my good nurse. So, for her's, your's and my own convenience, I will take up my residence wherever you may settle. Stop now, Ann, no thanks; I know all about your gratitude, for I was a pleased, though unintentional listener to a conversation between yourself and Henry, in which I found out how deep is your attachment to me."

Hers, then, was the sigh which had so alarmed me! It was all explained. I had no words to express my overflowing heart. My whole soul seemed melted. Henry's eyes were filled with grateful tears. He sank upon his knees and kissed the hem of Miss Nancy's dress.

"No, no, my brave-hearted man, do not kneel to me. I am but the humble instrument under Heaven; and, oh, how often have I prayed for such an opportunity as this to do good, and dispense happiness."

And so saying she glided out of the room.

" Well," exclaimed Biddy, " she is more than a saint, she is an angel," and she wiped the tears from her honest eyes.

" I have known her for some time," said Louise, " and never saw her do, or heard of her doing a wrong action. She is very different from her brother. Does he come here often, Ann ?"

" Not often ; about once a fortnight."

" He is too much taken up with business; hasn't a thought outside of his counting-room. He doesn't share in any of her philanthropic ideas."

" She hasn't her equal on earth," added Henry. " Mr. Moodwell is a good man, though not good enough to be *her* brother."

Thus passed away the evening, until the near approach of ten o'clock warned them to leave.

I was too happy for sleep. Many a wakeful night had I passed from unhappiness, but now I was sleepless from joy.

*   *   *   *   *   *   *

The next morning, after Miss Nancy had breakfasted, I asked her what I should read to her.

" Nothing this morning, Ann. I had rather you would talk with me. Let us arrange for the future ; but first tell me how much money does Henry lack to buy himself ?"

" About one hundred dollars."

" I think I can help him to make that up."

" You have already done enough, dear Miss Nancy. We could not ask more of you."

" No, but I am anxious to do all I can for you, my good girl. You are losing the greenest part of your lives. I feel that it is wrong for you to remain thus."

Seeing that I was in an unusually calm mood, she asked me to tell her the story of my life, or at least the main incidents. I entered upon the narrative with the same fidelity that I have observed in writing these memoirs. At many points and scenes I observed her weeping bitterly. Fearing that the excitement might prove too great for her strength, I several times urged her to let me stop; but she begged me to go on without heeding her, for she was deeply interested.

When I came to the account of my meeting with Mr. Trueman, she bent eagerly forward, and asked if it was Justinian Trueman, of Boston. Upon my answering in the affirmative, she exclaimed:

" How like him ! The same noble, generous, disinterested spirit !"

" Do you know him, Miss Nancy ?"

Oh yes, child, he is one of our prominent Northern men, a very able lawyer; every one in the State of Massachusetts knows him by reputation. but I have a personal acquaintance also."

Just as I was about to ask her something of Mr. Trueman's history, Biddy came running in, exclaiming:

" Oh, dear me! Miss Nancy ! what do you think? They say that Mr. Barkoff. the green grocer, has let his wife whip a colored woman to death."

" Oh, it can't be true," cried Miss Nancy, as she started up from her chair. " It is, I trust, some slanderous piece of gossip."

" Oh, the Lord love your saintly heart, but I do believe 'tis true, for, as I went down the street to market, I heard some awful screaming in there, and I asked a girl, standing on the pavement, what it meant; and she said Mrs. Barkoff was whipping a colored woman; then, when I came back there was a crowd of children and colored people round the back gate, and one of them told me the woman was dead, and that she died shouting."

" Oh, God, how fearful is this !" exclaimed Miss Nancy, as the big tears rolled down her pale cheeks. " Give me, oh, sweet Jesus, the power to pray as Thou didst, to the Eternal Father, ' to forgive them, for they know not what they do !' "

" Come, Ann," continued the impetuous Biddy, " you go with

16*

me, and we'll try to find out all about it. We will go to see the woman."

"I cannot leave Miss Nancy."

"Yes, go with her, Ann; but don't allow her to say anything imprudent. Poor Biddy has such a good, philanthropic heart, that she forgets the patient spirit which Christianity inculcates."

With a strange kind of awe, I followed Biddy through the streets, scarcely heeding her impassioned garrulity. The blood seemed freezing in my veins, and my teeth chattered as though it had been the depth of winter. As we drew near the place, I knew the house by the crowd that had gathered around the back and side gates.

"Let us enter here," said Biddy, as she placed her hand upon the heavy plank gate at the back of the lot.

"Stop, Biddy, stop," I gasped out, as I held on to the gate for support, "I feel that I shall suffocate. Give me one moment to get my breath."

"Oh, Ann, you are only frightened," and she led me into the yard, where we found about a dozen persons, mostly colored.

"Where is the woman that's been kilt?" inquired Biddy, of a mulatto girl.

"She ain't quite dead. Pity she isn't out of her misery, poor soul," said the mulatto girl.

"But where is she?" demanded Biddy.

"Oh, in thar, the first room in the basement," and, half-led by Biddy, I passed in through a mean, damp, musty basement. The noxious atmosphere almost stifled us. Turning to the left as directed, we entered a low, comfortless room, with brick walls and floor. Upon a pile of straw, in this wretched place, lay a bleeding, torn, mangled body, with scarcely life in it. Two colored women were bathing the wounds and wrapping greased cloths round the body. I listened to her pitiful groans, until I thought my forbearance would fail me.

"Poor soul!" said one of the colored women, "she has had

a mighty bad convulsion. I wish she could die and be sot free from misery."

" Whar is de white folks ?" asked another.

" Oh, dey is skeered, an' done run off an' hid up stairs."

" Who done it ?"

" Why, Miss Barkoff; she put Aunt Kaisy to clean de harth, an' you see, de poor ole critter had a broken arm. De white folks broke it once when dey was beatin' of her, and so she couldn't work fast. Well den, too, she'd been right sick for long time. You see she was right sickly like, an' when Miss Barkoff come back—she'd only bin gone a little while—an' see'd dat de harth wasn't done, she fell to beatin' of de poor ole sick critter, an' den bekase she cried an' hollered, she tuck her into de coal-house, gagged her mouth, tied her hands an' feet, an' fell to beatin' of her, an' she beat her till she got tired, den ole Barkoff beat her till he got satisfied. Den some colored person seed him, an' tole him dat he better stop, for Aunt Kaisy was most gone."

" Yes, 'twas me," said the other woman, " I was passin' 'long at de back of de lot, an' I hearn a mighty quare noise, so I jist looked through the crack, an' there I seed him a beatin' of her, an' I hollered to him to stop, for de Lor' sake, or she would die right dar. Den he got skeered an' run off in de house."

The narration was here interrupted by a fearful groan from the sufferer. One of the women very gently turned her over, with her face full toward me.

Oh, God have mercy on me! In those worn, bruised, anguish-marked features, in the glance of that failing, filmy eye, I recognized my long-lost mother! With one loud shriek I fell down beside her! After years of bitter separation, thus to meet! Oh that the recollection had faded from my mind, but no, that awful sight is ever before my eyes! I see her, even now, as there she lay bleeding to death! Oh that I had been spared the knowledge of it!

There was the same mark upon the brow, and, I suppose,

more by that than the remembered features, was I enabled to indentify her.

My frantic screams soon drew a crowd of persons to the room.

My mother, my dear, suffering mother, unclosed her eyes, and, by that peculiar mesmerism belonging to all mothers, she knew it was her child whose arms were around her.

" Ann, is it you ?" she asked feebly.

" Yes, mother, it is I ; but, oh, how do I find you !"

" Never mind me, child, I feel that I shall soon be at peace ! 'Tis for you that I am anxious.   Have you a good home ?"

" Yes ; oh, that you had had such !"

" Thank God for that.   You are a woman now, I think; but I am growing blind, or it is getting dark so fast that I cannot see you.   Here, here, hold me Ann, child, hold me close to you, I am going through the floor, sinking, sinking down. Catch me, catch me, hold me !   It is dark ; I can't see you, where, where are you ?"

" Here, mother, here, I am close to you."

" Where, child, I can't see you ; here catch me ;" and, suddenly springing up as if to grasp something, she fell back upon the straw——*a corpse !*

After such a separation, this was our meeting—and parting ! I had hoped that life's bitterest drop had been tasted, but this was as " vinegar upon nitre."

When I became conscious that the last spark of life was extinct in that beloved body, I gave myself up to the most delirious grief.   As I looked upon that horrid, ghastly, mangled form, and thought it was my mother, who had been butchered by the whites, my very blood was turned to gall, and in this chaos of mind I lost the faculty of reason.

＊   ＊   ＊   ＊   ＊   ＊   ＊   ＊

When my consciousness returned I was lying on a bed in my room, the blinds of which were closed, and Miss Nancy was seated beside me, rubbing my hands with camphor.   As I opened my eyes, they met her kind glance fixed earnestly upon me.

" You are better, Ann," she said, in a low, gentle voice. I was too languid to reply; but closed my eyes again, with a faint smile. When I once more opened them I was alone, and through one shutter that had blown open, a bright ray of sunlight stole, and revealed to me the care and taste with which my room had been arranged. Fresh flowers in neat little vases adorned the mantel; and the cage, containing Miss Nancy's favorite canary, had been removed to my room. The music of this delightful songster broke gratefully upon my slowly awakening faculties. I rose from the bed, and seated myself in the large arm-chair. Passing my hand across my eyes, I attempted to recall the painful incidents of the last few days; and as that wretched death-bed rose upon my memory, the scalding tears rushed to my eyes, and I wept long, long, as though my head were turned to waters !

Miss Nancy entered, and finding me in tears she said nothing; but turned and left the room. Shortly after, Biddy appeared with some nourishment,

" Laws, Ann, but you have been dreadfully sick. You had fever, and talked out of your head. Henry was here every evening. He said that once afore, when you took the fevers, you was out of your head, just the same way. He brought you flowers; there they are in the vase," and she handed me two beautiful bouquets.

In this pleasant way she talked on until I had satisfied the cravings of an empty stomach with the niceties she had brought me.

That evening Henry came, and remained with me about half an hour. Miss Nancy warned him that it was not well to excite me much. So with considerable reluctance he shortened his visit.

CHAPTER XXXVIX.

GRADUAL RETURN OF HAPPY SPIRITS—BRIGHTER PROSPECTS—
AN OLD ACQUAINTANCE.

When I began to gain strength Miss Nancy took me out in
a carriage of evenings ; and had it not been for the melancholy
recollections that hung like a pall around my heart, life would
have been beautiful to me. As we drove slowly through the
brightly-lighted streets, and looked in at the gaudy and flaunting
windows, where the gayest and most elegant articles of merchandise were exhibited, I remarked to Miss Nancy, with a
sigh, " Life might be made a very gay and cheerful thing—
almost a pleasure, were it not for the wickedness of men."

" Ah, yes, it might, indeed," she replied, and the big tears
rested upon her eyelids.

One evening when we had returned from a drive, I noticed
that she ate very little supper, and her hand trembled violently.

" You are sick, Miss Nancy," I said.

" Yes, Ann, I feel strangely," she replied.

" To-morrow you must go for my brother, and I will have a
lawyer to draw up my will. It would be dreadful if I were to
die suddenly without making a provision for you; then the
bonds of slavery would be riveted upon you, for by law you
would pass into my brother's possession."

" Don't trouble yourself about it now, dear Miss Nancy," I
said ; " your life is more precious than my liberty."

" Not so, my good girl. The dawn of your life was dark, I
hope that the close may be bright. The beginning of mine

[374]

was full of flowers; the close will be serene, I trust; but ah, I've outlived many a blessed hope that was a very rainbow in my dreaming years."

I had always thought Miss Nancy's early life had been filled with trouble; else why and whence her strange, subdued, melancholy nature! How much I would have given had she told me her history; yet I would not add to her sadness by asking her to tell me of it.

The next morning I went for Mr. Moodwell, who, at Miss Nancy's instance, summoned a notary. The will was drawn up and witnessed by two competent persons.

After this she began to improve rapidly. Her strength of body and cheerfulness returned. About this time my peace of mind began to be restored. Of my poor mother I never spoke, after hearing the particulars that followed her death. She was hurriedly buried, without psalm or sermon. No notice was taken by the citizens of her murder—why should there be? She was but a poor slave, grown old and gray in the service of the white man; and if her master chose to whip her to death, who had a right to gainsay him? She was his property to have and to hold; to use or to kill, as he thought best!

Give us no more Fourth of July celebrations; the rather let us have a Venetian oligarchy!

Miss Nancy, in her kind, persuasive manner, soon lured my thoughts away from such gloomy contemplations. She sought to point out the pleasant, easy pathway of wisdom and religion, and I thank her now for the good lessons she then taught me! Beneath such influence I gradually grew reconciled to my troubles. Miss Nancy fervently prayed that they might be sanctified to my eternal good; and so may they!

Louise came often to see me, and I found her then as now, the kindest and most willing friend; everything that she could do to please me she did. She brought me many gifts of books, flowers, fruits, &c. I may have been petulant and selfish in my grief; but those generous friends bore patiently with me.

Pleasant walks I used to take with Henry of evenings, and

he was then so full of hope, for he had almost realized the sum of money that his master required of him.

"Master will be down early in September," he said, as we strolled along one evening in August, "and I think by borrowing a little from Miss Nancy, I shall be able to pay down all that I owe him, and then, dearest, I shall be free—free! only think of it! Of *me* being a free man, master of *myself!* and when we go to the North we will be married, and both of us will live with Miss Nancy, and guard her declining days."

Happy tears were shining in his bright eyes, like dew-pearls; but, with a strong, manly hand he dashed them away, and I clung the fonder to that arm, that I hoped would soon be able to protect me.

"There is one foolish little matter, dearest, that I will mention, more to excite your merriment, than fear," said Henry with an odd smile.

"What is it?"

"Well, promise me not to care about it; only let it give you a good laugh."

"Yes, I promise."

"Well," and he paused for a moment, "there is a girl living near the G—— House. She belongs to Mr. Bodley, and has taken a foolish fancy to me; has actually made advances, even more than advances, actual offers of love! She says she used to know you, and, on one occasion, attempted to speak discreditably of you; though I quickly gave her to understand that I would not listen to it. Why do you tremble so, Ann?"

And truly I trembled so violently, that if it had not been for the support that his arm afforded me, I should have fallen to the ground.

"What is her name?" I asked.

"Melinda, and says she once belonged to Mr. Peterkin.'

"Yes, she did. We used to call her Lindy."

I then told him what an evil spirit she had been in my path; and ventured to utter a suspicion that her work of harm was yet unfinished, that she meant me further injury.

" I know her now, dearest. You have unmasked her, and, with me, she can have no possible power."

I seemed to be satisfied, though in reality I was not, for apprehension of an indefinable something troubled me sorely. The next day Miss Nancy observed my troubled abstraction, and inquired the cause, with so much earnestness, that I could not withhold my confidence, and gave her a full account.

" And you think she will do you an injury ?"

" I fear so."

" But have you not forestalled that by telling Henry who she is, and how she has acted toward you ?"

" Yes, ma'm, and have been assured by him that she can do me no harm ; but the dread remains."

" Oh, you are in a weak, nervous state ; I am astonished at Henry for telling you such a thing at this time."

" He thought, ma'm, that it would amuse me, as a fine joke ; and so I supposed I should have enjoyed it."

She did all she could to divert my thoughts, made Henry bring his banjo, and play for me of evenings ; bought pleasant romances for me to read ; ordered a carriage for a daily ride ; purchased me many pretty articles of apparel ; but, most of all, I appreciated her kind and cheerful talk, in which she strove to beguile me from everything gloomy or sad.

Once she sent me down to spend the day with Louise at the G—— House. There was quite a crowd at the hotel. Southerners, who had come up to pass their summer at the watering-places in Kentucky, had stopped here, and, finding comfortable lodgment, preferred it to the springs; then there were many others travelling to the North and East *via* L——, who were stopping there. This increased Henry's duties, so that I saw him but seldom during the day. Once or twice he came to Louise's room, and told me that he was unusually busy ; but that he had earned four dollars that day, from different persons, in small change, and that he would be able to make his final payment the next month.

All this was very encouraging, and I was in unusually fine

spirits. As Louise and I sat talking in the afternoon, she remarked—

"Well, Ann, early next month Henry will make his last payment ; and we have concluded to go North the latter part of
the°same month.   When will Miss Nancy be ready to go ?"

"Oh, she can make her arrangements to start at the same time.
I will speak to her about it this evening."

And then, as we sat planning about a point of location, a
shadow darkened the door. I looked up—and, after a long
separation, despite both natural and artificial changes, I recognized *Lindy !*   I let my sewing fall from my hands and
gazed upon her with as much horror as if she had been an ap-
parition !   Louise spoke kindly to her, and asked her to walk in.

"Why, how d'ye do, Ann ?   I hearn you was livin' in de
city, and intended to come an' see you."

I stammered out something, and she seated herself near me,
and began to revive old recollections.

"They are not pleasant, Lindy, and I would rather they
should be forgotten."

"Laws, I's got a very good home now; but I 'tends to marry
some man that will buy me, and set me free !   Now, I's got
my eye sot on Henry."

I trembled violently, but did not trust myself to speak
Louise, however, in a quick tone, replied :

"He is engaged, and soon to be married to Ann."

"Laws ! I doesn't b'lieve it ; Ann shan't take him from me."

Though this was said playfully, it was easy for me to detect,
beneath the seeming levity, a strong determination, on her part,
to do her very *worst*.   No wonder that I trembled before her,
when I remembered how powerful an enemy she had been in
former times.

With a few other remarks she left, and Louise observed :

"That Lindy is a queer girl.   With all her ignorance and
ugliness, she excites my dread when I am in her presence—a
dread of a supposed and envenomed power, such as the black
cat possesses."

" Such has ever been the feeling, Louise, that she has excited in me. She has done me harm heretofore ; and do you know, I think she means me ill now. I have uttered this suspicion to Henry and Miss Nancy, but they both laughed it to scorn— saying *she* was powerless to injure *me;* but still my fear remains, and, when I think of her, I grow sick at heart."

Upon my return home that evening I told Miss Nancy of the meeting with Lindy, and of the conversation, but she attached no importance to it.

No one living beneath the vine and fig-tree of Miss Nancy's planting, and sharing the calm blessedness of her smiles, could be long unhappy ! Her life, as well as words, was a proof that human nature is not all depraved. In thinking over the rare combination of virtues that her character set forth, I have marvelled what must have been her childhood. Certainly she could never have possessed the usual waywardness of children. Her youth must have been an exception to the general rule. I cannot conceive her with the pettishness and proneness to quarrel, which we naturally expect in children. I love to think of her as a quiet little Miss, discarding the doll and play-house, turning quietly away from the frolicsome kitten—seeking the leafy shade of the New England forests—peering with a curious, thoughtful eye into the woodland dingle—or straining her gaze far up into the blue arch of heaven—or questioning, with a child's idle speculation, the whence and the whither of the mysterious wind. 'Tis thus I have pictured her childhood ! She was a strange, gifted, unusual woman ;—who, then, can suppose that her infancy and youth were ordinary ?

To this day her memory is gratefully cherished by hundreds. Many little pauper children have felt the kindness of her charity ; and those who are now independent remember the time when her bounty rescued them from want, and " they rise up to call her blessed !"

Often have I gone with her upon visits and errands of charity. Through many a dirty alley have those dainty feet threaded a dangerous way ; and up many a dizzy, dismal flight of ricketty steps have I seen them ascend, and never heard a petulant word, or saw a haughty look upon her face! She never went upon missions of charity in a carriage, or, if she was too weak to walk all the way, she discharged the vehicle before she got in sight of the hovel. " Let us not be ostentatious," she would say, when I interposed an objection to her taking so long a walk. "Besides," she added, "let us give no offence to these suffering poor ones. Let them think we come as sisters to relieve them ; not as Dives, flinging to Lazarus the crumbs of our bounty !"

Beautiful Christian soul! baptized with the fire of the Holy Ghost, endowed with the same saintly spirit that rendered lovely the life of her whom the Saviour called Mother! thou art with the Blessed now ! After a life of earnest, godly piety, thou hast gone to receive thine inheritance above, and wear the Amaranthine Crown! for thou didst obey the Saviour's sternest mandate—sold thy possessions, and gave all to the poor !

CHAPTER XL.

I HAVE paused much before writing this chapter. I have taken up my pen and laid it down an hundred times, with the task unfulfilled—the duty unaccomplished. A nervous sensation, a chill of the heart, have restrained my pen—yet the record must be made.

I have that to tell, from which both body and soul shrink. Upon me a fearful office has been laid! I would that others, with colder blood and less personal interest, could make this disclosure; but it belongs to my history; nay, is the very nucleus from which all my reflections upon the institution of slavery have sprung. Reader, did you ever have a wound—a deep, almost a mortal wound—whereby your life was threatened, which, after years of nursing and skilful surgical treatment, had healed, and was then again rudely torn open? This is my situation. I am going to tear open, with a rude hand, a deep wound, that time and kind friends have not availed to cure. But like little, timid children, hurrying through a dark passage, fearing to look behind them, I shall hasten rapidly over this part of my life, never pausing to comment upon the terrible facts I am recording. "I have placed my hand to the ploughshare, and will not turn back."

Let me recall that fair and soft evening, in the early September, when Henry and I, with hand clasped in hand, sat together upon the little balcony. How sweet-scented was the gale that fanned our brows! The air was soft and balmy, and the sweet serenity of the hour was broken only by that ever-pleasant music of the gently-roaring falls!　Fair and queenly sailed the uprisen moon, through a cloudless sea of blue, whilst a few faint stars, like fire-flies, seemed flitting round her.

Long we talked of the happiness that awaited us on the morrow.　Henry had arranged to meet his master, Mr. Graham, on that day, and make the final payment.

"Dearest, I lack but fifty dollars of the amount," he said, as he laid his head confidingly on my shoulder.

"Ten of which I can give you."

"And the remaining forty I will make up," said Miss Nancy as she stepped out of the door, and, placing a pocket-book in Henry's hand, she added, "there is the amount, take it and be happy."

Whilst he was returning thanks, I went to get my contribution.　Drawing from my trunk the identical ten-dollar note that good Mr. Trueman had given me, I hastened to present it to Henry, and make out the sum that was to give us both so much joy.

"Here, Henry," I exclaimed, as I rejoined them, "are ten dollars, which kind Mr. Trueman gave me."

Miss Nancy sighed deeply.　I turned around, but she said with a smile:

"How different is your life now from what it was when that money was given you."

"Yes, indeed," I answered; "and, thanks, my noble benefactress, to you for it."

"Let me," she continued, without noticing my remark, "see that note."

I immediately handed it to her.　Could I be mistaken?　No; she actually pressed it to her lips!　But then she was such a philanthropist, and she loved the note because it was the means of bringing us happiness.　She handed it back to me with another sigh.

"When he gave it to me, he bade me receive it as his contribution toward the savings I was about to lay up for the purchase of myself. Now what joy it gives me to hand it to you, Henry." He was weeping, and could not trust his voice to answer.

"And Ann shall soon be free. Next week we will all start for the North, and then, my good friends, your white days will commence," said Miss Nancy.

"Oh, Heaven bless you, dear saint," cried Henry, whose utterance was choked by tears. Miss Nancy and I both wept heartily; but mine were happy tears, grateful as the fragrant April showers !

"Why this is equal to a camp-meeeting," exclaimed Louise, who had, unperceived by us, entered the front-door, passed through the hall, and now joined us upon the portico.

Upon hearing of Henry's good fortune, she began to weep also.

"Will you not let me make one of the party for the North ?" she inquired of Miss Nancy.

"Certainly, we shall be glad to have you, Louise ; but come, Henry, get your banjo, and play us a pleasant tune."

He obeyed with alacrity, and I never heard his voice sound so rich, clear and ringing. How magnificent he looked, with the full radiance of the moonlight streaming over his face and form ! His long flossy black hair was thrown gracefully back from his broad and noble brow; whilst his dark flashing eye beamed with unspeakable joy, and the animation that flooded his soul lent a thrill to his voice, and a majesty to his frame, that I had never seen or heard before. Surely I was very proud and happy as I looked on him then!

Before we parted, Miss Nancy invited him and Louise to join us in family devotion. After reading a chapter in the Bible, and a short but eloquent and impressive prayer, she besought Heaven to shed its most benign blessings on us ; and that our approaching good fortune might not make us forget Him from whom every good and perfect gift emanated ; and thus closed that delightful evening !

After Henry had taken an affectionate farewell of me, and

departed with Louise, he, to my surprise, returned in a few moments, and finding the house still open, called me out upon the balcony.

"Dearest, I could not resist a strange impulse that urged me to come back and look upon you once again. How beautiful you are, my love!" he said as he pushed the masses of hair away from my brow, and imprinted a kiss thereon. He was so tardy in leaving, that I had to chide him two or three times.

"I cannot leave you, darling."

"But think," I replied, "of the joy that awaits us on the morrow."

At last, and at Miss Nancy's request, he left, but turned every few steps to look back at the house.

"How foolish Henry is to-night," said Miss Nancy, as she withdrew her head from the open window. "Success and love have made him foolishly fond!"

"Quite turned his brain," I replied; "but he will soon be calm again."

"Oh, yes, he will find that life is an earnest work, as well for the freeman as the bondsman."

I lay for a long time on my bed in a state of sleeplessness, and it was past midnight when I fell asleep, and then, oh, what a terrible dream came to torture me! I thought I had been stolen off by a kidnapper, and confined for safe keeping in a charnel-house, an ancient receptacle for the dead, and there, with blue lights burning round me, I lay amid the dried bones and fleshless forms of those who had once been living beings; and the vile and loathsome gases almost stifled me. By that dim blue light I strove to find some door or means of egress from the terrible place, and just as I had found the door and was about to fit a rusty key into the lock, a long, lean body, decked out in shroud, winding-sheet and cap, with hollow cheek and cadaverous face, and eyes devoid of all speculation, suddenly seized me with its cold, skeleton hand. Slowly the face assumed the expression of Lindy's, then faded into that of Mr. Peterkin's. I attempted to break from it, but I was held with a vice-like power. With a loud, frantic scream I broke from the trammels of sleep. A cold, death-like sweat had broken out on my body. My screaming had aroused Miss Nancy and Biddy. Both came rushing into my room.

After a few moments I told them of my dream.

" A bad attack of incubus," remarked Miss Nancy, " but she is cold ; rub her well, Biddy."

With a very good will the kind-hearted Irish girl obeyed her. I could not, however, be prevailed upon to try to sleep again ; and as it wanted but an hour of the dawn, Biddy consented to remain up with me. We dressed ourselves, and sitting down by the closed window, entered into a very cheerful conversation. Biddy related many wild legends of the " *ould country*," in which I took great interest.

Gradually we saw the stars disappear, and the moon go down, and the pale gray streaks of dawn in the eastern sky !

I threw up the windows, exclaiming : " Oh, Biddy, as the day dawns, I begin to suffocate. I feel just as I did in the dream. Give me air, quick." More I could not utter, for I fell fainting in the arms of the faithful girl. She dashed water in my face, chafed my hands and temples, and consciousness soon returned.

" Why, happiness and good fortune do excite you strangely ; but they say there are some that it sarves just so."

" Oh no, Biddy, I am not very well,—a little nervous. I will take some medicine."

When I joined Miss Nancy, she refused to let me assist her in dressing, saying :

" No, Ann, you look ill. Don't trouble yourself to do anything. Go lie down and rest."

I assured her repeatedly that I was perfectly well ; but she only smiled, and said in a commendatory tone,

" Good girl, good girl !"

All the morning I was fearfully nervous, starting at every little sound or noise. At length Miss Nancy became seriously uneasy, and compelled me to take a sedative.

17

As the day wore on, I began to grow calm. The sedative had taken effect, and my nervousness was allayed·

I took my sewing in the afternoon, and seated myself in Miss Nancy's room. Seeing that I was calm, she began a pleasant conversation with me.

"Henry will be here to-night, Ann, a free man, the owner of himself, the custodian of his own person, and you must put on your happiest and best looks to greet him."

"Ah, Miss Nancy, it seems like too much joy for me to realize. What if some grim phantom dash down this sparkling cup; just as we are about to press it to our eager and expectant lips? Such another disappointment I could not endure.

"You little goosey, you will mar half of life's joys by these idle fears."

"Yes, Miss Nancy," put in Biddy. "Ann is just so narvous ever since that ugly dream, that she hain't no faith to-day in anything."

"Have you baked a pretty cake, and got plenty of nice confections ready to give Henry a celebration supper, good Biddy?" inquired Miss Nancy.

"Ah, yes, everything is ready, only just look how light and brown my cake is," and she brought a fine large cake from the pantry, the savory odor of which would have tempted an anchorite.

"Then, too," continued the provident Biddy, "the peaches are unusually soft and sweet. I have pared and sugared them, and they are on the ice now; oh, we'll have a rale feast."

"Thanks, thanks, good friends," I said, in a voice choked with emotion.

"Only just see," exclaimed Biddy, "here comes Louise, running as fast as her legs will carry her; she's come to be the first to tell you that Henry is free."

I rushed with Biddy to the door, and Miss Nancy followed. We were all eager to hear the good news.

"Mercy, Louise, what's the matter?" I cried, for her face terrified me. She was pale as death; her eyes, black and wild, seemed starting from their sockets, and around her mouth there was that ghastly, livid look, that almost congealed my blood.

"Oh, God!" she cried in frenzy, "God have mercy on us all!" and reeled against the wall.

"Speak, woman, speak, in heaven's name," I shouted aloud. "Henry! Henry! Henry! has aught happened to him?"

"Oh, God!" she said, and her eyes flamed like a fury's; "*he has cut his throat*, and now lies weltering in his own blood."

I did not scream, I did not speak. I shed no tears. I did not even close my eyes. Every sense had turned to stone! For full five minutes I stood looking in the face of Louise.

"Why don't you speak, Ann! Cry, imprecate, do something, rather than stand there with that stony gaze!" said Louise, as she caught me frantically by the arm.

"Why did he kill himself?" I asked, in an unfaltering tone.

"He went, in high spirits, to make his last payment to his master, who was at the hotel. 'Here, master,' he said, 'is all that I owe you; please make out the bill of sale, or my free papers.' Mr. Grahan took the money, with a smile, counted it over twice, slowly placed it in his pocket-book, and said, 'Henry, you are my slave; I hired you to a good place, where you were well treated; had time to make money for yourself. Now, according to law, you, as a slave, cannot have or hold property. Everything, even to your knife, is your master's. All of your earnings come to me. So, in point of law, I was entitled to all the money that you have paid me. Legally it was mine, not yours; so I did but receive from you my own. Notwithstanding all this I was willing to let you have yourself, and intended to act with you according to our first arrangement; but upon coming here the other day, a servant girl of Mr. Bodly's, named Lindy, informed me that you were making preparations to run off, and cheat me out of the last payment. She stated that you had told her so; and you intended to start one night this week. I was so enraged by it, that yesterday I sold you to a negro trader; and you must start down the river to-morrow.' "

" 'Master, it is a lie of the girl's; I never had any thought of running off, or cheating you out of your money.' Henry then told him of Lindy's malice.

" 'Yes, you have proved it was a lie, by coming and paying me : but nothing can be done now; I have signed the papers, and you are the property of Atkins. I have not the power to undo what I have done.'

" 'But, Master,' pleaded Henry, 'can't you refund the money that I have paid you, and let me buy myself from Mr. Atkins ?'

" 'Refund the money, indeed ! Who ever heard of such impertinence ? Have I not just shown that all that you made was by right of law mine ? No; go down the river, serve your time, work well, and may be in the course of fifteen or twenty years you may be able to buy yourself.'

" 'Oh, master!' cried out the weeping Henry, 'pity me, please save me, do something.'

" 'I can do nothing for you ; go, get your trunk ready, here comes Mr. Atkins for you.'

Henry turned towards the hard trader, and with a face contracted with pain, and eyes raining tears, begged for mercy.

" 'Go long you fool of a nigger ! an' git ready to go to the pen, without this fuss, or I'll have you tied with ropes, and taken.'

Henry said no more; I had overheard all from an adjoining room. I tried to avoid him; but he sought me out.

" 'Louise,' he said, in a tone which I shall never forget.

" 'I have heard all,' was my reply.

" 'Will you see Ann for me ? Take her a word from me ? Tell how it was, Louise; break the news gently to her.' Here he quite gave up, and, sinking into a chair, sobbed and cried like a child.

" 'Be a friend to her, Louise; I know that she will need much kindness to sustain her. Thank Miss Nancy for all her kindness; tell her that I blest her before I went. Tell Ann to stay with her, and oh, Louise'—here he wrung his hands in agony—' tell Ann not to grieve for me; but she mustn't forget me. Poor, wretched outcast that I am, I have loved her well! After awhile, when time has softened this blow, she must try to love and be happy with—— No, no, I'll not ask that; only bid her not be wretched;—but give me pen and ink, I'll write just one word to her.'

"I gave him the ink, pen and paper, and he wrote this."

As Louise drew a soiled, blotted paper from her bosom, I eagerly snatched it and read:

"Ann, dearest, Louise will tell you all. Our dream is broken forever! I *am sold;* but I shall be a slave *no more.* Forgive me for what I am going to do. Madness has driven me to it! I love you, even in death I love you. Say farewell to Miss Nancy—I *am gone!*"

I read it over twice slowly. One scalding tear, large and round, fell upon it! I know not where it came from, for my eyes were dry as a parched leaf.

The note dropped from my hands, almost unnoticed by me. Biddy picked it up, and handed it to Miss Nancy, who read it and fainted. I moved about mechanically; assisted in restoring Miss Nancy to consciousness; chafed her hands and temples; and, when she came to, and burst into a flood of tears, I soothed her and urged that she would not weep or distress herself.

"I wonder that the earth don't open and swallow them," cried the weeping Biddy.

"Hush, Biddy, hush!" I urged.

"They ought to be hung!"

"'Vengeance is mine, and I will repay, saith the Lord,'" I replied.

"Oh, Ann, you are crazy!" she uttered.

And so, in truth, I was. That granite-like composure was a species of insanity. I comprehended nothing that was going on around me. I was in a sort of sleep-waking state, when I asked Louise if she thought they would bury him decently; and gave her a bunch of flowers to place in the coffin.

And so my worst suspicion was realized! Through Lindy came my heaviest blow of affliction! I fear that even now, after the lapse of years, I have not the Christianity to ask, " Father, forgive her, for she knew not what she did !" Lying beside me now, dear, sympathetic reader, is *that note—his last brief words.* Before writing this chapter I read it over. Old, soiled and worn it was, but by his trembling fingers those blotted and irregular lines were penned; and to me they are precious, though they awaken ten thousand bitter emotions! I look at the note but once a year, and then on the fatal anniversary, which occurs to-day ! I have pressed it to my heart, and hearsed it away, not to be re-opened for another year. This is the blackest chapter in my dark life, and you will feel, with me, glad that it is about to close. I have nerved myself for the duty of recording it, and, now that it is over, I sink down faint and broken-hearted beside the accomplished task.

CHAPTER XLI.

MONTHS passed by after the events told in the last chapter—
passed, I scarce know how. They have told me that I wandered
about like one in the mazes of a troubled dream. My reason
was disturbed. I've no distinct idea how the days or weeks
were employed. Vague remembrances of kindly words, music,
odorous flowers, and a trip to a beautiful, quiet country-house,
I sometimes have; but 'tis all so misty and dream-like, that
I can form no tangible idea of it. So this period has almost
faded out of mind, and is like lost pages from the chronicle
of life.

When the winter was far spent, and during the snowy days of
February, my mind began to collect its shattered forces. The
approach of another trouble brought back consciousness with re-
kindled vigor.

One day I became aware that Miss Nancy was very ill. It
seemed as if a thick vapor, like a breath-stain on glass, had suddenly been wiped away from my mind; and I saw clearly.
There lay Miss Nancy upon her bed, appallingly white, with
her large eyes sunken deeply in their sockets, and her lips purple
as an autumn leaf. Her thin, white hand, with discolored nails,
was thrown upon the covering, and aroused my alarm. I rushed to her, fearing that the vital spark no longer animated that
loved and once lovely frame.

"Miss Nancy, dear Miss Nancy," I cried, "speak to me, only
one word."

She started nervously, "Oh, who are you? Ah, Ann—is it
Ann?"

" Yes, dear Miss Nancy, it is *I*. It appears as though a film had been removed from my eyes, and I see how selfish I have been. You have suffered for my attention. What has been the matter with me ?"

" Oh, dear child, a fearful dispensation of Providence was sent you; and from the chastisement you are about recovering. Thank God, that you are still the mistress of your reason ! For its safety, I often trembled. I did all for you that I could; but I was fearful that human skill would be of no avail."

" Thanks, my kind friend, and sorry I am for all the anxiety and uneasiness that I have given you."

" Oh, I am repaid, or rather was pre-paid for all and more, you were so kind to me."

Here Biddy entered, and I took down the Bible and read a few chapters from the book of Job.

" What a comfort that book is to us," said Biddy. " Many's the time, Ann, that Miss Nancy read it to you, when you'd sit an' look so wandering-like ; but you are well now, Ann, an' all will be right with us."

" *All* can never be, Biddy, as once it *was*," and I shook my head.

" Oh, don't spake of it," and she wiped her moist eyes with her apron.

Days and weeks passed on thus smoothly, during which time Louise came often to see us ; but the fatal sorrow was never alluded to. By common consent all avoided it.

Daily, hourly, Miss Nancy's health sank. I never saw the footsteps of the grim monster approach more rapidly than in her case. The wasting of her cheek was like the eating of a worm at the heart of a rose.

Her bed was wheeled close to the fire, and I read, all the pleasant mornings, some cheerful book to her.

Her brother came often, and sat with her through the evenings. Many of her friends and neighbors offered to watch with her at night; but she bade me decline all such kindness.

" You and Biddy are enough. I want no others. Let me die

calmly, in the presence of my own household, with no unusual faces around," she said in a low tone.

She talked about her death as though it were some long journey upon which she was about starting; gave directions how she should be shrouded; what kind of coffin we must get, tomb-stone, &c. She enjoined that we inscribe nothing but her age and name upon the tomb-stone.

"I wish no ostentatious slab, no false eulogium; my name and age are all the epitaph I deserve, and all that I will have."

Several ministers came to see her, and held prayer. She received them kindly, and spoke at length with some.

"I shall meet the great change with resignation. I had hoped, Ann, to see you well settled somewhere in the North; but that will be denied me. In my will, I have remembered both you and Biddy. I have no parting advice for either of you; for you are both, though of different faith, consistent Christians. I hope we shall meet hereafter. You must not weep, girls, for it pains me to think I leave you troubled."

When Biddy withdrew, she called me to her, saying,

"Ann, I am feeble, draw near the bed whilst I talk to you. I hold here in my hand a letter from my nephew, Robert Worth."

"Robert Worth? Why I—"

"Yes, he says that he was at Mr. Peterkin's and remembers you well. He also speaks of Emily Bradly, who is now in Boston; says that she recollects you well, and is pleased to hear of your good fortune. Robert is the son of my elder sister, who is now deceased; a favorite he always was of mine. He read law in Mr. Trueman's office, and has a very successful practice at the Boston bar. Long time ago, Ann, when I was a young, blooming girl, my sister Lydia (Robert's mother) and I were at school at a very celebrated academy in the North. During one of our vacations, when we were on a visit to Boston —for we were country girls—we were introduced to two young barristers, William Worth and Justinian Trueman. They were strong personal friends.

17*

" The former became much attached to my sister, and came frequently to see her. Justinian Trueman came also. By the force of circumstance, Mr. Trueman and I were thrown much together. From his lofty conversation and noble principles, I gained great advantage. I loved to listen to his candid avowal of free, democratic principles. How bravely he set aside conventionality and empty forms; he was a searcher after the soul of things! He was the very essence of honor, always ready to sacrifice himself for others, and daily and hourly crucified his heart !

" Chance threw us much together, as I have said. You may infer what ensued. Two persons so similar in nature, so united in purpose (though he was vastly my superior), could not associate much and long together without a feeling of love springing up ! Our case did not differ from that of others. *We loved.* Not as the careless or ordinary love; but with a fervor, a depth of passion, and a concentration of soul, which nothing in life could destroy,

" My sister was the chosen bride of William Worth. This fact was known to all the household. Justinian and I read in each other's manner the secret of the heart.

"At length, in one brief hour, he told me his story; he was the only child of a widowed mother, who had spent her all upon his education. Whilst he was away, her wants had been tenderly ministered to by a very lovely young girl of wealth and social position. Upon her death-bed his mother besought him to marry this lady. He was then inflamed with gratitude, and, being free in heart, he mistook the nature of his feelings. Whilst in this state of mind, he offered himself to her and was instantly accepted. Afterwards when we met he understood how he had been beguiled !

" He wrote to his betrothed, told her the state of his feelings, that he loved another; but declared his willingness to redeem his promise, and stand by his engagement if she wished.

" How anxiously we both awaited her reply ! It came promptly, and she desired, nay demanded, the fulfilment of the engagement; even reminded him of his promise to his mother, and of the obligation he was under to herself.

"No tongue can describe the agony that we both endured; yet principle must be obeyed. We parted. They were married. Twice afterwards I saw him. He was actively engaged in his profession; but the pale cheek and earnest look told me that he still thought lovingly of me! My sister married William Worth, and resided in Boston; but her husband died early in life, leaving his only child Robert to the care of Mr. Trueman. After my mother's death, possessing myself of my patrimony, I removed west, to this city, where my brother lived. I had been separated from him for a number of years, and was surprised to find how entirely a Southern residence had changed him. Owing to some little domestic difficulties, I declined remaining in his family.

"Last winter, when Justinian Trueman was here, I was out of the city; and it was well that I was, for I could not have met him again. Old feelings, that should be cradled to rest, would have been aroused! My brother saw him, and told me that he looked well.

"Now, is it not strange that you should have been an object of such especial interest to both of us? It seems as though you were a centre around which we were once more re-united. I have written him a long letter, which I wish you to deliver upon your arrival in Boston." Here she drew from the portfolio that was lying on the bed beside her, a sealed letter, directed to Justinian Trueman, Boston, Mass.

I was weeping violently when I took it from her.

She lingered thus for several weeks, and on a calm Sabbath morning, as I was reading to her from the Bible, she said to me—

"Ann, I am sleepy; my eyelids are closing; turn me over."

As I attempted to do it she pressed my hand tightly, straightened her body out, and the last struggle was over! I was alone with her. Laying her gently upon the pillow, I for the first time in my life pressed my lips to that cold, marble brow. I felt that she, holy saint, would not object to it, were she able to speak. I then called Biddy in to assist me. She was loud in her lamentation.

"She bade us not weep for her, Biddy. She is happier now;" but, though I spoke this in a composed tone, my heart was all astir with emotion.

Soon her brother came in, bringing with him a minister. He received the mournful intelligence with subdued grief.

We robed her for Death's bridal, e'en as she had requested, in white silk, flannel, and white gloves. Her coffin was plain mahogany, with a plate upon the top, upon which were engraved her name, age, and birth-place.

A funeral sermon was preached, by a minister who had been a strong personal friend. In a retired portion of the public burial-ground we made her last bed. A simple tombstone, as she directed, was placed over the grave, her name, age, &c., inscribed thereon.

Bridget and I slept in the same house that night. We could not be persuaded to leave it, and there, in Miss Nancy's dear, familiar room, we held, as usual, family devotion. I almost fancied that she stood in the midst, and was gazing well-pleased upon us.

That night I slept profoundly. My rest had been broken a great deal, and now the knowledge that duty did not keep me awake, enabled me to sleep well.

On the next day Mr. Worth arrived, and was much distressed to find that he was too late to see his aunt alive.

Though he looked older and more serious than when I last saw him, I readily recognized the same noble expression of face. He received me very kindly, and thanked Biddy and me for our attentions to his beloved aunt. He showed us a letter she had written, in which she spoke of us in the kindest manner, and recommended us to his care.

"Neither of you shall ever lack for friendship whilst I live," he said, as he warmly shook us by the hands.

He told me that he had ever retained a vivid recollection of my sad face; and inquired about "young Master." When I told him that he was dead, and gave an account of his life and sufferings, Mr. Worth remarked—

"Ah, yes, he was one of heaven's angels, lent us only for a short season."

I accompanied him to his aunt's grave.

* * * * * *

Upon the reading of the will, it was discovered that Miss Nancy had liberated me, and left me, as a legacy, four thousand dollars, with the request that I would live somewhere in the North. To Biddy she had left a bequest of three thousand dollars; the remainder of her fortune, after making a donation to her brother, was left to her nephew, Robert Worth.

The will was instantly carried into effect; as it met with no opposition, and she owed no debts, matters were arranged satisfactorily; and we prepared for departure.

Louise had made all her arrangements to go with us. I was now a free woman, in the possession of a comparative fortune; yet I was not happy. Alas! I had out-lived all for which money and freedom were valuable, and I cared not how the remainder of my days were spent. Why cannot the means of happiness come to us when we have the capacity for enjoyment?

On the evening before our departure, I called Louise to me and asked,

"Where is Henry's grave?" It was the first time since that fatal day that I had mentioned his name to her.

"He is buried far away, in a plain, unmarked grave; but, even if it were near, you should not go," she replied.

"Tell me, who found him, after—after—after *the murder ?*"

"Mr. Graham and Atkins went in search of him, and I followed them; though he had told me what he was going to do, Ann, I could not oppose or even dissuade him."

I wept freely; and, as is always the case, was relieved by it.

"I am glad to see that you can weep. It will do you good," said Louise.

CHAPTER XLII

CONCLUSION.

But little more remains to be told of my history.

When Louise, Biddy and I, under the protection of Mr. Worth, sailed on a pleasant steamer from the land of slavery, I could but thank my God that I was leaving forever the State, beneath the sanction of whose laws the vilest outrages and grossest inhumanities were committed !

Our trip would, indeed, have been delightful, but that I was constantly contrasting it in my own mind with what it might have been, had HE not fallen a victim to the white man's cupidity.

Often I stole away from the company, and, in the privacy of my own room, gave vent to my pent-up grief. Biddy and Louise were in ecstacies with everything that they saw.

All along the route, after passing out of the Slave States, we met with kind friends and genuine hospitality. The Northern people are noble, generous, and philanthropic ; and it affords me pleasure to record here a tribute to their worth and kindness.

In New York we met with the best of friends. Everywhere I saw smiling, black faces ; a sight rarely beheld in the cities and villages of the South. I saw men and women of the despised race, who walked with erect heads and respectable carriage, as though they realized that they were men and women, not mere chattels.

When we reached Boston I was made to feel this in a par_ticular manner. There I met full-blooded Africans, finely educated, in the possession of princely talents, occupying good positions, wielding a powerful political influence, and illustrating, in their lives, the oft-disputed fact, that the African intellect is equal to the Caucasian. Soon after my arrival in Boston I found out, from Mr. Worth, the residence of Mr. Trueman, and called to see him.

I was politely ushered by an Irish waiter into the study, where I found Mr. Trueman engaged with a book. At first he did not recognize me; but I soon made myself known, and received from him a most hearty welcome.

I related all the incidents in my life that had occurred since I had seen him last. He entered fully into my feelings, and I saw the tear glisten in his calm eyes when I spoke of poor Henry's awful fate.

I told him of Miss Nancy's kindness, and the tears rolled down his cheeks. I did not speak of what she had told me in relation to their engagement; I merely stated that she had referred to him as a particular personal friend, and when I gave him the letter he received it with a tremulous hand, uttered a fearful groan, and buried his face among the papers that lay scattered over his table. Without a spoken good-bye, I withdrew.

I saw him often after this; and from him received the most signal acts of kindness. He thanked me many times for what he termed my fidelity to his sainted friend. He never spoke of her without a quiver of the lip, and I honored him for his constancy.

He strongly urged me to take up my residence in Boston; but I remembered that Henry's preference had always been for a New England village; and I loved to think that I was following out his views, and so I removed to a quiet puritanical little town in Massachusetts.

And here I now am engaged in teaching a small school of African children; happy in the discharge of so sacred a duty. 'Tis surprising to see how rapidly they learn. I am interested, and so are they, in the work; and thus what with some teachers is an irksome task, is to me a pleasing duty.

I should state for the benefit of the curious, that Biddy is living in Boston, happily married to "a countryman," and is the proud mother of several blooming children. She comes to visit me sometimes, during the heat of summer, and is always a welcome guest.

Louise, too, has consented to wear matrimony's easy yoke. She lives in the same village with me. Our social and friendly relations still continue. I have frequently, when visiting Boston, met Miss Bradly. She, like me, has never married. She has grown to be a firmer and more earnest woman than she was in Kentucky. I must not omit to mention the fact, that when travelling through Canada, I by the rarest chance met Ben—Amy's treasure—now grown to be a fine-looking youth.

He had a melancholy story—a life, like every other slave's, full of trouble—but at length, by the sharpest ingenuity, he had made his escape, and reached, after many difficulties, the golden shores of Canada!

Now my history has been given—a round, unvarnished tale it is; and thus, without ornament, I send it forth to the world. I have spoken freely; at times, I grant, with a touch of bitterness, but never without truth; and I ask the wise, the considerate, the earnest, if I have not had cause for bitterness. Who can carp at me? That there are some fiery Southerners who will assail me, I doubt not; but I feel satisfied that I have discharged a duty that I solemnly owed to my oppressed and down-trodden nation. I am calm and self-possessed: I have passed firmly through the severest ordeal of persecution, and have been spared the death that has befallen many others. Surely I was saved for some wise purpose, and I fear nought from those who are fanatically wedded to wrong and inhumanity. Let them assail me as they will, I shall still feel that

> "Thrice is he armed who has his quarrel just,
>   And he but naked, though wrapped up in steel,
>   Whose bosom with injustice is polluted."

But there are others, some even in slave States, kind, noble, thoughtful persons, earnest seekers after the highest good in life and nature; to them I consign my little book, sincerely begging, that through my weak appeal, my poor suffering brothers and sisters, who yet wear the galling yoke of American slavery, may be granted a hearing.

From the distant rice-fields and sugar plantations of the fervid South, comes a frantic wail from the wronged, injured, and oh, how innocent African! Hear it; hear that cry, Christians of the North, let it ring in your ears with its fearful agony! Hearken to it, ye who feast upon the products of African labor! Let it stay you in the use of those commodities for which their life-blood, aye more, their soul's life, is drained out drop by drop! Talk no more, ye faint-hearted politicians, of "expediency." God will not hear your lame excuse in that grand and awful day, when He shall come in pomp and power to judge the quick and dead.

And so, my history, go forth and do thy mission! knock at the doors of the lordly and wealthy; there, by the shaded light of rosy lamps, tell your story. Creep in at the broken crevice of the poor man's cabin, and there make your complaint. Into the ear of the brave, energetic mechanic, sound the burden of your grief. To the strong-hearted blacksmith, sweating over his furnace, make yourself heard; and ask them, one and all, shall this unjust institution of slavery be perpetuated? Shall it dare to desecrate, with its vile presence, the new territories that are now emphatically free? Shall Nebraska and Kansas join in a blood-spilling coalition with the South?

Answer proudly, loudly, brave men; and answer, *No, No!* My work is done.

AFTERWORD.

TIME'S passage and a lack of historiographic interest have hidden the life of Mattie Griffith, a white woman from antebellum Kentucky, who in an act of racial cross-dressing, published *The Autobiography of a Female Slave*. To write a pseudoslave narrative was not an original decision, for many were published previously by Northern abolitionists. The most notable were *Slavery in the United States: A Narrative of the Life and Adventures of Charles Ball, A Black Man* (1836), probably by a white author who remains unknown, and historian Richard Hildreth's fraudulent memoirs, *The Slave; or Memoirs of Archie Moore* (1836).

What renders the Griffith text especially fascinating is not simply that a white woman adopted a black slave woman's voice but that at the date of her impersonation, Mattie Griffith herself owned slaves. Mattie Griffith's "autobiography" (often catalogued under her married name, Martha Browne) is simultaneously a fictional account of the life of a young African-American slave woman, a testimony of witness and statement of guilt from a participant in a slave economy, and an examination of the paradoxes under which she authored her text anonymously. The *Autobiography* constitutes a resonant psychological effort to break free of the ideological yoke of whiteness and imagine a life of blackness in the American South.

Although only Lydia Maria Child and Harriet Beecher Stowe surpassed Griffith in volume of antislavery fiction, Griffith remained largely a one-book phenomenon, increasingly unremembered during her own lifetime. Griffith was forgotten because she arrived one book too late: that book was the immense and overshadowing *Uncle Tom's Cabin*, after which any sentimental antislavery novel seemed redundant. Griffith's obscurity was aided by a general neglect of antebellum women writers that was not remedied until the recent generation of feminist literary scholarship. While she was familiar in abolition and women's suffrage circles, we know astonishingly little about a woman whose friends and collaborators included nearly every major name of those movements. Griffith's known oeuvre consists of an early volume of poetry, the *Autobiography* (1856), *Madge Vertner* (a serialized antislavery novel, published 1859-60), and some newspaper fiction. After a few brief years in the abolitionist and early suffrage limelight, Mattie Griffith faded into a domestic invisibility so profound that details about the majority of her long life remain obscure.

The *Autobiography* is especially notable for its uniqueness as a personal struggle with conscience by a woman raised and educated within slave culture. The singularity of Griffith's text—for antebellum Southern white-written pseudoslave narratives are the rarest of creatures in American literature—testifies to the domination of slave owning consciousness over white Southern literary production. Griffith, who viewed the *Autobiography* as a reenacted performance of her own witness of slavery, invented a countervoice to dramatize her rejection of a socially-designated racial role. However, the *Autobiography* can only be read with an awareness that it is a temporary visit into an imagined blackness.

Griffith's family arrived in northwest Kentucky at the turn of the nineteenth century along with an expanding stream of smallhold settlers who flowed south and west from Maryland and Virginia. Griffith was born sometime between 1825 and 1829. Her father, Thomas, a tavernkeeper and farmer who settled in Owensboro, Kentucky, died in 1830 and left six slaves to his already motherless young daughters. When Griffith was orphaned, her extended family took in Mattie and an older sister, Catherine. Most of Mattie's care as a child came from one of her own female slaves. The Griffith family valued schooling sufficiently and had enough income to provide Mattie with an education of some accomplishment. Little further, however, is known of Griffith's youth.

First public notice of Griffith arrived with her collected poems, published in New York in 1852. At this date, she was among the forerunners of Kentucky literature. Griffith's poetry does not reveal any sense of latent reform consciousness. At most, the poetry's elevated content and pale metaphysical style suggest an avoidance of precisely the degraded human scenery that she confronted in the *Autobiography*.

According to an account Griffith gave to writer Lydia Maria Child, her conscience was triggered by congressman Preston Smith Brooks (afterwards called "Bully Brooks" by outraged Northerners) and his caning assault of Massachusetts senator Charles Sumner on the Senate floor on May 22, 1856, two days after Sumner's famous "Crime Against Kansas" antislavery speech. Griffith reacted to the news by sending for a copy of Sumner's speech, which supposedly provided her first introduction to antislavery ideas and a world of social reform. This account is quite dubious, given that Griffith's book was published only five months later.

One of her friends, the reform educator, translator, and activist intellectual Elizabeth Palmer Peabody wrote a more plausible history of Griffith's antislavery conscience:

> Mattie has been known from childhood among her friends as opposed to slavery—but they never appreciated the depth & entireness of her soul's abhorrence of it—and treated it as an *eccentricity*—Nevertheless they have in some degree humoured her in the disposition of her negroes while she has been under age—& shielded her from the operation of the law—when she & also her agent have been at several times presented to the Grand Jury for violating the laws of the state in the privileges given to her negroes—The known conservatism of these families on the slavery question has been her protection. But as soon as she was of age she determined to make them free.

This description entirely parallels a long, obviously autobiographical passage in chapter 15 (129-31) of the *Autobiography*. Too, the social situation of Miss Bradly once her opposition to slavery becomes public—"Inuendoes, of most insulting character, had been thrown out...Foul slanders were in busy circulation about her, and she began to be a taboed person" (202)—carries the ring of personal knowledge.

What induced her political conversion and its literary form? Griffith's evolution as an abolitionist closely followed the outline suggested by Angelina Grimké, who joined the abolitionist cause a generation earlier. In her "Appeal to the Christian Women of the South," Grimké advocated, first, reading on the subject of slavery; second, praying over this subject; third, speaking on slavery and naming it as a sin; and fourth, acting against slavery through emancipation and all other means. Whatever the facts of her conversion to abolitionism, whether a political epiphany or long-resident sentiments, Griffith indicated the force of reading by singling out her memory of reading Sumner's "Crime Against Kansas" speech. Her copious reading brought her to journal literature and the cult of sensibility. Grimké's second stage finds ample expression in the many scenes of prayer throughout the *Autobiography*. The third and fourth steps—speaking and direct action—echo as the generative forces behind the writing of the *Autobiography* and the subsequent emancipation of her slaves. When Griffith visited at length with the Grimké sisters at their home in the experimentalist Raritan commune in northern New Jersey in 1859, her personification of Angelina Grimké's concept of a true Christian woman led to a lasting close friendship.

Griffith's major purpose in writing the *Autobiography*, according to Peabody, was to use the profits of a successful book to return to her slaves the value of the money they had earned for her, to establish them in freedom, and to support herself and her sister's impoverished family. Her plans for reparation did not fully succeed, although she was able to emancipate her slaves. She also intended the *Autobiography* to serve as her entrée to a writing career. As Peabody wrote, "She was sanguine that a conscientious & faithful picture of slavery *from a slaveholder* would *initiate* at least a literary life in the North." If the book was social testimony—as she told Child, she had witnessed every incident recounted—it nevertheless used recognized conventions of sentimentalism. Features of the *Autobiography*, such as the slaveowner's son Johnny Peterkin (essentially a male Little Eva) who dies of consumption after rejecting slavery, indicate the heavy influence that Stowe's *Uncle Tom's Cabin* (1852) had on Griffith's style.

Whether because of the imposture or the manuscript's politics, her New York publisher, Justin Starr Redfield, did not initially want to publish the *Autobiography*. Still, he was aware of the enormous public appetite for antislavery fiction. During one month alone in 1856, Harriet Beecher Stowe's antislavery novel *Dred* sold over one hundred thousand copies. When Redfield agreed to publish the book, he virtually condemned it to obscurity with a small press run of two thousand copies and almost no publicity. Redfield apparently did not wish to jeopardize his substantial Southern market by advertising the book in newspapers that travelled below the Mason-Dixon line. As remains occasional publishing practice today, Redfield advanced the correct year of publication—1856—to keep the book fresher, printing 1857 instead.

Autobiography of a Female Slave was extremely well received in abolitionist circles, which were initially unaware of the circumstances behind its authorship. That unfamiliarity changed rapidly as Griffith took steps to shed her imposture. Although the precise manner of that revelation remains unclear, Griffith's identity became known in the Philadelphia abolitionist community from at least mid-November 1856. Perhaps she revealed her identity because her imposture was less than successful or because prolonging any attempt at concealment would no longer serve its original purposes. In a letter written in early December 1856, Griffith introduced herself to abolitionist leader William Lloyd Garrison. In her letter, she advanced a theory of the book's narrative voice, claiming that the environment of slavery gave rise to a prose style that she described as a "sincere narration of stern fact" rather than sentimental or romantic.

The author's identity was still generally unknown when a front-page review appeared in the *Boston Evening Transcript* on December 3, 1856. The review stated that the book's "title indicates that it is an autobiography, yet it is not precisely so." While "the work will be read with a shudder,…the volume will be ignored by the people of the South, as an overwrought picture of scenes connected with their 'peculiar institution,' and as only existing in the sickly brain of some rabid abolitionist." Reviews in the abolitionist press consistently mentioned the book's convincing power and authenticity in its narration of conditions of domestic slavery. In Garrison's opinion, Griffith was "a young lady of rare personal accomplishments and of brilliant promise, who, ignorant of the radical abolition movement at the North, out of the depths of her own soul" wrote the *Autobiography*. Privately, Lydia Maria Child found Griffith's prose style overly sentimental and inflated, "but *that* belongs to her nineteen years, and will be outgrown" (a misimpression, since Griffith had quietly deducted about ten years from her age when she moved north).

When Charlotte Forten, a Massachusetts black woman who was really nineteen and destined to become an outstanding social activist, read the *Autobiography* three months after its publication—by which time she was well aware of the book's authorship—she wrote in her journal: "Some parts of it almost too horrible to be believed, did we not know that they cannot exceed the terrible reality. It is *dreadful, dreadful* that such scenes can be daily and hourly enacted in this enlightened age, and *most* enlightened republic. How long, Oh Lord, how long, wilt thou delay thy vengeance?" The next day, having finished the book, Forten wrote of Griffith that "hers must be a brave, true soul thus to surmount all obstacles, to soar above all the prejudices, which, from childhood must have been instilled into her mind." In Philadelphia, where Griffith finished the book, the abolitionist community received it equally well. Some radical abolitionists preferred Griffith's *Autobiography* over *Uncle Tom's Cabin*, for Stowe had advocated Liberian colonization schemes whereas Griffith explicitly rejected them.

Notice in the South, not unexpectedly, was not nearly as appreciative. The *Louisville Journal*, unaware that the *Autobi-*

ography's author was one of its own, managed both to scourge and praise the book:

> The tone of this book is exceedingly objectionable: it is filled with the foulest abolitionism that has ever been uttered. It contains the concentrated fanaticism of Garrison and Beecher and Phillips and Fred. Douglas [sic], but the story itself is of thrilling interest and artistic finish. It is the production of a practised pen. It abounds in beautiful thoughts and highly poetic expressions. Considered merely as a literary production, independent of its gross misrepresentations, false theories, and most disgusting ultra anti-slavery aspirations, it evinces a high order of talent and literary genius. We much regret to see a perversion of ability. We are pained to see a great genius thus grovelling in the mire of fanaticism, and soiling its brilliant plumage in the filth of ultra abolitionism.

Elizabeth Peabody reported that after the book's publication Griffith's "whole connection in the south was outraged in their opinion—to the last degree—& have denounced her—not however without holding out to her every temptation to return provided she will publish in all newspapers that she *did not write the book* & renounce her plans of emancipation." When Griffith could not be persuaded, according to Peabody, her family attempted to induce her brother-in-law, Dr. Thomas Slattery, Catherine's estranged husband, to claim their three children in order to raise them within the Church. This threat of possible child abduction caused the sisters to live very cautiously in Philadelphia until legal guardianship could be established under Pennsylvania law.

It is unclear what circulation or real influence the *Autobiography* achieved beyond an abolitionist audience. It would be exaggeration to say that Griffith had a formative intellectual impact on the abolitionist movement; still, abolitionists from Philadelphia to Boston seized upon and read her book. The text's popularity within the white abolitionist community suggests that it filled a need for sentimentalization of the slave experience; Griffith's account could recharge ideological commitment by employing an idealized almost-white heroine, another version of the noble mulatto protagonist. Through the irony of implicit expectations, few readers seemed to credit the narrative voice as one that belonged to a former slave. Rather, like the above reviewer, they assumed that the author was white, without any evidence. Given this reader resistance—despite many slave narratives published by African-Americans—to imagining black authorship, both among abolitionists and slavery's sympathizers, Griffith's narrative transvestism was fated from the beginning to appear against a presumption of whiteness.

If mid-nineteenth century readers found Griffith's intemperate outrage and impolitic condemnations to be "flaws," contemporary readers find her troubling for different reasons. Recurrent references to phenotypical and broadly racialized characterizations suggest how heavily the overflow of race science discourse controlled Griffith's writing. The white John Peterkin, for example, is racially elevated above black children: "Young master, with his pale, intellectual face, his classic head, his sun-bright curls, and his earnest blue eyes, sat in a half-lounging attitude, making no inappropriate picture of an angel of light, whilst the two little black faces seemed emblems of fallen, degraded humanity." (113) While Griffith remains trapped by phenotypical language in racial characterization of blacks, she ironically employs the same tropes to assail whites: "Oh, ye of the proud Caucasian race, would that your hearts were as fair and spotless as your complexions!" (75) Griffith, who is capable of inherently racist remarks, is also capable of moments of near-revolutionary thought, including the then-unthinkable acceptance of mixed-race marriages. Worthiness, personal and spiritual, Griffith writes, is the only valid crite-rion: "I care not if the skin be black as Erebus or fair and smooth as satin, so the heart and mind be right. I do not deal in externals or care for surfaces" (79-80).

Dissatisfied with the Church's silence regarding American slavery, Griffith converted from her native Catholicism to the Protestant evangelism that so heavily shapes the *Autobiography*. For Griffith, slavery, in its reliance on a black anti-enlighten-ment, frustrates a true Christian comprehension. Divinity has been falsely attributed to white masters who exercise dominion over enslaved lives, redirecting proper devotion away from a metaphysical god. The worst effect of slavery, in this view, was to create ignorant atheists of innocents. When Ann attempts to teach the doctrine of the immortality of the soul to Amy, a young slave girl whose mother has been sold away, she en-counters scathing cynicism. Through an ugly logic of race supremacy, creation itself has become endowed with whiteness:

> Who do you think made negroes?" I inquired.
> Looking up with a meaning grin, she said, "White folks made 'em fur der own use, I 'spect."
> "Why do you think that?"
> "Kase white folks ken kill 'em when dey pleases, so I 'spose dey make 'em." (63)

Although Ann is left momentarily without reply, the evan-gelical themes of the novel reverse this logic. Griffith argues, following a tradition of Anglo-American religious abolition-ism, that any social system which enacts possession of a soul as human property inevitably corrupts Christian subordination to the only true Creator. To define a soul as property alienates legitimate claims to self-possession by creatures made in the divine image by divine hands. Ann's dialogue with Amy exemplifies the effects of this submission: a complete alienation from and scorn for a Christianity that was indistinguishable from white racial oppression. As an obstacle to divine allegiance and spiritual self-improvement, slavery's establishment of human property, in Griffith's view, could only promote skepticism among those who needed salvation.

Although the Philadelphia years before and after publication of the *Autobiography* were difficult, both for economic and health reasons, Griffith was aided by an extensive support network there. Fearing for her protegé, Child was especially responsible for mobilizing friends to support Griffith. Equally important, Elizabeth Palmer Peabody initiated a vigorous letterwriting campaign to gather financial aid for her. Her friends brought her to Massachusetts during summer 1857 in order to introduce her to their society. Griffith captivated Ralph Waldo Emerson; the pair discussed European literature and other topics during their meetings. They corresponded briefly, and Emerson invited Griffith, "a presence so brilliant & glad," to visit his Concord home where he hoped "to claim to be one of your tutors, & to persuade you to come to me in my turn for a lesson, when I meant to wear the cowl with great dignity, and to wile all your beautiful stories out of you." What Peabody called her "subrosa society" of admiring Griffith supporters—Emerson among them—continued operating on a well-organized basis of quarterly subscriptions for at least another four years.

On the evidence of her fiction alone, Griffith believed Southern society to be profoundly corrupt and evil due to slavery's presence, a belief that contributed powerful impetus to her 'Yankee-fication' and rejection of her native culture. Together with this need to break from her birth culture in order to oppose it, Griffith evinced a powerful desire for personal expiation. After conversation with Griffith, Elizabeth Peabody wrote "I found a person more profoundly alive on the subject of human rights—and the sin & spiritual suicide of slaveholding—& who gave me a more terrible impression of the sum of human agonies that slavery is—than any thing I ever had seen or heard or imagined." Griffith was quite reticent about telling her personal story; it took Peabody three weeks of conversation to elicit details.

Having embraced radical abolitionism, Griffith needed to enact it. In 1858, with a one-hundred-dollar grant from Garrison's American Anti-Slavery Society, she travelled to Kentucky with the express purpose of freeing her slaves. State law required her to transport her freed slaves beyond state boundaries in order to prevent their re-enslavement. Emancipation under these circumstances was a mixed blessing since its terms required that manumitted slaves depart a familiar environment and relinquish the few social advantages they had achieved. In truth, the deed was far from the unmitigated act of benevolence that Griffith's admirers made out.

Griffith became active in the Anti-Slavery Society, helping organize its annual political and fundraising fairs, and its membership voted her a large and likely never paid sum. Acquiring the allegiance of a young former slaveowner was a political coup for the Society, and the imminent moral collapse of slavery was read into the event. Griffith's example was held up before the abolitionist community as a conversionary model, one which suggested with unwarranted hopefulness that the "peculiar institution" would collapse as a new Southern generation attained maturity.

After travelling with companions to visit British supporters of American abolitionism during 1860-61, Griffith resided in

New York City where she became intensely active in the Woman's National Loyal League in 1863. The League, led by Lucy Stone and Elizabeth Cady Stanton, drummed up public support for prosecution of the war, for immediate abolition, and for a full Emancipation Proclamation. Her activist reputation was such that, after the war, Stanton and Stone asked her to assist organizing for women's suffrage. Griffith lived above the offices of the Freedman's Aid Commission, where she watched as mobs tried to burn down the offices of this ex-slave assistance organization during the Draft Riots of July 1863, the country's deadliest-ever race riots, and then went to the aid of black victims.

Following the war, Griffith became active in the emergent women's rights movement and called for gender-neutral language that would link black and women's suffrage under the draft Fourteenth Amendment. In a "Petition for Universal Suffrage" presented to the House and Senate on February 21, 1866, Mattie Griffith's name follows close after those of Stanton, Stone, Susan B. Anthony, Antoinette Blackwell, and other movement stalwarts. Griffith wrote, "I thought I should never marry, but fight out life on the woman's rights plan—single and alone," but she decided to marry Albert Gallatin Browne, an attorney and former Union colonel, on June 27, 1866. Browne, a member of an old and wealthy Massachusetts family, had been an ardent abolitionist. As a Harvard law student in 1854, Browne had been charged with murder along with twelve other abolitionists, the majority of whom were black men, after a bloody attempt to rescue seized fugitive slave Anthony Burns from the Boston City Jail. Joined by shared militant abolitionism, the couple took up residence in a spacious home in Cambridge, Massachusetts.

In 1869, Griffith was elected as a vice-president of the Na-

tional Woman Suffrage Association. This was a period of pro-
grammatic infighting and fractiousness in the women's
movement, and with constitutional extension of the franchise
only to black men, the abolitionist and women's suffrage movements essentially parted company. Fighting this separation,
Griffith united with Sara Pugh, Frederick Douglass, Gerrit
Smith, and others to form the very short-lived Union Woman
Suffrage Society in New York in May 1870. There is little further
political record of Griffith, who moved in 1874 to New York
City, where Albert pursued a journalist's career. They returned
to Boston in 1887, when Browne assumed a position at a local
banking firm. The couple, who had no children, lived in a fashionable apartment on downtown Newbury Street.

Griffith's last known public appearance was at the inaugural
convention of the National Association of Colored Women,
held in Boston's Berkeley Hall in July 1895, where she read a paper on temperance and social purity. In her final years Griffith
joined the ranks of the second- and third-generation abolitionists who lent their support to black educational projects,
anti-lynching organizations, and the women's suffrage and
temperance movements. These white northern intellectuals
pursued an ameliorationist agenda, contributing heavily to
black colleges and institutions.

Griffith consumed books with a passion, acquiring a personal library estimated at a size "running into the thousands."
Her estate, inventoried after her death in Boston in 1906, listed
a stunning 4,619 pieces or sets of jewelry, including 122 combs,
79 fans, and 30 watches, with one-third of the jewelry being
valued as worthless. A rather exhausted-sounding executor reported that Griffith's clothes and linens (including 300 dozen
handkerchiefs) required "151 large pasteboard boxes, 9 large
chests, 11 large trunks, 8 unusually large drawers, 7 large rolls"

for packing and transport. Her favorite color was red, and Griffith was known to appear in Harvard Square dressed entirely in red, including gloves. The same ill-considered question that Griffith propounded rhetorically in the *Autobiography*—"Does not the African, in his love of gaud, show and tinsel, his odd and grotesque decorations of his person, exhibit a love of style?" (41)—could have been better directed toward Griffith herself. Narrative cross-dressing is an imaginative device of identity costuming, one that translates externalities into internalities and the reverse. Griffith's life was guided by the same richly decorative imagination that created the sentimental self-blackening of the *Autobiography*.

Although Griffith conceived her pseudoslave narrative as one of sympathetic identification and expiation, what she wrote was a novel of American cultural integration: black became white, white became black. Yet Griffith also remains an anomaly, unassimilable either as a representative regionalist or as a legitimate ex-slave narrator. Given the *Autobiography*'s character as a transgressive work, the text reads as a challenge to dominant histories and neat literary rubrics. That violation is phrased through a rejection of racial and sexual hierarchies in the plot construction and an authorial refusal to accept narrative confinements of either raciality or domesticity. Its violation of history lay in Griffith's assertion of an ambiguous identity, one that threatened the twin fixities of race and sex. Griffith was not alone in this transgressive culture that echoed through progressive and radical social thought during the 1850s, finding expression in such innovations as Amelia Bloomer's half-pant, half-dress "bloomers."

A final question remains: why should we study a pseudoslave narrative when so many real ones remain unresearched? Only an estimated tenth of African-American nineteenth-century

literary production is known or has been unearthed. By ex-
pending energies on a fake slave narrative, as opposed to a real
one, do we not risk repeating the terms of racial privilege under
which a white narrative voice disguised itself as a black voice?
A brief answer must be that whiteness needs blackness in order
to exist, and the reverse. Just as we need an elucidation of wrong
in order to discover what is right, so too we read white narratives of slavery to understand the construction of American
racism. Mattie Griffith arrived at a realization that as a slaveowner she was entirely in the wrong, and her pseudoslave
narrative testifies to her grappling with a perennial moral problem: what does a decent person do on the wrong side of an
inherited and ethically untenable social situation? Griffith's
case presents the classic attributes of a young person caught up
by horrified recognition of the injustice she, her family, and her
culture perpetuated. For all her narrative faults and problem-
atic representations of race, Mattie Griffith evinced an outraged
revulsion towards the institution of slavery. The same could not
be said about the great majority of white American opinion,
whether in the North or South, in the 1850s. Griffith's *Autobiography* ultimately is more than a would-be African-American
narrative; it reveals the problematics of a white American conscience attempting to bear witness against racial divisions and
slavery. The book argues against the concept of white supremacy, even while it echoes other prevalent racialisms of its
day. Its importance as an ethical work is in its fictionalizing of
an inner history that reshaped a slaveowner into an opponent
of slavery, a shift that caused Griffith to reject the spiritual
schismatics of the ideology we call "race."